AREA 7

At only 27 years of age, Matthew Reilly is the international bestselling author of four novels, *Contest*, *Ice Station*, *Temple* and now *Area 7*. He wrote his first two books while studying Law at the University of New South Wales, and now spends his time writing novels and screenplays.

Contest, *Ice Station* and *Temple* were all runaway bestsellers both in Australia and overseas, and rights to Matthew's novels have now been sold to over twelve countries including the UK, US and Germany. Film rights to *Contest* have been optioned.

A keen fan of Hollywood action blockbusters, Matthew hopes to direct one of his own action-adventure screenplays sometime in the near future. He lives in Sydney.

For more information on Matthew and his books, visit his website: www.matthewreilly.com

MATTHEW REILLY

AREA 7

MACMILLAN

First published in Great Britain 2001 by Macmillan
an imprint of Pan Macmillan Ltd
Pan Macmillan, 20 New Wharf Road, London N1 9RR
Basingstoke and Oxford
Associated companies throughout the world
www.panmacmillan.com

ISBN 0 333 90626 8 (Hardback)
ISBN 0 333 90625 X (Trade Paperback)

A CIP catalogue record for this book is available from
the British Library.

Printed and bound in Great Britain by
Mackays of Chatham plc, Chatham, Kent

For John Schrooten, my friend

Acknowledgements

I'll try to be quick. Sincere thanks once again to:

Natalie Freer—who gets to see (and put up with) my creative eccentricities up close. Her patience and generosity know no bounds;

My brother, Stephen Reilly—tortured writer, constructive and creative critic, and good friend; and to his wife, Rebecca Ryan, because they come as a package;

My wonderful parents—Ray and Denise Reilly—for encouraging me to build miniature movie sets for my *Star Wars* action-figures when I was a kid; my creativity comes directly from them;

My good friends, John Schrooten, Nik and Simon Kozlina, the whole Kay clan (notably Don, who made me shrink the size of the cats in *Temple*) and to Paul Whyte for accompanying me on an extraordinary trip to Utah while researching this book.

A special mention to two American friends—Captain Paul M. Woods, US Army, and Gunnery Sergeant Kris Hankinson, USMC (retired), who generously gave of their time and assisted me with the military details of this book. Any mistakes are mine, and were made over their objections.

And finally, once again, thanks to everyone at Pan Macmillan. This is our fourth outing together and it still rocks. Thanks to Cate Paterson (legend publisher), Jane Novak (legend publicist), Sarina Rowell (legend editor), and Paul Kenny (legend). And, of course, as always, to the sales reps at Pan for the countless hours they spend on the road between bookshops.

To anyone who knows a writer, never underestimate the power of your encouragement.

All right! Now on with the show . . .

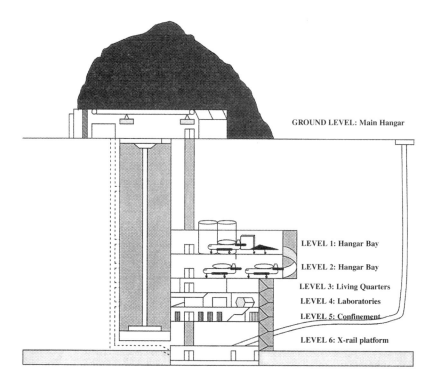

**UNITED STATES AIR FORCE
SPECIAL AREA (RESTRICTED) NO. 7**

GROUND LEVEL: Main Hangar

LEVEL 1: Hangar Bay

LEVEL 2: Hangar Bay

LEVEL 3: Living Quarters

LEVEL 4: Laboratories

LEVEL 5: Confinement

LEVEL 6: X-rail platform

GROUND LEVEL: MAIN HANGER

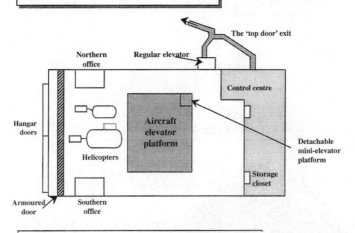

The 'top door' exit

Northern office

Regular elevator

Control centre

Hangar doors

Aircraft elevator platform

Detachable mini-elevator platform

Helicopters

Storage closet

Armoured door

Southern office

LEVEL 1: UNDERGROUND HANGAR BAY

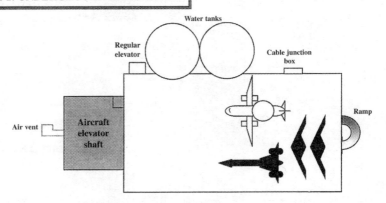

Water tanks

Regular elevator

Cable junction box

Ramp

Air vent

Aircraft elevator shaft

LEVEL 2: UNDERGROUND HANGAR BAY

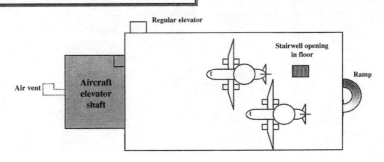

Regular elevator

Stairwell opening in floor

Ramp

Air vent

Aircraft elevator shaft

LEVEL 3: LIVING QUARTERS

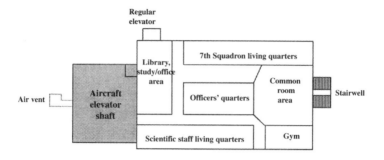

LEVEL 4: LABORATORIES AND QUARANTINE

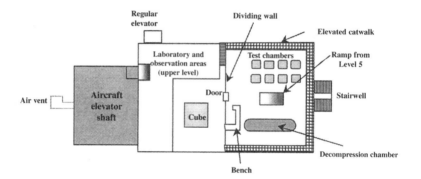

LEVEL 5: CONFINEMENT

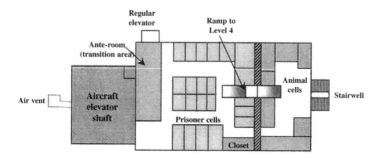

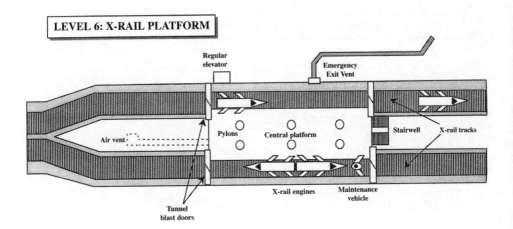

LEVEL 6: X-RAIL PLATFORM

Regular
elevator

Emergency
Exit Vent

Air vent

Pylons

Central platform

Stairwell

X-rail tracks

Tunnel
blast doors

X-rail engines

Maintenance
vehicle

*The single greatest fear that America faces today
is that its military forces no longer tolerate the
continuing incompetence of its civilian leadership.*

Mr George K. Suskind,
Defense Intelligence Agency,
Evidence given before the House
Sub-committee on the Armed Forces,
22 July 1996

*The difference between a republic and an empire is
the loyalty of one's army.*

Julius Caesar

INTRODUCTION

From: Katz, Caleb
The C.B. Powell Memorial Address: 'The Presidency'
**(Speech delivered at the School of Politics,
Harvard University, 26 February 1999)**

'There is no other institution in the world quite like the President of the United States.

All at once, the person who holds this title becomes the leader of the fourth most populous nation on earth, the commander-in-chief of its armed forces, and the chief executive officer of what Harry Truman called "the largest going concern in the world".

The use of the term "chief executive" has made comparisons with company structures inevitable, and to a certain extent, they are appropriate—although, what other corporate leaders in the world have 2 trillion dollar budgets at their fingertips, a licence to use the 82nd Airborne Division to enforce their will, and briefcases at their sides that can unleash an arsenal of thermonuclear devastation against their competitors?

Among modern political systems, however, the American President is unique—for the simple reason that he is both head of government *and* head of state.

Most nations separate these two functions. In the United

Kingdom, for instance, the head of state is the Queen; the head of *government* is the Prime Minister. It is a separation born out of a history of tyrants—kings who wore the crown, but who also governed at their often erratic pleasure.

But in the US, the man who runs the country is also the *symbol* of the country. In his words and his deeds, the President's every act is a barometer for the glory of the nation. For his strength is the people's strength.

John F. Kennedy staring down the Soviets over Cuba in 1962.

Harry Truman's nerves-of-steel decision to drop the atomic bomb on Japan in 1945.

Or Ronald Reagan's confident smile.

His strength is the people's strength.

But there are dangers in this arrangement of things. For if the President is the embodiment of America, what happens when things go wrong?

The assassination of John F. Kennedy.

The resignation of Richard Nixon.

The humiliation of William Jefferson Clinton.

The death of Kennedy was the death of America's innocence. Nixon's resignation drove a knife into the heart of America's optimism. And the humiliation of Clinton was the global humiliation of America—at peace summits and press conferences around the world, the first question asked of Clinton was invariably directed at his sexcapades in a study adjoining the Oval Office.

Be it in death or disgrace, decisiveness or courage, the President of the United States is more than just a man. He is an institution—a symbol—the walking, talking embodiment of a nation. On his back ride the hopes and dreams of 276 million people . . .' [pp.1–2]

From: Farmer, J.T.
'Coincidence or Co-ordinated Murder?
The Death of Senator Jeremiah Woolf'
Article from: *The Conspiracy Theorist Monthly*
[circulation: 152 copies]
(Delva Press, April issue, 2001)

'... The body was found in the woods surrounding the senator's isolated hunting cabin in the Kuskokwim Mountains in Alaska.

Truth be told, at the time of his death Jerry Woolf was no longer a senator, having retired abruptly from Congress only ten months earlier, surprising all the pundits, citing family reasons for the unexpected move.

He was still alive when they found him—no mean feat considering the high-velocity hunting bullet lodged in his chest. Woolf was immediately taken by helicopter to Blaine County Hospital, one hundred and fifty miles away, where emergency residents tried in vain to stem the bloodflow.

But the damage was too severe. After forty-five minutes of emergency treatment, former United States Senator Jeremiah K. Woolf died.

Sounds simple, doesn't it? A terrible hunting accident. Like so many others that happen every year in this country.

That's what your government would have you believe.

Consider this: Blaine County Hospital records show that a patient named Jeremiah K. Woolf was declared dead in the emergency ward at 4:35 p.m. on the afternoon of February 6, 2001.

That is the only record of the incident that exists. All other records of Woolf's examination at the hospital were confiscated by the FBI.

Now consider this: *on that very same day*—February 6, 2001—on the other side of the country, at exactly 9:35 p.m., Jeremiah Woolf's Washington townhouse was destroyed in an explosion, an explosion that killed his wife and only daughter. Investigators would later claim that this blast was caused by a gas leak.

The FBI believes Woolf—previously a vibrant young senator, crusader against organised crime, and potential presidential candidate—was the victim of an extortion racket: leave us alone, or we'll kill your family.

This is, without a doubt, a government smokescreen.

If Woolf was being blackmailed, well, one has to ask: *why?* He had retired from the Senate ten months previously. And if he was killed in a routine hunting accident, why were the records of his emergency room procedures at Blaine County Hospital taken by the FBI?

What *really* happened to Jerry Woolf? At the moment, we just don't know.

But consider this final point: owing to the time difference, 9:35 p.m. in Washington DC is 4:35 p.m. in Alaska.

So at the end of the day, after all the talk of hunting accidents and Mafia blackmail and faulty gas valves is cast aside, one fact remains: at the *exact* same moment that former United States Senator Jerry Woolf's heart stopped beating in an emergency room in Alaska, his home on the other side of the country exploded in a gigantic ball of flames . . .'

AREA 7

PROLOGUE

Protected Inmates' Wing,
Leavenworth Federal Penitentiary,
Leavenworth, Kansas,
20 January, 12:00 p.m.

It had been his last request.

To watch the inauguration ceremony on television.

Sure, it had delayed the trip to Terre Haute by an hour, but then—so the powers-that-be at Leavenworth had reckoned—if the condemned man's last request was reasonable, who were they to refuse him.

The television threw a flickering strobe-like glow onto the concrete walls of the holding cell. Tinny voices came from its speakers:

'... *do solemnly swear* ...'

'... *do solemnly swear* ...'

'... *that I will faithfully execute the office of President of the United States* ...'

'... *that I will faithfully execute the office of President of the United States* ...'

The condemned prisoner watched the television intently.

And then—despite the fact that he had less than two hours to live—a smile began to spread across his face.

★

The number on his prison shirt read: 'T-77'.

He was an older man, fifty-nine, with a round, weather-beaten face and slicked-down black hair. Despite his age, he was a big man, powerfully built—with a bull neck and broad shoulders. His eyes were a bottomless unreadable black and they glistened with intelligence. He'd been born in Baton Rouge, Louisiana, and when he spoke, his accent was strong.

Until recently, he had been a resident of T-Wing—that section of Leavenworth devoted to inmates who are not safe among the general prison population.

Two weeks ago, however, he had been moved from T-Wing to Pre-Transit—otherwise known as the Departure Lounge—another special wing where those awaiting execution stayed before they were flown out to Terre Haute Federal Penitentiary in Indiana for execution by lethal injection.

A former Civil War fort, Leavenworth is a maximum-security federal prison. This means it receives only those offenders who break *federal* laws—a class of individuals that variously includes violent criminals, foreign spies or terrorists, organised crime bosses, and members of the US armed forces who sell secrets, commit crimes or desert.

It is also perhaps the most brutal penitentiary in America.

But in that peculiar way of prisons the world over, its inhabitants—men who have themselves killed or raped—have, over the years, developed a strange sense of justice.

Serial rapists are themselves violated on a daily basis. Army deserters are beaten regularly, or worse, branded on their foreheads with the letter 'D'. Foreign spies, such as the four Middle Eastern terrorists convicted of the World Trade Centre bombing in 1993, have been known to lose body parts.

But by far the most ferocious treatment of all is reserved for one particular class of prisoner: traitors.

It seems that despite all their own crimes, all their own

atrocities, the American inmates of Leavenworth—many of them disgraced soldiers—still profess a deep love of their country. Traitors are usually killed within their first three days in the pen.

William Anson Cole, the former CIA analyst who sold information to the Chinese government about an impending Navy SEAL mission to the Xichang Launch Centre, the epicentre of China's space operations—information which led to the capture, torture and death of all six SEAL team members—was found dead in his cell two days after he had arrived at the prison. His rectum had been torn from repeated violations with a pool cue and he had been strangled, hog-style, with a bed leg tied across his throat—a crude simulation of the Chinese torture method of strangulation by bamboo pole.

Ostensibly, prisoner T-77 was in Leavenworth for murder—or more precisely, for *ordering* the murder of two senior Navy officers—a crime which in the US military carried the death sentence. However, the fact that the two Navy officers he'd had killed *had been advisers to the Joint Chiefs of Staff* elevated his crime to treason. High treason.

That—and his own previous high ranking—had earned him a place in T-Wing.

But even in T-Wing a man isn't entirely safe. T-77 had been beaten several times during his short residency there—on two occasions, so severely that he'd required blood transfusions.

In his former life, his name had been Charles Samson Russell and he had been a three-star Lieutenant General in the United States Air Force. Call-sign: *Caesar*.

He had a certified IQ of 182, genius level, and as such he had been a brilliant officer. Methodical and razor-sharp, he'd been the ultimate commander, hence his call-sign.

But most of all . . . *patient*, Caesar thought now as he watched the flickering television screen in front of him.

The two men on the screen—the Chief Justice of the

Supreme Court and the President-Elect—were finishing their duet. They stood in grey, wintry sunshine, on the West Portico of the Capitol Building. The new President had his hand on a Bible.

'... and will to the best of my ability ...'

'... and will to the best of my ability ...'

'... preserve, protect, and defend the Constitution of the United States, so help me God.'

'... preserve, protect, and defend the Constitution of the United States, so help me God.'

Fifteen years, Caesar thought.

Fifteen years, he had waited.

And now, at last, it had happened.

It hadn't been easy. There had been several false starts—including one who had made it to the election as a vice-presidential candidate, only to lose in a landslide. Four others had made it to the New Hampshire primary, but then failed to secure their parties' candidacy.

And of course, you always had some—like that Woolf fellow—who would quit politics before they had even begun to truly explore their presidential potential. It was an extra expense, but no matter. Even Senator Woolf had served a useful purpose.

But now ...

Now, it was different ...

Now, he had one ...

His theory had been borne out of a very simple fact.

For the last forty years, every American president bar one has hailed from two very elite clubs: state governors and federal senators.

Kennedy, Johnson, Nixon and Ford were all senators before they became President. Carter, Reagan and Clinton were all state governors. George Bush was the only exception—he was a member of the House of Representatives, not the Senate.

But, as General Charles Russell had *also* discovered, men

14

of influence were also men of extremely unpredictable health.

The ravages of their political lifestyles—high stress, constant travel, chronic lack of exercise—often took a great toll on their bodies.

And while getting the transmitter onto the heart of a sitting President was nigh on impossible, given the narrow source of American Presidents—senators and governors—getting it onto a man's coronary muscle *before* he became President wasn't out of the question.

Because, after all, a man is just a man before he becomes President.

The statistics for the next fifteen years spoke for themselves.

Forty-two per cent of US senators had had gall bladder surgery during their time in office, gallstones being a common problem for overweight middle-aged men.

Of the remaining fifty-eight per cent, only four would avoid some sort of surgical procedure during their political careers.

Kidney and liver operations were very common. Several heart bypasses—they were the easiest operations during which to plant the device—and not a few prostate problems.

And then there had been this one.

Halfway through his second term as governor of a large south-western state, he had complained of chest pains and laboured breathing. An exploratory procedure performed by a staff surgeon at the Air Force base just outside Houston had revealed an obstruction in the Governor's left lung, detritus from excessive smoking.

Through a deft procedure involving state-of-the-art fibre-optic cameras and ultra-small wire-controlled surgical instruments called nanotechnology, the obstruction was removed and the Governor told to quit smoking.

What the Governor did not know, however, was that during that operation the Air Force surgeon had attached a *second* piece of nanotechnology—a microscopic radio transmitter the size of a pin-head—to the outer wall of the Governor's heart.

Constructed of evanescent plastic—a semi-organic material which, over time, would partially dissolve into the outer tissue of the Governor's heart—the transmitter would ultimately take on a distorted shape, giving it the appearance of a harmless blood clot, thus masking it from discovery by any observation techniques such as X-rays. Anything larger or more regularly shaped would be detected on an incoming President's first physical, and that just couldn't be allowed to happen.

As a final precaution, it was inserted into the Governor's body 'cold'—unactivated. The White House's AXS-7 anti-bugging system would detect an unauthorised radio signal in an instant.

No.

Activation would occur later, when the time was right.

As usual, at the end of the procedure, one final operation was performed: a fine-grained plaster mould of the Governor's right hand was made.

It would also be necessary, when the time came.

The guards came for him ten minutes later.

Cuffed and chained, General Charles 'Caesar' Russell was escorted from his cell and taken to the waiting plane.

The trip to Indiana passed without incident, as did the sombre walk to the injection room.

The record would later show that as he lay spread-eagled on the injection table like a horizontal Christ, his arms and legs bound with worn leather straps, the prisoner refused to take the last rites. He had no last words, no final expression of remorse for his crimes. In fact, throughout the whole pre-injection ritual, he never said a word at all. This was consistent with Russell's post-trial actions—indeed, his execution had been fast-tracked because he had lodged no appeals of any kind.

The military tribunal that had sentenced him to death

had said that so heinous was his crime, he could never be allowed to leave federal custody alive.

They had been right.

At 3:37 p.m. on 20 January, the grim procedure took place. Fifty milligrams of sodium thiopental—to induce unconsciousness—was followed by ten of pancuronium bromide—to stop respiration—and then, finally, twenty milligrams of potassium chloride to stop Russell's heart.

At 3:40 p.m., three minutes later, Lieutenant General Charles Samson Russell was declared dead by the Terre Haute county coroner.

Since the General had no living relatives, his body was taken from the prison by members of the United States Air Force for immediate cremation.

At 3:52 p.m.—twelve minutes after he had been declared officially dead—as his body was being rushed through the streets of Terre Haute, Indiana, in the back of an Air Force ambulance, two electro-shock defibrillator paddles were applied to the dead General's chest and charged.

'Clear!' one of the Air Force medical personnel yelled.

The General's body convulsed violently as a wave of raw electric current shot through his vascular system.

It happened on the third applicaton of the paddles.

On the electro-cardiogram monitor on the wall, a small spike appeared.

The General's heartbeat had resumed.

Within moments, it was pulsing at a regular rhythm.

As General Russell well knew, death occurs when the heart is no longer able to deliver oxygen to the body. The act of respiration—breathing—oxygenates a person's blood, and then the person's heart delivers that oxygenated blood to the body.

It was the supply of *hyper*oxygenated blood coursing through Russell's arteries that had kept him alive for that crucial twelve minutes—blood that had been biogenetically crammed with oxygen-rich red cells; blood which during that twelve-minute period had continued to supply Russell's brain and vital organs with oxygen, even though his heart had stopped beating—blood which had been supplied to the General during the two transfusions that had been required after his unfortunate beatings at Leavenworth.

The military tribunal had said that he would never leave federal custody alive.

They had been right.

While all this was happening, in a stark empty cell in the Departure Lounge at Leavenworth Federal Penitentiary, the rickety old television remained on.

On it, the newly-crowned President—smiling, ecstatic, elated—waved to the cheering crowds.

O'Hare International Airport, Chicago, Illinois
3 July (Six months later)

They found the first one at O'Hare in Chicago, sitting inside an empty hangar at the farthest reaches of the airfield.

A regulation early-morning sweep with an electromagnetic reader had revealed a weak magnetic signal emanating from the suspect hangar.

The hangar had been completely deserted, except for the warhead standing in the exact centre of the cavernous interior space.

From a distance, it looked like a large silver cone about five feet tall mounted on a cargo pallet. Up close, one would recognise it more easily as a conical warhead designed to be inserted into a cruise missile.

Wires sprang out from its sides, connecting the warhead to a small upwardly-pointed satellite dish. Through a clear rectangular window set into the warhead's side, there could be seen a luminous purple liquid.

Plasma.

Type-240 blast plasma. An extremely volatile quasi-nuclear liquid explosive.

Enough to level a city.

Further investigations revealed that the magnetic signal that had been detected inside the hangar was part of a complex proximity sensor array surrounding the warhead. If anyone stepped within fifty feet of the bomb, a red warning light began to flash, indicating that the device had been armed.

Lease records revealed that the empty hangar belonged to the United States Air Force.

Then it was discovered that according to the airfield's log books, no Air Force personnel had set foot inside that hangar for at least six weeks.

A call was made to USAF Transportation Command at Scott Air Force Base.

The Air Force was vague, non-committal. It knew nothing about any plasma-based warheads at its civilian hangars. It would check with its people and get back to O'Hare ASAP.

It was then that reports came flooding in from around the country.

Identical warheads—all of them surrounded by magnetic proximity sensors; all with fold-out satellite dishes pointing up into the sky—had been found inside empty Air Force hangars at all three of New York's major airports: JFK, La Guardia and Newark.

And then Dulles in Washington called.

Then LAX.

San Francisco. San Diego.

Boston. Philadelphia.

St Louis. Denver.

Seattle. Detroit.

Fourteen devices in all, at fourteen airports across the country.

All armed. All set. All ready to go off.

All they were waiting for now was the signal.

FIRST CONFRONTATION

3 July, O6OO Hours

The three helicopters thundered over the arid desert plain, booming through the early morning silence.

They flew in tight formation—like they always did—shooting low over the tumbleweeds, kicking up a tornado of sand behind them, their freshly waxed sides glinting in the dawn light.

The giant Sikorsky VH-60N flew out in front—again, like it always did—flanked on either side by two menacing CH-53E Super Stallions.

With its pristine white roof and hand-polished dark-green flanks, the VH-60N is unique among American military helicopters. It is built for the United States government in a high security 'caged' section at the Sikorsky Aircraft plant in Connecticut. It is non-deployable—meaning that it is never used in any operational capacity by the United States Marine Corps, the branch of the military charged with its upkeep.

It is used for one thing, and one thing only. And it has no replicas on active duty—and for good reason, for no-one but a few highly-cleared Marine engineers and executives at Sikorsky can know all of its special features.

Paradoxically, for all this secrecy, the VH-60N is without a doubt the most recognised helicopter in the Western world.

On air traffic control displays, it is designated 'HMX-1', Marine Helicopter Squadron One, and its official radio call-sign is 'Nighthawk'. But over the years, the helicopter that ferries the President of the United States over short-to-medium distances has come to be known by a simpler name—Marine One.

Known as 'M1' to those who fly in it, it is rarely observed in flight, and when it is, it is usually in the most demure of circumstances—taking off from the manicured South Lawn of the White House or arriving at Camp David.

But not today.

Today it roared over the desert, transporting its famous passenger between two remote Air Force bases located in the barren Utah landscape.

Captain Shane M. Schofield, USMC, dressed in his full blue dress 'A' uniform—white peaked hat; navy-blue coat with gold buttons; medium-blue trousers with red stripe; spit-polished boots; white patent leather belt with matching white holster, inside of which resided an ornamental nickel-plated M9 pistol—stood in the cockpit of the Presidential helicopter, behind its two pilots, peering out through the chopper's reinforced forward windshield.

At five-ten, Schofield was lean and muscular, with a handsome narrow face and spiky black hair. And although they were not standard attire for Marines in full dress uniform, he also wore sunglasses—a pair of wraparound anti-flash glasses with reflective silver lenses.

The glasses covered a pair of prominent vertical scars that cut down across both of Schofield's eyes. They were wounds from a previous mission and the reason for his operational call-sign, 'Scarecrow'.

The flat desert plain stretched out before him, dull yellow against the morning sky. The dusty desert floor rushed by beneath the bow of the speeding helicopter.

In the near distance, Schofield saw a low mountain—their destination.

A cluster of buildings lay nestled at the base of the rocky hill, at the end of a long concrete runway, their tiny lights just visible in the early light. The main building of the complex appeared to be a large aeroplane hangar, half-buried in the side of the mountain.

It was United States Air Force Special Area (Restricted) 7, the second Air Force base they were to visit that day.

'Advance Team Two, this is Nighthawk One, we are on final approach to Area 7. Please confirm venue status,' the pilot of M1, Marine Colonel Michael 'Gunman' Grier said into his helmet mike.

There was no reply.

'I say again, Advance Team Two. Report.'

Still no reply.

'It's the jamming system,' Grier's co-pilot, Lieutenant Colonel Michelle Dallas, said. 'The radio guys at 8 said to expect it. These bases are all Level-7 classified, so they're covered at all times by a satellite-generated radiosphere. Short-range transmissions only, to stop anybody transmitting information out.'

Earlier that morning, the President had visited Area 8, a similarly isolated Air Force base about twenty miles to the east of Area 7. There, accompanied by his nine-man Secret Service Detail, he had been taken on a brief tour of the facility, to inspect some new aircraft stationed in its hangars.

While he had done so, Schofield and the other thirteen Marines stationed aboard Marine One and its two escort choppers had waited outside, twiddling their thumbs underneath Air Force One, the President's massive Boeing 747.

While they waited, some of the Marines had started arguing over why they hadn't been allowed inside the main hangar of Area 8. The general consensus—based solely on wild unsubstantiated gossip—had been that it was because the facility housed some of the Air Force's top secret new aeroplanes.

One soldier, a big-smiling, loud-talking African–American sergeant named Wendall 'Elvis' Haynes, said that he'd heard they had the *Aurora* in there, the legendary low-orbit spy plane capable of speeds over Mach 9. The current fastest plane in the world, the SR-71 Blackbird, could only reach Mach 3.

Others had proffered that a whole squadron of F-44s—ultra-nimble, wedged-shaped fighters based on the flying-wing shape of the B-2 stealth bomber—were stationed there.

Others still—perhaps inspired by the launch of a Chinese space shuttle two days previously—suggested that Area 8 housed the X-38, a sleek 747-launched offensive space shuttle. A black project run by the Air Force in association with NASA, the X-38 was reputedly the world's first fight-capable space vehicle, an attack shuttle.

Schofield ignored their speculation.

He didn't have to guess that Area 8 had something to do with top-secret aeroplane development, probably space-based. He could tell it from one simple fact.

Although the Air Force engineers had concealed it well, the regulation-size black bitumen runway of Area 8 actually *extended* another thousand yards in both directions—as a pale concrete landing strip hidden beneath a thin layer of sand and carefully-placed tumbleweeds.

It was an elongated runway, designed to launch and receive aircraft that needed an extra-long landing strip, which meant aircraft like space shuttles or—

And then suddenly the President had emerged from the main hangar and they were on the move again.

Originally, the Boss had intended to fly to Area 7 on Air Force One. It would be faster than Marine One, even though the distance was short.

But there had been a problem on Air Force One. An unexpected leak in the left wing's fuel tank.

And so the Boss had taken Marine One—always on stand-by for precisely this situation.

Which was why Schofield was now gazing at Area 7, lit up like a Christmas tree in the dim morning light.

As he peered at the distant hangar complex, however, Schofield had a strange thought. Curiously, none of his colleagues on HMX-1 knew any stories about Area 7, not even wild unsubstantiated rumours.

No-one, it seemed, knew what went on at Area 7.

Life in the immediate vicinity of the President of the United States was a world unto itself.

It was at the same time both thrilling and frightening, Schofield thought.

Thrilling because you were so close to one with so much power, and frightening because that man was surrounded by a great number of people who claimed his influence as their own.

Indeed, even in his short time on board Marine One, Schofield had observed that at any one time, there were at least three competing power clusters vying for the President's attention.

First was the President's own staff, those people—largely self-important Harvard types—whom the President had appointed to aid him on a range of matters: from national security and domestic policy; to the management of the press corps or the management of his political life.

No matter what their field of expertise, at least insofar as Schofield could see, each of the President's personal staff seemed to have one all-encompassing goal: to get the President outside, onto the streets, and into the public eye.

In direct contrast to this objective—indeed, in direct opposition to it—was the second group vying for the President's ear: his protectors, the United States Secret Service.

Led by the stoic, no-nonsense and completely impassive Special Agent Francis X. Cutler, the Presidential Detail was constantly at loggerheads with the White House staff.

Cutler—officially known as 'Chief of the Detail', but known to the President merely as Frank—was renowned for his coolness under pressure and his complete intransigence to pleas from political ass-kissers. With his narrow grey eyes and matching crew-cut hair, Frank Cutler could stare down any member of the President's staff and rebuff them with a single word, 'No'.

The third and last group pressing for presidential attention was the crew of Marine One itself.

Not only were they also subjected to the inflated egos of the presidential staff—Schofield would never forget his first flight on Marine One, when the President's Domestic Policy Adviser, a pompous twenty-nine-year-old lawyer from New York, had ordered Schofield to get him a double latte, and to 'make it quick'—they were also often at odds with the Secret Service.

Securing the President's safety may have been the job of the Secret Service, but when he was on HMX-1, so the Marine Corps reasoned, the Boss had at least six United States Marines on board with him at any given time.

An uneasy truce had been brokered.

While on board Marine One, the President's safety would be in Marine hands. As such, only key members of his Secret Service Detail—Frank Cutler and a few others—would fly with him. The rest of his personal Detail would fly in the two chase helicopters.

As soon as the President stepped off Marine One, however, his well-being was once again the exclusive responsibility of the United States Secret Service.

Gunman Grier spoke into his helmet mike. 'Nighthawk Three, this is Nighthawk One. Go and check on Advance Team Two for me. This radiosphere is screwing up our long-range comms. I'm picking up their All-Clear beacon, but I can't get any voice contact. They should be over at the exit vent. And if you get close enough, see if you can raise Area 8 again. Find out what's happening with Air Force One.'

'*Copy that, Nighthawk One,*' a voice replied over the short-wave. '*On our way.*'

From his position behind Grier and Dallas, Schofield saw the Super Stallion to their right peel away from the group and head off over the desert.

The two remaining choppers of Marine Helicopter Squadron-1 continued on their way.

In a darkened room somewhere, a blue-uniformed man wearing a radio headset and seated in front of an illuminated computer display spoke quietly into his wraparound microphone.

'—Initiating primary satellite signal test . . . *now*—'

He pressed a button on his console.

'What the hell—?' Dallas said, touching her earpiece.

'What is it?' Gunman Grier asked.

'I don't know,' Dallas said, swivelling in her seat. 'I just picked up a spike on the microwave band.'

She looked at the microwave display screen—it depicted a series of jagged spikes and troughs—then shook her head. 'Strange. Looks like an incoming microwave signal just hit us and then bounced away.'

'Anti-bugging was done this morning,' Grier said. 'Twice.'

Comprehensive sweeps for listening devices planted on Marine One—and her passengers—were done with rigorous regularity. It was nigh on impossible to plant a transmitting or receiving device on the President's helicopter.

Dallas peered at her screen, shrugging. 'The signal's too small to be a location beacon. Ditto, speech or computer data. It didn't send or take any information—it's as if it was just, well, checking to see if we were here.' She turned to Grier questioningly.

The Presidential Helicopter Pilot frowned. 'Most probably it's just a surge in the radiosphere, a deflected microwave signal. But let's not take any chances.' He turned to Schofield. 'Captain, if you wouldn't mind, would you please do a sweep of the aircraft with the magic wand.'

'—Return signal received,' the console operator in the darkened room said. 'Primary signal test successful. The device is operational. Repeat. *The device is operational.* Switching back to dormant mode. All right. Commencing test of secondary signal—'

Schofield stepped into the main cabin of Marine One, waving a AXS-9 digital spectrum analyser over the walls, seats, ceiling and floor, searching for anything that was emitting an outgoing signal.

As one would expect of the President's helicopter, the interior of M1 was plush. Indeed, with its deep maroon carpet and widely-spaced seats, it looked more like the first-class section of a commercial airliner than the hold of a military aircraft.

Twelve beige leather seats took up most of the main cabin. Each seat had the Seal of the President of the United States embroidered on it, as did the oversized armrests that adjoined each chair and the scotch glasses and coffee mugs, just in case anyone forgot in whose presence they were travelling.

At the rear of the central area, guarded at all times by a Marine in full dress uniform, was a polished mahogany door that led to the aft-most section of the helicopter.

It was the President's private office.

Small but elegantly appointed—and featuring an amazingly compact arrangement of phones, faxes, computers and televisions—Marine One's office allowed the Boss to monitor the nation's business wherever he happened to be.

At the very rear of the President's office, behind a small pressure-sealed door, was one final feature of Marine One which was reserved for use in only the most dire of circumstances—a small one-man ejection unit, the Presidential escape pod.

Schofield waved his spectrum analyser over the seats in the first-class section, searching for bugs.

Seated there were Frank Cutler and five of his Secret Service people. They peered out the windows, ignoring Schofield as he did his sweep around them.

Also there were a couple of the President's advisers—his Deputy Chief of Staff, his Communications Director—both of whom flicked through thick manila folders.

Standing above them, manning the two exit doors at either end of the main cabin, were a pair of straight-backed United States Marines.

There was one more person seated in the main cabin.

A stocky no-necked man dressed in an olive US Army uniform, sitting quietly at the back of the cabin, in the first-class seat closest to the President's office.

To look at him, with his carrot-red hair and bushy orange moustache, he didn't seem like anyone special, and truth be told, he wasn't anyone special.

He was an Army warrant officer named Carl Webster, and he followed the President wherever he went—not because of any special expertise or knowledge he possessed, but because of the extremely important object handcuffed to his right wrist: a stainless-steel briefcase that contained the codes and the activation switches to America's nuclear arsenal, a briefcase known as 'the Football'.

Schofield finished his sweep, including a short 'excuse me' check of the President's office.

Nothing.

There was not a single bug to be found on the helicopter.

He returned to the cockpit, just in time to hear Gunman Grier say into his mike:'Copy that, Nighthawk Three, thank you. Continue on to the vent.'

Grier turned to his co-pilot. 'Air Force One's back on

deck. It was just a valve leak. It'll stay at Area 8. We'll bring the Boss back after our little visit to Area 7. Scarecrow?'

'Nothing,' Schofield said. 'The helicopter's clean.'

Grier shrugged. 'Must have been the radiosphere. Thanks, Scarecrow.'

Suddenly Grier touched his helmet as another message came through.

He sighed wearily as the voice at the other end nattered into his ear.

'We'll do our best, Colonel,' he said, 'but I make no promises.' Grier switched off his mike and shook his head. 'Fucking Ramrod.'

He turned to Schofield and Dallas. 'Ladies and gentlemen, our esteemed White House Liaison Officer has asked us to pick up the pace a little. Apparently, the Boss has an afternoon tea with the Washington Ladies' Auxiliary to get to, and Liaison Officer Hagerty thinks we're not going fast enough to meet his schedule.'

Dallas snuffed a laugh. 'Good ol' Ramrod.'

When it came to the use of Marine One, all White House–Marine Corps correspondence went through a Marine colonel called the White House Liaison Officer, a position which for the last three years had been held by Colonel Rodney Hagerty, USMC.

Unfortunately, Hagerty, forty-one years old, tall and lanky, with a pencil-thin moustache and a far too proper manner, was regarded by many in HMX-1 as the worst kind of soldier—a ladder climber, but also a ruthless expert in office politics, someone more interested in getting stars on his shoulders than actually being a United States Marine. But as so often happens, the upper echelons of the Corps didn't see this and kept promoting him nonetheless.

Even Schofield disliked him. Hagerty was a bureaucrat— a bureaucrat who had obviously come to enjoy his proximity to power. Although his official call-sign was 'Hot Rod', his rigid adherence to procedure and protocol, even when it was patently impractical, had earned him an alternate call-sign among the troops: 'Ramrod'.

★

At that very same moment, the lone Super Stallion chopper that was Nighthawk Three was landing in a cloud of dust on the sandy desert plain. About half a mile to the west stood the low rocky mountain that housed Area 7.

As the big chopper's tyres hit the ground, four Marines dressed in full combat attire leaped out from it and ran over to a small trench carved into the rock-hard desert floor.

The trench housed Area 7's EEV—Emergency Escape Vent—the well-concealed exit point of a long underground tunnel that provided emergency egress from Area 7. Today it was the primary escape route from the complex, in the unlikely event that the President encountered any trouble there.

The lead Marine, a lieutenant named Corbin 'Colt' Hendricks, approached the dusty earthen hole, accompanied by his three subordinates, MP-5/10—sometimes called the MP-10, they were 10 mm versions of the Heckler & Koch MP-5—in hand.

A steady *beep*-pause-*beep* warbled in Hendricks' ear-piece: Advance Team 2's All-Clear beacon. The A-C beacon couldn't transmit voice messages, but its powerful digital signal still provided a worthwhile service: if Advance Team 2 encountered any kind of ambush or disturbance, its lead agent simply flicked off the All-Clear beacon and everyone else in the presidential entourage would know that danger was afoot. Its presence now was reassuring.

Hendricks and his squad came to the edge of the trench and looked down into it.

'Oh *shit* . . .' Hendricks breathed.

The other two Presidential helicopters raced toward Restricted Area 7.

'Hey, Scarecrow?' Gunman Grier turned in his seat to face Schofield. 'Where's your harem?'

Through his reflective silver sunglasses, Schofield offered a crooked smile to the Presidential Helicopter Pilot.

'They're over on Nighthawk Two today, sir,' he said.

Grier was referring to the two female members of Schofield's former unit who had joined him on his tour on board Marine Helicopter Squadron-1—Staff Sergeant Elizabeth 'Fox' Gant and Gunnery Sergeant Gena 'Mother' Newman.

As a former commander of a Marine Force Reconnaissance Unit, Schofield was something of a rarity on board Marine One.

Owing to the largely ceremonial duties associated with working on the President's helicopter and to the fact that time spent on board the helicopter is *not* counted as 'active deployed airtime', many Marines choose to avoid HMX-1 duty. Indeed, with few exceptions, most of the troops assigned to HMX-1 are relatively junior soldiers who won't miss any promotional opportunities.

So to have a former Recon commander on board was highly unusual, but something which Gunman Grier welcomed.

He liked Schofield. He'd heard on the grapevine that he was a gifted field commander—a man who looked out for his men, and as a result, got the very best out of them.

Grier had also heard about what had happened to Schofield on his last mission and he respected the young captain for it.

He also liked both Mother and Gant—admired their attitudes to their work and their fierce loyalty to their former commander—and his labelling of them as Schofield's 'harem' was a sign of affection from a man who rarely showed it.

Schofield, however, was used to being considered unusual.

Indeed, that was why he was stationed aboard Marine One.

About eighteen months previously, as a lieutenant, he'd been in command of a Marine Reconnaissance Unit that had been sent to a remote ice station in Antarctica, to investigate the discovery of a possible alien spacecraft.

In a word, the mission had gone to hell on an express elevator.

Including himself, only four of his twelve Marines had survived the nightmare, during which they had been forced to defend the station against two foreign military forces and infiltrators from within their own unit. To top it off, Schofield himself had been declared dead by some corrupt members of the Marine Corps hierarchy, men who had been prepared to make that lie a reality.

His eventual return to America—alive and well—had sparked a media frenzy.

His face appeared on every major newspaper in the nation. Wherever he went, even after the initial frenzy, tabloid journalists and photographers tried to snap his picture or coax information out of him. After all, he was a walking talking monument to the corruption of the United States military— the good soldier who had been targeted for extermination by the faceless generals of his own military leadership.

Which left the Marine Corps with a serious problem: *where to put him?*

In the end, the answer had been rather inventive.

The safest place to hide Schofield was right in front of the world's media, but in the one place where they wouldn't be able to touch him.

He would be assigned to Marine One.

The chopper was based at the Marine Corps Air Facility at Quantico, Virginia, so Schofield could live on the base, making access to him all but impossible. And he would work on board the President's VH-60N, which was only really ever seen landing at the White House, and even then, always at a safe distance from the press.

When the transfer was made, Mother and Gant had elected to go with Schofield. The fourth survivor of their Antarctic disaster, a private named Rebound Simmons, had decided to leave the Marine Corps after their ill-fated mission.

That had been a year ago.

In that time, Schofield—quiet at the best of times and not given to small talk—had made only a handful of friends in the White House: mainly people among the Secret Service and the domestic staff; the ordinary people. With his reflective silver anti-flash glasses, however, he was popular with the President's playful grandkids. As such, to their delight, he was nearly always assigned to guard them whenever they visited. And yet, despite this, he had never actually spoken conversationally with the President.

Area 7 loomed large in front of Marine One. Schofield could see the massive doors of the complex's enormous hangar slowly opening, revealing bright electric lighting inside.

Grier spoke into his helmet mike: 'Nighthawk Two, this is Nighthawk One, beginning descent now.'

In the belly of Nighthawk Two, Sergeant Elizabeth 'Fox' Gant sat hunched in a canvas jumpseat, trying vainly to read from a folder perched on her knees.

Unlike Marine One, the rotor noise inside Nighthawk Two was absolutely deafening. And since it never carried the President, its interior decor was about a thousand times more utilitarian. No upholstered seats or embroidered armrests here.

Now a staff sergeant, Libby Gant was twenty-eight years old, well, as of six hours ago.

Compact and fit, she had short blonde hair and sky-blue eyes, and in regular battle dress—fatigues, body armour and MP-10—she cut a smart figure. In full dress uniform—peaked hat, dress coat and trousers—she looked spectacular.

Since they were flying in restricted Air Force airspace, the mood on board Nighthawk Two was relaxed. The usual tensions of co-ordinating Marine One's flight path with those of civilian air traffic weren't an issue, so Gant—studying part-time for entry into Officer Candidate School—took the opportunity to brush up on some of her notes.

She was just getting to Course 9405, Advanced Tactical Command, when a soft voice invaded her consciousness.

'Happy birthday to you . . .

Happy birthday to you . . .

Happy birthday, dear Staff Sergeant Ga-ant . . .

Happy birthday to you.'

She looked up from her work and sighed.

Sliding into the empty seat beside her was Nicholas Tate III, the President's Domestic Policy Adviser. Tate was handsome in a European sort of way—with dark eyebrows, olive skin and a male model's jawline—and confident in the extreme. Today he wore a three-thousand-dollar Armani suit and matching Armani cologne. Apparently it was the latest thing.

Tate held out a small neatly-wrapped package for Gant to take.

'Twenty-eight, if I'm not mistaken,' he said.

'That's right, sir,' Gant said.

'Please, call me Nick.' He nodded at the gift. 'Well, go on. Open it.'

Reluctantly, Gant unwrapped the small package, unveiling an aqua-green box. She popped the lid, revealing an absolutely gorgeous silver necklace.

Small and thin, it looked like a length of the finest silver thread, its polished surface sparkling. A small but stylish diamond dangled like a teardrop from the front of the necklace.

'It's from Tiffany's,' Tate said.

Gant looked up at him. 'I'm not allowed to wear jewellery in uniform, Mr Tate.'

'I know. I was hoping you could wear it when I took you to dinner at Nino's next Saturday.'

Nino's was a restaurant in Georgetown, popular among Washington socialites and arguably the most expensive eatery in town.

Gant sighed. 'I'm seeing someone.'

It was kind of true. Only last weekend, after a tentative start, she and Shane Schofield had gone out on something resembling a date.

'Now, now, now,' Tate said, 'I heard about that. One date does not a relationship make.'

This was getting difficult. Gant held the necklace up to the light of the window. 'You know, this looks a lot like a necklace I saw in Paris once.'

'Oh, really?'

At Gant's mention of the word 'Paris', however, one of the other Marines sitting nearby cocked her head to the side. Tate never saw it.

'Yes,' Gant said. 'We were there a couple of months ago with the Boss, and I had a day off, so I—'

'Jesus H. Christ, would you take a look at *that*!' a lusty woman's voice cut Gant off.

'Hey there, Mother,' Gant said, as Gunnery Sergeant Gena 'Mother' Newman appeared in the narrow aisle next to her.

'How you doin' there, Birthday Babe?' Mother said with a knowing smile.

The 'Paris' code was one they had used several times before. When either of them encountered an unwanted male admirer, she would slip the word 'Paris' into the conversation and the other, hearing the signal, would come to the rescue. It was a common trick used by girlfriends worldwide.

Granted, at six feet four inches and an even 200 pounds, Mother rarely had to use it. With her dark, heavyset features, fully shaved head and gruff no-nonsense manner, she was almost the perfect antithesis of Libby Gant. Her call-sign, 'Mother', said it all, really. It wasn't indicative of any extraordinary maternal qualities. It was short for *motherfucker*. A gifted warrior, adept at all kinds of heavy weaponry and guncraft, she'd been promoted to the highly-respected rank of gunnery sergeant a year ago.

In addition to this—thanks to a close encounter with a killer whale during the disastrous mission to Antarctica— Mother had one other, highly unusual physical feature.

A prosthetic lower left leg.

The nasty incident with the killer whale had deprived her of everything below the left knee. That said, she'd done better than the killer had. It had received a bullet to its brain.

What Mother now had in place of her natural left foot and shin was a state-of-the-art prosthetic limb which, so its makers claimed, guaranteed total and undiminished body movement. Featuring titanium-alloy 'bones', fully rotating joints and hydraulic muscle simulators, its operation was so sophisticated—involving nerve impulse reception and automatic weight-shifting—that it required an internal prologic computer chip to control it.

Mother was gazing at the glistening Tiffany's necklace.

'Whoa, that is one mighty fine piece of jewellery,' she gawped. She turned to Nick Tate: 'That piece of string must have cost you a pretty penny, sonny Jim.'

'It was within my price range,' Tate said coolly.

'Probably cost more than I make in a *year*.'

'Probably did.'

Mother ignored him, turned to Gant. 'Sorry to rain on your parade, Birthday Babe, but the skipper sent me back to get you. He wants you up front for the landing.'

'Oh, okay.'

Gant stood, and as she did, she handed Tate back his

necklace. 'I'm sorry, Nicholas, but I can't accept this. I'm *seeing* someone else.'

And with that she headed up front.

Over at the Emergency Escape Vent, Colt Hendricks just stood with his mouth agape, staring down into the trench.

The sight before him was nothing short of horrific.

All nine members of the Secret Service's secondary advance team lay on the sand-covered floor of the trench, their bodies twisted at all angles, riddled with bullet holes. The size of the wounds indicated hollow-point ammunition had been used—bullets that expanded once they entered the wound, guaranteeing a kill. A few of the agents had been shot in the face—their heads had been all but blown off. Blood was everywhere, drying in the sand.

Hendricks saw the agent-in-charge of the Secret Service team, a man named Baker—mouth open, eyes wide, bullet hole in the forehead. In Agent Baker's outstretched hand was the Advance Team's All-Clear beacon switch. The attack must have happened so quickly that he hadn't even had time to flick the switch.

Beyond Baker, Hendricks saw a solid-looking steel door set into the dirt wall of the trench—the escape vent itself. It just stood there, resolutely closed.

Hendricks spun on his heel, yanked out his radio, headed back toward Nighthawk Three.

'Nighthawk One!'

Radio static.

'*Goddamn it!* Nighthawk One! This is—'

It was as if the desert just came alive.

The dusty desert floor parted—sand falling off canvas ambush covers—and suddenly, from *both* sides of Hendricks, about a dozen man-sized shapes rose from the sand, sub-machine guns raised and firing.

A second later, a 9-millimetre Silvertip bullet entered Hendricks's brain from the side. The subsequent gaseous expansion of the hollow-pointed projectile caused his head to explode.

Hendricks never saw the man who killed him.

Never saw the dark team of desert wraiths take down the rest of his men with clinical, ruthless efficiency.

And he never saw them take his helicopter and fly it back toward Area 7.

The two remaining Presidential helicopters descended together, landing in a whirlwind of sand in front of the massive main hangar of United States Air Force Special Area (Restricted) No. 7.

The giant hangar's enormous twin doors yawned wide, its interior brightly illuminated. The low mountain into which the hangar had been carved loomed over the squat four-building complex.

No sooner had the two choppers touched the ground than the Secret Service people from Nighthawk Two were dashing to their positions around Marine One.

A welcoming party stood on the runway in front of the hangar, standing silently in the cool morning air, silhouetted by the hangar light behind them.

Two Air Force officers—one colonel and one major—stood at the head of the welcoming unit.

Behind the two officers stood four rows of fully-armed commandos, ten men to a row. All of them were dressed in full combat gear—black battledress uniforms, black body armour, black helmets—and they all held high-tech Belgian-made P-90 assault rifles rigidly across their chests.

Looking out through Marine One's cockpit windshield, Schofield recognised their insignia patches at once. They were members of a unit rarely seen at US military

42

exercises, a unit which was shrouded in secrecy, a unit which many believed was used only in the most critical of missions.

It was the elite ground unit in the United States Air Force, the famous 7th Special Operations Squadron.

Based in West Germany for much of the Cold War, its official task during that time was the defence of US airfields against the elite Soviet Spetsnaz units. Its unofficial achievements, though, were far more spectacular.

Masterminding the defection of five senior Soviet nuclear missile specialists from a secret base in the Ukraine mountains. The assassination of KGB operations chief Vladimir Nakov in Moscow in 1990, before Nakov could himself assassinate Mikhail Gorbachev. And, finally, in 1997, the daring rescue of the CIA's captured Far Eastern Bureau Chief, Fred Conway, from the dreaded Xiangi Prison—the all but impregnable maze of grim cells and torture chambers belonging to the notorious Chinese External Intelligence Service.

Each man in the formation wore a special combat mask around his throat—an ERG-6 gas-mask. Black and hard, it looked like the lower half of a hockey mask, and it covered its wearer's mouth and nose in much the same way Jesse James's mask had covered his face in the old days.

Three other men stood out in front of the detachment of 7th Squadron members on the deserted runway. All three wore starched white labcoats. Scientists.

Once the Marine and Secret Service people from Nighthawk Two were in place, a set of Airstairs folded down from the forward left-hand side of Marine One.

Two Marines emerged from the helicopter first and took up their positions at the base of the stairs, backs straight, eyes forward.

A moment later, Special Agent Frank Cutler stepped out of the chopper, hand on his holster, eyes watchful. The Secret Service trusts nobody. Not even the United States Air Force. Even it could have a disgruntled soldier who might take a shot at the President.

The President came out next, followed by his staff.

Schofield and a young Marine corporal emerged last of all.

As usual, Marine One's two pilots, Gunman and Dallas, stayed on board just in case a rapid departure was called for.

The two parties faced each other on the runway in the early morning light—the Air Force detachment stationed at the complex; the President and his entourage.

Twisting coils of windswept sand swirled around their bodies. A sandstorm was due later in the day.

A young Air Force captain guided the President over to the colonel at the head of the Air Force formation—a severe-looking man with grey hair and eyebrows. As the President came closer, the colonel stepped forward and crisply saluted his Commander-in-Chief.

'Good morning, Mister President,' he said. 'My name is Colonel Jerome T. Harper, United States Air Force Medical and Surgical Command, and commanding officer of United States Air Force Special Area (Restricted) 7. This is Major Kurt Logan, commander of the 7th Squadron forces here at the base. Your two Secret Service advance teams are waiting for you inside. We're honoured to have you, sir. Welcome to Area 7.'

'Thank you, Colonel,' the President replied. 'It's a pleasure to be here. Lead the way.'

As soon as the President was taken away, disappearing inside the enormous main hangar with his highest-level entourage in tow, the major in charge of the 7th Squadron detachment came up to Schofield.

Major Kurt Logan was about six-one, with closely shaved hair and heavily pockmarked skin. Schofield had actually met him before, although he doubted Logan would remember him.

It had been at a special command and leadership course run by the Navy at their SEAL compound in Fort Lauderdale in 1997. Through a combination of smart tactics and ruthless follow-through, the softly-spoken Logan had come first in the class by a clear forty points. He could assess any battlefield situation in an instant, and when it came to engaging the enemy, he was uncompromising. Schofield, then just a budding Recon Unit commander, had come tenth in a class of sixteen.

From the looks of things, Logan hadn't changed much. His whole bearing—hands clasped firmly behind his back, steely level gaze—indicated a powerful, confident inner strength. Battle-hardened strength.

'Excuse me, Captain,' Logan said in a soft Southern drawl. He offered Schofield a sheet of paper. 'Our personnel list for your records.'

Schofield took the list, then gave one of his own to Logan in return.

It was common practice at presidential inspections for both sides to swap personnel lists, since the President's people wanted to know who was at the base they were inspecting, and the base people wanted to know exactly who was in the presidential convoy.

Schofield glanced at the Area 7 list. Columns of meaningless names ran down it.

UNITED STATES AIR FORCE
SPECIAL AREA (RESTRICTED) 07
ON-SITE PERSONNEL
CLASSIFICATION: TOP SECRET

NAME	UNIT	NAME	UNIT	NAME	UNIT
COMMAND UNIT					
Harper, JT (CO)					
7TH SQUADRON					
Alvarez, MJ	A	Dillan, ST	D	Logan, KW (MAJ)	A
Arthurs, RT	C	Doheny, FG	A	McConnell, BA	B
Atlock, FD	B	Egan, RR	B	Messick, K	E
Baines, AW	A	Fraser, MS	C	Milbourn, SK	D
Bennett, B	E	Fredericks, GH	A	Morton, IN	C
Biggs, NM	C	Frommer, SN	E	Nance, GF	D
Boland, CS	B	Gale, A	D	Nystrom, JJ	D
Boyce, LW	D	Giggs, RE	B	Oliver, PK	E
Calvert, ET	E	Golding, DK	D	Price, AL	C
Carney, LE	E	Goldman, WE	A	Rawson, MJ	C
Christian, FC	A	Grayson, SR	E	Sayles, MT	B
Coleman, GK	E	Hughes, R	A	Sommers, SR	C
Coles, M	B	Ingliss, WA	B	Stone, JK	C
Crick, DT	D	Johnson, SW	D	Taylor, AS	B
Criece, TW	A	Jones, M	D	Willis, LS	C
Davis, AM	E	Kincaid, R	B	Wolfson, HT	A
Dayton, AM	E	Littleton, SO	E		
CIVILIAN STAFF					
Botha, GW	MED				
Franklin, HS	MED				
Shaw, DE	MED				

46

He did notice something, though.

There were more names here than there were 7th Squadron men on the tarmac. While there had been forty commandos out on the tarmac, there were fifty 7th Squadron members on the list. He figured there must be another ten-man unit inside the base somewhere.

As Schofield looked at the list, Logan said, 'Captain, if you wouldn't mind, we'd like you to move your—'

'What appears to be the problem, Major?' a voice said from behind Schofield. 'Don't bother with Captain Schofield. *I* am in command here.'

It was Ramrod Hagerty, the White House Liaison Officer. With his Englishman's moustache and distinctly *un*battle-hardened posture, Hagerty was everything Kurt Logan was not.

Before he answered him, Logan looked Hagerty up and down. What he saw obviously didn't impress him.

'I was led to believe that Colonel Grier was in ultimate command of Marine One,' Logan said coolly—and correctly.

'Well, ah, yes . . . yes, *technically*, he is,' Hagerty said. 'But, as White House Liaison, anything to do with the movement of these helicopters must go through me first.'

Logan looked at Hagerty in stony silence.

Then he said, 'I was about to ask the captain here if he wouldn't mind rolling your helicopters into the main hangar while the President is at the base. We wouldn't want enemy satellites knowing that we had the Boss visiting, now would we?'

'No, no, of course not. Of course not,' Ramrod said. 'Schofield. Make it happen.'

'Yes, sir,' Schofield said drily.

The giant double doors of the hangar closed with a resounding *boom*.

The two lead helicopters of Marine Helicopter Squadron-1 were now parked inside the main hangar of Area 7, their rotors and tail booms folded into their stowed positions.

Despite their own considerable size, the two Presidential helicopters were dwarfed by the cavernous hangar.

Having supervised the roll-in of the choppers, Schofield now stood in the middle of the massive interior space, alone, scanning it silently.

The rest of the Marine, White House and Secret Service contingent—those who hadn't been senior enough to go with the President, about twenty people—variously milled about the helicopters or drank coffee in the two glass-walled offices that flanked the main doors.

The size of the hangar stunned Schofield.

It was *gigantic*.

Completely illuminated by brilliant white halogen lights, it must have stretched at least a hundred yards into the mountain. A ceiling-mounted rail system ran for its entire length. At the moment, two large wooden crates hung from the rails at either end of the hangar.

At the far end of the vast space—facing the doors that led out to the runway—stood a two-storey, completely *internal* building that ran for the full width of the hangar. This building's upper floor had angled glass windows that looked out over the hangar floor.

A small unobtrusive personnel elevator sat quietly underneath the overhang created by the building's upper level, sunk in the hangar's northern wall.

Apart from the Presidential helicopters, there were no other aircraft in the hangar at present. Some large white-painted towing vehicles not unlike those seen at airports lay scattered around the hangar floor—indeed, Schofield had used two of them to bring in the choppers.

By far the most striking feature of the immense hangar, however, was the massive aircraft elevator platform that lay in its centre.

It was *huge*, unbelievably huge, like the enormous hydraulic elevators that hang off the sides of aircraft carriers—a giant square-shaped platform in the very centre of the hangar.

At 200 feet by 200 feet, the platform was large enough to hold an entire AWACS Boeing 707—the Air Force's famous radar-detecting aeroplanes, known for the thirty-foot flying-saucer-like rotodomes mounted on their backs.

Supported by an unseen hydraulic lift system, the giant platform took up nearly the whole of the central area of the hangar. As with similar aircraft elevators, to maximise efficiency, on the north-eastern corner of the platform was a small *detachable* section which was itself a working elevator, capable of operating independently of the larger platform. To do this it ran on rails attached to the wall of the elevator shaft rather than on the main platform's telescoping hydraulic strut—a kind of 'platform within a platform', so to speak.

Today, however, the Air Force personnel at Area 7 were putting on the whole show.

As he stood at the edge of the enormous elevator shaft, Schofield could see the President—with his nine-man Secret Service Detail and his high-ranking Air Force tour guides—standing on the full-sized platform, getting smaller and smaller as they descended the wide concrete shaft on it.

At that very same moment, as Shane Schofield stood in the centre of the vast hangar bay, looking down into the wide elevator shaft, someone else was watching *him*.

The watcher stood in Area 7's darkened control room, on the upper floor of the internal building that formed the eastern wall of the hangar. Around him, four uniformed radio operators spoke softly into headset microphones:

'—Alpha Unit, cover the Level 3 common room—'

'—Echo Unit advises that the Marine investigatory team from Nighthawk Three had to be neutralised out at the EEV. They found the secondary advance team. Echo is parking their chopper in one of the outside hangars now. Returning to the main hangar when they're done—'

'—Bravo and Charlie Units are to remain in main hangar—'

'—Delta Unit reports that it is now in position—'

'—the Secret Service are trying to contact their primary

advance team on Level 6. The simulated All-Clear signal, however, appears to be working—'

Major Kurt Logan arrived at the side of the shadowy figure. 'Sir. The President and his Detail just arrived on Level 4. All units are in position.'

'Good.'

'Shall we move now?'

'No. Let him take the tour,' the faceless man said. 'There is still one more thing that has to be taken care of before we can begin.'

'Good morning.'

Schofield turned, and saw the smiling faces of Libby Gant and Mother Newman.

'Hey there,' he said.

'Ralph's still pissed at you,' Mother said. 'He wants a rematch.'

Ralph was Mother's husband. A short nugget of a man with a moon-shaped smiling face and a limitless ability to put up with Mother's eccentricities, he was a trucker, owning his own Mack eighteen-wheeler. It had a painting of an arrow-struck heart on its side with the word '*Mother*' flowing over it. With his short stature and ready smile, Ralph was widely regarded in the Marine community as a bona fide legend.

He was also the proud owner of a new barbecue, and at the obligatory Sunday afternoon lunch at Mother's place a few weeks ago, he'd challenged Schofield to a shoot-off on the garage basketball hoop. Schofield had let him win and Ralph knew it.

'Maybe next weekend?' Schofield said. 'How about you? How'd that check-up on the leg go yesterday?'

'In a word, Scarecrow, sen-*fucking*-sational,' Mother said. 'I got full movement and I can run just as fast as I used to. That seemed to satisfy the docs. Hell, I told 'em that just last week

I bowled 275, but that didn't seem to mean much. Either way, since I'm now part machine, I want a new nickname: Darth Fucking Vader.'

Schofield laughed. 'Okay, Darth.'

'You having trouble with Ramrod again?' Gant asked seriously.

'The usual,' Schofield said. 'Hey, happy birthday.'

Gant smiled. 'Thanks.'

'I got you something.' Schofield reached into his dress coat pocket. 'It's not huge or anything, but . . .' he frowned, patted his other pockets. 'Damn, it's here somewhere. Maybe it's back on the chopper . . .'

'Don't worry about it.'

'Can I give it to you later?'

'Sure.'

Mother gazed at the enormous hangar around them. 'What the fuck is this place? Looks like Fort Knox.'

'More than that,' Schofield said.

'What do you mean?'

'Look at the floor just inside the hangar doors.'

Mother and Gant did. A series of box-shaped indentations ran in a line across the concrete floor in front of the doors. Each indentation was at least a yard square and deep.

'Now look up.'

They did, and saw a series of thick, tooth-like metal protrusions—protrusions which, when lowered, would fit perfectly into the box-shaped indentations on the floor.

'Piston-driven armoured door,' Schofield said, 'like the ones they have on Nimitz-class carriers. They're used to divide the ship's hangar bays into self-contained zones in case of fire or explosion. But, you'll notice that there aren't any other armoured doors in this hangar. That's the only one, which means it's the only exit.'

'So what are you saying?' Mother asked.

'I'm saying,' Schofield said, 'that whatever they're doing in this complex is more important than you or I could possibly imagine.'

The wide elevator platform holding the President of the United States jolted to a halt in front of a giant steel door marked with an enormous black-painted '4'.

The wide concrete elevator shaft stretched up into the air above the President and his Secret Service Detail like an oversized vertical tunnel. The bright artificial light of the ground-level hangar was but a small square of white now— three hundred feet straight up.

No sooner had the elevator stopped than the massive steel door in front of it rumbled upward. Colonel Jerome Harper led the way, walking and talking quickly:

'This facility was once the headquarters for the North American Air Defence Command—NORAD—before NORAD was moved to a more modern facility built underneath Cheyenne Mountain in Colorado in 1975.

'The complex is surrounded by a two-foot-thick titanium outer wall, which is itself buried beneath one hundred feet of solid granite. Like the Cheyenne Mountain complex, it is designed to withstand a direct hit from a thermonuclear missile.'

Harper handed the President a sheet of paper, on which was a schematic diagram of the subterranean structure.

The hangar appeared at the top of the diagram—at ground level, capped by the low mountain—then the wide aircraft elevator shaft led downwards, until it met a multi-levelled structure built deep within the earth.

Harper said, 'The underground complex contains six levels, the first two of which—Levels 1 and 2—are storage hangars for high-risk aircraft, much like the ones you saw at Area 8 earlier this morning. Level 3 houses communications and staff living quarters. Level 5 is confinement. And Level 6 is the X-Rail system.

'Each level is completely sealable to both radiation and airborne contagions, and the whole facility, if locked down, is capable of living off a self-contained supply of oxygen for thirty days. Food supplies are kept in a storage area on Level 3. Water supply is kept in a 100-millon-gallon tank in the Level 1 hangar.'

Their group came to a short upwardly-sloping corridor, at the end of which sat a squat solid-looking door that looked like a gigantic safe. An Air Force man hurriedly began opening it.

'Project Fortune was stationed here four years ago, after the first viable embryo reached maturity,' Harper said. 'Now, at last, it has reached a stage where it can be put to use.'

The President waited patiently while the three-foot-thick door was pulled open.

Frank Cutler and the eight other members of the President's personal Detail stood behind him—silent, impassive, invisible. At three-minute intervals, Cutler would silently check his earpiece for the All-Clear beacons from both of his advance teams. The beacons came in loud and clear.

Then, finally, the door swung open, and the President looked casually beyond it.

And his jaw dropped.

'Oh . . . my . . . *God* . . .'

'My money's on the superbomb,' Elvis Haynes said as he leaned back in his chair.

Elvis, Schofield, Gant and Mother were sitting in one of the glass-walled offices by the main doors of the hangar. With them were Colonels Grier and Dallas, all the other Marines stationed on board the Presidential helicopters, as well as the three remaining Secret Service agents.

In a not-so-subtle division of management and labour, all the White House people who had remained up in the hangar either sat in the *other* glass-walled office on the southern side of the hangar or worked inside their helicopters, which, they said, were more suited to their rank than the spartan Air Force offices.

They also—so Nicholas Tate had said to Gant when he had invited her to stay on Marine One with him—had better coffee, plunger stuff.

Gant went with Schofield and the others.

Ramrod Hagerty, on the other hand, sat over with the White House people.

'No way, man,' a small bespectacled corporal named Gus Gorman said. 'The superbomb doesn't exist.'

Gorman was a thin, nerdy-looking individual, with thick glasses, a big nose and a narrow scrawny neck. Not even full dress uniform could make him look sexy. Popular with the other troops for his almost-photographic memory and sharp wit, his call-sign 'Brainiac' was a compliment, not an insult.

'Bullshit,' Elvis said, 'DARPA made it in the nineties, in conjunction with the Navy—'

'But they could never make it *work*. Thing depended on some element only found in meteorites and they could never find a live specimen of it.'

'You guys'll believe anything,' a softly-spoken voice said from the other side of the office.

Everybody turned, Schofield included.

The speaker was a new sergeant to the unit—an intense young man with a heavy-browed face, pug nose and deep brown eyes. He didn't talk much, so when he did it was something of a special occasion for the team. At first, it had been a trait which some had mistaken for contempt. But soon it was discovered that Sergeant Buck Riley Jnr just didn't like to talk unnecessarily.

Riley Jnr was the son of a highly-regarded Marine staff sergeant. His father, Buck Riley Snr, had also been a man Shane Schofield had known better than most.

They had met under fire—back when Schofield had been in a god-almighty mess in Bosnia and Riley Snr had been on the rescue team. They had become good friends and Riley Snr had become Schofield's loyal staff sergeant. Sadly, he had also been on that fateful mission to Antarctica— where he had been murdered in the most brutal fashion by an enemy whose name Schofield had been forbidden to mention by the Official Secrets Act.

Sergeant Buck Riley Jnr—silent, intense and serious—bore his father's call-sign with pride. He was known throughout the unit simply as 'Book II'.

Book II looked at Elvis and Brainiac. 'Do you guys seriously believe that DARPA has built a bomb that can destroy a third of the earth's mass?'

'Yes,' Elvis said.

'No,' Brainiac said.

'Well, they haven't. The superbomb is an urban myth,' Book II said, 'designed to keep the conspiracy theorists on the Internet and the gossipy old women in the United States Marine Corps happy. Want me to give you a couple more examples? That the FBI sends agents into prisons as deep cover operatives. That the United States Air Force has nuclear bombers stationed in commercial hangars at every major airport in the United States for use in the event of a sudden outbreak of war. That USAMRIID has developed a cure for AIDS but hasn't been allowed to release it. That the Air Force has developed a magnetic-propulsion system that allows vehicles to float on air. That the *losing* tenderer in the bid to build the stealth bomber proposed a supersonic plane that could attain complete invisibility through the use of nuclear-powered air refraction—and built the plane anyway, even after they *lost* the bid. Heard any of those?'

'No,' Elvis said, 'but they're *way* cool.'

'What about you, Captain?' Book II turned to Schofield. 'You heard any of those before?'

Schofield held the young sergeant's gaze. 'I've heard about the last one, but not the others.'

He turned away from the debate, scanning the office around him.

He frowned. Someone was missing.

And then it hit him.

'Hey, where's Warrant Officer Webster?' he said.

The President of the United States stared out through the slanted observation windows, his mouth agape.

Through the windows, in the middle of a high-ceilinged, hall-like room, he saw a large freestanding *cube* made of a clear glass-like substance.

It just sat there in the middle of the hall, not quite reaching the ceiling, not quite reaching the walls, a glass cube the size of a large living room, bounded on two sides by the elevated L-shaped observation structure.

It was what lay *inside* the glass cube, however, that seized the President's attention.

Indeed, he couldn't take his eyes off it.

'The cube is made of high-tensile polyfibre, and has its own separate oxygen supply. It is completely airtight,' Colonel Harper said. 'Should its structural integrity be compromised, the cube's internal air pressure is automatically raised, so that no contagions can enter it.'

Harper gestured to one of the three scientists who had been up on the tarmac earlier. 'Mr President, I'd like you to meet Doctor Gunther Botha, the guiding force behind Project Fortune.'

The President shook Botha's hand. Botha was a fat, wide-faced, balding man of fifty-eight, and he spoke with a guttural South African accent: 'It's a pleasure to meet you, Mister President.'

'Doctor Botha is from—'

'I know where Doctor Botha is from,' the President said, a trace of disapproval in his voice. 'I saw his file yesterday.'

Gunther Botha was a former member of the South African Defence Force's notorious Medical Battalion. Though not widely known, throughout the 1980s South Africa was second only to the Soviet Union in the creation and stockpiling of biological weapons, principally for use against the black majority.

But with the fall of the apartheid regime, Gunther Botha quickly found himself out of a job and directly in the firing line of the Truth and Reconciliation Commission. His clandestine hiring by the United States government in 1996 was not unlike its harbouring of Nazi scientists after World War II. Specialists in Botha's chosen field of expertise were exceedingly hard to come by.

The President turned back to look out through the observation windows. 'So this is the vaccine . . .' he said, gazing down at the clear fibreglass cube.

'Yes, sir, it is,' Botha said.

'Tested?' The President didn't turn as he spoke.

'Yes.'

'In serum-hydrate form?'

'Yes.'

'Against the latest strain?'

'We tested it against 9.1 yesterday afternoon, as soon as it arrived.'

'Mister President,' Colonel Harper said, 'if you'd like, we can give you a demonstration.'

A pause.

'All right,' the President said. 'Do so.'

'Where did he go?' Schofield asked as he stood in the middle of the wide main hangar of Area 7 with Libby Gant.

Warrant Officer Carl Webster—the man in charge of the Football—wasn't in either of the two Presidential helicopters, nor was he in the hangar's two offices. And a quick check with the Secret Service people had revealed that he hadn't gone with the President on the tour of the facility.

Warrant Officer Webster was nowhere to be found.

It was cause for concern because there were strict rules of protocol as to Webster's movements. If he wasn't with the President, he was supposed to stay close to Marine One at all times.

'Take a look at the welcoming committee, the famous 7th Squadron,' Gant said, eyeing the three groups of P-90-armed commandos stationed at various points around the hangar bay. The crack Air Force troops just watched Schofield and Gant impassively.

'They look pretty mean to me,' Schofield said.

'They're jacked up,' Gant said.

'What?'

'Yellow tinges to their eyes.'

'Steroids?'

'Uh-huh,' Gant said.

'No wonder they look so edgy,' Schofield said.

'Elvis doesn't like them,' Gant said. 'Says he heard somewhere that they're, quote, "unofficially racist". You'll notice that there are no black members in these squads.'

It was true. Apart from a couple of Asian–American

members scattered among them, the 7th Squadron units in the hangar were absolutely lily-white.

'Yes, I've heard those rumours, too,' Schofield said. Although no-one liked to admit it, in some sections of the armed forces, racism—particularly against black soldiers— was still a problem. And with their brutal selection courses, special forces units like the 7th Squadron could easily wield subtle discriminatory powers.

Schofield nodded at the leaders of the three ten-man groups, distinguished from the others by the fact that they didn't have to hold their P-90s in their hands. Their machine guns were secured behind their shoulderblades, in back-mounted holsters. 'You know what they call the five 7th Squadron unit commanders at exercises?'

'What?'

'The Five Snakes. As the overall squadron leader, Kurt Logan commands one ten-man team, the first one, Alpha Unit. The other four units are run by four captains— McConnell, Willis, Stone and Carney. And they're good. When they've cared to show up at the inter-service combat exercises at Bragg, they've always come in at number one. One time, a lone 7th Squadron unit took out three SEAL defensive teams all by itself—and that was *without* Logan.'

'Why do they call them the Five Snakes?' Gant asked.

'It started out as a jealous joke among the other field commanders. Three reasons. One, because tactically they resemble snakes: they strike quickly and with maximum force, and with a total lack of mercy. Two, because, person-ally, they're all very cold individuals. They would never mix with their counterparts in the other services. Always stuck together.'

'And the third reason?'

'Because each of their call-signs is a variety of aggressive snake.'

'Nice,' Gant said wryly.

They kept walking. Gant changed the subject: 'You know, I had a good time last Saturday night.'

'You did?' Schofield turned to face her.

'Yeah. Did you?'

'Oh, *yeah.*'

Gant said, 'I was just wondering, you know, because, well, you didn't . . .'

'Wait a second,' Schofield said suddenly. 'Something's wrong here.'

'What?'

Schofield looked at the three 7th Squadron units stationed around the hangar again.

One squad stood guard over by the regular elevator. The second group of ten men stood beside the wide aircraft elevator shaft. The third unit stood on the south-eastern side of the hangar, over by a door that led into the two-storey control building.

It was at that moment that Schofield saw the sign on the door behind the third group of 7th Squadron men.

And then, in his mind's eye, he saw it.

'Come on,' he said, heading back toward the offices. 'Quickly.'

'The arming codes have been entered, sir,' Logan said. 'The Football is ready. Warrant Officer Webster was most . . . forthcoming.'

The radio operators inside the control room continued their verbal updates:

'—emergency sealing system ready—'

'—self-contained oxygen supply ready—'

'Major Logan,' one of them said, 'I'm still picking up those trace heat signatures in sector nine outside, out by the EEV.'

'Size?'

'Same as before. Between twelve and seventeen inches. I'm not sure, sir, but I'd swear they've moved closer to the vent since the last time I looked.'

Logan looked at the satellite image. A zoomed-in black-and-white shot of the desert to the east of the main complex showed about twenty-four rod-shaped white blobs arrayed in a wide three-hundred-yard circle around the Emergency Escape Vent.

'Twelve to seventeen inches.' Logan peered closely at the image. 'Too small to be men. Probably just a pack of desert rats. Get an enhanced image from the satellite, just to be sure. Keep an eye on them.'

The shadowy figure turned to face Logan. 'Where is the President now?'

'He's down in the testing lab on Level 4.'

'Contact Harper. Give him the green light. Tell him we're ready. Tell him the mission is go.'

'Subject One has *not* been immunised with the vaccine,' Dr Gunther Botha said in a neutral scientific voice.

The President now stood in near darkness, in another area of Level 4, facing two brightly-lit test chambers.

Inside each chamber stood a completely naked man. Both men, in perverse contrast to their nakedness, wore gas-masks and a series of electrodes attached to their chests.

'Subject One is a white, Caucasian male, five foot seven inches, one hundred and sixty pounds, age thirty-six. Subject is wearing a standard-issue anti-contagion gas-mask. Releasing the agent now.'

There was a soft hissing sound as a light mist of mustard-yellow aerosol particles was released into the first man's chamber. He was a thin man, gangly. He looked about himself fearfully as the gas entered his air-tight room.

The President said, 'Where did you get the virus?'

'Changchun,' Botha said.

The President nodded.

Changchun was a remote town in northern Manchuria. Although the Chinese government denied it, Changchun was the Chinese Army's chief biological weapons testing facility. It was said that political prisoners and captured foreign spies were sent there and used as guinea pigs for virus and nerve agent testing.

The naked man in the gas chamber was still standing, still looking nervously about himself.

'Secondary infection occurs via indirect ingestion through dermatological orifices—hair follicles in the skin, open cuts,' Botha said blandly. 'Without administration of an effective vaccine, death will occur approximately thirty minutes after contact. For indirectly ingested nerve agents, this is a relatively fast kill-rate.

'But,' Botha held up a finger, 'when compared with the effects of *direct* inhalation of this agent, it is highly *in*efficient.'

He pressed an intercom switch and addressed the man in the chamber. 'Would you please remove your mask.'

In response, the man gave Botha the finger—firmly.

Botha just sighed and pressed a button on a nearby console. Subject One received a severe shock through his chest electrodes.

'I said, would you please remove your gas-mask.'

Subject One slowly took off his mask.

And immediately—*violently*—the virus took effect.

The man clutched his stomach and coughed a deep, hacking cough.

'As I said, *far* more efficient,' Botha said.

The man doubled over, started wheezing.

'Gastrointestinal irritation begins within approximately ten seconds of onset.'

The man vomited explosively, splatting brown-green vomit all over the test booth's floor.

'Stomach liquefication within thirty seconds . . .'

The man dropped to his knees, gasping for air. A chunky liquid dribbled down his chin. He clutched at the booth's glass wall, right in front of Botha.

'Liver and kidney liquefication within a minute . . .'

The subject puked a bloody black sludge all over the window. Then he fell to the ground, shuddering and shivering.

'Total organ failure within ninety seconds. Death within two minutes.'

Soon, the naked man inside the chamber—coiled in the foetal position—lay still.

The President watched, trying to hide his revulsion.

It was beyond cruel, this method of death, even for a man such as this.

Nevertheless, he tried to justify Subject One's grisly death in the light of what Subject One had done during his life. With a friend, Leon Roy Hailey had tortured nine women in the back of his van, laughing at them as they begged for mercy. The two men had recorded the girls' death throes on a video recorder for later gratification. The President had seen those tapes.

He also knew that Leon Roy Hailey had been sentenced to four hundred and fifty-two years in prison for his crimes. He was never to leave prison alive. And so, after five brutal years in jail, he—like every other test subject at Area 7, all of them serving multiple life sentences—had elected to submit himself to scientific testing.

'Subject Two,' Botha said tonelessly, 'has been given the vaccine in serum-hydrate form. Serum was mixed into a glass of water he drank exactly thirty minutes ago. Subject is a white, Caucasian male, six feet eight inches, two hundred and fifteen pounds, age thirty-two. Releasing the agent now.'

Again, the hissing came, followed by the sudden puff of mustard-yellow aerosol mist.

The man in the second chamber saw the gas enter his booth, but unlike the first test subject, he didn't do anything in response. He was much bigger than the first man—a massive six-eight—broadchested, too, with bulging biceps, enormous fists and a small elliptical head that seemed way too tiny for his body.

With his gas-mask on and the yellow mist falling all around him, he just stared out through the one-way glass of the test chamber, as if a painful agonised death didn't worry him in the slightest.

No coughing. No spasming. With the gas-mask on, the virus hadn't affected him yet.

Botha flicked the intercom switch: 'Take off your mask, please.'

Subject Two obeyed Botha's command without objection, removed his mask.

The President saw the man's face, and this time he caught his breath.

It was a face he had seen many times before—on television, in the newspapers. It was the evil tattooed face of Lucifer James Leary, the serial killer known across America as 'the Surgeon of Phoenix'.

He was the man who had killed thirty-two hitch-hikers, most of them young backpackers, whom he had picked up on the interstate between Las Vegas and Phoenix between 1991 and 1998. In every case, Leary had left his trademark— a piece of the victim's jewellery, usually a ring or necklace, lying on the roadway at the spot where the victim had been abducted.

A disgraced former medical student, Leary would take his victims to his home in Phoenix, amputate their limbs and then *eat* those limbs in front of them. The discovery of his house by FBI agents—complete with blood-smeared basement and two live but partially-eaten victims—had horrified America.

Even now, Lucifer Leary looked like the picture of evil. The entire left-hand side of his face was covered by a black tattoo depicting five vertical claw marks, as if Freddy Krueger himself had slashed his razor-tipped fingers viciously down Leary's cheek. The tattooed slash-marks were impressive in their detail—torn ragged skin, imitation blood—designed to evoke maximum revulsion.

At that moment, to the President's horror, Leary *smiled* at the observation window, revealing hideous yellow teeth.

It was then that it hit the President.

Even though his gas-mask was off, Leary didn't seem to be affected by the airborne virus.

'As you will see,' Botha said proudly, 'even when the virus is inhaled *directly* into the lungs from the air, an orally-administered vaccine delivered in serum-hydrate form is effective in preventing infection. The vaccine neutralises the invading virus by restricting the release of the protein

66

diethylpropanase by the virus, a protein which attacks the pigmentation enzyme metahydrogenase and the blood group protein, DB—'

'In English, please,' the President said tersely.

Botha said, 'Mr President, what you have just seen is a quantum leap forward in biotechnological warfare. It is the world's first genetically-engineered biological weapon, a completely synthetic agent, so there are no natural cures. And it works with a degree of efficiency the likes of which I have never seen before. It is a purely *constructed* virus, and make no mistake, it has been constructed in a very particular way.

'It is an ethnic bullet, designed to kill only *certain* races of people, people possessed of certain ethnically exclusive genes. In this case, it attacks only those people who are possessed of the enzyme metahydrogenase and DB blood protein. These are the enzymes which cause white skin pigmentation, the characteristic enzymes of Caucasian people.

'Mister President, the same enzyme that makes our skin white makes us susceptible to this virus. It is extraordinary. I don't know how the Chinese did it. My government in South Africa tried for years to develop a virus that it could put in the water supply which would make only black people sterile, but we never succeeded.

'But from the look of this agent, it would not be difficult to adapt the genetic make-up of the virus so that it would also attack African–Americans, since their pigmentation enzyme is a variant of metahydrogenase—'

'Bottom line,' the President said.

'The bottom line is simple, Mister President,' Botha said. 'The only people safe from this virus are people of Asian origin, because they do not possess these pigmentation enzymes *at all*. As such, they would be immune from the agent while Caucasians and African–Americans everywhere would die.

'Mister President. Allow me to introduce you to the latest Chinese biological weapon. Meet the Sinovirus.'

'I'm telling you, there's something not right here,' Schofield said.

'Bullshit, Captain,' Ramrod Hagerty waved his hand dismissively. 'You've been reading too many comic books.'

'What about Webster, then? I can't find him anywhere. He's not allowed to just disappear.'

'Probably in the john.'

'No, I checked there,' Schofield said. 'And Nighthawk Three? Where are they? Why hasn't Hendricks called in?'

Hagerty just stared at him blankly.

Schofield said, 'Sir, with all due respect, if you would just look at where these 7th Squadron guys are standing . . .'

Hagerty turned in his chair. He, Schofield and Gant were in the southern office of the main hangar, with the small group of White House people. Hagerty casually looked out through the office's windows at the 7th Squadron commandos spaced around the hangar outside.

'Looks like they're guarding every entrance,' Hagerty shrugged. 'To stop us going into areas we're not supposed to.'

'No, sir, they're not. Look *closely*. The group to the north are guarding the regular elevator. The middle group are guarding the aircraft elevator. They're both fine. But look at the group over by the control building, the group in front of the door.'

'Yeah, so . . .'

'Sir, they're guarding a storage closet.'

Hagerty looked from Schofield to the Air Force commandos. It was true. They were standing in front of a door marked 'STORAGE'.

'That's very nice, Captain. I'll put your observations in my report.' Hagerty resumed his paperwork.

'But sir . . .'

'I *said*, I'll put your observations in my report, Captain Schofield. That will be all.'

Schofield straightened.

'With respect, sir, have you ever been in combat?' he said.

Hagerty froze, looked up. 'I'm not sure if I like your tone, Captain.'

'*Have you ever been in combat?*'

'I was in Saudi during Desert Storm.'

'Fighting?'

'No. Embassy staff.'

'Sir, if you'd ever been in combat, you'd know that those three groups of Air Force commandos are not standing in defensive positions. Those are *offensive* positions. More than that, those men are perfectly placed to rout *these two offices*—'

'Rubbish.'

Schofield grabbed the sheet of paper Hagerty had been writing on and scribbled a quick map of the hangar:

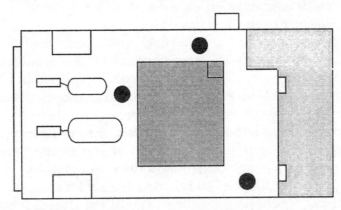

'This is where they are now,' Schofield tapped the three big black dots on the diagram. 'Twelve o'clock, ten o'clock

and four o'clock. But when they move like this . . .'
Schofield added some arrows to his diagram:

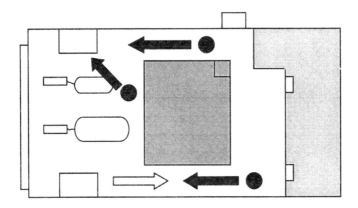

'. . . we've got serious trouble. All the Marines and Secret Service people over in the northern office will face the full force of the attack, while the White House people here in the southern office will naturally run the other way—right into the the third unit of 7th Squadron soldiers.'

Hagerty looked at Schofield's diagram for a long moment.

Then he said, 'That has got to be the stupidest thing I've ever heard, Captain. These are *American* servicemen.'

'For Christ's sake, just *listen* to me—'

'No, you listen to me,' Hagerty spat. 'Don't think for a moment that I don't know who you are. I know all about Wilkes Ice Station. I know what happened there. But just because you were some kind of hero once doesn't give you a licence to spout out fucking conspiracy theories and expect to be believed. I've been in this Corps for twenty-two years and I have risen to where I am by—'

'—what? Pushing pencils,' Schofield said.

Hagerty fell silent. His face grew beetroot red.

'That's it, Schofield. For the sake of the Corps, I won't make a scene here, but when we get back to Quantico, as soon as we touch down, you will be taken into custody and held for court martial on charges of gross insubordination. Now get *the fuck* out of my sight.'

Schofield just shook his head in exasperation and left.

'And these, sir, are the men who brought back the Sinovirus,' Colonel Harper said, guiding the President around the test booths on Level 4.

A giant thirty-foot-long quarantine chamber stood before them. Through a small glass window set into the side of the reinforced chamber, the President saw four men, all seated on sofas watching a television and bathed in blue ultra-violet light. All of them, he noted, were of Asian extraction.

As soon as they saw the President, two of the men inside the chamber rose to their feet and stood to attention.

'Mister President, meet Captain Robert Wu and Lieutenant Chet Li from the 7th Squadron—'

Just then Harper's cell phone buzzed.

The colonel excused himself and stepped away to take the call.

'It's a pleasure to meet you both, gentlemen,' the President said, stepping forward. 'Your country owes you a debt of gratitude.'

'Thank you, sir.'

'Thank you.'

'How long do you have to stay in there for?' the President inquired, asking the obligatory personal question.

'Another couple of hours, I think, sir,' the one named Wu said. 'We got back yesterday with the new strain, but we have to stay in here for twenty-four hours. The chamber is operated on a time-lock. Can't be opened until 0900 hours. So they can be sure there are no other bugs on us.'

'Well, I won't be here come nine o'clock,' the President said, 'but rest assured, you'll be receiving something from me in the very near future.'

'Thank you, sir.'

'Thank you, sir.'

Having finished his call, Colonel Harper returned.

'And that concludes our tour, Mister President,' he said. 'Now, if you'll come this way, I have one last thing to show you.'

Schofield and Gant stood inside Marine One, behind Brainiac.

Brainiac was seated at the helicopter's communications console, typing quickly on a keyboard.

'Anything from Nighthawk Three or the two advance teams?' Schofield asked.

'Nada from Nighthawk Three,' Brainiac said. 'And just the beacons from the Secret Service teams.'

Schofield thought for a moment. 'Are we plugged into Area 7's local network?'

'Yep. So the President can collect secure transmissions by the landline.'

'Okay then, can you bring up the complex's security camera system for me?'

'Sure.'

The President was led up a set of firestairs to Level 3, the living quarters of Area 7.

With his nine-man Secret Service Detail he was brought into a wide low-ceilinged common room—couches, coffee tables, kitchenette and, taking pride of place over by the wall, a big-screen Panasonic TV.

'If you would just wait here for a moment, Mister President,' Colonel Harper said, 'I'll send someone down in a minute.'

And then he left the room, leaving the President and his Detail alone.

A series of black-and-white monitors flickered to life in the communications bay of Marine One.

Each monitor depicted a grid of views from the multitude of security cameras around Area 7.

'We have contact,' Brainiac said.

From various angles, Schofield saw empty stairwells—the main hangar—something that looked like a subway station—the interiors of the glass-walled offices in the main hangar, one of them filled with Marines and Secret Service people, the other containing White House staff members—and, in grainy black-and-white, the inside of an elevator—

Schofield froze at the final image.

The elevator was packed with ten fully-armed 7th Squadron commandos.

And then suddenly movement from one of the other monitors caught his eye.

It was the view from one of the stairwell cameras.

A whole stream of armed 7th Squadron commandos were storming down the stairwell.

'This is going to be very painful,' he said flatly.

Schofield stepped out of Marine One onto the hangar floor, Gant and Brainiac close behind him.

Although nothing *physical* about it had changed, somehow the hangar now looked very different.

Now it looked menacing.

Dangerous.

Schofield saw the three groups of 7th Squadron commandos arrayed around the enormous interior space—saw the commander of one of the groups touch his ear as he caught a radio transmission.

'Stay here,' Schofield said.

'Okay,' Brainiac said.

'Hey,' Gant said.

'What?'

'Try not to look so spooked.'

'I'll do my best,' Schofield said as he stepped out from the cover of Marine One and started walking casually across the hangar floor, toward the northern glass-walled office.

He was about halfway there when it happened.

Loud and sudden.

Boom!

Like a curtain falling at the end of a stage show, a giant piston-driven titanium door thundered down in front of the hangar's main doors. Its leading edge—lined with nasty-looking tooth-like protrusions—lodged firmly into the series of box-like indentations that ran across the entry to the hangar.

And with the falling of the massive armoured door, Schofield gave up any pretence of trying to appear calm.

He broke into a run just as the two nearest groups of 7th Squadron commandos—the ones at twelve o'clock and ten o'clock—raised their P-90s and the air around him became awash with sizzling bullets.

It had been five minutes now and nobody had come for them and the President of the United States was not accustomed to waiting.

The President and his protective Detail just stood in the common room on Level 3, looking about themselves, waiting in the silence.

'Frank,' the President said to the Chief of the Detail, 'see what's going on—'

The big-screen television came on.

The President and his Detail whirled around.

'What the fuck . . .' somebody said.

On the screen, large and bold, was the bright yellow insignia of the Emergency Broadcast System—the special all-spectrum broadcast network that was capable of cutting off regular broadcasting in the event of a national emergency.

Then, abruptly, the EBS symbol disappeared, and a face appeared in its place.

'What the hell . . .' this time it was the President who spoke.

The face on the screen was that of a dead man.

It was the face of Lieutenant General Charles Samson Russell, USAF, call-sign: 'Caesar.'

★

On every television screen in Area 7—and, it appeared, every television in the United States—the round, heavy-browed face of Charles Russell began to speak.

'Mister President. People of America. Welcome to Area 7. My name is General Charles Russell, United States Air Force. For too long, I have watched this country eat itself. I will do so no longer.' His tone was measured, his Louisiana accent thick.

'Our representatives at both federal and state levels are incapable of genuine leadership. Our free press is no longer the tool for controlling government that it was intended to be. To every man who has ever fought or died for this country, this state of affairs is a disgrace. It can no longer be allowed to continue.'

In the common room, the President just stared at the big-screen television.

'And so I propose a challenge, Mister President—both to you and to the system you represent.

'Implanted on your heart is a radio device. It was attached to the outer tissue of your cardiac muscle during an operation on your left lung four years ago.'

Frank Cutler spun to face the President, a look of horror spreading across his face.

'I will initiate its signal now,' Caesar said. He pressed some buttons on a small red unit that he held in his hand. The compact unit had a black stub antenna sticking out from its top.

Frank Cutler pulled a debugging wand from his coat—a spectrum analyser used to detect any signal-emitting device—and waved it over the President's body.

Feet and legs . . . okay.

Waist and stomach . . . okay.

Chest . . .

The wand went crazy.

★

'My challenge to you, Mister President, is simple.' Russell's voice echoed throughout the underground base.

'As you well know, at every major airport in the United States there are at least three hangars devoted to the storage of United States Air Force bombers, fighters and ordnance.

'Right now, inside fourteen of those hangars, sit fourteen Type-240 blast plasma warheads. The airports include John F. Kennedy, Newark and La Guardia in New York, Dulles in Washington, O'Hare in Chicago, LAX in Los Angeles, and airports in San Francisco, San Diego, Seattle, Boston, Philadelphia and Detroit. Each plasma warhead, as you know, has a blast radius of sixteen miles and a detonation yield of ninety megatons. All are armed.'

In the common room on Level 3, everyone was silent.

'The only thing that will stop the detonation of these warheads, Mister President,' Charles Russell said with a smile, 'is the continued beating of your heart.'

Russell went on.

'All the devices at the airports are patched in to a single satellite in geosynchronous orbit above this base. That satellite, Mister President, emits a high-powered microwave signal which is picked up and bounced back to it by the transmitter placed on your heart.

'But the radio transmitter on your heart, once started, is kinetically operated. If your heart should stop beating, the transmitter will cease to operate, and the satellite's signal will *not* be bounced back to it—in which case, the satellite will instruct the bombs in the airports to detonate.

'Mister President. If your heart should stop, America as we know it dies. If your heart keeps beating, America lives.

'You are the symbol of a bankrupt culture, sir: a *politician*, a man who seeks power for power's sake, but, like the people you represent, one who lives safe in the knowledge that he will never ever be called upon to stand up and fight for the system that gives him that power.

'Well, you have lived safely for too long, Mister President. Now you have been called to account. Now you have been called to fight.

'I, on the other hand, am a warrior. I have spilled my blood for this country. What blood have you spilt? What sacrifices have you made? None. *Coward*.

'But like an honest patriot, I will give you and the system you represent a final chance to prove your worth. For the people of this country need proof. They need to see you flounder—see you fall—see you *sell them out* to save your skin. They elected you to represent them. Now you shall do that—literally. If you die, they die with you.

'This facility has been completely sealed. It is designed to withstand the full force of a nuclear blast, so there is no way out of it. Inside it with you is a fifty-man detachment of the best ground force this country has to offer, the 7th Special Operations Squadron. These men have orders to kill you, Mister President.

'With your Secret Service Detail, you will face them in a fight to the death. Whoever wins, gets the country. Whoever loses, dies.

'Of course, the American people must be kept appraised of the score in this challenge,' Caesar said. 'Therefore, every hour on the hour, I shall address them via the Emergency Broadcast System and give them an update on the pursuit.'

The President looked up at the nearest security camera. 'This is ridiculous! You couldn't *possibly* have put a—'

'Jeremiah K. Woolf, Mister President,' Caesar Russell said from the TV screen. The President immediately fell silent.

No-one else spoke.

'I will assume from your silence that you have seen the FBI file.'

Of course the President had seen the file—the peculiarities of the ex-senator's death had demanded it.

At the exact moment that Jeremiah Woolf had died in Alaska, his home in Washington DC had exploded. No culprit—for either incident—had ever been found. It was a coincidence too bizarre to ignore, but in the absence of any evidence to explain it, to the mass media it had remained simply that, a tragic coincidence.

As the President knew, however, one particular aspect of the ex-senator's death had never been made public: namely, the elevated levels of red blood cell production in his bloodstream, plus extremely low alveolar and arterial phosphate pressures. All of these symptoms indicated a prolonged period of hyperventilation *before* Woolf had been shot—a period during which the ex-senator had experienced a heightened state of 'fight or flight' physiology.

In other words, the ex-senator had been running from someone when he'd been shot. He had been hunted.

And now it made sense.

Woolf had been implanted with a transmitter . . .

. . . and then in Alaska he had been hunted and shot, and when, finally, his heart had stopped, his home on the other side of the country had been destroyed.

Caesar Russell's voice invaded his thoughts. 'Former Senator Woolf's unexpected retirement from government left me with an extra transmitting device. And so he became a guinea pig, a test run. A test run for today.'

The President exchanged a look with Frank Cutler.

Caesar said, 'Oh, and just in case you're harbouring ambitions of escaping this facility . . .' He lifted an object into view.

It was a stainless steel briefcase.

Warrant Officer Carl Webster's steel briefcase.

The case's handle still had the pair of handcuffs attached to it—only now the open-ended cuff was no longer attached to anything. It was splattered all over with blood.

It was the Football.

And it was open.

The President saw the briefcase's flat-glass palm-print analyser and keypad. The palm-print analyser was an identification feature programmed to recognise the President's palm-print, so that only he could activate—and de-activate—America's thermonuclear arsenal.

Somehow, though, Russell had managed to falsify the President's palm-print and enter the arming codes. But how could he have got a copy of the President's *hand*?

In addition to the transmitter on your heart, Mister President,' Russell said, 'all the devices in the airports have been networked to a recycling timer of exactly ninety minutes, as is shown on the Football's display screen. Only the application of *your palm-print* to the analyser—once every ninety minutes—will reset that timer and stop the plasma warheads from going off, so don't think of leaving. The Football, for your information, will be kept up here in the main hangar.

'This is a great day in the history of the nation, Mister President, a day of reckoning. Come the dawn of tomorrow, the glorious Fourth of July, we shall see if we all awake in a new, reborn America. Good luck, Mister President, and may God have mercy on your soul.'

At that moment, as if right on cue, the main doors to the common room burst open and a team of 7th Squadron commandos—led by Major Kurt Logan and wearing their fearsome ERG-6 gas-masks—rushed into the room, their devastating P-90 machine guns blazing.

The challenge had begun.

SECOND CONFRONTATION

3 July, 0700 Hours

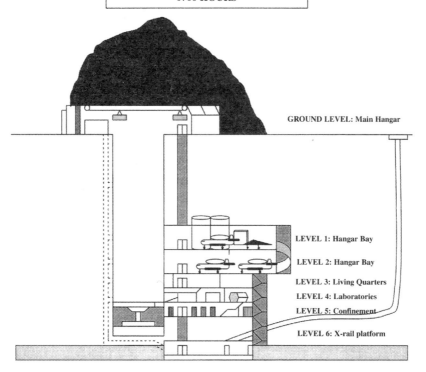

**UNITED STATES AIR FORCE
SPECIAL AREA (RESTRICTED) NO.7
0700 HOURS**

GROUND LEVEL: Main Hangar

LEVEL 1: Hangar Bay

LEVEL 2: Hangar Bay

LEVEL 3: Living Quarters

LEVEL 4: Laboratories

LEVEL 5: Confinement

LEVEL 6: X-rail platform

The main hangar had become a battlefield.

Bulletholes raked the floor at Shane Schofield's feet as he raced for the doorway to the northern glass-walled office.

He poked his head around the doorway: 'Marines! *Scatter!*'

But that was all he could say before the window next him shattered into a thousand fragments and he dived away, crawling for the cover of the two Presidential helicopters and their towing vehicles.

He looked back just in time to see a couple of full-dress-uniformed Marines burst out through the windows of the office a moment before the small structure was hit by a Predator shoulder-launched missile and its walls blasted outwards in a shower of glass and billowing fire.

Schofield slid under Marine One, and found himself lying next to Libby Gant and Brainiac.

Gunfire echoed out all around them. And then bizarrely, above the gunshots, Schofield heard a voice booming out from the hangar's loudspeaker system: '—*ood luck, Mister President, and may God have mercy on your soul.*'

'Holy *shit!*' Brainiac yelled.

'This way!' Schofield said, crawling on his stomach underneath the big helicopter.

He arrived at a wide grille in the floor. It came away easily.

An air vent opened up beneath it. The steel-walled vent plunged down into the earth, disappearing into darkness.

'Let's go!' Schofield yelled above the gunfire.

Abruptly, a metal panel in the bottom of Marine One burst open—almost decapitating Schofield—and a figure with an M-16 dropped down behind him, the gun levelled at his forehead.

'*Fuck!* It's you,' Mother said as she lowered herself out of the helicopter's emergency escape hatch onto the ground.

'Here, happy birthday,' she said, tossing an MP-10 machine pistol to Gant. 'Sorry, Scarecrow, nothing for you. That was all I could find in the basic arms cabinet on board. There's more in the forward armoury, but Gunman's got the key to that.'

'Never mind,' Schofield said, 'the first thing we've got to do is get out of here and regroup. Then we have to figure out a way of taking these bastards down. This way.'

'Did you catch any of that shit on the television?' Mother said as she crawled over to the vent.

Gant and Brainiac climbed down into the vent first, bracing their legs against its walls, shimmying themselves down into it.

'No,' Schofield said, 'I was too busy dodging bullets.'

'Then I've got a lot to tell you,' Mother said as they lowered themselves into the shaft.

The President of the United States was moving faster than he had ever moved before. In fact, his feet barely even touched the ground.

At the first sight of the 7th Squadron commandos storming the common room, his nine-man Protective Detail had thrown itself into action.

Four men immediately took up defensive positions in between the President and the oncoming assault troops, throwing their coats open to reveal Uzi sub-machine guns. The Uzis buzzed as they unleashed a brutal wave of gunfire at a crushing 600 rounds per minute.

The other five members of the Detail crash-tackled the President out into the nearby fire escape, practically lifting him off his feet as they gang-rushed him out of the room, covering his body with their own.

The door to the fire stairs slammed shut behind them, but not before they saw the 7th Squadron troops clinically take up covering positions behind couches, doors and cupboards and leap-frog each other and tear to shreds the four Secret Service men who had remained behind—drowning out the buzz of their Uzis with the whirring drone of their P-90 assault rifles.

The Uzis might have fired at 600 rounds per minute. But the P-90, made by the FN Herstal company in Belgium, fired at an astonishing 900 rounds per minute. Indeed, with its rounded hand guard, internal blowback system, and incredible hundred-round magazine mounted above the barrel, it looked like something out of a science fiction movie.

'Down the stairs! *Now!*' Frank Cutler yelled as bullets slammed into the other side of the firedoor. 'Head for the alternate exit!'

The President and what was left of his Detail flew down the stairs, taking them four at a time, hurling themselves around every turn. Every one of them had a weapon in his or her hand now—Uzis, SIG-Sauers, anything.

The President himself could do nothing but run with them, so tightly was he flanked by his bodyguards.

'Advance Team One! Come in!' Cutler yelled into his wrist microphone as he ran.

No reply.

'Advance Team One! Come in! We are approaching Exit Point One with Patriot and we need to know if it is open!'

He received no reply.

Up in the main hangar, Book II was in hell.

Bullets strafed the floor all around him, glass rained down on his head.

He was tucked up against the outside of the northern

office with Elvis—in the tiny gap between it and the hangar's armoured door—the two of them having dived out through the office's bullet-shattered windows a moment before it had been blasted to smithereens by the Predator missile.

The three ten-man teams of 7th Squadron men were every-where, moving with precision and speed, racing around the helicopters, leaping over dead men, their guns pressed against their shoulders, eyes looking straight down the barrels.

On the other side of the hangar, Book saw the White House people come streaming out of the southern glass-walled office—about ten people in total—screaming, look-ing about themselves, only to be met by the 7th Squadron unit that had been stationed on the eastern side of the floor.

The White House men and women were cut down where they stood, hit head-on by a wave of merciless fire. Their bodies convulsed and shuddered under the weight of the brutal onslaught.

And then suddenly Book II heard a shout and he looked up and saw Gunman Grier burst out of the remains of the northern office, yelling with rage, his nickel-plated Beretta up and firing.

No sooner had he appeared, however, than Grier's chest literally *exploded* in a gout of red as two 7th Squadron troopers blasted him at the same time.

The force of their fire pummelled Grier's body, keeping him standing long after he was dead—sending him stagger-ing backwards, reeling with each impact, until he slammed into a wall and fell to the ground in a heap.

'This is a real fucked-up situation!' Elvis yelled above the gunfire. 'There's no way out of here!'

'Over there!' Book II pointed at the regular elevator on the northern side of the hangar. 'That's the only way out I can see!'

'But how do we get there?'

'We drive!' Book II shouted, nodding at one of the big towing vehicles attached to the tail boom of Nighthawk Two, ten yards away.

★

The four radio men inside the control room spoke rapidly into their headsets.

'—Bravo Unit, close down all remaining hostile agents inside that northern office—'

'—Alpha Unit is in pursuit of Presidential Detail down the eastern fire stairs—'

'—Charlie Unit, break off from the main hangar, I have visual on four Marines heading down the primary air vent—'

'—Delta Unit, be patient, maintain your position—'

'What do you mean, they attached a radio transmitter to his heart?' Schofield said as he made his way down the vertical ventilation shaft, his feet splayed wide, pressed against its silver steel walls.

Gant and Brainiac were further down, shimmying their way quickly down the vent, a seemingly bottomless drop beneath them.

'If his heart stops, the bombs go off, in every major airport, in every major city,' Mother said.

'Jesus,' Schofield said.

'And he's got to report in every ninety minutes, to reset a timer on the Football. Again, if he doesn't, *boom.*'

'Every ninety minutes?' Schofield pressed a button on his old digital watch, starting a timer of his own. He gave it a few minutes head-start. It started ticking down from 85:00 minutes—85:00 . . . 84:59 . . . 84:58—when abruptly, he heard a clattering noise from somewhere above him and he snapped his head up—

Bullets sprayed everywhere.

Peppering the metal walls all around him and Mother.

Schofield saw a P-90 rifle sticking over the rim of the ventilation shaft—held by someone out of sight—firing wildly down into it.

'*Scarecrow!*' Gant called from ten feet below them. She was crouched inside a small horizontal tunnel that branched off the main vertical shaft. 'Down here!'

'Go, Mother! Go!' Schofield yelled.

Both he and Mother released their footholds on the shaft's walls and let themselves slide down the vertical vent.

Whooosh!

They shot down the narrow vertical tunnel, sizzling-hot bullets impacting all around them, before—*reeeech!*—they dug their heels into the shaft's walls just short of the horizontal tunnel.

Mother came to a perfect halt right in front of it. Schofield, however, overshot the cross-vent, but somehow managed to throw his hands out and grip it with his fingertips, a split second before he fell several hundred feet to his death.

Mother stepped inside the cross-vent first, then hauled Schofield into it after her, not a moment before a long abseiling rope dropped down the vertical shaft above them.

The 7th Squadron were coming.

Up ahead, Gant ran in the lead, closely followed by Brainiac. The silver-walled tunnel was about five feet square, so they all had to crouch slightly to run through it.

Gant came around a slight bend on the tunnel and saw light up ahead. She sped up—and then lurched to a sudden halt, clutching desperately for a handhold.

She stopped so suddenly that Brainiac almost bowled right into her. It was lucky he pulled up in time. A collision would have sent both of them falling a hundred and eighty feet straight down.

'Fuck me . . . ' Brainiac said.

'What's the hold-up—?' Mother said as she and Schofield arrived on the scene. 'Oh . . .'

Their tunnel ended at the main elevator shaft.

The giant concrete-walled chasm, two hundred feet across, yawned before them.

On the other side of it, directly opposite them, they saw an enormous heavy steel door with a black-painted '1' on it. It looked like a hangar door of some sort.

And nearly two hundred feet *below* them—parked at the

fourth underground level—they saw the wide hydraulic elevator platform.

'You know, it's at times like this I wish I had a Maghook,' Schofield said. A Maghook was a combined grappling hook and high-powered magnet—the signature weapon of Marine Recon Units.

'There are a couple upstairs in Nighthawk Two,' Mother said.

'Wouldn't do us any good,' Gant said. 'Distance is too far. A Maghook has a maximum rope length of a hundred and fifty feet. This is at least two hundred.'

'Well, we better think of something,' Brainiac said, looking back down the cross-vent, listening to the whizzing sounds of the 7th Squadron men abseiling down the main vertical shaft beyond it.

Schofield looked at the wide concrete chasm in front of them. It was clearly well used—covered in grime and grease.

Indented at regular intervals on its walls, however, were a series of thin rectangular conduits—small horizontal gutters cut into the shaft's concrete walls. Each gutter was about six inches deep and ran right around the enormous elevator shaft, circling it. They were designed, it seemed, to house wires and cabling without hindering the elevator platform's upward and downward movement.

But right now, they afforded Schofield no escape.

Boom!

He spun. It was the sound of heavy boots clanging on metal.

The 7th Squadron men had arrived at the other end of the horizontal tunnel.

The Air Force men moved fast, racing half-crouched down the cross-vent, guns up.

There were four of them—all wearing black combat gear: helmets, gas-masks, body armour. Unsure of which cross-tunnel Schofield's group had taken, the others in their unit had gone further down the vertical vent to check the other levels.

The two lead men rounded the bend in the tunnel—and stopped.

They had come to the end of the horizontal cross-vent, to the point where it met the massive elevator shaft.

But there was no-one here.

The end of the tunnel was empty.

When the President of the United States visits a certain venue, the Secret Service has always plotted in advance at least three alternate exit routes, in case of emergency.

In big city hotels, this usually comprises a back entrance, a service entrance—say, through the kitchen—and the roof, for lift-out via helicopter.

At Area 7, the Secret Service had sent two advance teams to secure and then guard the alternate exit points that they had chosen.

Alternate Exit Point 1 was on the lowest level of Area 7— Level 6. The exit itself was the eight-hundred-yard-long Emergency Exit Vent that opened onto the desert floor about half a mile from the low mountain that covered the base. The first Secret Service advance team was stationed down on Level 6, the second up at the Vent's exit on the desert floor itself.

The President and his five-man Detail charged down the fire stairs, a hailstorm of bullets sizzling past their cheeks, shooting right through their flailing coats. The 7th Squadron's first unit—Alpha Unit, led by Major Kurt Logan—was close behind them.

They came to a firedoor that read: 'LEVEL 4: LABORATORY FACILITIES'. Dashed past it.

More stairs, another landing, another door. This one had a larger sign on it:

LEVEL 5: ANIMAL CONTAINMENT AREA
NO ENTRY
THIS DOOR FOR EMERGENCY USE ONLY
ENTER VIA ELEVATORS AT OTHER END OF FLOOR

The President ran right past it.

They arrived at the bottom of the stairwell—at a door marked: 'LEVEL 6: X-RAIL STATION'.

Frank Cutler was running in the lead. He came to the door, yanked it open—

—and was immediately assaulted by a ferocious barrage of automatic gunfire.

Cutler's face and chest became a ragged bloody mess as a relentless wave of bullets rammed into it. The Chief of the Detail went flying back into the stairwell, skidding across the floor, the man immediately behind him *also* going down.

Another agent—a young female agent named Juliet Janson—dived forward and slammed the door shut again, but before she did she got a fleeting, horrifying glimpse of the area beyond it.

The sixth and lowest level of Area 7 looked like an underground subway station—with a flat, raised platform sitting in between two sets of extra-wide railway tracks. The door to the Emergency Exit Vent—their goal—lay buried in the concrete wall of the right-hand track.

Positioned on the train tracks in front of that door, however, and covered by the station's chest-high platform, was a whole *other* unit of 7th Squadron soldiers, all with their P-90s trained on the fire escape.

In front of the 7th Squadron men, lying face-down in their own blood, lay the bullet-riddled bodies of the nine members of the Secret Service's Advance Team One.

The door slammed shut and Special Agent Juliet Janson turned.

'Quickly!' she shouted. 'Back up the stairs! Now!'

★

94

'—All units, be aware, Delta Unit has engaged the enemy—' one of the radio men in the control room said. 'Repeat, Delta Unit has engaged the enemy—'

Shane Schofield tried not to breathe, tried not to make a sound.

All they had to do was look over the edge.

He was hanging by his fingertips from one of the horizontal cabling gutters carved into the concrete wall of the elevator shaft, a bare three feet below the mouth of the cross-vent he had been standing in only moments before.

Standing in that cross-vent right now were the four heavily-armed 7th Squadron men who had stormed it only seconds earlier.

Beside him, Mother, Gant and Brainiac were also clinging to the cabling gutter with their fingers.

Above them, they could hear one of the 7th Squadron men speaking into his helmet mike.

'Charlie Six, this is Charlie One, they're not in the Level 1 cross-vent. Copy that, we're on our way.'

Heavy footsteps, then nothing.

Schofield sighed with relief.

'Where to now?' Brainiac asked.

'There,' Schofield said, jerking his chin at the giant steel hangar door on the opposite side of the wide elevator shaft.

'*You ready?*' Book II yelled to Elvis.

'Ready!' Elvis shouted back.

Book II looked out at the big white-painted Volvo towing vehicle attached to the tail boom of Nighthawk Two ten yards away. With its oversized tyres, low-slung body and small two-man driver's cabin, it looked like either a brick on wheels or a giant cockroach. Indeed, it was this resemblance that had earned the towing vehicle the nickname 'cockroach' among airport workers around the world.

At the moment, Nighthawk Two's cockroach was facing outwards, pointed at the armour-plated titanium door that had thundered down into place only minutes earlier, sealing the hangar.

Book II was now holding two nickel-plated Berettas in his hands, one his own, the other pilfered from a dead Marine nearby. He shouted to Elvis: 'You take the wheel! I'll go for the other side!'

'You got it!'

'Okay! *Now!*'

The two of them leapt to their feet and dashed out into the open together, their legs moving in time.

Almost instantly, a line of bullets raced across the ground behind them, nipping at their heels.

Elvis flung himself into the driver's seat, slammed the door shut behind him. Book II made for the passenger side, but he was met with a brutal volley of gunfire, so instead he just dived onto the towing vehicle's flat steel roof and yelled, 'Elvis! *Punch it!*'

Elvis keyed the ignition. The Volvo's big 600-horsepower engine roared to life. Then Elvis jammed it into gear and floored it.

The towing vehicle's tyres squealed as they shot off the mark, heading straight for the armoured door that cut the hangar off from the outside world, taking Nighthawk Two, a full-sized CH-53E Super Stallion transport helicopter, with it!

The two remaining units of 7th Squadron men in the hangar—twenty men in total—swept across the hangar on foot, pursuing the speeding cockroach with their guns.

A wave of supercharged bullets pummelled the big Volvo's sides.

Elvis yanked on the steering wheel and the big cockroach swung around, rocketing toward the southern glass-walled office.

On its roof, Book II raised himself on one knee and fired both his pistols at the oncoming 7th Squadron commandos.

It didn't do much good—the Air Force assassins had him outgunned. It was like attacking a battery of Patriot missiles with a pea-shooter. He ducked back behind the cockroach's cabin amid a flurry of return fire.

'*Oh, crap!*' Elvis shouted from the driver's cabin.

Book II looked up.

A lone 7th Squadron commando stood about thirty yards in front of them—*right in their path*—on the southern side of the central elevator shaft, with a Predator anti-tank rocket launcher hefted onto his shoulder!

The commando pulled the trigger.

There was a puff of smoke before a small cylindrical object came blasting out of the launcher, shooting toward the speeding cockroach at phenomenal speed, leaving a dead-straight vapor-trail in the air behind it.

Elvis reacted quickly, did the only thing he could think to do.

He yanked his steering wheel hard to the left.

The massive Volvo towing vehicle rose onto two wheels as it swung violently left—and for a moment it looked like it was going to drive straight into the yawning chasm that was the elevator shaft.

But it just kept turning . . . turning . . . wheels screeching . . . until suddenly it was heading north, along the narrow section of floor *in between* Marine One and the elevator shaft.

Nighthawk Two wasn't so lucky.

Since it was bouncing along—in reverse—behind the runaway cockroach, Elvis's sudden turn had brought it directly into the missile's line of fire.

The Predator hit it, slamming into Nighthawk Two's reinforced glass cockpit at tremendous speed.

The result was nothing short of spectacular.

The whole front section of the CH-53E Super Stallion exploded magnificently—blasting out in an instant, showering the area behind the quickly moving helicopter with glass and twisted metal, leaving the chopper with a jagged metal *hole* where the glass bubble of its cockpit was supposed to be!

The impact of the missile had also destroyed the landing

wheels under the nose of the chopper. So now the giant heli-copter was being hauled behind Elvis's towing vehicle with its nose—or what was left of it—dragging wildly on the floor, kicking up sparks.

'Elvis!' Book II yelled. 'Go for the elevator! The regular elevator!'

7th Squadron soldiers dived out of the way as the speed-ing cockroach thundered in amongst them, wildly out of control.

Elvis saw the elevator doors off to his right, and yanked the steering wheel hard over. The cockroach responded, swinging right, cutting the corner of the aircraft elevator shaft—so that for the briefest of moments, Book II, partially hanging off the roof of the vehicle, saw nothing but a wide chasm of emptiness falling away beneath him.

Three seconds later, the cockroach—with the semi-destroyed helicopter behind it—skidded to a squealing halt right in front of the elevator doors on the northern side of the hangar.

Book II leapt off the top of the big Volvo and hit the call button, Elvis joining him, when suddenly two armed men leapt over the big towing vehicle behind them.

Book II spun, snapping his guns up, triggers half-pulled.

'Whoa! Whoa! Whoa!' one of the armed men said, holding his pistol up.

'Easy, Sergeant,' the other one said calmly. 'We're with you.'

Book II eased back on his triggers.

They were Marines.

The first was Sergeant Ashley Lewicky, an extraordinarily ugly career sergeant with a thick monobrow, battered pug nose, and mile-wide grin. Short and stout, his call-sign was a slam-dunk: 'Love Machine'. Of roughly equal age and rank, he and Elvis had been buddies for years.

The second Marine, however, couldn't have been more different from Love Machine. Tall and handsome in a clean-cut kind of way, he was a twenty-nine-year-old captain named Tom Reeves. A promising young officer, he'd been tagged for rapid promotion. Indeed, he'd already been promoted over several more-experienced lieutenants. Despite his obvious skills, the men called him 'Calvin', because he looked like a Calvin Klein underwear model.

'Jesus H. Christ, Elvis,' Love Machine said, 'where the hell did you learn to drive! A demolition derby?'

'Why? Where have you two been?' Elvis asked.

'Where do you think, knucklehead? Inside Nighthawk Two. We both dived in there when the shit hit the fan. And we *were* kinda happy there until you guys drove us into the sights of that rocket laun–'

Just then, a volley of bullets smacked into the wall above their heads.

Ten 7th Squadron men—Bravo Unit—were charging across the wide hangar after them.

'I presume you had a plan when you drove over here, Sergeant,' Calvin Reeves said to Book II.

At that moment, the elevator pinged and its metal doors slid open. Thankfully, it was empty.

'This was it, sir,' Book II said.

'I approve,' Calvin said and they all rushed inside. Book II went straight to the control panel and hit 'DOOR CLOSE'.

The doors began to close. A bullet sizzled inside, smacked against the back wall of the lift.

'Hurry *up* . . . ' Elvis urged.

The doors kept closing.

They heard boots thud onto the roof of the cockroach outside, heard machine-gun bolts cock—

The doors came together . . .

. . . a bare second before they erupted with dome-like welts from the barrage of bullets outside.

It had taken them a while, but moving hand over hand, hanging by their fingertips from the cabling gutter that ran all the way around the elevator shaft, they had eventually made it to the wide hangar door on the other side.

Hanging one-handed from the horizontal gutter, Schofield hit a button on a control panel beside the hangar door. Instantly, the massive steel door began to rumble upward.

Schofield climbed up onto level ground first, made sure there were no enemy troops around, then turned to help the others up behind him.

When they were all up, they gazed at the area before them.

'Whoa, *mama* . . . ' Mother breathed.

A cavernous—completely *underground*—aircraft hangar stretched away from them.

In the control room overlooking the main ground-level hangar, the wall of black-and-white television monitors flashed an array of images from the underground complex:

Juliet Janson and the President running up the stairwell.

Book II, Calvin Reeves, Elvis and Love Machine inside

the regular elevator, punching out the ceiling hatch and climbing up through it.

Schofield and the others stepping up into the doorway of the underground hangar.

'—okay, Charlie Unit, I have them. The ones who were in the ventilation shaft. Level 1 hangar bay. Four Marines: two male, two female. They're all yours—'

'—Bravo Unit, your targets have just exited the personnel elevator through the ceiling hatch. About to lose visual contact. But they're in the shaft. Sealing all elevator shaft doors except yours. Okay, they're shut in. Take them out—'

'—sir, Echo Unit has cleaned out the rest of the main hangar. Awaiting further instructions—'

'Send them to help Charlie,' Caesar Russell said, eyeing the monitor with Shane Schofield on it.

'—Echo, this is Control, proceed to Level 1 hangar bay for rendezvous with Charlie Unit—'

'—Alpha Unit, Presidential Detail is climbing the stairs. Coming right for you. Delta Unit, the Level 6 fire door is unguarded. You are free to enter the stairwell and engage—'

It was absolutely gigantic.

An enormous subterranean hangar, roughly the same size as the one up at ground level, perhaps even larger.

It had several aircraft in it, too.

One converted Boeing 707 AWACS plane, with the characteristic flying-saucer-like rotodome mounted on its back. Two sinister-looking B-2 stealth bombers, with their black radar-absorbent paint, futuristic flying-wing design, and angry furrowed-brow cockpit windows. And parked directly in front of the stealth bombers, one Lockheed SR-71 Blackbird, the world's fastest operational aircraft, with its sleek super-elongated fuselage and twin rear thrusters.

The massive aeroplanes towered above Schofield and his team, dominating the cavernous space.

'What do we do now?' Mother asked.

Schofield was momentarily silent.

He was staring intently at the AWACS plane. It just stood there silently, pointing towards the wide aircraft elevator shaft.

Then he said, 'We find out if what they're saying about the President's heart is true.'

The air in the fire stairs was filled with flying bullets.

The Presidential Detail, down to three now, guided their charge up the stairs, leading with their guns, a makeshift array of Uzis, SIG-Sauers and spare ankle revolvers.

A young male agent named Julio Ramondo led the way, spraying the stairs above them with his Uzi, despite a bullet wound to his shoulder.

Special Agent Juliet Janson came after him, having assumed command of the Detail more by action than protocol. She guided the President along behind her.

The third and last surviving agent of the Detail—his name was Curtis—covered their rear, firing down the stairs behind them as they moved.

At twenty-eight, Juliet Janson was the most junior member of the President's Detail, but that didn't seem to matter now.

She had degrees in criminology and psychology, could run a hundred metres in 13.8 seconds and was an excellent marksman. The daughter of an American businessman father and a Taiwanese university lecturer mother, she had a flawless Eurasian complexion—smooth olive skin, a sharply defined jawline, beautiful almond-brown eyes and shoulder-length jet-black hair.

'Ramondo! Can you see it!' she shouted above the gunfire.

After the horror of their attempt to get to Level 6 and the bloody death of Frank Cutler, the President and his Detail had been left in the middle of a 7th Squadron sandwich.

The unit down on Level 6 was coming up after them, while the unit that had chased them out of the common room on Level 3 was closing in on them from above.

What that had left them with was a race—a race to get to one of the floors *in between* Level 6 and Level 3 before they faced fire from both above and below.

'Yes! I see it!' Ramondo yelled back. 'Come on!'

Juliet Janson arrived on the landing next to Ramondo, with the President beside her. Thumping footfalls echoed down the stairwell above them, bullets ripped apart the walls all around them.

Janson saw the nearest door, saw the sign on it:

LEVEL 5: ANIMAL CONTAINMENT AREA
NO ENTRY
THIS DOOR FOR EMERGENCY USE ONLY
ENTER VIA ELEVATORS AT OTHER END OF FLOOR

'I think this qualifies as an emergency,' she said, before blasting the door's locks with three shots from her SIG-Sauer.

Then she kicked open the door and hauled the President into Level 5.

Book II looked up into the darkness of the regular elevator shaft, saw the outer doors that led to the ground-level hangar about fifty feet above him.

He was standing on top of the personnel elevator—now stopped midway down the shaft—with Calvin, Elvis and Love Machine. A few widely-spaced fluorescent lights illuminated the enclosed concrete elevator well.

'Why did we have to get out of the elevator?' Elvis asked.

'Cameras,' Book II said. 'We couldn't stay—'

'We'd have been sitting ducks if we'd stayed inside it,' Calvin Reeves said, cutting in. 'Gentlemen, as the ranking officer here, I am taking command.'

'So what's the plan then, Captain America?' Love Machine asked.

'We keep moving—'Calvin began, but that was all he got out, because at that moment, the outer doors above them burst open and almost immediately three P-90 gunbarrels appeared, bright yellow flashes bursting forth from their muzzles.

A flurry of ricochets impacted all around the elevator.

Book II ducked and spun—and saw a series of vertical counterweight cables running down the wall of the shaft, disappearing down the side of the stationary elevator.

'The cables!' he yelled, scampering over to the wall, not caring for the chain of command. 'Everybody down! *Now!*'

Shane Schofield burst into the forward cabin of the AWACS plane in the hangar on Level 1.

'Brainiac.'

'Already on it,' Brainiac headed aft, disappearing inside the main cabin of the aircraft.

'Close the door,' Schofield said to Mother, who had come in last.

Schofield charged aft. The interior of the AWACS was very similar to that of a commercial airliner—albeit a commercial airliner that had had all its seats ripped out and replaced by large flat-topped surveillance consoles.

Brainiac was already at one of the consoles. It was whirring to life as Schofield took a seat beside him. Mother and Gant went straight for the plane's two door-windows, peered out through them.

Brainiac started typing at the console.

'Mother said it was a microwave signal,' Schofield said. 'The satellite beams it down and then the radio chip on the President's heart bounces the signal back up.'

Brainiac typed some more. 'Makes sense. Only a microwave signal could penetrate the radiosphere over this base—and then only if it knew the trapdoor frequency.'

'Trapdoor frequency?'

Brainiac kept typing. 'The radiosphere over this base is like an umbrella, a giant hemispherical dome of scrambled electromagnetic energy. Basically, this umbrella of garbled energy stops all unauthorised signals from either entering or escaping the base. But, like all good jamming systems, it has a designated frequency for use by *authorised* transmissions. This is the trapdoor frequency—a microwave bandwidth that wends its way through the radiosphere, avoiding the jamming signatures. Kind of like a secret path through a minefield.'

'So this satellite signal is coming in on the trapdoor frequency?' Schofield said.

'That's my guess,' Brainiac said. 'What I'm doing now is using the AWACS' rotodome to search all the microwave frequencies *inside* this base. These birds have the best bandwidth detection systems around, so it shouldn't take— bingo. Got it.'

He slammed his finger down on the 'ENTER' key and a new screen came up.

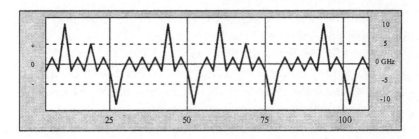

'Okay, you looking at this?' Brainiac printed out the screen. 'It's a standard rebounding signature. The satellite sends down a search signal—they're the tall spikes on the positive side, about 10 gigahertz—and then, soon after, the receiver on the ground, the President, bounces that signal back. Those are the deep spikes on the negative side.'

Brainiac circled the spikes on the printout.

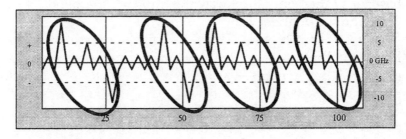

'Search and return,' he said. 'Interference aside, the rebounding signature seems to repeat itself once every twenty-five seconds. Captain, that Air Force general ain't lying. There's something down here bouncing back a secure satellite microwave signal.'

'How do we know it isn't just a beacon or something?' Schofield said.

'The irregularity of it,' Brainiac said. 'See how it isn't quite a perfectly replicating sequence? See how, every now and then, there's a medium-sized spike in between the search and the return signals?' Brainiac tapped the mid-sized spikes inside two of the circles.

'So what does that mean?'

'It's an interference signature. It means that the source of the return signal is moving.'

'Jesus,' Schofield said. 'It's real.'

'And it just got worse,' Gant said from the window set into the escape door on the left-hand side of the cabin. 'Have a look at this.'

Schofield came over to the small window, looked out through it.

And his blood went cold.

There must have been at least twenty of them.

Twenty 7th Squadron soldiers running quickly across the hangar outside—P-90 assault rifles in their hands, ERG-6 masks covering their faces—forming a wide circle around the AWACS plane, surrounding it.

It was the smell that hit them first.

It smelled like a zoo—that peculiar mix of animal excrement and sawdust in a confined space.

Juliet Janson led the way into Level 5, pulling the President along behind her. The other two Secret Service agents hurried in after them, jamming the stairwell door shut behind them.

They were standing in a wide, dark room, lined on three sides with grim-looking cages—forged steel bars set into walls of solid concrete. On the fourth side of the room were some more modern-looking cages: these cages had clear, floor-to-ceiling fibreglass walls and were filled with inky black water. Janson couldn't see what lurked inside the sloshing opaque water.

A sudden grunting sound made her spin.

There was something very large inside one of the steel cages to her right. In the dim light of the dungeon, she could make out a big, hairy, lumbering shape moving behind the thick black bars.

There came an ominous scratching sound from the cage—like someone dragging a fingernail slowly and deliberately down a chalkboard.

Special Agent Curtis went over to the cell, peered into the darkness beyond the bars.

'Don't get too close,' Janson warned.

Too late.

A hideous bloodcurdling roar filled the dungeon as an enormous black head—a blurred combination of matted hair, wild eyes and flashing six-inch teeth—burst out from behind the bars and lunged at the hapless agent.

Curtis fell back from the cage, landing on his butt as the animal—enraged, ferocious, frenzied—reached in vain for him with a long hairy claw, held back only by the super-strong bars of the cell.

The would-be ambush over, Janson now got a better look at the creature.

It was huge, at least nine feet tall, and covered in shaggy black fur—and it looked completely out of place in a concrete underground cell.

Janson couldn't believe it.

It was a *bear*.

And it didn't seem to be a very happy bear either. Its fur was matted and stringy, sweat-stained, growing in clumps. The animal's own faeces clung to the fur on its hindquarters, making the world's largest living land carnivore look like some deranged horror movie monster.

The three other cages on the northern side of the dungeon held more bears—four females and two cubs.

'Jesus . . . ' the President breathed.

'What the hell is going on in this place?' Julio Ramondo whispered.

'I don't care,' Janson said, pulling the President toward a heavy-looking door on the far side of the dungeon. 'Whatever it is, we can't stay here.'

The hangar bay on Level 1 was silent.

The giant AWACS plane stood in the centre of the vast hangar, surrounded by the ring of 7th Squadron commandos.

'This isn't the situation I was hoping for,' Schofield said.

'How do they keep knowing where we are?' Mother asked.

Gant looked at Schofield. 'I would imagine a base like this is wired up the kazoo.'

'Agreed,' Schofield said.

'What are you talking about?' Mother said.

'Cameras,' Schofield said. 'Surveillance cameras. Somewhere in this base, someone's in a room watching a bank of monitors and telling these guys where we—'

Whump!

There came a heavy thump from somewhere outside.

Gant peered out through the window in the escape door. 'Shit! They're on the wing!'

'Oh, *Christ*,' Schofield said, 'they're going for the doors . . .'

He exchanged a look with Gant.

'They're going to storm the plane,' he said.

They looked like ants crawling over a toy aeroplane. Eight 7th Squadron men—four to each side—stalking along the wings of the giant Boeing 707.

Captain Luther 'Python' Willis, commander of the 7th Squadron's third sub-unit, Charlie Unit, stood on the hangar floor, watching his men move along the wings of the stationary plane.

'The Avengers are on the way up,' his master sergeant said.

Python said nothing, just nodded coldly.

Inside the AWACS plane, Schofield was charging down the central aisle, checking the plane's rear entry points. Gant and Brainiac manned the two side windows.

'There's nobody back here!' Schofield called from the aft section of the plane, where there were two emergency doors. 'Fox!'

'I got four on the left wing!' Gant yelled.

'I got four on the right!' Brainiac said.

'Mother!' Schofield called.

No answer.

'Mother!'

Schofield strode quickly through the main cabin, moving forward.

There was no sign of Mother anywhere. She was supposed to be checking the plane's forward entrances—the bail-out door in the floor of the forward cabin, and the roof hatches in the cockpit above the pilots' ejection seats.

As he hurried forward, Schofield looked out through the nearest window, saw the armed commandos on the left-hand wing.

He frowned: *what were they doing out there?*

They couldn't just burst in through the wing doors. Even with their nickel-plated pistols, Schofield and his Marines could easily repel a single-file entry through such a small entrance.

It was at that moment, however—out through the window in the side door of the Boeing 707—that he saw the Avengers.

There were two of them and they entered the hangar bay from the vehicle access ramp at the far eastern end of the floor.

The Avenger air-defence vehicle is a modified Humvee. It has the basic wide-bodied chassis of a Humvee, but mounted on its back are two square-shaped pods, which each hold four Stinger surface-to-air missiles. Attached to the underside of these missile launchers is a pair of powerful fifty-calibre machine guns. It is basically a highly-efficient, highly-mobile aeroplane killer.

'Okay, now I know what they're going to do,' Schofield said aloud.

They were going to blast the plane with the Stingers and then, in the smoke and confusion that followed, make a forced entry.

Good plan, Schofield thought. And very painful for him and his three Marines.

The two Avengers split up as they raced across the wide-open floor of the hangar, one heading for the right flank of the AWACS, the other heading for the left.

Schofield saw them go, disappearing from his limited field of vision.

Shit.

He had to do something, and fast—

VROOOM!

The wing-mounted engines of the AWACS plane thundered to life. In the enclosed space of the hangar, their roar was positively deafening.

Schofield spun where he stood. 'Mother,' he said.

The Avengers skidded to a halt on either side of the AWACS plane just as the massive Boeing 707 began to roll forward, its engines filling the hangar with the thunderous roar of blasting air.

At the sudden movement of the plane, the eight men on its wings were jolted off balance.

Schofield charged into the cockpit of the AWACS.

Mother was sitting in the captain's seat.

'Hey there, Scarecrow!' she yelled above the din. 'Want to join me for a Sunday drive!'

'You ever driven a plane before, Mother?'

'I saw Kurt Russell drive one in a movie once! Hell, it can't be much different from driving Ralph's eighteen-wheel—'

Whack-whack-whack-whack-whack!

A volley of bullets assaulted the windshield of the cockpit, shattering it, sending glass flying all over Mother and Schofield, the upwardly-directed shots punching into the ceiling.

And then Schofield saw one of the Avengers skid to a halt off to the left of the AWACS plane, saw its twin missile pods tilt upward on their hinges, getting ready to fire at the cockpit.

'Mother! Quickly! Go left!' he shouted.

'*What?*' Going left would put them on a collision course with the Avenger.

'Just do it!' Schofield leapt into the right-hand co-pilot's seat and using the plane's pedal-operated steering controls, brought her hard to port, at the same time as he pushed forward on the plane's thrusters.

The giant AWACS plane responded immediately.

It picked up speed, moving quickly inside the confines of the enormous hangar, swinging sharply to the left—*heading directly for the Avenger!*

The 7th Squadron men on the Avenger saw what was going to happen.

Abandoning their efforts to get a lock on the plane with their Stingers, they dived from the missile-mounted Humvee a bare second before the enormous forward wheels of the Boeing thundered right over the top of the Avenger, crushing it like a tin can, rolling over its crumpled remains like a monster truck at a car rally.

'Yee-hah!' Mother yelled as the aeroplane bounced wildly over what was left of the Humvee.

'It's not over yet,' Schofield said. 'There's still another one out there. *Fox!* Where's that other Avenger!'

Gant and Brainiac were still in the main cabin of the AWACS, covering the wing-entry doors on either side of the plane—Gant with her MP-10, Brainiac with his Beretta.

'It's behind us to the left!' Gant yelled. Out her window, she saw the Humvee on the hangar floor outside, over by the northern wall, its missile pods raised and ready. Then, without warning, there came a puff of smoke from one of the pods.

'Bracing positions!' she called. 'Missile away!'

There came a sudden *monstrous* explosion and abruptly the whole AWACS plane shuddered violently as its rear wheels were lifted clear off the ground.

Billowing smoke rushed into the main cabin, shooting forward from the rear as the giant plane came back down to earth, jouncing on its suspension.

'They've hit our tail!' Gant yelled.

It was worse than that.

The second Avenger had reduced the entire tail section of their 707 to a smoking, gaping hole. The high tail fin of the plane lay bent and broken on the floor of the hangar, completely detached from the plane.

The AWACS continued to turn in a wide circle, its massive wheels rolling quickly, at the same time as it was pummelled by a continuous rain of fire from the 7th Squadron soldiers on the ground.

In the enormous space of the underground hangar, the plane's movement seemed almost comical—for something so big and so heavy to move so quickly and so recklessly was a sight to behold.

The plane came around 180 degrees—the tip of its right wing bouncing off the flank of the parked SR-71 Blackbird—so that now it was facing the *opposite* direction from which it had started, its open rear end now exposed to the withering fire of the 7th Squadron men on the ground.

Bullets raked the interior of the central cabin, smashing into the ceiling and walls. Gant and Brainiac hit the deck as fragments of plastic and plaster rained down all around them.

'Fuck!' Brainiac yelled. 'They don't teach *this* at Parris Island!'

Book II was also moving fast.

He slid quickly down one of the vertical counterweight cables that ran up the side of the regular elevator shaft. Calvin, Elvis and Love Machine slid down the cables after him, lowering themselves down the shaft.

After avoiding the barrage of fire up on the roof of the elevator, they now had to find a way out of the shaft, before the 7th Squadron men up there got around the elevator that now formed an obstacle between them.

Book II stopped at a pair of outer doors marked with a large black-painted '1', and immediately heard the muffled sounds of a firefight—clattering automatic gunfire, booming explosions, squealing tyres.

'Not this one,' Calvin Reeves said as he came alongside Book II. 'Let's try the next one.'

They slid further down the shaft.

Inside the hangar bay, Python Willis watched the AWACS plane as it sped in a wild circle around the enormous hangar.

He spoke without emotion into his headset mike: 'Avenger Two. Go for the cockpit. Two missiles.'

In the cockpit of the AWACS plane, Schofield pumped on the steering pedals.

'Mother!' he yelled. 'Get back in the main cabin! Cover the tail! Make sure no-one gets in through there! I'll take care of the driving up here!'

Mother grabbed her M-16 and headed aft.

As she left, Schofield saw the second Humvee appear in front of him, over by the northern wall. It swung around quickly, taking up a new position, getting ready to fire again.

He keyed the plane's intercom.

'*Brainiac!*' Schofield's voice boomed over the plane's speaker system. '*Engage electronic countermeasures!*'

Back in the main cabin, Brainiac looked up at the sound of Schofield's voice. 'Oh, yeah. Of course!'

'What is he talking about?' Gant yelled as Mother joined them in the main cabin.

But Brainiac was already clambering toward one of the consoles. He slid into the seat, began typing quickly.

Gant peered out her door-window—saw the walls of the hangar streaking by outside—saw the surviving Humvee skid to a halt over by the wall, preparing to fire another of its missiles.

'It's going to hit us again!' she called.

'*Brainiac* . . .' Schofield's voice said expectantly over the speakers.

Brainiac typed fast. The words 'ENGAGE MF SCRAMBLER' appeared on his screen.

'Bracing positions!' Gant yelled.

Two clouds of smoke puffed out from the Humvee's missile pods—

—at exactly the same moment as Brainiac slammed his finger down on the 'ENTER' key.

A pair of Stinger missiles shot out from the pods on the back of the Humvee, twin smoke-trails zooming out behind them. They were heading directly for the forward section of the AWACS plane, flying in perfect formation.

And then, all of a sudden, the Stingers went crazy.

Despite the fact that the missiles were heat-seekers, the AWACS's powerful anti-missile countermeasures still affected them—disrupting their chip-to-chip electronics, scrambling their internal-logic systems. It was as if a tidal wave of electronic noise, blasting invisibly outward from the AWACS's enormous rotodome, had slammed into the two Stingers.

The two missiles responded accordingly.

They went haywire.

They broke formation in an instant, parting in a looping Y-shape—one rolling wildly to the right, the other swinging left. The right-hand one shot quickly *underneath* the rolling AWACS plane, while the left-hand one sailed clear *over* it.

From the cockpit of the AWACS Schofield watched in amazement as one of the missiles shot across his bow and then—bizarrely—headed *back toward* the Humvee that had launched it!

A second later the missile *slammed* into the concrete wall above the Humvee—thundering at tremendous speed right into a ten-foot-high box-shaped compartment mounted above the floor of the hangar.

The missile detonated—sending an enormous gout of concrete spraying out from the wall all around the

116

compartment. The compartment's wide steel door was blasted off its hinges by the stunning impact and went bouncing across the hangar, a twisted metal wreck. Large chunks of concrete rained down on the very Humvee that had fired the missile.

Whatever that compartment was, Schofield thought, it was toast now.

But there was still one more out-of-control missile swooping around the hangar.

This second missile swung around the destroyed rear section of the moving AWACS plane, rolling wildly through the air, before it too doubled back and hit the hangar's northern wall, right alongside the regular elevator's doors.

A hailstorm of concrete blasted out from the wall, showering chunks everywhere.

This blast of concrete, however, was followed by a most peculiar sight.

A shockingly powerful geyser of water—yes, *water*—began to shoot out from the newly formed hole in the wall, jetting outward with tremendous force.

Schofield frowned. 'What the hell . . . ?'

An ominous explosion shook the walls of the regular elevator shaft.

Book II, now hanging with his group next to the outer doors of Level 3—the doors to Level 2 had also been locked, so they'd moved down to the next floor—looked up sharply at the sound.

The sight that met him was as terrifying as it was unexpected.

A whole section of the concrete wall alongside the Level 1 doorway sixty feet above them just blasted outward, showering the shaft with chunks of concrete.

And then, right behind the concrete, came the water.

It rained down on Book II and the others like spray from a goddamned firehose.

Torrents and torrents of pouring water, roaring like a waterfall down the narrow elevator shaft, gushing out of the hole in the wall on Level 1, pounding down against their bodies.

It was all they could do to hold on to their cables.

But as soon as he felt the surging weight of the waterfall, Book II saw the future: the wall of water was just too strong.

They were going to fall.

'—All units, be aware. We have rupture of the long-term water tanks on Level 1. Repeat: integrity of water tanks on Level 1 has been broken—'

'—Water from the tanks is entering the regular elevator shaft—'

'Initiate airtight countermeasures,' Caesar Russell said calmly. 'Seal off the shaft. Keep that water contained. Let it flood the shaft.'

'Yes, sir.'

Love Machine fell first.

In the face of the powerful waterfall, he lost his grip on the counterweight cable and dropped straight past Book.

He fell fast—falling away from Book II in a kind of nightmarish slow motion; eyes wide, mouth open, his shout drowned out by the roar of the waterfall—before he disappeared into the inky darkness of the shaft.

Book II swore. 'Damn it!'

And then he did the only thing he could think to do.

'Sergeant! *No!*' Calvin yelled, but it was too late.

Book II loosened his grip on his cable and slid like a bullet down the shaft after Love Machine, disappearing into the darkness.

Book II dropped into blackness.

He slid for a long time, whizzing down the counterweight

cable, sliding fast, the heat from the cable burning through his white formal gloves.

Then suddenly, with a splash, he entered water—*deep* water—at the bottom of the shaft.

Just as he had hoped.

The elevator shaft was approximately ten feet square and if all its exit doors were sealed, then with the monumental quantities of water rushing out of the hole on Level 1, he'd figured it wouldn't take long for it to accumulate at the bottom and fill to a reasonable depth.

Sure enough, Love Machine hovered in the pool of water next to him, gasping for air, coughing water. But alive.

'You okay!' Book II yelled.

'Uh-huh!'

Calvin and Elvis arrived at the base of the shaft a few moments later, sliding down the counterweight cables. The roaring waterfall thundered into the pool all around them, kicking up spray.

'Okay, Captain Fantastic,' Elvis said to Calvin, 'our nice safe elevator shaft is now filling with water! What do you suggest we do now?'

Calvin hesitated.

Book II didn't. He nodded at the pair of outer doors a few feet above them. 'Simple. We bust out!'

'Mother*fucker* . . . ' Brainiac said as he peered out from the rear of the AWACS plane's main cabin.

A high-pressure geyser of water was now shooting out of the hole in the wall over by the personnel elevator, throwing a carpet of water all over the concrete floor of the hangar. 'What the hell is this ride?'

'Just another day of mayhem and destruction with the Scarecrow,' Mother said.

'Hey,' Gant said, looking out through her door-window. 'What happened to the guys on the wings?'

Mother and Brainiac spun to look out at the plane's wings.

The AWACS's wings were bare.

The 7th Squadron men who had been out there before were nowhere to be seen.

It was only then that they heard the ominous sound of thumping footsteps on the roof.

The AWACS plane continued on its rampaging circuit of the hangar, now travelling through a layer of water one inch deep.

It had almost come full circle—so that now it was facing the empty section of the hangar that led to the wide-open doorway of the aircraft elevator shaft.

Schofield pumped on the steering pedals, trying to keep the enormous surveillance plane under control.

He saw the doorway to the aircraft elevator shaft directly in front of him. At the moment, a shallow film of water cascaded over it like Niagara Falls, dropping out of sight into the shaft.

The big hydraulic elevator platform was almost certainly the best way out of this jam, but the last he had seen, it was stopped down on one of the lower levels—

And then, more suddenly than Schofield could possibly have anticipated, the roof above him exploded in a shower of sparks.

In actual fact, it wasn't the roof—it was one of the blast hatches *set into* the roof of the cockpit, one of the hatches that blew open when the pilot's ejection seat was activated.

No sooner had the hatch blasted open than a veritable *hailstorm* of gunfire flooded down through it, smashing into the aeroplane's dashboard, shattering all its gauges and dials.

This torrent of bullets was quickly followed by a second volley which ripped through the empty pilot's seat—the left-hand seat; the seat Mother had been sitting in before—tearing it to shreds.

Schofield saw what was going to happen next and he quickly dived out of his seat, rolling forward into the tiny section of floorspace in front of it.

Not a moment later, a pair of combat boots landed with a thump on the pilot's seat—boots that belonged to a fearsome-looking 7th Squadron commando.

The masked commando spun quickly, his P-90 assault rifle pressed firmly against his shoulder, searching for enemies at the rear of the cockpit. Then he turned to look forward, and downward—where, to his complete surprise, he saw Schofield lying curled up on the floor.

Gunless and defenceless, Schofield saw the masked commando's black-gloved trigger finger begin to squeeze—

And so he lashed out with his foot.

Not at the man's legs, but at the lever that ran alongside the flight seat underneath him—the ejection lever.

Schofield's kick connected.

The lever snapped backward.

And with a loud, blasting *whoosh!* the pilot's ejection seat shot up through the hole in the cockpit's roof—taking the 7th Squadron commando with it!

Python Willis watched in complete and utter astonishment as one of his men went rocketing up at incredible speed *out* of the cockpit of the AWACS and past his shocked colleagues on the roof of the plane, on top of an ejection seat!

The man shot into the air like a bullet, before smashing—violently, concussively—into the concrete ceiling of the hangar.

The crack of the man's neck echoed sickeningly throughout the underground hangar bay—it was distinct even above the roar of the AWACS's engines, so hard did his body hit the ceiling. He was killed instantly, the force of the three-hundred-pound ejection seat snapping his spine like a twig as it squashed him against the concrete roof.

In the meantime, Schofield had got his own Beretta pistol out and, sliding on his back onto the floor behind the pilots' seats, was firing it up at the roof of the cockpit—trying to deter anyone else from following their comrade into the flight deck.

In seconds, his gun went dry and he stood up and looked out through the forward windshield—

—and saw that the plane was heading directly for the massive doorway leading to the elevator shaft!

'Oh, this just keeps getting better and better,' he said.

In a fleeting second, he tried to find a solution to the situation.

The plane was heading for the shaft.

The 7th Squadron were all over its roof—all over the hangar for that matter.

And he and Gant and Mother and Brainiac were stuck inside the plane.

What was the solution?

Simple.

Get out of the hangar.

But there is no way out. We're stuck in this plane, and if we leave it, we're dead.

Unless, of course, we get out of the hangar while we're still on board the plane . . .

Oh, yeah . . .

And with that Schofield climbed back into the co-pilot's seat and took control of the plane again. Despite the bullet damage, the controls still worked.

He pushed forward on the collective, speeding up the big Boeing 707, keeping it pointed directly at the enormous steel doorway that led out to the elevator shaft.

'What the hell is he doing . . . ?' Python said.

The giant AWACS plane was picking up speed, rumbling across the wide expanse of the hangar, heading straight for the open elevator doorway.

★

The commandos on the roof of the plane felt it surge forward, gaining momentum.

They looked forward, saw where it was heading, and their eyes widened.

'He can't be serious,' Python breathed, as he watched his men leap off the roof of the moving aeroplane as it careered toward the open doorway.

In the cockpit of the speeding plane, Schofield was strapping on his seatbelt. As he did so, he keyed the intercom switch.

'Ladies and gentlemen, this is your captain speaking. Find a chair and buckle up tight, because we're about to take off.'

Back in the main cabin, Gant and the other two Marines spun to look forward.

Through the AWACS's cabin, they could see all the way through to the cockpit—could see the open elevator shaft looming ahead of them, rapidly approaching.

'Is he thinking what I think he's thinking?' Gant said to Mother.

Mother paused before she spoke. 'Yes, he is.'

They leapt as one for the nearest available seats and clutched desperately for the seatbelts.

The converted Boeing 707—deprived of its entire tail section—thundered across the wide subterranean hangar bay, the wet concrete floor rushing by beneath it, heading straight for the open elevator shaft.

And then, before anyone could even hope to stop it, the plane shot through the doorway and tipped off the edge and fell down into the shaft, disappearing from view.

124

The AWACS plane soared down the elevator shaft fast—nose-first—looking like a crazed kamikaze fighter.

Down the wide concrete shaft it went—down, down, down—before it crashed, loudly, on the massive hydraulic elevator platform resting on Level 4, one hundred and eighty feet below.

The nose of the AWACS plane crumpled instantly as it thundered into the elevator platform. Loose parts flew everywhere, blasting outward like shrapnel. Two of the plane's jet engines bounced high into the air as they smashed into the platform.

The plane itself, however, seemed to teeter on its broken nose for an eternity. And then, with a loud metal-on-metal groan, like a slow-falling California redwood, it fell, landing with a colossal thump on its left-hand wing, snapping the wing in an instant, before the whole ruined aircraft slammed down against the elevator platform with a resounding *boom*.

Inside the AWACS plane, the world was tilted forty-five degrees to the left.

Mother, Gant and Brainiac all sat comically in their seats, strapped in, but hanging dramatically to the side. They were starting to unbuckle themselves from their seatbelts when Schofield hurried into the main cabin from the cockpit.

'Come on,' he said, helping Mother with her belt, 'we can't stay here. They'll be down soon.'

'Where are we going?' Gant asked, as she dropped out of her seat and stood up.

Schofield pursed his lips. 'We have to find the President.'

'—Jesus! He just drove the plane off the fucking edge—'

'—Charlie and Echo Units, initiate pursuit—'

'—President is on Level 5, heading into the confinement area. Delta Unit, you are free to enter the animal quarters—'

'—Copy that, Bravo leader. Yes, they're in the water at the bottom of the shaft. Good idea—'

'What's Boa doing?' Caesar Russell asked. Captain Bruno 'Boa' McConnell was in command of Bravo Unit, one of the Five Snakes.

'He's on top of the personnel elevator, sir. He's going to lower the elevator down the shaft. Drown the bastards. And if they try to crawl up the sides, shoot them dead.'

Book II and the others hovered in the ever-deepening pool of water at the base of the regular elevator shaft.

The super-heavy rain of water blasted down all around them. It showed no sign of stopping and the elevator shaft was flooding rapidly, the water level rising fast, lifting them to the nearest pair of outer doors.

And then abruptly, above the roar of falling water, a loud clunking noise echoed down the shaft, followed by the hum of mechanical movement.

Book II looked upwards—just as the rain of water stopped.

Well, sort of stopped. Now it started raining down the *sides* of the shaft, covering the counterweight cables with a curtain of gushing water.

'What's happening?' Love Machine said.

126

And then Book II saw it.

Saw a shadow superimposed on the darkness above them—a *box-shaped* shadow, growing larger and larger as it came closer and closer.

'What is *that*?' Calvin Reeves said.

'Oh, damn . . . ' Book II breathed. 'It's the elevator.'

The personnel elevator edged its way down the shaft, water pounding onto its roof and cascading off its sides.

High above it, in the open doorway up on ground level, two 7th Squadron snipers lay with night-scoped rifles at the ready, aimed down into the shaft.

Their guns were trained on the roof of the elevator, waiting for anyone to emerge from the gaps on either side of the lift, the only points where the enemy could climb out from underneath the downward-moving elevator.

'Not nice,' Book II said flatly. 'Not nice.'

Either they drowned as the elevator pushed them under the surface, or they climbed up the sides of the lift, where no doubt, the bad guys would be waiting . . .

He looked quickly at the pair of outer doors two feet above him. They had a large '5' painted on them.

Level 5.

He wondered what was on this level, then decided he didn't care. These doors were the only way out. Period.

He hauled himself out of the water, stood on his toes on the edge of the doorway. A curtain of water poured down onto his head.

Like all the other outer doors in this elevator shaft, he saw, these two were closed tight, air-sealed.

The elevator above him continued its descent, moving slowly and steadily downward.

The rising water reached the base of the doorway, splashed against his boots, moving equally steadily upward.

Calvin Reeves appeared at his side. 'How the hell do we open these doors, Sergeant!'

Book guessed that the doors' release mechanism was contained somewhere within the wall.

'I can't see it!' he shouted back. 'It must be hidden inside the wall!'

The elevator was close now, looming one floor above them, grinding inexorably downward.

Water continued to pour.

And then Book II saw it—a thick insulated cable running out from the concrete wall to the right of the doors and *down* into the pool of water beneath him.

'Of course!' he yelled. An emergency release lever wouldn't be on this level. It would be situated either *above* or *below* the floor, so that the doors could be opened when the elevator was stopped here.

Without so much as a second thought, Book II took a deep breath and dropped into the pool of water beneath him.

Silence.

The eerie quiet of the underwater world.

Book II swam downwards, his fingers feeling their way along the thick black cable attached to the concrete wall.

After about nine feet, he came to a steel utility box sunk into the wall. He opened it, felt for a lever, found a row of six, and yanked the fifth one.

He immediately heard a sharp *shoosh!* from somewhere above him—the sound of a pressure door being released.

He swam upward, fast. Came to the surface, broke it—

'—Book! *Quickly!* Come on!' were the first words he heard.

He'd come up a few feet away from the now-opened doors and immediately saw Calvin Reeves and Elvis standing up on level ground. Love Machine clung to the edge of the doorway, reaching out for Book II with an outstretched hand.

Then Book II looked up.

The descending elevator was barely three feet above his head and coming down fast!

He threw out a hand and Love Machine grabbed it, and hauled him over to the doorway, pulling him through the water. Then Elvis and Calvin grabbed them both and yanked them out of the water, *just as* the elevator slid past the edge of the doorway and abruptly came to a halt—right in front of the doorway.

Everybody froze.

Water began to ooze up around the floor of the lift, rising up from beneath it, hungrily searching for an escape from the shaft. It immediately began to spread out across the concrete floor of Level 5.

Book II waited tensely for the elevator's doors to open— waited for a phalanx of 7th Squadron men to burst out from it with their guns blazing.

But none did.

The lift was empty.

They were safe, for the moment.

Book II turned to face the room around him. A layer of expanding water had already started filling it.

It was a wide anteroom of some sort. Some wooden desks, a Lexan glass cabinet full of shotguns and riot gear. Plus a couple of holding cells.

Book II frowned.

It was almost as if he was standing in the reception room of a *jail*.

'What in God's name is this place?' he said aloud.

At that very same moment, on the other side of Level 5, Juliet Janson and the President of the United States found themselves standing in a whole new kind of hell.

Juliet had thought the animal cage room had been bad.

This was worse.

After bursting through the heavy-looking door on the western side of the animal cage room, she now found herself staring at a far more frightening part of Area 7.

A wide, dark, low-ceilinged room stretched away from her. It was sparsely lit, with only one in every three lights turned on, a policy which had the effect of leaving small patches of the vast room hidden in perfect blackness.

But the low light couldn't hide the true nature of this level.

It was *filled* with cells.

Old rusty concrete cages—thick-walled, with anodised black bars sunk deep into concrete dividers. The cells were quite obviously aged, and in the half-light of Level 5, they took on a positively Gothic appearance.

It was, however, the groans and hoarse whispers coming from the darkness behind the bars that betrayed the nature of their occupants.

These were not animal cells, Juliet realised in horror.

They were *human* cells.

★

The prisoners heard the heavy door burst open—heard Juliet and the President and the other two Secret Service agents charge through it—and they rushed as one to the doors of their cells to see what the commotion was.

'Oh, hey, *baby*!' one toothless individual cried as Juliet, striking and purposeful as she held her silver SIG-Sauer pistol in her hand, charged past his cell, pulling the President behind her.

'Ramondo!' she yelled. 'Block that door behind us!'

A row of steel lockers lined the wall near the door leading back to the animal cage room. Ramondo yanked the first three of them down from their upright positions, strewing the lockers in front of the door.

The prisoners began to shout and cry out.

Like all lifers, they could sense fear instantly, and they took pleasure in heightening it. Some yelled obscenities, others rattled their bars with enamel drinking mugs, others still just wailed a constant ear-piercing '*Ahhhhhhhhh!*'

Juliet bolted through the nightmare, grim-faced and determined.

She saw a gently-sloping ramp off to her right—fenced off by a big barred gate. The ramp seemed to lead up to the next level. She made for it.

'Hey, baby! You wanna go for a spin . . . on top of my flagpole!'

The President stared wide-eyed at the chaos all around him. Prisoners in blue denim uniforms, unshaven and crazed, leaned out from their cages, trying to grab him.

'Hey, old man. I bet you got a *nice* soft marshmallow ass—'

'Come on,' Juliet yanked the President away from the voices.

They came to the barred gate.

As one would expect on a cell block, its lock was thick and strong. They couldn't shoot through it.

'Curtis,' Juliet said crisply. 'Lock.'

Special Agent Curtis slid to his knees in front of the gate and pulled a high-tech-looking lock-picking device from his coat pocket.

As Curtis unfolded his lock-picker, Janson scanned the area around them.

There was movement and noise everywhere. Arms flailed out of cell doors. Snarling faces tried to squeeze through the bars. And the shouting, the constant shouting.

'Ahhhhhhhh!'

None of the prioners seemed to recognise the President. They all just seemed to enjoy making noise, inciting fear—

Then abruptly, there came a loud *boom* from somewhere behind them.

Juliet spun, pistol up.

She was met by the sight of a Marine, his full dress uniform completely saturated, charging toward her with a Remington pump-action shotgun raised.

Behind the first man were three more Marines, also soaked to the skin.

The lead Marine lowered his shotgun when he saw Juliet and the President.

'It's okay! It's okay!' Book II said, coming closer, lowering the shotgun he had pilfered from the arms cabinet in the anteroom. 'It's us!'

Calvin Reeves stepped forward, spoke seriously. 'What's happened down here?'

Juliet said, 'We've lost six people already, and those Air Force bastards are in the next room, right on our asses.'

Behind her, Special Agent Curtis inserted his lock-picker into the gate's lock, pressed a button.

Zzzzzzzzz!

The lock-picking device emitted a shrill dentist-drill-like buzz. The lock clicked loudly and the gate swung open.

'What's your plan from here, Agent Janson?' Calvin asked.

'To be where the bad guys aren't,' Juliet said. 'First of all, by going up this ramp. Let's move.'

Special Agents Curtis and Ramondo headed up the ramp first, followed by Calvin. Juliet pushed the President after them. Love Machine and Elvis went next. Book II fell into step beside Juliet, covering the rear.

Just as they were about to head up the ramp, however, they both heard a voice above the din.

'—not a prisoner—a scientist!—*know this facility*—can help you!'

Juliet and Book II spun.

It took them a second to locate the owner of the voice.

Three cells down from the ramp, in the cell closest to the animal cage room.

The owner of the voice was standing up against the bars of his cell—which in the surrounding chaos had only made him look just like all the other prisoners.

But upon closer inspection, he looked considerably different from the others.

He wasn't wearing a blue denim inmate uniform. Rather, he wore a white labcoat over shirtsleeves and a loosened tie.

Nor did he look deranged or menacing. Quite the opposite, in fact. He was short, with glasses and thinning blond hair that looked like it had been combed every day of his life.

Juliet and Book came to his cell.

'Who are you?' Juliet shouted above the din.

'My name is Herbert Franklin!' he replied quickly. 'I'm a doctor, an immunologist! Until this morning, I was working on the vaccine! But then the Air Force people locked me in here!'

'You know this facility?' Book II yelled. Beside him, Juliet stole a glance at the heavy door leading back to the animal cage room. It was banging from the other side.

'Yes!' the man named Franklin said.

'What do you think?' Book II asked Juliet.

She pondered it for a moment.

Then she shouted up the ramp: 'Curtis! Quickly! Get back here! I got another lock I need opened!'

Two minutes later, they were all heading up the ramp, now with a new member added to their group.

As they raced up the sloping walkway, however, making for the next floor, none of them noticed the layer of expanding water that lapped up against the bottom of the ramp.

When Schofield's runaway AWACS plane had crashed down onto it, the massive aircraft elevator platform had been parked on Level 4—at the spot where the President's entourage had left it nearly an hour earlier.

Now, the crumpled remains of the Boeing 707 lay sprawled across the width of the elevator platform.

Gnarled pieces of metal lay everywhere. A couple of tyres had been thrown clear with the impact. The plane itself lay pointed downwards, tilted over on its side, its nose dented sharply inwards, its left-hand wing broken in half, crushed beneath the plane's tremendous weight. Miraculously, the AWACS plane's thirty-foot flying-saucer-like rotodome had survived the fall completely intact.

Shane Schofield stepped out of the wreck of the plane, followed by Gant, Mother and Brainiac. They jumped over the debris as they ran for the giant steel door that led to Level 4.

A smaller door set into the base of the gigantic door opened easily.

No sooner had they opened it than Schofield raised his gun and fired. The shot smashed into a wall-mounted security camera, blasting it to oblivion in a shower of sparks.

'No cameras,' he said as he walked. 'That's how they're following us.'

The four of them made their way up a short upwardly-sloping corridor. A squat solid-looking door loomed at the end of it.

Mother spun the flywheel on it and the big door swung open.

Schofield stepped through the doorway first, his nickel-plated pistol leading the way.

He emerged inside a laboratory of some sort. Super-computers lined the walls, their lights blinking. Keyboard terminals and data screens and clear-plastic experiment boxes occupied the remaining bench space.

Otherwise, the lab was deserted—

Blam!

Gunshot.

Blam!

Another.

It was Gant, exterminating a couple of security cameras.

Schofield continued to scan the wide room.

The most dominant feature of the laboratory was a line of slanted glass windows that lay directly opposite the entrance.

He stepped up to the observation windows and peered out through them—

—and found himself looking out over a wide, high-ceilinged room, in the centre of which stood a gigantic glass cube.

The cube was freestanding, occupying the centre of the hall-like room, but without touching its ceiling or walls.

The wall on the far side of the cube—a wall which divided this level in two—didn't quite reach the ceiling. Rather, it stopped about seven feet short of it, replaced by thick glass. Through that glass, Schofield saw a series of criss-crossing catwalks suspended above whatever was on the other side of the floor.

But it was the cube in front of him that held his immediate attention.

It was about the size of a large living room. Such a conclusion was easy to come to, given that the glass cube was filled with regular household furniture—a couch, a table, chairs, a TV with Playstation 2 and, most strangely of all, a single bed draped with a Jar Jar Binks doona cover.

Some toys lay strewn about the glass-enclosed living room. Matchbox cars. A bright yellow *Episode I* spaceship. Some picture books.

Schofield shook his head.

It looked like the bedroom of a little boy.

It was at that precise moment that the occupant of the glass cube ambled casually out from a discreetly curtained-off corner of the cube—the toilet.

Schofield's jaw dropped.

'What on earth is going on here?' he breathed.

There was a set of stairs on the northern side of the elevated lab leading down to the cube.

When he reached the base of the stairs, Schofield walked alongside the dividing wall that sealed this section off from the eastern side of the floor. Gant walked with him. Mother and Brainiac stayed up in the observation lab.

Schofield and Gant came to a halt before the giant free-standing cube, gazed into it.

The occupant of the glass cube saw them coming, and casually walked over to the edge of the completely sealed structure.

The occupant arrived at the clear glass barrier in front of Schofield, cocked his head to one side.

'Hey, mister,' the little boy said.

'—Sir, I have complete visual blackout in the labs on Level 4. They've started shooting the surveillance cameras—'

'I'm surprised it took them this long,' Caesar Russell said. 'Where is the President?'

'Level 5, moving up the ramp to Level 4.'

'And our people?'

'Alpha Unit is in position, waiting in the decompression area on Level 4. Delta Unit has been stopped in the animal containment area on Level 5.'

Caesar smiled.

Although Delta was momentarily halted, the theory behind its movements was sound. Delta was forcing the President up through the complex—to where Alpha was waiting . . .

'Tell Delta to get through that doorway and push up the ramp, and cut off the President's retreat.'

He couldn't have been more than six years old.

And with a bowl-shaped shock of brown hair that came down to his eyes, Disneyland T-shirt and Converse sneakers, he looked like any of a million American kids.

Only this kid lived inside a glass cube, in the belly of a top-secret United States Air Force base.

'Hey there,' Schofield said warily.

'Why are you frightened?' the boy asked suddenly.

'Frightened?'

'Yes, you're frightened. What are you scared of?'

'How do you know I'm frightened?'

'I just know,' the boy said cryptically. He spoke with such a serene, even voice that Schofield felt like he was in some kind of dream. 'What's your name?' the boy asked.

'Shane. But most people call me Scarecrow.'

'Scarecrow? That's a funny name.'

'What about you?' Schofield said. 'What's your name?'

'Kevin.'

'And your last name?'

'What's a last name?' the boy asked.

Schofield paused.

'Where are you from, Kevin?'

The boy shrugged. 'Here, I guess. I've never been any-where else. Hey, do you want to know something?'

'Sure.'

'Did you know that Twinkies give kids half their daily glucose requirement as well as giving them a tasty snack?'

'Uh, no, I didn't know that,' Schofield said.

'And that reptiles are so sensitive to variations in the earth's magnetic field that some scientists say they can pre-dict earthquakes? Oh, and *nobody* knows news like NBC,' the boy said earnestly.

'Is that so?' Schofield exchanged a glance with Gant.

Just then, a loud mechanical noise echoed out from the other side of the dividing wall.

Schofield and Gant spun, and through the glass section at the top of the wall, saw the lights on the other side of Level 4 suddenly and unexpectedly go out.

The President of the United States moved cautiously up the ramp that linked Level 5 to Level 4, surrounded by three Secret Service agents, four United States Marines and a lone bookish scientist.

138

At the top of the ramp was a large retractable grill—kind of like a garage door mounted horizontally.

Juliet Janson hit a switch on the wall and the horizontal door began to slide open, revealing ominous darkness above it.

'Ramp door is opening . . .' one of the ten 7th Squadron commandos inside the Level 4 decompression area whispered into his radio mike.

The other nine members of Alpha Unit were arrayed around the eastern section of the floor in various hiding places—their guns focused on the ramp in the centre of the room. With their half gas-masks and night-vision goggles they looked like a gang of insects waiting for the kill.

The horizontal door slid slowly open, casting a wide beam of light up into the darkened room. The only other light in the area came through the section of glass at the top of the wall which divided this level in two.

'Stay out of sight until they're all up on level ground,' Kurt Logan said from his position. 'No-one gets out alive.'

The two Secret Service agents Curtis and Ramondo stepped up into the semi-darkness first, armed with their Uzis. They were followed by Calvin Reeves and Elvis.

The President came next, with Juliet Janson by his side. He held a small SIG-Sauer P-228 pistol awkwardly in his hand. Juliet had given it to him, just in case.

Behind them came the scientist, Herbert Franklin, and bringing up the rear, Book II and Love Machine, both armed with pump-action shotguns.

As soon as he stepped up into the semi-darkness, Book II didn't like it.

Various structures loomed around them. To his immediate right, on the southern side of the enormous room, was a long hexagonal chamber. To his left, shrouded in deep shadow, he saw eight telephone-booth-sized chambers. In the hazy light filtering through from the other side of the floor, he could just make out a series of catwalks high up near the ceiling, twenty feet above the floor.

As soon as Book II stepped clear of the floor-level doorway, its horizontal door slid smoothly back into place near his feet, sealing the exit.

Calvin had hit a switch in the floor nearby, closing it.

Book II swallowed. He would have preferred to keep that door open.

He flicked on a heavy police flashlight he had taken from the Level 5 anteroom. Holding it under the barrel of his shotgun, he played its beam over the room around them.

Calvin Reeves assumed command of strategy.

'You two,' he whispered to Curtis and Ramondo, 'check behind those telephone booths, then take the stairwell door. Haynes, Lewicky, Riley'—he said, using Elvis's, Love Machine's and Book II's surnames—'the area behind this decompression chamber, then secure that other door,' he pointed toward the dividing wall. 'Janson. You and I stay with the Boss.'

Curtis and Ramondo disappeared in amongst the test chambers, then, moments later, reappeared at the stairwell end.

'No-one back there,' Ramondo said.

Book II, Elvis and Love Machine entered the darkness behind the decompression chamber. A narrow, empty section of floor greeted them. Nothing.

'Clear back here,' Book II said, as the three Marines emerged from behind the long hexagonal chamber. They headed for the door in the dividing wall.

Reeves was following standard tactics in close-quarter, indoor engagements—where there is no sign of the enemy, secure all exits, then consolidate your position.

It was his biggest mistake.

Not only because it limited his options for retreat, but because it was exactly what Kurt Logan—already *inside* the room—was expecting him to do.

★

While Elvis and Love Machine headed for the dividing wall, Book II played his flashlight over the thirty-foot-long decompression chamber. It was absolutely huge.

At the end of the elongated chamber, he found a small glass porthole, and shone his light in through it.

What he saw made him jump.

An Asian face stared back at him, a man's face, pressed up against the glass.

The Asian man was smiling cheerfully.

And then he pointed up—toward the roof of the decompression chamber.

Book II followed the man's finger with his flashlight and peered up at the top of the decompression chamber—

—and found himself staring into the mantis-like face of a 7th Squadron commando wearing night-vision goggles and a gas-mask!

The flashlight was the only thing that saved Book II's life.

Primarily because it blinded the man hiding on top of the decompression chamber, if only for a moment. The man shied away from the light as his night-vision goggles magnified its beam by a factor of 150.

That was all the time Book II needed.

His shotgun boomed, blasting the commando's goggles to pieces, sending him flying off the top of the chamber.

It was a small victory, for at that exact moment, gunfire erupted around the darkened room as a legion of dark figures emerged from their positions *on top of* the decompression chamber and *inside* the telephone-booth-like test chambers and rained hell on Book's hapless group in the centre of the floor.

Over by the stairwell door, Curtis and Ramondo were assaulted by a barrage of P-90 gunfire from both flanks. They were cut down where they stood, their bodies riddled with bloody wounds.

Juliet Janson crash-tackled the President, hurling him to the floor at the base of the decompression chamber, just as a volley of rounds whistled past their heads.

Calvin Reeves wasn't so lucky.

The crossfire of bullets ripped into the back of his head, and he jolted suddenly upright, then dropped to his knees, a look of stunned dismay on his face—as though he had done everything right, and still lost. Then his face smacked down hard against the floor, right next to the spot where Herbert Franklin lay with his head in his hands.

Bullets sizzled through the air.

Juliet yanked the President to his feet, firing with her free hand, dragging him toward the cover of the lab benches over by the dividing wall, when suddenly she saw a 7th Squadron commando rise up from the roof of the decompression chamber and take aim at the President's head.

She brought her gun around. Not fast enough—

Blam!

The 7th Squadron man's head exploded, his neck snapping backwards. His body tumbled off the decompression chamber.

Juliet spun to see who had fired the killing shot, but strangely she saw no-one.

Book II, Elvis and Love Machine all dived together behind a lab bench just as the benchtop was raked with gunfire. They returned fire, aiming at three Air Force commandos taking cover among the test booths.

But it quickly became clear that the Marines' makeshift assortment of shotguns and pistols was going to be no match for the rapid-fire P-90 machine guns of the 7th Squadron troops. The shelves around them shattered and splintered under the phenomenal weight of enemy fire.

Elvis ducked for cover. 'Goddamn!' he yelled. 'This is seriously *fucked up*!'

'No kidding,' Book II shouted. He shucked his pump-action and snapped up to fire, but when he appeared above the benchtop and loosed a couple of shots, he saw a very strange thing happen: he saw all three of the shadowy 7th Squadron shooters get yanked clean off their feet from behind.

Their guns went silent, and Book II found himself staring at an empty area of the battlefield.

'What the . . . ?'

From his own position near the stairwell door, Alpha Unit's leader, Kurt Logan, saw what was happening.

'Fuck! There's someone else in here!' he yelled angrily into his microphone. 'Somebody's picking us off!'

Suddenly the trooper beside Logan took a hit to the side of the head and half his skull exploded, spraying blood and brains everywhere.

'*Fuck!*' Logan had expected to lose maybe two of his men in the shootout—but now he had lost six. 'Alpha Unit, pull out! Everybody back to the stairwell now! Take emergency evac measures!'

He threw open the stairwell door, just as a line of bullets punctured the wall all around it, almost taking his head off. His remaining men dashed past him, out through the door, into the shelter of the eastern stairwell—but not before they had brutally fired down at their fallen comrades' bodies, peppering the corpses and the floor all around them with bullets.

Logan himself mercilessly strafed the body of a dead 7th Squadron man on the ground beside him. Then, when he was done, he disappeared through the doorway after the others and abruptly there was silence.

Book II was still crouched behind his lab bench with Elvis and Love Machine, acrid gunsmoke rising into the air all around them.

Silence.

Deafening silence.

Juliet Janson and the President lay on the floor five feet away from Book and the others, shielded by another bench, covered in dust and broken bits of plastic. Juliet still had her gun raised—

Whump!

A pair of boots landed with a loud thud on the benchtop above them.

They all snapped to look up—and found themselves staring at Captain Shane M. Schofield, USMC, dressed in full dress uniform, with two nickel-plated Berettas gripped in his hands.

He smiled at them. 'Hey there.'

Meanwhile, in bars and offices and homes around America and the world, people sat glued to their television sets.

Because there was so little footage, CNN and the overseas news networks just kept broadcasting the existing few minutes' worth of tape over and over again. Experts were brought in to give their opinions.

Government people sprang into action, although no-one could really do anything substantive, since the exact location of the nightmarish affair was known only to a select few.

In any case, in a few minutes it would be eight o'clock Mountain Daylight Time and the people of the world tensely awaited the next hourly update.

THIRD CONFRONTATION

3 July, 0800 Hours

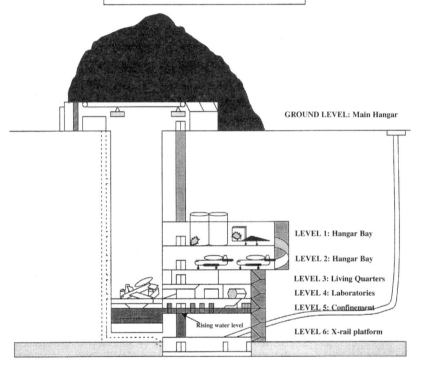

**UNITED STATES AIR FORCE
SPECIAL AREA (RESTRICTED) NO.7
0800 HOURS**

GROUND LEVEL: Main Hangar

LEVEL 1: Hangar Bay

LEVEL 2: Hangar Bay

LEVEL 3: Living Quarters

LEVEL 4: Laboratories

LEVEL 5: Confinement

Rising water level

LEVEL 6: X-rail platform

Space Division, that part of the Defense Intelligence Agency which deals with foreign powers' space capabilities, is located on the second-to-bottom floor of the Pentagon, three storeys directly below the famous Pentagon Situation Room.

And although its title may sound exotic and exciting, as David Fairfax knew such a perception couldn't have been farther from the truth.

In short, you got sent to Space Division as punishment, because nothing ever happened in Space Division.

It was nearly 10.00 a.m. on the East Coast as Fairfax—oblivious to any commotion going on in the outside world—tapped away on his computer keyboard, trying to decipher a collection of phone taps that the DIA had picked up over the past few months. Whoever had been using the phones in question had fitted them with sophisticated encoders, masking their content. It was up to Fairfax to crack that code.

It's funny how times change, he thought.

David Theodore Fairfax was a cryptanalyst, a code-breaker. Of medium height, lean, with floppy brown hair and thin wireframe glasses, he didn't look like a genius. In fact, in his Mooks T-shirt, jeans and sneakers, he looked more like a gawky university student than a government analyst.

It was, however, his brilliant undergraduate thesis on theoretical non-linear computing that had brought him to the attention of the Defense Intelligence Agency, the Department of Defense's chief intelligence-gathering organisation. The DIA worked in close consultation with the NSA, America's chief signals gatherer and codebreaker. But that didn't prevent it from running its own team of codecrackers—who often spied *on* the NSA—of which Dave Fairfax was a part.

Fairfax had taken to cryptanalysis immediately. He loved the challenge of it, the battle between two minds: one which hopes to conceal, the other which hopes to reveal. He lived by the maxim: *No code is unbreakable.*

It didn't take him long to get noticed.

In the early 1990s, US authorities were confounded by a man named Phil Zimmerman and his unbreakable encryption software, 'PGP'. In 1991, Zimmerman had posted PGP on the Internet, to the great consternation of the US government—principally because the government couldn't crack it.

PGP employed a cryptographic system known as the 'public key system,' which involved the multiplication of very large prime numbers to obtain the code's all-important 'key'. In this case 'very large prime numbers' meant numbers with over 130 digits.

It was unbreakable.

It was claimed that it would take all the supercomputers in the world twelve times the age of the universe to check all the possible values for a single message.

The government was annoyed. It became known that certain terrorist groups and foreign governments had started using PGP to encrypt their messages. In 1993, a grand jury investigation into Zimmerman was initiated on the basis that by uploading PGP onto the Internet, he had exported a *weapon* out of the United States, since encryption software came under the government's definition of a 'munition'.

And then strangely, in 1996, after hounding Zimmerman for three years, the US Attorney General's office dropped the case.

Just like that.

They claimed that the horse had bolted and the case was no longer worth pursuing, so they closed the file.

What the Attorney General never mentioned was the call she had received from the Director of the DIA on the morning she dropped the case, saying that PGP had been cracked.

And as anyone in cryptography knows, once you crack your enemy's code, you don't let them know you've cracked it.

And the man who cracked PGP: an unknown twenty-five-year-old DIA mathematician by the name of David Fairfax.

It turned out that Fairfax's theoretical non-linear computer was no longer theoretical. A prototype version of it was built for the express purpose of breaking PGP, and as it turned out, the computer, with its unimaginable calculative abilities, could factor extremely large numbers with considerable ease.

No code is unbreakable.

History, however, is tough on cryptanalysts—for the simple fact that they cannot talk about their greatest victories.

And so it was with Dave Fairfax. He might have cracked PGP, but he could never talk about it, and in the great maze of government work, he had simply been given a small pay rise and then moved on to the next job.

And so here he was in Space Division, analysing a series of unauthorised phone transmissions coming into and out of some remote Air Force base in Utah.

In a similarly isolated room across the hall from him, however, was where all the good stuff was happening today. A joint taskforce of DIA and NSA cryptanalysts were tracking the encrypted signals coming out of the Chinese space shuttle that had launched from Xichang a few days earlier.

Now that was interesting, Fairfax thought. Better than decrypting some phone calls from a stupid Air Force base in the desert.

The recorded phone calls appeared on Fairfax's computer screen as a waterfall of cascading numbers—the mathematical representation of a series of telephone conversations that had taken place in Utah over the last couple of months.

A huge pair of headphones covered Fairfax's ears, emitting a steady stream of garbled static. His eyes were fixed on the screen.

One thing was clear: whoever had made these calls had encrypted them well. Fairfax had been at this for the last two days.

He tried a few older algorithms.

Nothing.

He tried a few newer ones.

Nothing.

He could do this all month if he had to.

He tried a program he had developed to crack Vodafone's newest encryption system—

'—*Kan bevestig dat in-enting plaasvind*—'

For a brief second, a strange guttural language materialised in his ears.

Fairfax's eyes glowed to life.

Gotcha . . .

He tried the program on some of the other telephone conversations.

And in a miraculous instant, formless static suddenly became clear voices speaking in a foreign tongue, interspersed with the odd sentence of English.

'—*Toetse op laaste poging word op die vier-en-twientigste verwag. Wat van die onttrekkings eenheid?*—'

'—*Reccondo span is alreeds weggestuur*—'

'—*Voorbereidings onderweg. Vroeg oggend. Beste tyd vir onttrekking*—'

'—*everything is in place. Confirm that it's the third*—'

'—*Ontrekking kan 'n probleem wees. Gestel ons gebruik die Hoeb land hier naby. Verstaan hy is 'n lid van Die Organisasie*—'

'—*Sal die instruksies oordra*—'

'—*mission is a go*—'

'—*Die Reccondos is gereed. Verwagte aankoms by beplande bestemming binne nege dae—*'

Fairfax's eyes gleamed as he gazed at the screen.

No code is unbreakable.

He reached for his phone.

After the short battle in the decompression area, Schofield and the others retreated to the opposite side of Level 4, to the observation lab overlooking the giant cube—locking the doors behind them and then blasting the security keypads with gunshots.

Of all the places Schofield had seen so far, this area was the most easily defended.

Barring the regular personnel elevator, it had only two entrances: the short ramp leading back to the aircraft elevator and the doorway leading to the staircase that went down to the cube.

Juliet Janson flopped to the floor of the lab, exhausted.

The President did the same.

The Marines—Book II, Elvis, Love Machine, Mother and Brainiac—formed a huddle and quickly told each other of their respective adventures inside flooding elevator shafts and runaway AWACS planes.

The last member of their rag-tag group—the labcoat-wearing scientist, Herbert Franklin—took a seat in the corner.

Schofield and Gant remained standing.

They had a few weapons now, gear that they had scavenged from the bodies of the 7th Squadron men in the decompression area—guns, a few radio headsets, three extremely high-powered grenades made of RDX compound, and two thumbtack-sized lock-destroying explosives known as Lock-Blasters.

Logan's men, however, had spoiled well.

The brutal gunfire that they had directed at their own fallen men *hadn't* been intended as kill shots—it had been intended to destroy any weapons the dead men might offer their enemy. Consequently, only one P-90 assault rifle had been salvaged from the battlefield. All the others had been shattered, as had many of the fallen men's semi-automatic pistols.

'Mother,' Schofield said, tossing the P-90 to her, 'keep an eye on the ramp entrance. Elvis, the stairs going down to the cube.'

Mother and Elvis dashed off.

Although just about everyone else in the world would have gone straight over to the President at that time, Schofield didn't. He could see that the President hadn't been injured—still had all his fingers and toes—and so long as his heart was still beating, he was all right.

Instead, Schofield went over to Juliet Janson.

'Update,' was all he said.

Janson glanced up at Schofield, looked into the reflective silver lenses of his wraparound anti-flash glasses.

She'd seen him around the Presidential helicopters before, but had never really talked to him. She'd heard about him from the other agents, though. He was the one from that thing in Antarctica.

'They ambushed us in the Level 3 common room, just after the message came over the Emergency Broadcast System,' she said. 'Been right on our tails ever since. We hit the stairwell, made for the Emergency Exit Vent down on Level 6, but they were waiting for us. We came back *up* the stairs—they were waiting for us again. We diverted through 5 and came up the ramp to 4—and they were waiting for us again.'

'Casualties?'

'Eight agents from the President's Personal Detail killed.

Plus the whole Advance Team down on Level 6. That makes seventeen in total.'

'Frank Cutler?'

'Gone.'

'Anything else?'

Janson nodded at the little labcoated man. 'We picked him up on 5, before we walked into that ambush in the decompression room. Says he's a scientist working here.'

Schofield glanced over at Herbert Franklin. Small and bespectacled, the little man just bowed his head in silence.

'What about you?' Janson asked.

Schofield shrugged. 'We were up in the main hangar when it went down. Scrambled down the ventilation shaft, arrived in one of the underground hangars, destroyed a Humvee, crashed an AWACS plane.'

'The usual,' Gant added.

'How did you know about the ambush next door?' Janson asked.

Schofield shrugged. 'We were down next to the cube when the lights went out in the decompression area. We were hoping it was someone friendly, trying to hide from the security cameras. So we checked it out from above, from the catwalks. When we saw who it was, saw them surrounding that ramp in the middle of the room, we figured they were waiting for the big score'—he nodded at the President—'so we set up a little counter-ambush of our own.'

On the other side of the room, Brainiac sat down next to the President.

'Mister President,' he said with deference.

'Hello,' the President replied.

'How you feelin', sir?'

'Well, I'm still alive, which is a good start, considering the circumstances. What's your name, son?'

'Gorman, sir. Corporal Gus Gorman, but most of the guys just call me Brainiac.'

'Brainiac?'

'That's right, sir,' Brainiac hesitated. 'Sir, if you don't mind, I was wondering, if it wasn't too much trouble, if I could ask you a question.'

'Why not?' the President said.

'Okay, then. Okay. Well, you bein' President and all, you'd know certain things, right?'

'Yes . . . '

'Right. Cool. Because what I always wanted to know was this: is Puerto Rico a United States protectorate because it has the highest number of UFO sightings in the world per annum?'

'*What?*'

'Well, think about it, why the hell else would we want to hold onto Puerto-fucking-Rico, there ain't nothing there—'

'*Brainiac,*' Schofield said from across the room. 'Leave the President alone. Mister President, you better come and see this. It's almost eight o'clock and Caesar will be giving his hourly update any second.'

The President went over to join Schofield—but not before he gave Brainiac a strange look.

At the tick of eight o'clock, Caesar Russell's face appeared on every television set in Area 7.

'My fellow Americans,' he boomed, 'after one hour's play, the President is still alive. His cause, however, is not looking good.

'His personal Secret Service Detail has been decimated, with eight of its nine members already confirmed dead. Two more Secret Service units—advance teams, one stationed down in the lowest floor of this facility, another at one of the exterior exits, consisting of nine men each—were also eliminated, bringing the total of presidential losses to twenty-six men. On both occasions, no losses were sustained by my 7th Squadron men.

'That said, some knights in shining armour *have* arrived on the scene. A small band of United States Marines—members of the President's ornamental helicopter crew, looking very pretty in their dress uniforms—have come to his defen—'

Just then, completely without warning, the television sets throughout Area 7 abruptly died, their screens shrinking to black.

At the same moment, all the lights in the complex blinked out, plunging Area 7 into darkness.

Inside the lab on Level 4, everybody looked up at the sudden loss of power.

'Uh-oh . . . ' Gant said, eyeing the ceiling.

Then, a second later, the lights whirred back to life and the TV system rebooted, Caesar's face still looming large, still talking.

'—which leaves us with five 7th Squadron units versus a handful of United States Marines. Such is the state of play at eight o'clock. I shall see you again for another update at 0900 hours.'

The TV screens cut to black.

'Liar,' Juliet Janson said. 'That son of a bitch is distorting the truth. The advance team down on Level 6 was already dead when we got there. They were killed before all this started.'

'He also lied about his losses,' Brainiac said. 'Sneaky bastard.'

'So what do we do?' Gant asked Schofield. 'They have us outnumbered, outflanked and outgunned. Plus, this is their turf.'

Schofield was wondering exactly the same thing.

The 7th Squadron had them completely on the run. They had all the leverage, and more importantly, he thought, looking down at his formal full dress uniform, they had come prepared to fight.

'Okay,' he said, thinking aloud. 'Know your enemy.'

'What?'

'First principles. We have to even things up, but to do that, we need knowledge. Rule Number One: know your enemy. Okay. So who are they?'

Janson shrugged. 'The 7th Squadron. The Air Force's crack ground unit. The best in the country. Well trained, well armed—'

'And on steroids,' Gant added.

'More than just steroids,' another voice said.

Everyone turned.

It was the scientist, Herbert Franklin.

'Who are you?' Schofield said.

The little man shuffled nervously. 'My name is Herbie

Franklin. Until this morning, I was an immunologist on Project Fortune. But they locked me up just before you all arrived.'

Schofield said, 'What did you mean, "more than just steroids"?'

'Well, what I meant was that the 7th Squadron men at this base have been . . . *augmented* . . . for want of a better word.'

'Augmented?'

'Enhanced. *Improved* for better performance. Ever wondered why the 7th Squadron do so well at inter-service battle competitions? Ever wondered why they can keep fighting while everyone else is falling over with exhaustion?'

'Yes . . . '

Franklin spoke quickly: 'Anabolic steroids to enhance muscle and fitness levels. Artificial erythropoietin injections for increased blood oxygenation.'

'Artificial erythropoietin?' Gant repeated.

'EPO for short,' Herbie said. 'It's a hormone that stimulates production of red blood cells by the bone marrow, thus increasing the supply of oxygen in the bloodstream. Endurance athletes, mainly cyclists, have been using it for years.

'The 7th Squadron are stronger than you, and they can run all day long,' Herbie said. 'Hell, Captain, these men were tough when they got here, but since their arrival they have been augmented by the latest pharmacological technology to fight harder, better and longer than anybody else.'

'Okay, okay,' Schofield said, 'I think we get the picture.'

He was thinking, however, of a small boy named Kevin, living fifty feet away, inside a glass cube. 'So is that what you do here? Is that what this base is all about? Enhancing elite soldiers?'

'No . . . ' Herbie said, casting a wary glance over at the President. 'The augmentation of the 7th Squadron troopers is only performed as an ancillary task, since they guard the base.'

'So what the hell *is* this place?'

160

Again Herbie looked at the President. Then he took a deep breath before answering—

It was another voice, however, that spoke.

'This base houses the most important vaccine ever developed in the history of America,' it said.

Schofield spun.

It was the President.

Schofield appraised him. The President was still wearing his charcoal-coloured suit and tie. With his neatly-combed light-grey hair and familiar wrinkled face, he looked like a middle-aged country businessman—albeit a businessman who had been sweating hard for the last hour.

'A vaccine?' Schofield said.

'Yes. A vaccine against the latest Chinese genetic virus. A virus that targets Caucasian people by way of their pigmentation DNA. An agent known as the Sinovirus.'

'And the source of this vaccine . . . ?' Schofield said.

' . . . is a genetically-constructed human being,' the President said.

'A *what?*'

'A person, Captain Schofield, who since the embryonic stage of his existence has been *purpose-built* to withstand the Sinovirus, whose very blood can be harvested to produce antibodies for the rest of the American population. A human vaccine. The world's first genetically-tailored human being, Captain, a boy named Kevin.'

Schofield's eyes narrowed.

It explained a lot—the tight security surrounding the complex, the presidential visit, and a boy living inside a glass cube. He was also struck by one other aspect of what the President had just said: the President knew his name.

'You *created* a boy to use as a vaccine?' Schofield said. 'With respect, sir, but doesn't that bother you?'

The President grimaced. 'My job is not made up of black and whites, Captain. Just grey, infinite grey. And in that world of grey, I have to make decisions—often difficult ones. Sure, Kevin existed long before I became President, but once I knew about him, I had to make the call to continue the project. I made that call. I may not like it, but in the face of an agent like the Sinovirus, tough decisions are necessary.'

There was a short silence.

Book spoke. 'What about the prisoners downstairs?

'And the animals. What are they used for?' Juliet said.

Schofield frowned. He hadn't seen Level 5, so he didn't know about any animals or prisoners.

Herbie Franklin answered. 'The animals are used for both projects, the vaccine and the 7th Squadron augmentation. The Kodiak bears are utilised for their blood toxins. All bears have extremely high blood-oxygen levels for use when they hibernate. The blood enhancement research for the 7th Squadron came from them.'

'So what about the other cages, the water-filled ones?' Janson asked. 'What's in them?'

Herbie paused. 'A rare breed of monitor lizard known as the Komodo dragon. The largest lizard in the world, about thirteen feet long, as big as a regular crocodile. We have six of them.'

'And what are they used for?' Schofield asked.

'Komodos are the most ancient reptilian species on earth, found only on the scattered middle islands in Indonesia. They're great swimmers—been known to swim between islands—but they're equally fast on land, easily capable of running down a man, which they do regularly. Their internal antibiotic system, however, is extraordinarily robust. They are all but impervious to illness. Their lymph nodes produce a highly-concentrated antibacterial serum that has protected them against disease for thousands of years.'

The President said, 'The Komodo dragons' blood by-products have been reconfigured to match the structure of human blood, and as such form the basis of Kevin's immune system. We then harvest Kevin's genetically-constructed blood plasma to produce a serum that can be inserted into America's water supply—a serum-hydrate solution—thereby immunising the general population against the Sinovirus.'

'You spike the water supply?' Schofield said.

'Oh, it's been done before,' Herbie said. 'In 1989, against botulinum toxin, and in 1990—because of Iraq—against anthrax. Although Americans don't know it, they're resistant to all the world's major biological weapons.'

'What about the human prisoners?' Book II asked. 'What are they here for?'

Herbie looked to the President, who nodded silently.

The little scientist shrugged. 'The human prisoners are another story altogether. They're not here to provide any sort of blood by-product or serum. Their role is simple. They're guinea pigs for the testing of the vaccine.'

★

'*Jesus Christ*,' Gant breathed when she saw the list of prisoner names.

After Herbie had told them the purpose of the prisoners downstairs, he had brought up a list of their names on one of the laboratory's computer terminals.

There were forty-two of them in total, all multiple lifers or death-row candidates who had somehow escaped the chair.

'The worst of the worst,' Herbie said, nodding at the list of names.

Schofield had heard of many of them.

Sylvester McLean—the child-murderer from Atlanta. Ronald Noonan—the Houston baker turned clock-tower sniper. Lucifer Leary—the serial killer from Phoenix. Seth Grimshaw—the notorious leader of the Black League, an ultra-violent terrorist organisation that believed the US government was preparing America for a United Nations takeover.

'Seth Grimshaw?' Gant said, seeing the name. She turned to Juliet Janson. 'Wasn't he the one who –?'

'Yes,' Janson said, glancing nervously at the President over on the far side of the lab. 'In early February. Just after the inauguration. He's a genuine 18-84.'

Gant said, 'Oh, man, do I hope their cages are sturdy.'

'All right. Great,' Schofield said, bringing everyone back to the present. 'Which brings us back to the here and now. We're shut in here. They want to kill the President. And because of the radio transmitter on his heart, if he dies, fourteen major cities go up in smoke.'

'And all right in front of the people of America,' Janson said.

'Not necessarily,' the President said, 'because Caesar wouldn't know about the LBJ Directive.'

'What's the LBJ Directive?' Schofield asked.

'It's a feature of the Emergency Broadcast System, but known only to the President and the Vice-President. It's essentially a safety valve, brought in by Lyndon Johnson in 1967, to stop the EBS from being used too soon.'

'So what does it do?'

'It provides for a forty-five-minute delay of any broadcast sent over the system, unless a presidential override code is entered. In other words, except in the most urgent circumstances, it stops a panic broadcast from being sent out, effectively allowing for a forty-five-minute cooling-off period.

'Now, since it's 8:09, Caesar's initial broadcast has got out there, but if we were to find the EBS transmission box inside this complex, we could stop all his subsequent transmissions.'

Schofield pursed his lips, thinking. 'That has to be a secondary consideration. Something to do only if we happen to be in the right place at the right time.'

He turned to Herbie. 'Tell us about this complex.'

Herbie shrugged. 'What's there to know? It's a fortress. Used to be NORAD headquarters. When it shuts down, it *shuts down*. The thing is, I don't think anyone ever expected it to be used to keep someone locked *in*.'

'But even a total lockdown must have a release procedure,' Schofield said. 'Something which opens the doors when the crisis is over.'

Herbie nodded. 'The time-lock.'

'Time-lock?'

'In the event of total lockdown, a timer-controlled security system is activated. Every hour on the hour, those people still alive inside the base have a five-minute window period to enter one of three possible codes.'

'What kind of codes?' Gant asked.

'Remember,' Herbie said, 'this facility was intended for use in a full-scale US–Soviet nuclear exchange. The codes reflect that. As such, there are three possible entry codes.

'The *first* code simply continues the lockdown. The nuclear crisis is still going, so the facility remains locked down. The *second* code assumes the crisis has been resolved. It calls an end to the lockdown—armoured blast doors are retracted and all entrances and exits are re-opened.'

'And the third code?' Gant asked.

'The *third* code is a halfway measure—it allows for messenger escape. It authorises the opening of individual exits and entrances for messengers to leave the facility.'

Schofield was listening to Herbie carefully.

'What happens when *no code* is entered during the hourly window period?' he asked.

'You're fast, Captain. You see, that's the kicker, isn't it. If no code is entered, the complex's computer is warned that the facility may have been taken by the enemy. It then gives you one chance to re-enter one of the other codes at the *next* hourly window period. If no code is entered at that time, then the computer assumes that the facility has been taken by the enemy, at which point the facility's self-destruct mechanism is activated.'

'*Self-destruct mechanism,*' Brainiac blurted. 'What the fuck is that?'

'A one-hundred-megaton thermonuclear warhead buried beneath the complex,' Herbie said simply.

'Oh, Christ . . . ' Brainiac said.

Gant said, 'Surely they removed that when the Soviet Union collapsed.'

'I'm afraid not,' Herbie said. 'When this base was reconfigured as a chemical weapons facility, it was decided that the self-destruct device still had value. If there was an accident and a virus spread throughout the facility, the whole contaminated complex—virus included—could be destroyed by a superheated nuclear blast.'

'Okay,' Schofield said, 'so if we want to leave, we have to wait for the hourly window period, find a computer connected to the central network, and then enter the correct code.'

'That's right,' Herbie said.

'So what are the codes?' Schofield asked.

Herbie shrugged helplessly. 'That I don't know. I can initiate a lockdown if there's been an outbreak, but I don't have clearance to undo one. Only the Air Force guys can do that—'

'Uh, excuse me,' Juliet Janson said, 'but aren't we forgetting something?

'Like what?' Brainiac said.

'Like the Football,' Janson said. 'The President's briefcase. The one that's been rigged to *stop* him from escaping this complex. He has to press his palm against the analyser plate on the Football once every ninety minutes, otherwise the plasma bombs in the cities go off.'

'Damn it,' Schofield said. He had forgotten all about that. He looked at his watch.

It was 8:12 a.m.

This had all started at 7:00 a.m. Which meant they had to get the President's hand onto the Football by 8:30.

He looked up at the others. 'Where are they keeping the Football?'

'Russell said it would be kept in the main hangar, up on ground level,' the President said.

'What do you think?' Gant said to Schofield.

'I don't think we have much choice. Somehow, we have to get his hand onto the Football.'

'But we can't keep doing that forever.'

'No,' Schofield said, 'we can't. At some point, we'll have to come up with a more long-term solution. But until then, we deal with the short-term ones.'

Janson said, 'It'd be suicide to bring the President out into the open upstairs, they'll almost certainly be waiting.'

'That's right,' Schofield stood up. 'Which is why we don't do that. What we do is quite straightforward. We bring the Football to him.'

'The first thing we have to do,' Schofield said, rounding every-one up, 'is take care of those security cameras. While they're still operating, we're screwed.' He turned to Herbie Franklin. 'Where's the central junction box in this place?'

'In the Level 1 hangar bay, I think, on the northern wall.'

'Okay,' Schofield said. 'Mother, Brainiac, I want you guys to take care of those cameras. Cut the power if you have to, I don't care, just shut down the camera system. You got me?'

'Got it,' Mother said.

'And take Doctor Franklin with you. If he's lying, shoot him.'

'Got it,' Mother said, eyeing Herbie suspiciously. Herbie gulped.

'What about the rest of us?' Juliet asked.

Schofield headed toward the short ramp that led to the wide aircraft elevator shaft.

'The rest of us are going upstairs to play some football.'

'—System reboot is complete—'

'Status?' Caesar Russell asked.

Ten minutes previously, during Caesar's second EBS broadcast, the entire complex had experienced an abrupt power shutdown, causing all its interior systems to switch off.

'—Confirm: main power supply has been cut,' one of the radio operators said. 'We're running on auxiliary power now. All systems operational.'

'—We lost that enhanced satellite image of the EEV that was coming through. Renewing contact with the satellite now—'

Another operator: 'Copy that. Main power supply was switched off at the Level 1 junction box at exactly 0800 hours, by operator 008-72—'

'8-72?' Caesar frowned, thinking.

'—Sir, we have no visual feed. All cameras went down with the cutting of the main power supply—'

Caesar's eyes narrowed. 'All units, report in.'

'—*This is Alpha,*' Kurt Logan's voice said. '*Initiate frequency swap. Possibility that enemy has obtained some of our radio equipment—*'

'—Frequency swap complete,' the senior operator said. 'Go ahead, Alpha Leader—'

'—*We are in the Level 2 hangar bay. Heading for the personnel elevator for rendezvous up in the main hangar. Report six dead—*'

'—*This is Bravo Leader, we're up in the main hangar, covering the Football. All men present and accounted for. No casualties—*'

'—*This is Charlie Leader. We are moving in tandem with Echo through the common room area on Level 3. We have one dead, two wounded from that AWACS shit before. Understand targets were last sighted on Level 4. Preparing for joint assault through floor-to-ceiling hatches between 3 and 4. Please advise—*'

'—Charlie, Echo, this is Control. We have lost all visual contact on the Level 4 lab area—'

'Engage at will, Charlie and Echo,' Caesar Russell cut in sharply. 'Keep them moving. They can't run forever.'

'—*This is Delta. We are still on 5. No casualties. By the time we broke down that door on 5, the targets had already gone up the ramp to Level 4. Be advised, there is substantial flooding in the Level 5 confinement area. Awaiting instructions—*'

'—Delta, this is Caesar,' Russell said coolly, 'head back down to Level 6. Cover the X-rail exits.'

'—*Affirmative, that, sir—*'

★

Twenty black-clad 7th Squadron commandos hurried down one of the corridors of the Level 3 living area, their boots thundering on the floor—the men of Charlie and Echo Units.

They came to a pressure-sealed manhole in the carpet. A code was entered and the circular hatch came free with a sharp hiss, revealing a crawlspace between the floor of Level 3 and the ceiling of Level 4. Another pressure hatch lay directly beneath this one—the entry to Level 4.

One of the commandos lowered himself through the manhole.

'Control, this is Charlie Leader,' Python Willis said into his headset mike. 'We are at the manhole leading to the observation lab on Level 4. Preparing to storm the floor from above.'

'*Do it,*' Caesar's voice replied.

Python nodded to his man in the crawlspace.

The commando released the pressure valve and let the hatch drop to the floor ten feet below him. Then he jumped down to the ground after it, three others close behind him, their P-90s aimed and ready.

Nothing.

The lab around them was empty.

There came a loud mechanical rumbling from within the walls.

The 7th Squadron men whirled around as one.

It was the sound of the hydraulic aircraft elevator platform.

The commandos of Charlie and Echo Units hurried down the short sloping walkway that led from the observation lab to the aircraft elevator shaft.

They got there just in time to see the underside of the giant elevator platform rising up into the shaft above them, heading for the main hangar.

Python Willis spoke into his helmet mike. 'Control, this is Charlie Leader. They're going for the Football.'

The gigantic aircraft elevator groaned loudly as it lumbered up the wide concrete shaft.

It moved slowly, carrying the crumpled remains of the crashed AWACS plane on its back.

The plane lay tilted forward, like a wounded bird, its nose lower than its destroyed rear section, its broken wings splayed wide. The plane's rotodome—still intact—towered high above the whole sorry image.

The massive elevator rumbled up the greasy concrete shaft.

As it passed the open doorway to the Level 1 hangar bay, however, three tiny figures quickly leapt off it, hustling into the underground hangar.

It was Mother and Brainiac and, puffing along behind them, Herbie Franklin.

They were heading for the central junction box that Franklin had said was located in the Level 1 hangar bay, to disable Area 7's camera system.

The hangar was deserted now, the 7th Squadron men long gone. The two stealth bombers and the lone SR-71 Blackbird still stood silently in the cavernous space, like a trio of sleeping sentinels.

Mother checked her watch as she skirted the left-hand wall of the hangar.

8:20.

Ten minutes to get the President to the Football.

As she moved along the concrete wall, watchful for enemy soldiers, she saw a large box-shaped compartment at the far end of it. The compartment's ten-foot-tall steel door was twisted and bent, partially destroyed.

'Oh, yeah,' she said.

'What?' Herbie asked from behind her.

'Our little run-in with the 7th Squadron up here earlier,' Mother said. 'They got a couple of Stingers off—one hit that compartment, the other punctured some water tanks inside the wall over by the personnel elevator.'

'Oh,' Herbie said.

'Let's see what's left,' Mother said.

Upstairs, the giant elevator platform rose slowly into the main hangar.

The remains of the AWACS plane appeared first, rising above the rim of the square-shaped shaft.

Then the exploded rear section of the fuselage . . .

. . . followed by the intact rotodome . . .

. . . then the snapped wings . . .

The rest of the battered plane rose slowly into view and then, with a loud *boom!*, the platform came level with the hangar floor and stopped.

There was a long silence.

The ground-level hangar bore the scars of the battle that had taken place there nearly an hour and a half before.

Marine One—still attached to its towing vehicle—stood on the western side of the elevator platform, while its semi-destroyed sister chopper, Nighthawk Two, and its cockroach stood on the northern side of the platform, over by the personnel elevator.

On the eastern side of the AWACS plane, however, stood something entirely new: a team of ten 7th Squadron

172

commandos—Bravo Unit—positioned in between the elevator platform and the internal building, standing inside a semi-circular barricade of wooden crates and Samsonite containers.

On a chair in the centre of the barricade sat a familiar stainless-steel briefcase, folded open, revealing a series of red and green lights, a keypad, and a flat-glass analyser plate.

The Football.

Captain Bruno 'Boa' McConnell—the grey-eyed leader of Bravo Unit—gazed at the crumpled AWACS plane suspiciously.

The broken plane just sat there in the centre of the enormous hangar—silent, unmoving—a great big pile of junk.

More silence.

'How's it going down there, Mother?' Schofield's voice whispered in Mother's earpiece, borrowed from one of the dead Secret Service agents.

Down on Level 1, Mother surveyed the damaged electricity junction box in front of her. Fully half the switchboard had been destroyed by the missile impact. The other half was a mixed bag—some parts were intact, others were just mounds of melted wires. At the moment, Herbie Franklin was tapping the keys on a computer terminal that had survived the impact.

'Just a second,' she said into her wrist microphone. 'Yo, Poindexter. What's the story?'

Franklin frowned. 'It doesn't make sense. Somebody's been here already, about twenty minutes ago at eight o'clock. They cut the main power. The whole base is running on auxiliary power . . . '

'Can you cut the cameras?' Mother asked.

'Don't have to. They were shut down when the main power was disabled.' Herbie turned to face Mother. 'They're already off.'

★

Up in the main hangar, the regular elevator's doors opened.

Out of the lift stepped Kurt Logan and the three other survivors from Alpha Unit. They met up with Boa McConnell and the men of Bravo Unit.

'What's happening?' Logan asked.

'Nothing . . . ' Boa replied. 'Yet.'

'—*Control, this is Charlie Leader,*' Python Willis's voice said over the control room's speakers. '*There's no-one down here on Level 4.*'

'—Copy, Charlie Leader. Bring your team up to the main hangar in the personnel lift. Echo, stay down there. Caesar wants you roving around the lower levels. We've lost all camera visuals and we need some eyes down there—'

On Level 1, Mother keyed her wrist mike. 'Scarecrow, this is Mother. Cameras are down. Repeat: Cameras are down. We're heading for the aircraft elevator shaft.'

'*Thanks, Mother.*'

'All right, we're in business,' Schofield said, turning to the President, Book II and Juliet. They were in a dark place.

He looked at his watch:

8:25:59

8:26:00

This was going to be close.

'Fox, Elvis, Love Machine, get ready. On my mark. In three . . . '

The main hangar was silent.

'Two . . . '

Marine One stood about thirty feet away from the wreck of the AWACS plane, shining in the harsh artificial light.

'One . . . '

The men of Bravo Unit eyed the shattered AWACS bird cautiously, guns up, trigger fingers tensed.

' . . . mark.'

Schofield pressed a button on a small hand-held unit—it was the remote detonation switch for one of the RDX-based grenades that he had found on the 7th Squadron men in the decompression room. Pound for pound, aluminised RDX is about six times more powerful than C4—it blows big and it blows wide, a *super*blasting charge.

As soon as he hit the button, the RDX charge that he had left in the cockpit of the AWACS plane exploded—blasting outwards, showering the hangar with a star-shaped rain of glass and shrapnel.

And then everything happened at once.

The men of Bravo Unit dived away from the explosion.

Sizzling-hot pieces of the plane's cockpit shot low over their heads, lodging in the barricade all around them like darts smacking into a corkboard.

As they clambered back to their feet, they saw movement, saw three shadows climb out from the air vent *underneath* Marine One.

'*There!*' Boa pointed.

One of the shadows ran out from beneath the President's helicopter, while the other two slithered up through a hatch in its underbelly.

A moment later, Marine One's engines roared to life.

Its tail boom folded into place from its stowed position, as did its rotor blades. No sooner were the rotor blades extended than they began to rotate, despite the fact that the President's helicopter was still attached to its towing vehicle.

Gunfire erupted as the lone Marine who had dashed out from underneath the chopper—Love Machine—*disengaged* the cockroach attached to its tail and climbed inside the towing vehicle's tiny driver's cabin.

'What the fuck . . . ?' Kurt Logan said as the cockroach skidded out from behind Marine One and swung *around* the elevator platform, heading directly for the 7th Squadron men guarding the Football.

'Open fire,' Logan said to Boa and his men. 'Open fire now.'

They did.

A barrage of P-90 fire assaulted the speeding towing vehicle's windscreen, shattering it.

Inside the driver's cabin, Love Machine ducked below the dashboard. Bullets tore into the seatback behind him, sending the fluffy innards of the seat showering everywhere.

The cockroach careered across the hangar, bouncing wildly, taking fire.

Then suddenly, behind it, Marine One rose into the air—inside the hangar—the deafening *thump-thump-thump* of its rotor blades reverberating off the walls, drowning out all other sound.

Inside its cockpit, Gant worked the controls while Elvis hit switches everywhere.

'Elvis! Give me missiles!' she shouted. 'And whatever you do, don't hit the Football, okay!'

Elvis slammed his finger down on a launch button.

Shoom!

A Hellfire missile shot out from a pod mounted on the side of the Presidential helicopter, a finger of smoke extending through the air behind it, the missile shooting at tremendous speed toward the internal building on the eastern side of the hangar.

The missile hit the exact centre of the building—right above the Bravo troops guarding the Football—and detonated.

The middle section of the internal building blasted outwards in a shower of glass and plasterboard. A section of the glassed-in upper level collapsed to the ground behind the Bravo men guarding the Football.

The 7th Squadron commandos leapt clear of the falling debris—only to have to roll again a split-second later to avoid a second source of danger: the oncoming cockroach driven by Love Machine.

It was chaos.

Mayhem.

Pandemonium.

Exactly as Schofield had planned.

Schofield watched the confusion from his position inside the destroyed AWACS plane. His watch read:

8:27:50

8:27:51

Two minutes left.

'Okay, Book, let's go.' He turned to Juliet and the President. 'You two stay here until we've checked the status of the Football. If we can get it, we'll bring it back to you. If not, you'll have to come out.'

And with that Schofield and Book II leapt down from the gaping hole at the rear of the AWACS plane and ran out into the open.

At exactly the same moment, a six-barrelled Vulcan mini-gun popped out from a compartment underneath the nose of Marine One and began spewing out a devastating stream of supermachine-gun fire.

The 7th Squadron men—already scattered everywhere—were dispersed even more. Some dived behind their barricade for cover, others found shelter among the ruins of the AWACS plane and fired up at the President's helicopter.

Gant sat at the controls of Marine One as her enemy's bullets left scratches on the Lexan windshield. And the armour-plated walls of the big Sikorsky were built to withstand missile impacts, so gunfire wasn't a problem.

Beside her, Elvis was yelling, '*Yee-ha!*' as he rained hell on the 7th Squadron men with the mini-gun.

Schofield and Book II ran eastward, sidestepping quickly toward the 7th Squadron men guarding the Football.

They moved in tandem, guns up, firing—*bizarrely*—at Love Machine's runaway cockroach and up at Marine One.

178

The fact that they were firing at their own people was probably best explained by the fact that they were dressed in the black fatigues, black body armour and half-face gas-masks of the 7th Squadron—slightly damaged uniforms they had pilfered from the dead Air Force commandos in the decompression area down on Level 4.

Schofield and Book danced sideways, edging toward the barricade in front of the Football, firing hard at their own men—but missing woefully.

They reached the barricade, and Schofield immediately saw the Football on the chair.

Then he saw the tether.

'Damn it!'

The presidential briefcase was anchored to a tie-down stud on the floor by a thick metal cord. It looked like titanium thread.

Watch.

8:28:59

8:29:00

'Shit,' Schofield keyed his wrist mike. 'Janson! The Football's tethered to the floor. We can't move it. You're going to have to bring the President out into the open.'

'Okay,' came the reply.

'Fox! Love Machine! I need another thirty seconds of mayhem! Then you know what to do.'

Fox's voice: 'Whatever you say, Scarecrow!'

Love Machine: 'Roger that, Boss!'

And then Schofield saw Janson and the President leap out from the rear section of the AWACS plane—also dressed in full 7th Squadron attire and brandishing pistols, which they fired determinedly at Love Machine's cockroach.

Janson fired her SIG-Sauer with a firm two-handed grip. The President wasn't as fluid, but he did all right for a guy who'd never served in the military.

Marine One banked in a wide circle around the enormous hangar, drawing fire, the roar of its speed-blurred rotor blades thunderous in the enclosed space.

Love Machine's towing vehicle swung past the barricade protecting the Football, then veered left, heading
north, *smashing* through some broken pieces of the
AWACS plane and then disappearing behind it.

From the first-floor control room of the internal building,
Caesar Russell watched the chaos unfolding below him.

He saw the Presidential helicopter performing death-
defying passes *inside the enclosed hangar!* He saw the speeding cockroach blasting through the remains of the AWACS
plane on the elevator platform.

And he saw his own men—scattered and dispersed—firing
wildly at both of these two crazy threats, as if they had been
prepared for any ordered attack but not a totally insane one.

'Goddamn it!' he roared. 'Where is Charlie?'

'Still coming up in the personnel elevator, sir.'

And then, in an instant of total clarity, as he watched his
men down on the hangar floor, Caesar saw him, and his jaw
dropped.

'No . . . '

Caesar watched in stunned amazement as one of his own
men raced over to the Football—which, of course, was still
surrounded by a few men from Bravo Unit, all of them facing
outwards—pulled off one of his black leather gloves, and
under the watchful eye of three other black-clad impostors,
moved his hand toward the palm-print analyser inside the
steel briefcase.

Schofield's watch ticked ever forward.

8:29:31

8:29:32

Amid the roar of the rampaging helicopter and the
cacophony of gunfire all around him, and guarded by
Schofield, Book II and Juliet Janson, the President stepped
up to the Football.

He yanked off his glove, took a final look around himself,

and then, as he strode past the Football, he inconspicuously placed his hand on the palm-print analyser, just as the countdown timer on its display hit 0:24.

The briefcase beeped and the timer instantly ticked over from 0:24 to 90:00 and started counting down again.

When Schofield saw that the deed was done, he and Book II fell into step alongside Juliet and the President.

'Remember, guns up and firing,' he said. He held his wrist mike to his lips, 'Fox, Elvis, Love Machine: get out of here. We'll meet you downstairs. Mother, the platform. *Now.*'

Mother stood inside the enormous hangar doorway down on Level 1, looking up into the elevator shaft.

Two hundred feet above her, she could see the underside of the massive aircraft platform, beyond which she could hear the sounds of the battle.

She hit the call button, and immediately the giant elevator platform high above her jolted sharply and slowly began to descend.

Up in the main hangar, the shattered remains of the AWACS plane—and the platform on which they stood—began to disappear into the floor.

The elevator was going down.

Schofield, Book II, Juliet and the President charged toward it, firing up at Marine One as they did so—acting like good 7th Squadron soldiers.

In the control room overlooking the hangar, Caesar grabbed a microphone.

'Boa! Logan! The President is there! He walked right in among you and hit the analyser and now he's heading for the elevator platform. For Christ's sake, he's wearing one of *our own goddamn uniforms!*'

★

In the main hangar, Kurt Logan spun around where he stood, and he saw them—saw four 7th Squadron people leaping down onto the slowly descending elevator platform, now completely ignoring Marine One and the runaway cockroach.

'The platform!' he yelled. 'Bravo Unit! Converge on the platform! Alpha, take out the helicopter and kill that fucking cockroach!'

Marine One was already swooping toward the ground again—her diversionary mission accomplished.

Gant landed the big chopper right where she had found it—over the air vent in the floor on the western side of the elevator shaft—and with Elvis's help, she manoeuvred the big bird around so that her floor hatch stopped directly above the ventilation shaft.

Once the helicopter was stopped, she leapt out of the pilot's seat and headed for the floor hatch, while Elvis dashed for the rear left-hand door and threw it open for Love Machine.

Love Machine was in a world of pain.

His Volvo towing vehicle wasn't as bulletproof as Marine One and he was taking all kinds of shit from the 7th Squadron men.

Tyres squealed, bullets impacted, glass shattered.

And now he had to get over to Marine One.

His biggest problem, however, was that he had just swung his cockroach around for another pass at the 7th Squadron men on the *eastern* side of the platform when Schofield's call had come in.

He was now on the *other* side of the shaft from Marine One, heading northward, and the elevator platform—now sinking slowly into the shaft—was no longer there to drive on.

He'd have to go around.

More bullets hit his cockroach as three 7th Squadron commandos appeared right in front of him and assailed his vehicle with a harrowing wave of gunfire.

Bullets riddled the driver's compartment.

Two slugs slammed into Love Machine's left shoulder, spraying blood.

Love Machine roared.

A separate volley hit both of his front tyres and they punctured loudly, and suddenly he was skidding out of control, sliding precariously close to the edge of the elevator shaft and the now ten-foot drop to the slowly descending platform.

Somehow, he didn't fall into the shaft. Instead, he bounced across the north-eastern corner of the great square hole, shooting past the 7th Squadron men who had hammered him with gunfire, and slammed at tremendous speed into the remains of Nighthawk Two, which still sat near the northern wall of the hangar—attached to its own towing vehicle, its cockpit blasted open—right where Book II had left it ninety minutes earlier.

Elvis saw the crash from his position inside Marine One, saw Love Machine's cockroach plough into Nighthawk Two and lurch to a thunderous halt, the brick-like towing vehicle half-buried in the helicopter's crumpled side.

And then he saw the three 7th Squadron men rushing toward the crashed cockroach.

'Oh, no . . . ' he breathed.

Meanwhile, Schofield, Book II, Juliet and the President—still dressed in their black 7th Squadron uniforms—were fighting their own unique kind of battle.

Since it was now descending into the square-shaped shaft, the aircraft elevator platform had effectively become a great walled pit, the four walls of the shaft bounding it on every side. And with the remains of the AWACS plane still strewn about the platform, it was also now a twisted steel maze.

Seven members of Bravo Unit moved among the pieces of the plane, searching for them, hunting them.

Schofield guided his people along the eastern edge of the platform, leading the way, hurdling broken pieces of plane, eyes watchful for the enemy, but searching the floor for something else, something he had planted—

There.

The broken section of wing was right where he had left it.

Schofield hurried over to it. It was resting on the ground at the corner of the moving elevator platform, up against the northern and eastern walls. With Book II's help, he lifted the portion of wing off the elevator's floor, revealing a wide square hole in the platform.

The hole was about ten feet square. It was that part of the platform that usually housed the detachable mini-elevator.

Right now, the detachable section of the elevator platform lay about fifteen feet *below* them, further down the shaft—nestled in the corner, unmoving, waiting for them.

By placing the broken section of wing over the top of it earlier, Schofield had ensured that the 7th Squadron didn't know this exit existed.

It was their escape route.

'Love Machine! You still alive?' Elvis yelled into his mike from the cockpit of Marine One.

'*Aw, fuck . . .*' came the pained reply.

'Can you move?'

'*Get out of here, man. I'm gone. I'm hit and my ankle was busted in the crash—*'

'We don't leave anyone behind,' another voice said firmly over the same frequency.

It was Schofield's voice.

'*Elvis. You and Fox get clear. I'm closer—I'll take care of Love Machine. Love Machine, sit tight. I'm coming for you.*'

★

On the downward-moving elevator platform, Schofield spun and looked upwards.

'What are you doing?' Book II asked.

'I'm going to get Love Machine,' he said, eyeing the destroyed fuselage of the AWACS plane above him. It was still tilted sharply forward—nose down, ass up. The elevated rear section of the plane was still above the rim of the hangar floor. But not for long. Soon the downward movement of the platform would bring it below the rim.

'Take the President down,' he said to Book II and Juliet.

'What are you going to do?' Juliet said.

'I'm going to get my man,' Schofield said. 'I'll meet you downstairs.'

With that he took off into the twisted metal forest around them.

Book II and Juliet could only watch him go. And then they set about their own task of leaping down to the detachable mini-elevator in the shaft below them.

Schofield ran.

Up the steeply sloping left-hand wing of the destroyed AWACS plane.

He reached the top of the wing, then used some dents in the side of the fuselage to climb up onto the battered plane's roof. It was then that he was spotted by two of the Bravo Unit men on the platform below him.

Their P-90 assault rifles erupted.

But Schofield never stopped moving. He just kept running, dancing up the slanted roof of the plane, heading aft—toward the point where the rear section of the downward-moving plane was about to swing past the rim of the shaft.

He hit the rear edge of the plane's roof *just as* it swooped past the rim and he jumped—diving forward, leaping full-stretch—and landed with a thud, face-first, out of the line of fire, on the main hangar's shiny concrete floor, twenty feet away from Love Machine's crashed cockroach.

He looked up just in time to see the three 7th Squadron commandos arrive at the cockroach's door.

Love Machine sighed as he saw the muzzle of a P-90 assault rifle appear a few inches in front of his face.

The features of the 7th Squadron commando holding the gun were obscured by the soldier's half-faced gas-mask, but the man's eyes weren't covered. They glinted with satisfaction.

Love Machine closed his eyes, waited for the end.

Blam!

No end.

Confused, he opened his eyes again—to see his executioner, now with only half a head, sway unsteadily on his feet, and then fall in a kind of stunned slow motion to the ground.

The other two commandos spun instantly, only to be cut down by a ferocious volley of semi-automatic pistol fire. They were hurled out of view and then to Love Machine's complete surprise, he saw, standing in their place—

The Scarecrow.

Dressed in his black 7th Squadron clothing.

'Come on,' Schofield said. 'Let's get you out of here.'

Book II landed on the non-skid deck of the mini-elevator, next to Juliet and the President, eight feet below the downward-moving main platform.

It was dark down here, in the shadow of the principal platform.

As soon as they were all on the detachable deck, Juliet hit a button on a small console built into its floor.

The detachable deck began to glide quickly down the side of the shaft, travelling on its own set of wall-mounted rails, moving faster than the gigantic main platform above it.

Pulling away.

Schofield began to haul Love Machine out of the cockroach.

As he did so, he saw several weapons strewn about the exploded-open cockpit of Nighthawk Two—a couple of MP-10s, some grenades, a chunky .44 calibre 'Desert Eagle' semi-automatic pistol, and, most pleasing of all for Schofield, two gun-like weapons, still in their black-leather back-holsters, that must have spilled out of Nighthawk Two's weapons cabinet when it had been blown apart earlier.

They looked like high-tech Tommy guns, each possessed of a short stubby barrel and two handgrips. Sticking out of each gun's barrel, however, was a chrome grappling hook with a bulbous magnetic head.

It was the famous Armalite MH-12 Maghook, a grappling hook which also contained a high-powered magnet for adhesion to sheer metallic surfaces.

'Oh, *yes* . . . ' Schofield said, grabbing the two Maghooks and handing one of them to Love Machine. He also grabbed an MP-10, and the big Desert Eagle pistol, which he shoved into his belt—

Ping!

At that moment, the doors to the nearby personnel elevator abruptly opened—

—*revealing ten fully-armed 7th Squadron men!*

Python Willis and the men of Charlie Unit.

Python's eyes nearly popped out of his head when he saw Schofield standing so close and dressed in 7th Squadron attire.

His men raised their P-90s instantly.

'Oh, *shit*,' Schofield said as he shoved Love Machine back into the cockroach's driver's compartment and clambered in there with him as a volley of bullets slammed into the cockroach's frame.

Schofield jammed the stick into reverse—hoped to God it would still go—and planted the gas pedal to the floor.

The cockroach squealed off the mark, its rear tyres smoking, shooting backwards out of the wreck of Nighthawk Two, impact sparks chasing it across the floor.

The cockroach rushed across the hangar floor in reverse, narrowly missing the edge of the elevator shaft as it rocketed toward the now-abandoned barricade on the eastern side of the shaft.

Schofield turned in his seat as he drove—saw the barricade rushing toward him a second too late.

He hit the brakes and the big three-ton towing vehicle did a wild 180-degree spin. The front end of the cockroach came swinging around like a baseball bat and took out the barricade with one devastating swipe, sending crates and Samsonite containers flying everywhere.

188

The cockroach jolted to a halt.

In its driver's compartment, Schofield lurched forward. When he looked up to see where he was, he was surprised to see that, right next to his door, not three feet away, stood the chair upon which sat the President's briefcase—the Football.

Holy shit.

The briefcase's handgrip was still tethered to the floor by the length of superstrong titanium cord, but now, since the President had successfully reset its ninety-minute timer, it had been abandoned by the 7th Squadron men, rightfully assuming that the President's sole objective was now to get out.

So now the Football just sat there, alone, completely unguarded.

Schofield saw the opportunity, and took it.

He leapt out of the driver's compartment and slid to the floor beside the Football.

The men of Charlie Unit were charging across the hangar, guns blazing, pummelling the exposed rump of the cockroach with a million rounds of lead.

Sheltered by the big towing vehicle, Schofield brought one of the tiny 7th Squadron Lock-Blasters out of his pocket, attached it to the tie-down stud in the floor that held the Football to the ground, hit the activate button, and dived away.

One, one-thousand . . .

Two, one-thousand . . .

Three—

The blast was short and sharp.

With a loud *crack!* the tie-down stud broke free from the floor, and suddenly the Football—with the length of titanium cord still attached to it—was free.

Schofield scooped it up and dived back into the cab of the cockroach, just as the first 7th Squadron men arrived.

Two of them leapt up onto the back of the cockroach, landing on it at the exact same moment that Schofield floored the accelerator and the cockroach took off, the sudden lurch of motion sending one of the commandos falling ass-over-head off the back of the towing vehicle.

The second man had better reflexes. He discarded his P-90, giving himself an extra hand, and somehow managed to hang on to the roof of the speeding vehicle.

Schofield swung the cockroach around the southern side of the enormous elevator shaft—tyres squealing, engine roaring, and now with an extra passenger on its back.

He saw Marine One up ahead, standing on the western side of the shaft, its rotor blades still turning.

That was where he wanted to go. Pull alongside Marine One, race inside it and then leap down into its floor hatch and escape into the ventilation shaft below it.

But his hopes were dashed when he saw the three black-clad men from Alpha Unit appear from the other side of the Presidential helicopter, guns up.

Ready for him.

But for some reason, they didn't fire.

Why weren't they fi—?

With shocking suddenness, the small rear window of the driver's compartment behind Schofield's head exploded all around him, showering Schofield and Love Machine with glass, and a pair of black-gloved hands appeared on either side of Schofield's head, one of them brandishing a knife!

It was the 7th Squadron commando on the back of the cockroach. With his head held above the driver's compartment, he was reaching in with his hands to kill Schofield.

On a reflex, Schofield grabbed the man's knife-hand, while the assassin's other hand clutched madly at his face.

They were still rushing toward Marine One, the cockroach—its two front tyres punctured, its driver fighting for his life—carooming wildly across the shiny hangar floor.

Grappling with the commando behind him, Schofield saw Marine One ahead of them, saw its rapidly spinning vertical tail rotor, a blurring circle of motion about six feet off the ground, a few inches higher than the roof of the cockroach . . .

Schofield didn't miss a beat.

He threw the fast-moving cockroach into a skid, fishtailing the big vehicle sideways—sliding it *underneath* the tail

190

rotor of Marine One, so that the buzz-saw-like blades of the vertical rotor passed low over the cockroach's roof.

Then he heard the commando behind him scream in terror before—abruptly—the yell was cut short as the tail rotor sheared the commando's head clean off his body and a shocking waterfall of blood gushed down from the roof of the driver's compartment.

The three men of Alpha Unit standing near Marine One hurled themselves clear of the sliding towing vehicle as it shot beneath the tail boom of the President's helicopter.

The cockroach emerged on the other side of the chopper, skidding to a sideways halt, so that now the bullet-battered towing vehicle was facing the great square hole that was the elevator shaft.

Schofield saw the yawning shaft before him—with its wide hydraulic platform inside it, still making its ponderous descent; saw the AWACS plane's flying-saucer-like rotodome about ten feet below the floorline.

He revved the engine.

Love Machine saw what he was thinking.

'You are *out* of your *mind*, Captain.'

'Whatever works,' Schofield said. 'Hang on.'

He gunned it.

The cockroach shot forward, rear tyres squealing, rushed toward the edge of the shaft.

Speed is everything, Schofield thought as he drove. He needed enough forward velocity so that the cockroach would reach the . . .

The cockroach rushed toward the rim.

Bullet sparks exploded all around it.

Schofield drove hard.

Then the cockroach hit the edge of the elevator shaft and launched itself out into the air . . .

The cockroach soared—wheels spinning, nose high.

Then, as it fell, its forward bumper began to droop and it resumed the appearance of three tons of steel that was never intended to fly.

By this time, the elevator platform had descended about thirty feet below floor-line, but the body of the destroyed AWACS plane—and its intact rotodome—made the fall for the soaring cockroach only about ten feet.

The cockroach landed—*smash!*—right on top of the AWACS plane's downward-slanted rotodome.

The rotodome, titanium-based and very rigid, resisted the downward energy of the falling vehicle valiantly.

Its support struts, however, did not.

They buckled instantly, snapping like twigs, as did the body of the aeroplane underneath the rotodome.

The AWACS's cylindrical fuselage just *crumpled* like an aluminium can under the weight of the falling towing vehicle, effectively cushioning the roach's fall.

The rotodome was driven down into the fuselage, creating a ramp-like effect which allowed Schofield's cockroach to skip off the other side of the plane and bounce down onto its destroyed left-hand wing.

Schofield and Love Machine were thrown about like rag

dolls as the cockroach bounced and jounced and thundered forward.

Somehow, Schofield managed to hit the brakes and the cockroach skidded and spun, before slamming to an abrupt halt against the far wall of the shaft, right next to the square-shaped hole that normally housed the detachable mini-elevator.

Schofield was already moving when the cockroach stopped, helping Love Machine out of the driver's cabin just as the first 7th Squadron men emerged from the twisted steel forest around them and opened fire.

But their bullets were too slow.

Indeed, they could only watch in stunned amazement as Schofield handed Love Machine the Football, draped the wounded man's arms over his shoulders, and without even a blink, jumped with Love Machine down into the hole in the platform, disappearing into the blackness beneath it.

Like a pair of tandem skydivers, Schofield and Love Machine dropped down the side of the massive elevator shaft, dwarfed by its immense size.

As instructed, Love Machine gripped Schofield's shoulders as hard as he could—holding onto the Football as he did so. That didn't stop him screaming *'Arrrrrgghh!!!'* all the way down.

The grey concrete wall rushed past them as they freefell down the side of the shaft.

As he dropped, Schofield looked down and saw a square of white light stretching out from the hangar on Level 1, illuminating the tiny mini-elevator platform stopped there—two hundred feet below.

He unholstered his newly-acquired Maghook, snapped open its grappling hook.

He couldn't fire it up at the underside of the main platform. Maghooks only had one hundred and fifty feet of rope. It wouldn't be long enough.

No, he had to wait until they dropped about fifty feet, and then—

As he dropped past it, Schofield lodged the Maghook's grappling hook into a metal bracket sticking out from the greasy concrete wall. The bracket kept a series of thick cables running down the side of the shaft bundled together.

As the Maghook gripped the bracket, Schofield and Love Machine continued to fall, the hook's rope playing out above them, unspooling rapidly, wobbling through the air.

The mini-elevator's deck rushed up toward them at shocking speed.

Faster, faster, faster . . .

Jolt.

And they stopped, *three feet* above the mini-elevator's deck, in front of the massive doorway that led into the Level 1 hangar bay.

Schofield released his grip on a black button on the Maghook's forward grip—it was a trigger that initiated a clamping mechanism that bit into the Maghook's unspooling rope. He'd hit it just in time. He and Love Machine were lowered the final three feet.

Their boots touched the ground and they turned to find that they had company.

Standing in front of them just inside the hangar bay doors were Book II, Juliet and the President. With them were Mother, Brainiac and the scientist, Herbie Franklin.

'If anybody makes a joke about "dropping in",' Mother said, 'I will personally rip that person's throat out.'

'We have to keep moving,' Schofield said when he'd reeled in his Maghook. The giant aircraft elevator was still lumbering down the shaft above them—with its cargo of 7th Squadron commandos.

Schofield's group headed for the vehicle ramp at the far end of the enormous underground hangar bay, Book II and Mother carrying the wounded Love Machine between them.

Juliet Janson came alongside Schofield. 'So, now what?'

'We've got the President,' he said. 'And we've got the Football. Since the Football was the only thing keeping the President here, I say we ditch this party. That means finding a networked terminal. We use the computer to open up an exit during the next hourly window period and then we get out of Dodge.

'Doctor Franklin,' he turned as they all started down the circular vehicle access ramp. 'Where's the nearest security computer? Something that will open up an exit during the next window period.'

Herbie said, 'There are two on this level—one in the hangar's office, the other in the junction box.'

'Not here,' Schofield said. 'The bad guys'll be here any minute.'

'Then the nearest one is on 4, in the decompression area down there.'

'Then that's where we're going.'

A woman's voice came through Schofield's earpiece as he moved: *'Scarecrow, this is Fox. We are at the bottom of the ventilation shaft. What do you want us to do?'*

'Can you cut across the bottom of the aircraft elevator shaft?'

'Yeah, I think so.'

'Meet us in the Level 4 lab,' Schofield said into his wrist mike.

'Got it. Oh, and Scarecrow, we—uh—picked up a couple of new passengers.'

'Wonderful,' Schofield said. 'See you soon.'

They raced down the vehicle ramp to Level 2, where they came to an opening in the floor that accessed the emergency stairwell. The eight of them hurried down the stairs until they arrived at the heavy firedoor that led to the decompression area on Level 4.

Brainiac tested the door.

It opened easily.

Schofield was immediately worried. This was one of the doors they had locked and then disabled earlier. Now it was unlocked. He made a hand signal: 'Proceed with caution.'

Brainiac nodded.

He quickly and silently swung the door open as Book II and Mother slipped inside, an M-16 and a P-90 pressed against their respective shoulders.

No fire was necessary.

Aside from the bodies on the floor—from their previous encounter with the 7th Squadron here—the decompression area was empty.

Juliet and the President went in next, stepping over the bodies. Schofield followed, with Love Machine draped over his shoulder.

A couple of computer terminals sat sunk into the wall on their right, partially hidden behind the telephone-booth-sized test chambers.

'Doctor Franklin, pick a terminal,' Schofield said. 'Brainiac, go with him. Find out what we have to do to get out of this rat-maze. Book, take Love Machine. Mother, check the lab next door for a first-aid kit.'

Mother headed for the doorway leading to the other side of the floor.

Book II lowered the grimacing Love Machine to the ground, then made to shut the door behind them.

'What the hell . . . ?' he said as he looked at the door.

Schofield came over. 'What is it?'

'Look at the lock.'

Schofield did so, and his eyes narrowed.

The door's bolt mechanism—the thick rectangular part of the lock that extended out from the door and secured itself inside a matching slot in the doorframe—had been sheared off.

Cleanly.

Perfectly.

Indeed, the cut was so clean that it could only have been done by some sort of *laser* . . .

Schofield frowned.

Somebody had been through here since the battle.

'Scarecrow,' someone said.

It was Mother.

She was standing in the doorway leading to the western side of Level 4. Standing with her was Libby Gant, who had appeared from the other side of the floor.

'Scarecrow. You better see this,' Mother said.

Schofield went over to the doorway set into the white wall that divided Level 4.

He checked the lock on the door as he met Gant and Mother. Its bolt had also been sheared off with a laser cutting device.

'What is it?' he said.

He looked up and was surprised to see, standing with Gant, Colonel Hot Rod Hagerty and Nicholas Tate III, the President's slick Domestic Policy Adviser. Gant's new passengers.

Gant jerked her thumb at the area behind her—the high-ceilinged hall-like space that housed the great glass cube.

Schofield looked into it . . .

. . . and immediately felt his blood run cold.

The cube looked like a bomb had hit it.

Its clear walls lay at all angles, shattered and broken. Entire sections of glass had fallen in on the bedroom inside it, exposing the room to the outside air. Toys lay on their sides. The colourful furniture had been overturned, hurled roughly aside.

There was no sign of the boy, Kevin.

'Looks like they took a whole bunch of stuff from up in the lab, too,' Gant said. 'The entire area has been ransacked.'

Schofield bit his lip in thought as he looked at the scene before him.

He didn't want to say it. Didn't even want to think it. But there was no denying it now.

'There's someone else in here,' he said.

The language was Afrikaans.

The official language of the white regime that had ruled South Africa up until 1994, but which now, for obvious reasons, was no longer the country's official language.

After consulting with the DIA's two African language specialists, Dave Fairfax now had all of his recorded conversations translated and ready for presentation to the Director.

He looked at the transcript again and smiled. It read:

COMM-SAT SECURE WIRE TRACE E/13A-2
DIA-SPACEDIV-PENT-DC
OPERATOR: T16-009
SOURCE: USAF-SA(R)07

29-MAY	22:10:56	AFRIKAANS – ENGLISH
VOICE 1:	Kan bevestig dat in-enting plaasvind.	*Can confirm that vaccine is operational.*

13-JUN	18:01:38	AFRIKAANS – ENGLISH
VOICE 1:	Toetse op laaste poging word op die vier-en-twientigste verwag. Wat van die onttrekkings eenheid?	*Test on latest strain expected on the third. What about the extraction unit?*

VOICE 2:	Reccondo span is alreeds weggestuur.	*Reccondo team has already been dispatched.*

15-JUN	14:45:46	AFRIKAANS – ENGLISH

VOICE 1:	Voorbereidings onderweg. Vroeg oggend. Beste tyd vir onttrekking.	*Preparations under way. Early morning. Optimal time for extraction.*

16-JUN	19:56:09	ENGLISH – ENGLISH

VOICE 3:	Everything is in place. Confirm that it's the third.	*Everything is in place. Confirm that it's the third.*

21-JUN	07:22:13	AFRIKAANS – ENGLISH

VOICE 1:	Ontrekking kan 'n probleem wees. Gestel ons gebruik die Hoeb land hier naby. Verstaan hy is 'n lid van Die Organisasie.	*Extraction is the biggest problem. Plan is to use the Hoeb land nearby. Member of Die Organisasie.*
VOICE 2:	Sal die instruksies oordra.	*Will pass on those instructions.*

22-JUN	20:51:59	ENGLISH – ENGLISH

VOICE 3:	Mission is a go.	*Mission is a go.*

23-JUN	01:18:22	AFRIKAANS – ENGLISH

VOICE 1:	Die Reccondos is gereed. Verwagte aankoms by beplande bestemming binne nege dae.	*Reccondos are in place. Estimate arrival at target destination in nine days.*

'That is some seriously weird shit, my friend,' one of the African language experts said as he was putting on his jacket to leave. He was a short, pleasant fellow named Lew Alvy. 'I mean, Reccondo Units. Die Organisasie. Jesus.'

'What do you mean?' Fairfax asked. 'What are they?'

Alvy took a quick look around himself.

'The Reccondos,' he said, 'are the baddest of the bad when it comes to elite units. They're the South African Reconnaissance Commandos. Before Mandela, they were *the* crack assassination squad of the white regime. Specialists in cross-border raids, covert hits—usually on black resistance leaders—*trained* to be ghosts. They would never leave a trace of their presence, but you'd know they'd been there because of all the cut throats.

'Tough bastards, too. I heard once, in Zimbabwe, a squad of Reccondos lay in ambush for nineteen *days*, not moving, hiding in the veldt under heat-deflecting dirt covers, until their target arrived. The target came by, thinking the area was secure, and—*boom*—they nailed him. Some say that in the eighties they bolstered their numbers by enlisting Angolan mercenaries, but the argument became academic in 1994 when Mandela took power and the unit was disbanded in light of its previous missions. Suddenly they all became mercenaries, a crack hit squad for hire.'

'*Shit*,' Fairfax breathed. 'And Die Organisasie? What's that?'

Alvy said, 'Part myth, part reality. No-one's really sure. But MI6 has a file, so does the CIA. It's an underground organisation of exiled white South Africans who actively plot the demise of the ANC government in the hope of returning South Africa to the bad old days. Rich bastards— rich, racist bastards. Also known as the "Third Force", or the "Spider Network". Hell, it was listed last year on Interpol as an active terrorist organisation.'

Fairfax frowned as Alvy departed.

What could an ultra-rich right-wing South African organisation and an elite light commando unit possibly want with a remote US Air Force base?

Typically, Hot Rod Hagerty and Nicholas Tate went straight over to the President. Elvis, on the other hand, rushed over to check on his wounded buddy, Love Machine.

Schofield stood in the centre of the decompression area on Level 4, with Gant at his side.

Gant nodded at Hagerty and Tate. 'We found them inside Marine One, holed up inside the Presidential escape pod. Hiding.'

'He'll take command,' Schofield said.

'He *is* the ranking officer,' Gant said.

'He's never been under fire.'

'Shit.'

A few yards to their left, over by the test chambers, Brainiac and Herbie Franklin sat before a computer terminal.

Schofield stepped up behind them. 'So, what's the story?

'This is very odd,' Herbie said. 'Here, look,' he pointed at the screen. It read:

S.A.(R) 07-A
SECURITY ACCESS LOG
7-3-010229027

TIME	KEY ACTION	OPERATOR	SYSTEM RESPONSE
06:30:00	System status check	070-67	All systems operational
06:58:34	Lockdown command	105-02	Lockdown enacted
07:00:00	System status check	070-67	All systems operational (lockdown mode)
07:30:00	System status check	070-67	All systems operational (lockdown mode)
07:37:56	WARNING: Auxiliary power malfunction	System	Malfunction located at terminal 1-A2 Receiving no response from systems: TRACS; AUX SYS-1; RAD COM-SPHERE; MBN; EXT FAN
07:38:00	WARNING: Auxiliary power capacity: 50%	System	Terminal 1-A2 not responding
08:00:15	Main power shutdown command (terminal 3-A1)	008-72	Main power disabled
08:00:18	Auxiliary power enabled	Aux System	Auxiliary power start up
08:00:19	WARNING: Auxiliary power operational. Low power protocol enabled	Aux System	Low power protocol in effect: non-essential systems disabled
08:01:02	Lockdown special release command entered (terminal 3-A1)	008-72	Door 003-V opened
08:04:34	Lockdown special release command entered (terminal 3-A1)	008-72	Door 062-W opened
08:04:55	Lockdown special release command entered (terminal 3-A1)	008-72	Door 100-W opened
08:18:00	WARNING: Auxiliary power capacity: 35%	Aux System	Terminal 1-A2 not responding
08:21:30	Security camera system shutdown command (terminal 1-A1)	008-93	SYSTEM ERROR: Security camera system already disabled per low power protocol

'Okay,' Herbie said. 'Well, it starts out all right. Standard system checks by a local operator. Probably one of the console operators up in the main hangar on ground level. Then comes the lockdown at 6:58, keyed in by operator number 105-02. That's someone high up. A 105 prefix indicates a colonel or above. Probably Colonel Harper.

'But *then*, at 7:37, something must have happened up on Level 1. At that time nearly half the complex's auxiliary power supply went up in smoke.'

'A missile hit the junction box,' Schofield said, recalling his battle with the missile-mounted Humvees up in the Level 1 hangar bay earlier. His tone made it sound like this sort of thing happened every day.

'O-*kay*,' Herbie said. 'That would explain it. That junction box housed the auxiliary power generators. The unfortunate consequence of that, however, happened here,' he pointed at another line:

08:00:15	Main power shutdown command (terminal 3-A1)	008-72	Main power disabled

'Somebody turned off the main power supply,' Herbie said. 'That was why I couldn't disable the cameras before. See here, you can see my entry at 8:21. I'm operator 008-93.

'The problem was *somebody else*—operator number 008-72—had already turned the cameras off by shutting down the main power supply. As soon as anyone shuts off the main power, the system switches over to auxiliary power— but now, because of your missile impact, this place only has *half* its auxiliary power remaining, which as you can see, is draining fast.

'But ... when the auxiliary power supply kicks in, the system switches off all non-essential power drains—things like excess lighting and the security camera network. That's the low power protocol that keeps getting mentioned.'

'So by cutting the power, he cut the cameras ... ' Schofield thought aloud.

'Yes.'

'He didn't want to be seen . . . '

'More than that,' Herbie said. 'Look at what he did next. He keyed in three special lockdown release codes—once at 8:01 and twice at 8:04—opening three exit doors.'

'The five-minute window period,' Schofield said.

'That's right.'

'So which doors did he open?'

'Just a second, I'll find out. ' Herbie tapped some keys. 'Now, the first one was 003-V.' A schematic diagram of the Area 7 complex came up on his screen. 'There it is. The Emergency Exit Vent.'

'And the other two?'

'062-W and 100-W . . . ' Herbie said aloud, scanning the screen. 'Door 062-W stands for door sixty-two/west. But that would mean it was part of the . . . '

'What?' Schofield said.

Herbie said, '62-West is the blast door that seals off the westward X-rail tunnel down on Level 6.'

'And the other one? 100-West?'

'It's where that X-rail tunnel ends, over by Lake Powell, about forty miles west of here. 100-West is the security door leading out to the lake.'

Brainiac asked, 'Why would he open those three doors?'

'You open the Emergency Exit Vent to let your companions in. To help you steal the booty,' Schofield said.

'And the other two doors?'

'You open them so all of you can get out.'

'So why cut the power?' Gant asked.

'To disable the security cameras,' Schofield said. 'Whoever did this didn't want the Air Force people to see him doing it.'

'See him doing what?' Brainiac said.

Schofield exchanged a look with Gant.

'See him taking the boy,' he said.

'Quickly,' Schofield said to Herbie, 'can you find out who operator number 008-72 is?'

'Sure.' Herbie began typing fast.

A moment later, he said, 'Got it.' A list appeared on his

screen. Schofield scanned the list until he found the entry he was looking for:

008-72 BOTHA, Gunther W.

'Who's Gunther Botha?' Schofield asked.

'Son of a bitch,' a voice said from behind them.

It was the President. He stepped up behind Schofield's shoulder.

'Botha,' he spat. 'I should have known.'

'South African scientist, working here on the vaccine,' the President said. 'You make a deal with the Devil, and it comes back to bite you in the ass.'

'Why would he want to take the boy?'

'The Sinovirus kills both white people *and* black people, Captain,' the President said. 'Only people of Asian origin are safe from it. That boy, however, has been genetically designed to be a universal vaccine, for *both* blacks and whites. But if only white people are given the vaccine, then only white people would survive an outbreak of the Sinovirus. And if Botha is working for who I think he's working for . . .'

'So what do we do now?' Herbie said.

'We go after the boy,' Schofield said instantly. 'And we—'

'*No, you do not*, Captain,' Hot Rod Hagerty said, appearing suddenly behind Schofield. 'You will stay here and you will guard the President.'

'But . . .'

'In case you haven't been paying attention, if the President dies, so does America. One little boy can wait. I think it's time you got your priorities straight, Captain Schofield.'

'But we can't just leave him—'

'Yes, we can, and yes we will,' Hagerty said, his face reddening. 'In case you have forgotten, *Captain*, I am your superior officer, and I am now ordering you to obey me. The United States government pays me to do the thinking for you. So this is what you will think: your country is more important than the life of one little boy.'

Schofield didn't move a muscle. 'I wouldn't want to live in a country that leaves a little boy to die . . . '

Hagerty's eyes blazed. '*No. From now on, you will do as I say, how I say, and when I say—*'

The President himself seemed about to interfere when Schofield stepped forward, right in front of Hagerty.

'No, *sir,*' he said firmly, 'I will not follow you. Because if you'd waited for me to finish what I was going to say earlier, you would have heard me say: "We go after the boy, *and we take the President with us*". Because in case *you* haven't been paying attention, that Botha guy and whoever's with him opened up an *exit* to this place! They've given us a way out.'

Hagerty fell silent, grinding his teeth.

'Now, if you don't mind,' Schofield said, 'and if nobody else has any better ideas, what do you say we all get the hell out of this place.'

Up in the control room overlooking the main hangar, Caesar Russell's four radio operators were working overtime.

'—main power's down, no cameras operational at all. All systems running on auxiliary power supply—'

'—Sir, someone's initiated the lockdown release codes. The western X-rail door has been opened—'

'Who?' Caesar Russell asked pointedly.

The console operator frowned. 'It looks like it was Professor Botha, sir.'

'Botha,' Caesar said quietly. 'How predictable.'

'Sir,' another operator said, 'I have movement on the X-rail system. Someone heading westward toward the canyons—'

'Oh, Gunther. You couldn't help yourself, could you? You're trying to snatch the boy,' Caesar smiled sadly. 'What's the ETA on that X-rail train at the lake?'

'Forty miles of track at one hundred and seventy miles per hour. About fourteen minutes, sir.'

'Get Bravo down to Level 6 on the double, to pursue Botha on the X-rail. Then open the top door and send Charlie out in the AH-77s to cut him off at the lake—we'll get him from in front and behind. Now go. Go. Although Gunther could never know it, we *need* that boy. This will all be for nothing if we don't have that child.'

★

Schofield, Mother, Gant and Book II flew down the fire stairs at full speed.

Schofield ran with his Desert Eagle held out in front of him. The Football now dangled from his waist, its hand-grip attached to a clip on his 7th Squadron combat webbing.

Behind them came the President and Juliet, Herbie the scientist, Hot Rod Hagerty and Nicholas Tate. Bringing up the rear were Elvis and Brainiac, carrying Love Machine between them.

They came to the Level 6 doorway. Frank Cutler's bloodied and broken body still lay on the floor beside it.

'Be careful,' Juliet said to Schofield as he put his hand on the doorknob. 'This was where they got us before.'

Schofield nodded.

Then—quickly, silently—he whipped open the door, and took cover.

There was no sound.

No gunshots went off.

No bullets whistled into the stairwell.

'Holy *Christ!*' Mother said, as she looked beyond the doorway.

The massive aircraft elevator lumbered down the shaft.

On its back, amid the pieces of the destroyed AWACS plane, stood the ten men of Bravo Unit. They were moving down through the complex, heading for Level 6, in pursuit of Gunther Botha and the boy.

The gigantic elevator platform rumbled down the shaft, the dirty grey concrete walls sliding past the Beta Unit men.

They swung by Level 3, moving downward . . . then Level 4 . . . then—

—the elevator platform *plunged into water*!

As it came to Level 5, the cell block level, the elevator platform rushed down into a wide body of water that had formed at the bottom of the shaft. Several tons of water immediately gushed onto the platform, slithering in amongst the pieces of the crumpled AWACS plane.

'Goddamn!' the leader of Bravo Unit, Boa McConnell, exclaimed as the water rushed up to his waist.

He reached for his radio mike.

'—Bravo Unit reports substantial flooding on Level 5. It's starting to fill the main elevator shaft. Only access to Level 6 is via the eastern firestairs or the western ventilation shaft. Bravo is going for the ventilation shaft—'

'—Sir. That enhanced satellite image of the Emergency Escape Vent is coming through now.'

A sheet of high-gloss paper edged out of a nearby printer. A radio operator tore it clear, checked the timecode at the top. 'This one's from ten minutes ago. Another one coming through—*what the fuck*—?'

'What is it?' Caesar Russell said, taking the printout from the operator. Russell recalled the subject of the satellite scans: the twenty-four rod-like objects that had been picked up on the infra-red satellite earlier, the ones that had been fanned out in a wide circle around the EEV.

Caesar's eyes narrowed.

The enhanced satellite image showed a few of the 'rods' very clearly. They weren't rods at all.

They were combat boots—sticking out from underneath heat-deflecting covers.

The second satellite scan came through. Caesar grabbed it. It was more recent than the first. Only a minute old.

It showed the same image as the first scan: the Emergency Exit Vent and the desert floor around it.

Only now the cluster of combat boots surrounding the Vent was nowhere in sight.

They were gone.

'Mmmm, *very* clever, Gunther,' Caesar said softly. 'You brought the Reccondos with you.'

There were bodies everywhere.

Christ, Schofield thought. *It looked like a war had been fought down here.*

He wasn't far wrong.

Level 6 resembled a subway station—with a central elevated concrete platform, flanked on either side by train tracks. Like a regular train station, at both ends of the extremely elongated space were a pair of train tunnels that disappeared into darkness. Unlike a regular train station, however, three of those four tunnels were sealed off by heavy grey-steel blast doors.

On the central platform lay nine corpses, all dressed in suits.

The nine members of the Secret Service's Primary Advance Team.

Their bodies lay at all angles, bathed in blood, their suits ripped to shreds by the penetration of countless bullets.

Beyond them, however, lay *another* set of bodies—ten of them—all dressed in black combat clothing.

7th Squadron men.

All dead.

Three of them lay spread-eagled on the platform, with enormous star-shaped holes in their chests. Exit wounds. It seemed that these men had been shot in their backs as they'd clambered up onto the platform from the right-hand railway track, their ribcages exploding outwards with the sudden gaseous expansion of the hollow-pointed bullets that had hit them.

More 7th Squadron men lay sprawled on the track itself, in various states of bloodiness. Three of them, Schofield saw, bore very precise bullet holes in their foreheads.

Four of the 7th Squadron commandos, however, had not been shot.

They lay slumped next to a steel door sunk into the wall of the right-hand track—the entrance to the Emergency Exit Vent.

Their throats had been slit from ear to ear.

They had been the first to die, Schofield thought, *when their assailants had emerged from the vent behind them.*

Schofield stepped out from the stairwell doorway, onto the platform.

The underground station was empty.

It was then that he saw them.

They sat on either side of the central platform, one to each track: X-rail engines.

'Whoa,' he breathed.

X-rail systems are high-speed underground railway systems used by the US military for equipment delivery and transport. X-rail engines—or 'railcars' as they are known—move so fast that they require *four* railway tracks for stability: two tracks on the ground and two fastened to the ceiling above the railcar.

The X-railcars that Schofield saw now *exuded* power and speed.

They were about sixty feet long—about the size of regular subway carriages—but their sleek curves and sharp pointed noses were quite clearly designed for one purpose: to slice through the air at tremendous speed.

Each train's design was based on that of the most well-known high-speed train in the world, the Japanese Bullet Train. A steeply slanted nose, aerodynamically grooved sides, even a couple of wing-like canards jutting out from the bow of each train were all included as part of the relent-less pursuit of speed.

The X-rail train to Schofield's left was actually made up of *two* carriages connected by way of an accordion-like pas-sageway. The two railcars were positioned back-to-back, their sharpened noses pointed in opposite directions. Both engines were painted glistening white, so that they looked like a pair of space shuttles connected tail-to-tail.

It was only when Schofield saw their struts, however, that he realised why the system was called an 'X'-rail.

Jutting out from both the front and rear edges of each engine, swept back like the wings of a fast-flying bird, were four elongated struts, which when seen from head-on would look like an 'X'. The lower struts reached down to the wide railway-like tracks beneath the railcar, while the upper struts reached up to an identical pair of tracks attached to the ceiling of the tunnel. All the struts, top and bottom, were contoured like aeroplane wings to allow for maximum speed.

Nestled up against the blast door behind the double-engined train was a smaller type of X-rail vehicle—a kind of miniature car that was barely a third the size of the longer engines. It was little more than a round two-person cockpit mounted in the centre of a set of four struts.

'Maintenance vehicle,' Herbie said. 'Used for tunnel upkeep and cleaning. Faster than the bigger engines, but it only holds two.'

'Now why don't they have *these* on the New York sub-way?' Elvis said, eyeing the double-engined X-rail train.

'Hey, over there,' Brainiac said, pointing at the open tunnel door at the far end of the left-hand railway track. It was the only tunnel that wasn't sealed off by a blast door.

'That's door 62-West,' Herbie Franklin said. 'That's how they got out.'

'Then that's where we're going,' Schofield said.

They all hurried for the twin-engined X-rail train, dashing out into the open, halfway down the length of the station's platform.

Schofield reached the forward engine's side door and hit

a button. With a soft *shoosh*, all the side doors of the two rail-cars—two doors per car—slid open.

Schofield stood inside the lead railcar's forward door-way, the Football hanging from his waist, as he ushered the others inside. Book II dashed in first, headed straight for the driver's cabin, Herbie close behind him.

The President and Juliet came next, rushing in through the lead car's rear doorway. They were flanked by Gant and Mother, and followed by Hot Rod Hagerty and Nick Tate—always keen to stay close to the President.

Trailing last of all, still making their way across the plat-form, were Elvis and Brainiac with the wounded Love Machine draped between them.

'Elvis! Brainiac! Pick it up! Come on!'

Schofield looked back into the interior of the railcar. The inside of the car looked like a cross between a standard subway carriage and a freight car. It had a few rows of pas-senger seats near the back, and a wide open empty space near the front for cargo boxes and the like to be stored.

Schofield saw the President over by the rear door, about forty feet away, slumping into a passenger seat in exhaustion.

And then it happened.

Completely without warning.

One moment, Schofield was looking down the interior of the railcar, looking at the seated figure of the President; the next, *every single window* on the platform side of the railcar just exploded, glass spraying inwards under the weight of a shocking amount of automatic gunfire, blasting tiny shards of glass all over the inside of the carriage.

More gunfire followed—loud, relentless, booming. It impacted hard against the right-hand flank of the X-rail engine, so hard in fact that it caused the entire carriage to shudder violently.

Schofield ducked, shielding his face from the rain of flying glass. Then he spun and peered out through the shattered window beside him—

—and saw a phalanx of 7th Squadron commandos come leaping out of the air vent at the far *western* end of the platform, armed with P-90 rifles and a couple of devastating six-barrelled mini-guns.

The mini-guns whirred, spewing out an unbelieveable storm of bullets, pummelling the side of the railcar.

'You okay?' Schofield yelled to Juliet and the President, his voice barely audible above the thunderous gunfire.

The President, now lying face-down on the floor, nodded feebly in reply.

'Stay down!' Schofield called.

Abruptly, the X-rail engine beneath them roared to life.

Schofield snapped around to see Book II and Herbie in the driver's compartment, flicking switches, pushing throttles. The railcar's power system thrummed loudly, warming up.

Let's go, Schofield thought anxiously. *Let's go . . .*

And then suddenly a voice exploded in his earpiece: '*Hey!* Wait for us!'

It was Elvis.

Elvis, Brainiac and Love Machine were still out on the platform.

Lagging behind the others under Love Machine's weight, they hadn't been able to make it to the two connected railcars by the time the 7th Squadron commandos had appeared at the other end of the underground station.

Now they were pinned down behind a concrete pillar, only ten feet away from the rearmost door of the second railcar, the area all around them shredded by the 7th Squadron's brutal mini-gun fire.

'All right! We have to move! Get ready!' Elvis yelled. 'Okay, now!'

They burst out from their position. Bullets slammed into the pillars all around them. Chunks of concrete flew everywhere. Two bullets blasted clean through Elvis's left shoulder.

'Come on, Love Machine, stay with us!' he yelled.

They reached the rear door of the second railcar, began to

shove Love Machine inside it when—

Smack!

Love Machine's head jolted violently to the left, snapping at an unnatural angle, smacking hard against the side of Elvis's shoulder.

'Oh, man,' Brainiac said, seeing it. 'No.'

Elvis turned.

Love Machine's head lolled lifelessly against his shoulder, a goopy syrup of brains and blood dripping slowly out of a bullet hole in the back of it.

Love Machine was gone.

Elvis just froze, oblivious to his own wounds.

Brainiac said, 'Elvis, come on. Get him inside. The train's about to go.'

Elvis didn't reply. He just looked at the lifeless body of Love Machine, slumped against his shoulder.

'Elvis . . .'

'Go,' Elvis said softly, as bullets hit all around them. He lowered Love Machine's body to the ground beside the X-railcar. Then he looked Brainiac square in the eyes: 'Go. Now.'

'What are you doing?' Brainiac said.

'I'm staying here with my friend.'

And then Brainiac saw the sadness in Elvis's eyes—saw Elvis look lethally over at the 7th Squadron men sidestepping their way toward them from the far end of the platform.

Brainiac nodded. 'Take care of yourself, Elvis.'

'Never,' Elvis said.

'*Brainiac!*' Schofield yelled, gun in hand, trying to see what was happening at the back of the train without getting his head blown off. 'What's going on back there!'

Brainiac's voice said, '*We lost Love Machine, sir, and Elvis has—oh, fuck!*'

Just then, two loud puncture-like booms echoed out through the underground station.

Thawump!

Thawump!

Schofield turned—

—just in time to see two black baseball-sized grenades come rocketing through the air toward him and the X-railcar!

They had been shot from a pair of M-203 grenade launchers held by the 7th Squadron commandos.

The two high explosive rounds shot in through the blasted-open windows of the lead X-railcar—one entering near the front of the car, right next to Schofield; the other rocketing in through a broken window near the rear of the car, near Gant and Mother and the President.

The grenade near Schofield bounced off the far wall and spun to a halt on the floor a couple of yards away from him.

Schofield didn't waste a second.

He dived forward—*toward* the grenade, sliding across the floor on his chest—and swiped the charge back out

218

through the open door of the railcar with his hand. The grenade whipped across the hard floor of the carriage and disappeared through the door. Schofield then ducked back behind the wall as the grenade detonated outside, sending a vicious ball of flames rushing in through the doorway.

At the other end of the carriage, Gant and Mother weren't so lucky.

Their grenade had landed in among the passenger seats that occupied the rear half of the carriage. There was no way anyone could get to it before it detonated.

'Everybody! This way!' Gant said, yanking the President to his feet and shoving him toward the accordion-like tunnel that connected the two X-railcars.

A glass door slid sideways as Gant pushed the President through the passageway. Mother, Juliet, Hot Rod and Tate clambered through behind them.

The glass door slid shut as a second connecting door opened and Gant and the President dived through it— entering the second railcar—and threw themselves sprawling to the floor, closely followed by the others, just as the grenade in the first railcar exploded brilliantly, spreading fire in every direction, shattering the first connecting door, but only cracking the second one, its flaming claws left to scratch hungrily at the glass.

Schofield was thrown to the ground by the blast of the second grenade.

He staggered to his feet, spoke into his radio-mike: 'Fox! Mother! You guys all right?'

Gant's voice: *'We're still here, and we've still got the President. We're in the second carriage now.'*

'Brainiac,' Schofield said. 'Are you on board?'

'Yeah, I'm in the back of the second car . . .'

'Book!' Schofield yelled forward. 'Have you figured out how to drive this thing yet?'

'I think so!'

'Then punch it!'

A moment later, the X-rail train began to move forward on its tracks, heading toward the oncoming 7th Squadron soldiers.

'*Sir,*' it was Brainiac's voice. '*I have to tell you something. We lost Love Machine . . .*'

'Ah, shit,' Schofield said sadly.

'*. . . and we're about to lose Elvis.*'

'What?' Schofield said, perplexed and horrified at the same ti–

But he didn't get to discuss it further, for at that moment, three more puncture-like whumps reverberated through the underground station.

Thwump!

Thwump!

Thwump!

Three rocket-launched grenades sped across the width of the station, zeroing in on the slow-moving X-rail train, three thin lines of smoke cutting through the air behind them, before suddenly—*swoop!-swoop!-swoop!*—one after the other they shot in through the shattered windows of the second X-railcar.

The X-railcar that held the President.

As if on cue, Schofield heard Mother's voice roar over his earpiece: '*Oh, fuck me!*'

The twin-engined X-rail train began to pick up speed, heading for the tunnel.

In the second railcar, Gant couldn't believe what was happening.

Three grenades!

All in her carriage.

She saw the options in a nanosecond: *If we stay, we die for sure. If we get out, we take our chances with the 7th Squadron. In that case, death is probable, but not certain.*

'We can't stay here!' she yelled instantly. 'Out! *Out!*'

She and Juliet immediately grabbed the President by his

coat and hauled him toward the door. They didn't miss a step as they ran through the doorway and dived out of the moving train onto the platform, rolling quickly as they landed.

Hot Rod Hagerty and Nicholas Tate jumped nervously from the moving railcar, landing awkwardly.

A split second later, the figure of Mother—obviously not wanting to wait in line behind Hagerty and Tate—came flying out through one of the broken windows next to the doorway. She somersaulted as she hit the platform, gun tucked up against her chest, rolled to her feet.

A moment later, the three grenades went off—three consecutive blasts, *booming* out from the second railcar.

A trio of brilliant fireballs expanded laterally throughout the interior of the railcar—illuminating the entire carriage like a spectacular elongated light-bulb—consuming every available inch of space within it.

Angry flames billowed out from the windows of the carriage, snapping the window-frames like twigs, cracking the car's walls.

The fireballs fanned out over the underground platform, expanding over Gant and the others' heads as they scurried behind the station's concrete pillars to avoid the fire of the advancing 7th Squadron men.

The entire X-rail train rocked with the triple grenade explosion, but it kept on going, picking up speed with every yard.

In the front carriage, Schofield was almost knocked off his feet by the blast. When he managed to regain his balance and look back down the track, he felt a rush of horror sweep through him.

He saw the President—flanked by Gant and Mother and Juliet—taking cover on the underground station's platform.

Damn it!

The President was off the train!

The accelerating X-rail train was now approaching the western end of the station, coming alongside the 7th

Squadron commandos positioned there. Schofield saw the 7th Squadron men, right alongside his carriage, but they paid him no heed.

They only had eyes for the President.

And suddenly Schofield had a decision to make.

Leap off the train and stay with the President—the President on whose back the fate of the country rested.

Or go after the boy . . .

Then, in a fleeting instant, just as the train was about to disappear into the tunnel, Schofield saw *him*, and he knew then that the President would get away—at least away from the Level 6 station. And he knew that Gant and Mother would see it, too.

And with that, he made his decision to go after Kevin.

A second later, Schofield's view of the X-rail station—the image of the ten 7th Squadron commandos leapfrogging their way down the platform toward the President of the United States and his last few guardians—was replaced with that of the impenetrable black wall of the tunnel.

Gant ducked, covering her head from the chunks of concrete that were raining down all around her.

They were screwed.

The 7th Squadron had them.

There was nowhere they could go, nowhere they could run. They were stuck out in the very middle of the platform, outnumbered, outgunned and out of goddamned luck.

And then she saw Elvis.

Walking like a robot—an automaton, completely out in the open—*toward* the advancing 7th Squadron men, despite the raging gunbattle going on all around him.

He had no weapon in his hands. Indeed, his massive fists were clenched firmly on either side of his body as he walked. His face was entirely devoid of emotion—his eyes fixed, his jaw set.

Elvis, it seemed, had his own mission now.

'Oh, Jesus,' Gant breathed. 'Take care, Elvis.'

Then she turned to the others, 'Get ready, people. We're leaving.'

'*What?*' Hot Rod Hagerty blurted. '*How?*'

'Elvis is going to buy us some time. Take cover and get ready to move.'

Sergeant Wendall 'Elvis' Haynes, USMC, strode purposefully toward the oncoming 7th Squadron commandos, *in between* them and the President's group.

The 7th Squadron men slowed slightly, if only because this was such an odd thing for Elvis to do. He was quite obviously unarmed and yet he just kept moving slowly forward—twenty yards from them, twenty yards from the President—completely calm.

The 7th Squadron commandos never heard the mantra he was repeating softly to himself as he walked. 'You killed my friend. You killed my friend. You killed my friend . . . '

Quickly and efficiently, one of the 7th Squadron men raised his P-90 and fired a short burst. The volley ripped Elvis's chest to shreds and he fell, and the 7th Squadron men resumed their advance.

It was only when they reached Elvis that they heard him speaking, gurgling through his own blood: 'You killed my friend . . . '

And then they saw his bear-like right hand open like a flower—

—to reveal, resting in his palm, a high-powered RDX hand grenade.

'You killed my . . . '

Elvis drew his final breath.

And his hand relaxed completely—releasing the grenade's spoon—and to the utter horror of the men of Bravo Unit standing close around it, the powerful RDX grenade went off with all its terrible force.

The X-rail train rocketed through the tunnel system.

Sleek and streamlined, with its bullet-shaped nose and its flat X-framed fuselage, the twin-carriage train whipped through the wide tunnel at a cool two hundred miles per hour—and this despite its blasted-out windows and bullet-battered walls.

It moved with little noise and surprising smoothness. This was because it was propelled not by an engine, but rather by a state-of-the-art magnetic propulsion system that had been developed to replace the ageing steam-operated catapults on the Navy's aircraft carriers. Magnetic propulsion required few moving parts yet yielded phenomenal ground speeds, making it very popular among engineers who lived by the rule that the more parts a piece of machinery has, the more parts it has that can break.

Book II sat in the driver's compartment, hands on the controls. Herbie sat beside him. The driver's compartment was the only part of the X-railcar that hadn't had all its windows blasted to pieces.

'Aw, *shit!*' Schofield's voice yelled from behind them. *'Shit! Shit! Shit!'*

Schofield strode into the driver's compartment.

'What's wrong?' Book II asked.

'This is what's wrong,' Schofield said, indicating the silver Samsonite briefcase dangling from his combat webbing. The Football. 'Damn it! Everything was happening too fast. I

224

never even thought about it when the President dived off the train. What time is it?'

It was 8:55.

'Great,' he said. 'We now have just over an hour to get this suitcase *back* to the President.'

'Should we turn around?' Book II asked.

Schofield paused, thinking fast, a thousand thoughts swirling through his head.

Then he said decisively: 'No. I'm not leaving that boy. We can get back in time.'

'Uh, but what about *the country*?' Book II said.

Schofield offered him a crooked smile. 'I've never lost to a countdown yet, and I'm not about to start today.' He turned to Herbie. 'All right, Herbie. Twenty-five words or less: tell me about this X-rail system. Where does it go?'

'Well, it's not exactly my area of expertise,' Herbie said, 'but I've travelled on it a few times. So far as I know, it's actually made up of *two* systems. One heads west from Area 7, taking you to Lake Powell. The other heads east, taking you to Area 8.'

As Herbie explained, they were on the system that extended forty miles to the west, out to Lake Powell.

Schofield had heard of Lake Powell before. Truth be told, it was not so much a lake as a vast one hundred-and-ninety-mile-long maze-like network of twisting water-filled canyons.

Situated right on the Utah–Arizona border, Lake Powell had once looked like the Grand Canyon, an enormous system of gorges and canyons that had been carved into the earth by the mighty Colorado River, the same river that would create the Grand Canyon further downstream.

Unlike the Grand Canyon, however, Lake Powell had been dammed by the US government in 1963 to generate hydroelectric power—thus backing up the river, creating the lake, and turning what was already a striking vista of rock formations into a spectacular desert canyonland *that was half-filled with water*.

Now giant sand-yellow mesas rose majestically out of the

lake's sparkling blue waters, while towering temple-like buttes lorded over its flat blue horizon. And, of course, there were the chasms and canyons, now with canals at their bases instead of dusty rocky paths.

Kind of like a cross between the Grand Canyon and Venice, really.

Like any large project, the damming of the Colorado River in 1963 had raised howls of protest. Environmentalists claimed that the dam raised silt levels and threatened the ecosystem of a two-centimetre-long variety of tadpole. This seemed like nothing, however, to the owner of a tiny rest-stop gas station, who would see his store— built on the site of an old western trading post—covered by a hundred feet of water. He was compensated by the government.

In any case, with its ninety-three named gorges and God-only-knew how many others, for a few years Lake Powell became a popular tourist destination for houseboaters. But times had changed, and the tourist trade had slackened off. Now it lay largely silent, a ghost-like network of winding chasms and ultra-narrow 'slot canyons', in which there was to be found no flat ground, only sheer vertical rock and water, endless water.

'This X-rail tunnel meets the lake at an underground loading bay,' Herbie said. 'The system was built for two reasons. First, so that the construction of Areas 7 and 8 could be kept absolutely secret. Materials would be hauled on barges up the lake and then delivered forty miles underground to the building site. We still use it occasionally as a back-door entrance for supplies and prisoner delivery.'

'Okay,' Schofield said. 'And the second reason?'

'To act as an escape route in the event of an emergency,' Herbie said.

Schofield looked forward.

X-rail tracks rushed by beneath him—and *above* him—at incredible speed. The wide rectangular tunnel in front of the train bent away into darkness.

A sudden noise made him spin, pistol up.

Brainiac froze in the doorway to the driver's compartment, his hands snapping into the air.

'Whoa-whoa-whoa! It's me!'

Schofield lowered his gun. 'Knock next time, will you.'

'Sure thing, boss.' Brainiac sat down in a spare seat.

'Where have you been?'

'In the back of the second carriage. I got separated from the others when those rocket grenades came flying in. Dived into a storage compartment just as the three grenades went off.'

'Well, it's good to have you here,' Schofield said. 'We need all the help we can get.' He turned to Herbie. 'Can we get telemetry on any of the other trains on this system?'

'I think so,' Herbie said. 'Just give me a second here...'

He punched some keys on the driver's console. A computer monitor on the dashboard came to life. In a few seconds, Herbie brought up an image of the X-rail system.

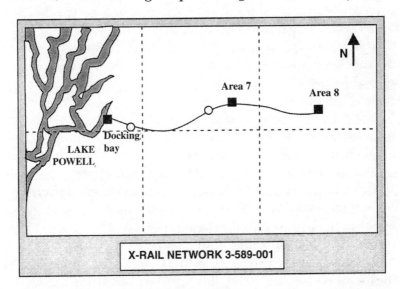

X-RAIL NETWORK 3-589-001

Schofield saw an elongated S-bend that stretched horizontally from Area 7 to the network of canyons that was Lake Powell. He also saw two blinking red dots moving along the track-line toward the lake.

'The dots are X-rail trains,' Herbie said. 'That's us closer to Area 7. The other one must have left about ten minutes ahead of us.'

Schofield stared at the first blinking dot as it arrived at the loading bay and stopped.

'So, Herbie,' he said, 'since we've got a bit of time, this Botha character. Who is he?'

No sooner had Elvis's hand grenade gone off than Gant and Mother and Juliet were up on their feet and firing their guns hard, covering the President as they all ran back toward the fire stairwell from which they had entered Level 6.

The blast of Elvis's RDX grenade had killed five of the 7th Squadron men instantly. Their bloodied limbs now lay splayed across the X-rail tracks on either side of the central platform.

The five remaining members of Bravo Unit had been further away from the grenade when it had gone off. They had been knocked over by the concussion wave, and were now scrambling to find cover—behind pillars and down on the X-rail tracks—in the face of Gant and the others' retreating fire.

Into the firestairs.

Gant led the President up the stairwell. She was breathing hard, legs pumping, heart pounding, Mother, Juliet, Hagerty and Tate close behind her.

The group came to the Level 5 firedoor.

Gant reached for the door's handle—then pulled her hand back sharply.

Small jets of water spurted out from the edges of its frame. The jets of water shot out from the door's rubber seal, mainly from down near the floor, losing intensity as they moved higher. No water sprayed out from the top of the door.

It was as if there was a waist-high body of water behind the fireproof door, just waiting to break through.

And then, from behind the door, Gant heard some of the most hideous shrieking sounds she had ever heard in her life. It was horrific—pained, desperate. The cries of trapped animals . . .

'Oh, no . . . the bears,' Juliet Janson said as she came alongside Gant and saw the firedoor. 'I don't think we want to go in there.'

'Agreed,' Gant said.

They raced up the stairs and came to Level 4. After checking the decompression area beyond the door, Gant gave the all-clear.

The six of them entered, fanned out.

'*Hello again!*' a voice boomed out suddenly from above them.

Everyone spun. Gant snapped her gun up fast, and found herself drawing a bead on a wall-mounted television set.

Caesar's face was on it, grinning.

'*People of America, it is now 9:04, and thus time for your hourly update.*'

Caesar gave his report smugly.

'*—and your Marines, inept and foolish, have yet to inflict any losses on my men. They do little but run. Indeed, His Highness was last seen making a desperate bid for freedom down on the lowest level of this facility. I am informed that a firefight has just taken place down there, but await a report on the result of that exchange . . .*'

As far as Gant was concerned, it was all bullshit. Whatever Caesar said, whatever lies he told, it didn't affect their situation. And it certainly didn't help to watch him gloat.

So while Caesar spoke on the television and the others watched him, Gant investigated the sliding door set into the floor that led down to Level 5.

She could just make out muffled shouts coming from the other side of it. People yelling.

She hit the 'DOOR OPEN' switch, raised her gun. The horizontal door slid away.

The shouts became screams as the prisoners down on Level 5 heard the door grind open.

Gant peered down the ramp.

'Good God,' she breathed.

She saw the water immediately, saw it lapping against the ramp below her. In fact, the ramp simply disappeared into it.

While Caesar's voice continued to boom, she edged down the sloping walkway, until her spit-polished dress shoes stepped ankle-deep into the water.

She crouched down on the ramp, looked out over Level 5.

What she saw shook her.

The entire level was flooded.

Easily to chest height.

It was terribly dark as well, which only served to make the flooded cell block look all the more frightening.

The inky-black indoor lake stretched away from her, to the far end of the floor, its liquid form slipping in through the bars of all the cells—cells which held an assortment of the most wretched-looking individuals Gant had ever seen.

And then the prisoners saw her.

Screams, shrieks, wails. They shook the bars of their cells, cells that they would ultimately drown in if the water level continued to rise.

Like Schofield, Gant hadn't seen the cell bay before. She had only heard the President talk about it when he'd told them about the Sinovirus and its vaccine, Kevin.

'We'd better go.' Juliet appeared at her shoulder. Caesar's broadcast, it seemed, had concluded.

'They're going to drown . . . ' Gant said, as Janson pulled her gently back up the ramp to Level 4.

'Believe me, drowning's too good for the likes of them,' the Secret Service agent said. 'Come on. Let's find somewhere to hole up. I don't know about you, but I sure as hell need a rest.'

She hit the 'DOOR CLOSE' button and the horizontal door slid shut, cutting off the prisoners' pained shouts.

Then, with the President and Mother and Hot Rod and Tate in tow behind them, Gant and Juliet headed for the western side of the floor.

None of them noticed the long decompression chamber as they departed.

Although from a distance it appeared normal, had they looked at it more closely, they would have seen that the timer-activated lock on its pressurised door had timed out and unlocked itself.

The door was no longer fully closed.

The decompression chamber was now empty.

It was 9:06 a.m.

'—Bravo Leader, come in. Report —' one of the radio operators said into his microphone.

'—*Control, this is Bravo Leader. We have suffered serious casualties on the X-rail platform. Five dead, two wounded. One of their guys had an RDX grenade and did a fucking kamikaze—*'

'—What about the President?' the radio man cut in.

'—*The President is still in the complex. I repeat: The President is still in the complex. Last seen heading back up the firestairs. Some of his Marine bodyguards, though, took off down the tunnel in the second X-rail train—*'

'—And the Football?'

'—*No longer with the President. One of my boys swears that he saw that Schofield guy with it on the train—*'

'—Thank you, Bravo Leader. Bring your wounded up to the main hangar for treatment. We'll get Echo to flush the lower floors for the President now—'

'Gunther Botha used to be a colonel in South Africa's Medical Battalion,' Herbie said, as the X-railcar hurtled down the tunnel toward the desert lake.

'The Meds,' Schofield said distastefully.

'You've heard of them?'

'Yes. Not a very nice group to be involved with. They

were an *offensive* bio-medical unit, a specialised subdivision of the Reccondos. Elite troops who used biological weapons in the field.'

'That's right,' Herbie said. 'See, before Mandela, the South Africans were the world leaders in bio-warfare. And, boy, did we love them. Ever wondered why we didn't do all that much about defeating apartheid? Do you know who brought us the Soviet flesh-eating bug, necrotising fasciitis? The South Africans.

'But as good as they were, one thing still eluded them. They'd been trying for years to develop a virus that would kill blacks but not whites, but they never found it. Botha was one of their leading lights and apparently he was on the verge of a breakthrough when the apartheid regime was overthrown.

'As it turned out,' Herbie said, 'Botha's core research could be adapted for use on something the American government was working on—a vaccine against the Sinovirus, a virus that distinguishes between races.'

'So we brought him here,' Schofield said.

'That's right,' Herbie said.

'And now it seems we're discovering that Professor Botha isn't all that trustworthy.'

'It would seem so.'

Schofield paused for a moment, thinking.

'And he's not working alone,' he said.

'How do you know?'

Schofield said, 'All those dead 7th Squadron men we saw when we arrived on Level 6 earlier. I've never met Gunther Botha before, but I'm pretty sure he couldn't wipe out an entire 7th Squadron unit all by himself. Remember, Botha opened three doors, the two X-rail doors and the Emergency Escape Vent—which opens onto Level 6.

'He let a team of men in through that vent. They were the ones who killed the 7th Squadron men there. Judging by the bullet wounds in their backs and the amount of slashed throats, I presume Botha's friends caught the 7th Squadron men from behind.' Schofield bit his lip. 'But that still doesn't tell me what I want to know.'

'And what is that?'

Schofield looked up. 'If Botha is selling us out, what I want to know is: who is he selling us out *to*?'

'It was a security risk from the start, but we couldn't have done it without him,' the President said.

He and the others were sitting in the observation lab overlooking the smashed glass cube on Level 4, catching their breath.

When they'd arrived moments earlier, they'd been confronted by the sight of a thick circular ceiling hatch lying on the floor of the lab.

The 7th Squadron had been through here.

Which hopefully meant they wouldn't be coming back soon. It would be a good place to hide, for a while.

Libby Gant was the only one who stood—still on edge—gazing down at the destroyed cube. The underground complex had grown strangely silent since Caesar's last update, as if the 7th Squadron weren't prowling around it anymore, as if they had stopped hounding the President, at least for the moment.

Gant didn't like it.

It meant something was up.

And so she had just asked the President about Gunther Botha, the man who had taken Kevin.

'Botha knew more about racially-targeted viruses than all of our scientists put together,' the President went on. 'But he had a history.'

'With the apartheid regime?'

'Yes, and beyond that. What we feared the most were his links with a group called Die Organisasie, or the Organisation. It's an underground network comprising former apartheid ministers, wealthy South African landowners, former elite troops from the South African armed forces, and ousted military leaders who fled the country when apartheid collapsed, rightfully fearing that the new government would have their heads for past crimes. Most intelligence agencies believe that Die Organisasie only wants to retake South Africa, but we're not so sure.'

'What do you mean?' Gant asked.

The President sighed. 'You have to realise what's at stake here. Ethnically-selective bio-weapons like the Sinovirus are like no other weapon in the history of mankind. They are the ultimate bargaining tool, because they have the power to sentence a *defined population* to death while absolutely, without question, protecting another.

'Our fears about Die Organisasie don't just relate to what they'd do to the Republic of South Africa. It's what they'd do to *the entire African continent* that frightens us.'

'Yes . . .'

'Die Organisasie is a racist organisation, pure and simple. They actually *believe* white people are genetically superior to black people. They *believe* that black people should be slaves to whites. They don't just hate South African black people, they hate *all* black people.

'Now, if Die Organisasie has the Sinovirus *and* the vaccine to it, they could release it Africa-wide, and give the cure only to those white groups who supported them. Black Africa would die, and the rest of the world wouldn't be able to do a thing about it, because we wouldn't have the vaccine to the Sinovirus.

'Do you remember in 1999 when Ghaddafi spoke of uniting Africa like never before. He spoke of creating "the United States of Africa", but it was regarded as a joke. Ghaddafi could never have made that happen. There are far too many tribal issues to overcome to unite the various black-African nations. But,' the President said, 'an organisation that had the Sinovirus *and* its cure in its possession could rule Africa with an iron fist. It could turn Africa—resource-rich Africa, complete with a billion-strong black slave workforce—into its own private empire.'

Schofield's battered X-railcar raced through the underground tunnel.

They had been travelling for ten minutes now and Schofield was beginning to feel anxious. They would be arriving at the loading dock adjoining the lake soon and he didn't know what to expect.

One question about Area 7, however, was still bothering him. 'Herbie, how did the Air Force get a sample of the Sinovirus?'

'Good question,' Herbie said, nodding. 'It took a while, but eventually we managed to turn two Chinese lab workers at the biowarfare facility in Changchun. In return for a one-way trip to America and twenty million US dollars each, they agreed to smuggle several vials of the virus out of China.'

'The guys in the decompression chamber,' Schofield said, recalling the Asian faces he had seen inside the chamber on Level 4 earlier.

'Yes.'

'But there were *four* men inside the chamber.'

'That's right,' Herbie said. 'As you'd probably under-stand, in China, top-secret government lab workers can't just up and leave the country that easily. We had to get them out. The other two men inside that quarantine chamber were the two 7th Squadron soldiers who extracted them from China—two Chinese–American officers named Robert Wu and Chet Li. Wu and Li used to be a part of Echo Unit, one of the five 7th Squadron teams based at Area 7, which was why they were chosen—'

Abruptly, Schofield held up his hand, moved to the front windshield.

'Sorry, Doctor Franklin,' he said, 'but I'm afraid that'll have to do for the moment. I have a funny feeling that things are about to get a little hairy.'

He nodded at the tunnel ahead of them.

At the end of the long concrete tunnel, beyond its rapidly streaking grey walls, was a tiny luminous speck of light— growing larger as they approached it—the familiar glow of artificial fluorescent lighting.

It was the loading dock.

They had arrived at the end of the tunnel.

'Don't go in,' Schofield said to Book. 'They could be waiting for us inside. Stop in the tunnel. We'll walk the rest of the way.'

The bullet-riddled X-rail train slowed to a halt in the darkness of the tunnel, a hundred yards short of the illuminated loading dock.

Schofield was out of it in an instant—Desert Eagle in one hand, the Football flailing from his waist—leaping down to the concrete next to the tracks. Brainiac, Book II and Herbie followed close behind him.

They ran down the tunnel toward the light, guns up.

Schofield came to the end of the tunnel, peered around the concrete corner.

Brilliant white light assaulted his eyes. He found himself staring at a giant rocky cavern that had been converted into a modern loading dock—a curious mix of flat concrete and uneven rocky surfaces.

Two sets of X-rail tracks lay on either side of a long central platform. The track on Schofield's side of the platform was empty, while the track on the other side was occupied by another X-rail train—Botha's.

It lay still, unmoving.

Some black steel cranes ran on wall-mounted rails, leading from the X-rail tracks to a wide pool of water at the far end of the enormous rocky cavern.

The water in the pool glowed a brilliant aquamarine green, enriched by the minerals of Lake Powell. The pool itself disappeared to the west, winding its way into a twisting black cave that Schofield could only assume led out to the lake. Three ordinary-looking houseboats and a couple of strange-looking sand-coloured speedboats bobbed on its surface, tied to the loading bay's concrete dock.

There was one other thing that Schofield noticed about the immense underground loading bay.

It was empty.

Completely and utterly empty.

Deserted.

Schofield stepped cautiously out from the tunnel, and climbed up onto the central platform between the two X-rail tracks, dwarfed by the sheer size of the cavern.

And then he saw it.

Standing at the other end of the platform, over by the pool of water leading out to the lake.

It looked like some bizarre kind of supermarket display: a small chest-high 'pyramid' of yellow ten-gallon barrels, in front of which sat a chunky Samsonite trunk—black and solid and high-tech. The trunk's lid was open.

As he approached them, Schofield saw that the yellow barrels had words stencilled on their sides.

'Oh, *damn* . . .' he said as he read them.

AFX-708: EXPLOSIVE FILLER.

AFX-708 was a shockingly powerful explosive epoxy, used in the famous BLU-109 bombs that had ripped Saddam Hussein's bunkers to shreds in the Gulf War. A 109's superhardened nose would drive down into a solid concrete bunker and then the AFX-708 warhead inside it would detonate—hard—and blow the bunker up from the inside.

With Book II, Brainiac and Herbie behind him, Schofield looked inside the open Samsonite trunk that sat in front of the collection of AFX barrels.

A timer display stared back up at him.

00:19

00:18
00:17

'Mother of God . . .' he breathed. Then he turned to the others, 'Gentlemen! *Run!*'

Seventeen seconds later, a bone-crunching explosion ripped through the loading bay.

The cluster of AFX-708 barrels sent a devastating ball of white-hot light shooting out in every direction, expanding radially.

The rock-and-concrete walls of the loading bay cracked under the weight of the explosion, blasting outwards in a million lethal chunks, one entire wall just disintegrating to powder in the blink of an eye. Gunther Botha's X-rail train—so close to the source of the blast—was simply vapourised.

Schofield never saw it.

Because by the time the explosives went off, he and the others were no longer inside the loading bay.

They were outside.

FOURTH CONFRONTATION

3 July, 0912 Hours

NORTH-EASTERN LAKE POWELL, UTAH, U.S.A.

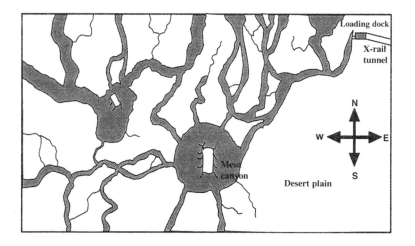

The heat hit them like a blast furnace.

Blistering desert heat.

It was everywhere. In the air. In the rock. Against your skin. Enveloping you, surrounding you, as if you were standing in an oven. The complete opposite of the subterranean cool of Area 7 and the X-rail tunnel.

Out here, the blazing desert sun ruled.

Shane Schofield sped down a narrow water-filled canyon at breakneck speed, blasting through the heat, sitting at the controls of a very odd-looking—but very fast—speedboat.

With him in the boat was Book II, while behind them, in a similar craft of their own, were Brainiac and Herbie.

Technically, Schofield's boat was called a PCR-2—patrol-craft, river, two-man—but it was more commonly known as a 'bipod', a small two-man jet-propelled rivercraft built by the Lockheed Shipbuilding Company for the US Navy. The bipod was known for its unique design configuration. Basically, it looked as if someone had joined two small bullet-shaped jet-boats with a thin seven-foot crossbeam, in effect creating a catamaran-type vehicle with two pods at either end of the beam. Since both open-topped pods were possessed of powerful two-hundred-horsepower Yamaha pump-jet engines, it made for an extremely fast—and extremely stable—boatframe.

Schofield's bipod was painted in desert camouflage colours—brown blobs on a sandy yellow background—and it shot over the water at incredible speed, kicking up twin ten-foot sprays of water behind it. Schofield sat in the left-hand pod, driving, while Book II sat in the right-hand one, manning the boat's sinister bow-mounted 7.62 mm machine gun.

The sun shone—burning hot.

It was already 100 degrees in the shade.

'How you guys doing over there?' Schofield said into his wrist mike as he looked back at the other bipod behind him—Brainiac was driving, Herbie sat in the gunner's pod.

Brainiac's voice: *'I'm okay, but I think our scientist friend here is turning green.'*

They were speeding down a twenty-foot-wide slot canyon that wended its way southward, toward the main body of Lake Powell.

The pool of water at the far end of the loading bay had indeed led out to the lake, a tight, dark, winding cave whose exterior door—a brilliantly camouflaged plate-steel gate designed to look like a wall of rock—had been left open by the escaping thieves.

Schofield and his men had emerged from the cave at the end of a dead-end canyon and powered off not a moment before the entire wall of rock behind them had been blasted outward by the monstrous AFX explosion.

The two bipods sped around a wide bend in the water-filled canyon.

When viewed from above, this canyon resembled a race-car track, a never-ending series of twists, turns and full 180-degree bends.

That wasn't so bad.

The trouble started when it met up with all the *other* narrow canyons of Lake Powell—then the canyon system resembled a giant high-walled maze of interconnecting natural canals.

They came to an intersection of three canyons, arriving at it from the north-east.

At first Schofield didn't know what to do.

Two rock-walled canals stretched away from him—a fork in the watery road. And he didn't know *where* Botha was going. Presumably the South African scientist had a plan—but what?

And then Schofield saw the waves. Saw a collection of ripples lapping against the sheer stone walls of the canyon branching away to the left—barely perceptible, but definitely there—the residual waves of a motorboat's wash.

Schofield gunned it, swinging left, heading south.

As he travelled down the canyonways, banking with the bends, he looked upward. The rocky walls of these canyons rose at least two hundred feet above the water level. At their rims, Schofield saw clouds of billowing sand, blowing viciously, offering sporadic relief from the blazing sun.

It was the sandstorm.

The sandstorm that had been forecast to occur that morning, but which the members of HMX-1 had expected to miss.

It was absolutely *raging* up there, Schofield saw, but down here, in the shelter of the canyons, it was relatively calm—a kind of meteorological haven below the canyon system's high rocky rim.

Relatively calm, Schofield emphasised.

Because at that moment, he rounded a final corner and, completely unexpectedly, burst out into wide open space—into an enormous crater-like formation with a giant flat-topped mesa rising out of the water in its centre.

Although the crater was bounded by magnificent sheer rock walls, it was too wide to offer total protection from the wild sandstorm above. Flurries of sand whipped down into the vast expanse of open water, swirling maniacally.

It was then that through the veil of wind-hurled sand, Schofield saw them.

They were rounding the right-hand base of the mesa, speeding away.

Five boats.

One large white powerboat that looked like a hydrofoil, and four nimble bipods, also painted sand-yellow.

To Schofield's horror, at least a half-dozen slot canyons branched out from the walls of this circular crater, like the points on a clock, offering a multitude of escape routes.

He hit the gas, charged into the sandstorm, heading for the southern end of the central mesa, hoping to take the South Africans by surprise on the other side.

His bipod skipped over the water at incredible speed, propelled by its powerful mini-jet engines. Brainiac and Herbie's bipod bounced along beside it, kicking up spray, jouncing wildly through the horizontal rain of flying sand.

They rounded the left-hand end of the mesa—and saw the five South African boats heading for a wide vertical canyon that burrowed into the western wall of the crater.

They gave chase.

The South Africans must have seen them, because right then two of their bipods peeled away from the main hydrofoil, turning in a wide 180-degree arc, angling menacingly toward Schofield's boats, their 7.62 mm machine guns flaring to life.

Then suddenly—*shockingly*—the left-hand South African bipod exploded.

It just blew out of the water, consumed in a geyser of spray. One second it was there, the next it was replaced by a ring of foaming water and a rain of falling fibreglass.

For its part, the *right-hand* South African bipod just wheeled around instantly, abandoning this confrontation, and took off after the other South African boats.

Schofield spun. *What the—?*

SHOOOOOM!!

Without warning, three black helicopters came bursting out of the sandstorm above the crater and plunged into the canyon system from behind him!

The three choppers swung into the relative shelter of the crater like World War II divebombers, banking sharply before righting themselves without any loss of speed. They thundered over Schofield and his team, powering toward the South African boats as they disappeared inside the slot canyon to the west.

The choppers just shot into the narrow canyon after them.

Schofield's jaw dropped.

In a word, the three helicopters looked *awesome*. Sleek and mean and fast. They looked like nothing he had ever seen before.

They were each painted gunmetal black and looked like a cross between an attack helicopter and a fighter jet. Each helicopter had a regular helicopter rotor and a sharply pointed nose, but they were also possessed of downwardly canted *wings* that extended out from their frames.

They were AH-77 Penetrators—medium-sized attack choppers; a new kind of fighter-chopper hybrid that combined the hovering mobility of a helicopter with the superior straight-line speed of a fighter jet. With their black radar-absorbent paint, swept-back wings and severe-looking cockpits, they looked like a pack of angry airborne sharks.

The three Penetrators shot forward, banking into the narrow canyon after the four South African speedboats, completely ignoring Schofield and his men.

And in a fleeting instant, Schofield had a strange thought. *What the hell were the Air Force people doing out here? Weren't they after the President? What did they care about Kevin?*

In any case, this was now a three-way chase.

'*Sir!*' Brainiac's voice came in. '*What do we do?*'

Schofield paused. Decision time. A tornado of thoughts whizzed through his mind—Kevin, Botha, the Air Force, the President, and the unstoppable countdown on the Football that at some point would force him to give up on this chase and turn back . . .

He made the call.

'We go in after them,' he said.

Schofield's bipod roared into the canyon the South Africans and the Penetrators had taken, Brainiac and Herbie's bipod close behind it.

It was a particularly winding canyon, this one—left then right, twisting and turning—but, thankfully, sheltered from the sandstorm.

About a hundred yards in, however, it forked into two sub-canyons, one heading left, the other right. Little did any of them know that the sub-canyons of Lake Powell have a habit of swinging back on each other, like inter-weaving pieces of string, forming multiple intersections . . .

Schofield saw the three Air Force choppers split up at the fork—one going left, two going right. The four South African rivercraft up ahead of them must have already split up.

'Brainiac!' he yelled. 'Go left! We'll take the right! Remember, all we want is the boy! We get him and then we high-tail it out of here, okay!'

'*Got it, Scarecrow.*'

The two bipods parted—taking separate canyons— Schofield peeling right, Brainiac banking left.

For Schofield, it was like entering a fireworks show—a

spectacular display of tracer bullets, missiles and dangerously exploding rock.

He saw the two black choppers eighty yards up ahead—trailing the lead hydrofoil and one of the South African bipods. The two speeding helicopters stayed below the canyon's rim—the raging sandstorm above the canyon system preventing them from going any higher—banking and turning with the bends of the winding canyon, their rotor blades thumping.

Tracer bullets streamed out from their nose-mounted Vulcan cannons. Air-to-ground missiles streaked out from their wings and *blasted* into the rocky walls of the canyon all around the two South African speedboats.

For their part, the South Africans weren't exactly shy either.

The men in the bipod had come prepared to protect the lead hydrofoil—they had a shoulder-mounted Stinger missile launcher. While one man drove the bipod, the gunner thrust the Stinger onto his shoulder and fired it up at the trailing Penetrators.

But the Penetrators must have had the same ultra-powerful electronic countermeasures that the AWACs planes inside Area 7 had, because the Stingers just shot past them, spiralling wildly, careering into the walls of the canyon where they detonated, sending showers of car-sized boulders splashing down into the canal below—boulders which Schofield had to swerve to avoid.

And then suddenly Schofield saw a long, white object drop out of a hatch in the belly of one of the black choppers and, dangling from a small drogue parachute, splash down into the water.

A second later, the water beneath the chopper churned into a froth and he saw a finger of bubbles stretch out from the roiling section of water, *heading straight for the South African bipod.*

It was a torpedo!

Five seconds later, completely without warning, the speeding bipod exploded violently.

The force of the blast was so strong that it lifted the fast-moving bipod clear off the water's surface. Indeed, such was the bipod's velocity that it tumbled end over end, totally out of control, bouncing across the water's surface like a skimming stone until it *slammed*—top-first—into the hard rock wall of the canyon and blew apart.

Schofield drove hard, closing in, now fifty yards behind the action. He needed to catch up, but the South Africans had had too much of a head-start.

And then abruptly the canyon turned . . .

. . . and intersected with its twin from the left—the sub-canyon that Brainiac and Herbie had taken in pursuit of the other two South African bipods—so that now the two canyons formed a giant X-shaped junction.

And it happened.

The white South African hydrofoil shot into the intersection from the top-right-hand corner of the X—*at exactly the same time* as one of its own bipods entered the junction from the bottom-right.

Speeding rivercaft shot every which way.

The hydrofoil and the bipod swerved to avoid each other. Both fishtailed wildly on the water, sending a wall of spray flying into the air—and losing all of their forward momentum in an instant.

The second South African bipod from Brainiac's canyon never even had a chance to slow down.

It just shot straight through the X-shaped junction like a bullet—*between* the two boats that had been forced to stop, blasting spectacularly through their spray—before zooming off down the canyon ahead of it, heading west.

The three Air Force Penetrators—two from Schofield's canyon, one from the other canyon—were also thrown into chaos. One managed to haul itself to a halt, while the other two whipped through the airspace *above* the junction, crossing paths, missing each other by inches, and overshooting the momentarily stalled boats below.

250

It was all Schofield needed.
Now he could catch up.

In his bipod, Brainiac was still eighty yards short of the X-junction.

He saw the mayhem in front of him—saw the restarting hydrofoil, and the stalled South African bipod.

His gaze fell instantly on the hydrofoil, which was now rotating laterally in the water, preparing to resume its run down the canyon to the bottom-left of the X.

Brainiac cut a beeline for it.

Schofield arrived at the junction just as the hydrofoil peeled away to the south and Brainiac's bipod swooped into the narrow canyon fast behind it.

'I'm going after the hydrofoil, sir!'

'I see you!' Schofield yelled.

He was about to follow when some movement to his right caught his eye. He spun to look down the long high-walled canyonway that stretched away from him to the west.

He saw one of the South African bipods disappearing down the elongated canyonway—all on its own.

It was the bipod that had shot straight through the intersection, from the bottom-right corner to the top-left. Curiously, it was not even *trying* to return to give aid to the hydrofoil.

Then, in a blink, the tiny bipod was gone, vanishing down a narrow side canyon at the far end of the larger canyonway.

And it hit Schofield.

The boy wasn't in the hydrofoil.

He was in the bipod.

That bipod.

'Oh, no,' Schofield breathed as he snapped round and saw Brainiac's speeding bipod disappear around a bend in the southern canyon in pursuit of the hydrofoil. 'Brainiac . . .'

★

Brainiac's sand-coloured bipod was moving fast.

Really, really fast.

It came alongside the speeding South African hydrofoil, the two rivercraft hurtling down the narrow rock-walled canal like a pair of runaway stock cars, with two of the Air Force Penetrators firing wildly down on them as they did so.

'*Brainiac, can—you hear—e—?*' Schofield's garbled voice said in Brainiac's ears, but in the roar of bullets, engines and helicopter rotors, the young Marine couldn't make out Schofield's words.

Brainiac got Herbie to use his pod's controls and bring the bipod in close to the speeding hydrofoil while Brainiac himself climbed out of his seat.

He watched the hydrofoil as they sped alongside it—saw its two strut-like bow-mounted skids carving through the water—but he couldn't see inside the big speedboat's smoked-glass windows.

Then, with a deep breath, he jumped—across the gap between the two speeding boats—landing on his feet, on the foot-wide side decking of the moving hydrofoil.

'*—ainiac—out—of there!—*'

Schofield's voice was a blur.

Brainiac grabbed a handhold on the roof of the speeding hydrofoil. He wasn't sure what he expected to happen next. Perhaps some resistance—like someone throwing open one of the hydrofoil's side doors and firing on him. But no resistance came.

Brainiac didn't care. He just dive-rolled onto the hydrofoil's forward deck and blasted out the vehicle's windshield. Glass flew everywhere and a second later, when the smoke cleared, he saw the inside of the boat's cabin.

And he frowned.

The hydrofoil's cabin was empty.

Brainiac climbed inside—

—and saw the hydrofoil's steering controls moving of their own accord, guided by some kind of computer-controlled navigation system, an anti-impedance system that directed the vehicle away from all other objects, rock walls and boats alike.

Then suddenly, in the silence of the cabin, Schofield's voice was loud and alive in Brainiac's ear.

'For God's sake, Brainiac! Get out of there! The hydrofoil is a decoy! The hydrofoil is a decoy!'

And at that moment, to his absolute horror, Brainiac heard a shrill *beep* that would signal the end of his life.

A second later, the entire hydrofoil blew, its windows blasting outwards in a shockingly violent explosion.

The force of the blast flipped Herbie's bipod, too, causing the little speedboat to flip over onto its top and skid in a gigantic spraying mess across the surface of the canal, before it smashed into the wall of the canyon and stopped.

After the impact, the crumpled bipod just lay still, droplets of water raining down all around it.

Back at the X-intersection, Schofield was about to take off after the rogue South African bipod that had skulked away from the fight when, from completely out of nowhere, a line of bullet geysers shattered the water all around his boat.

It was the fourth and last South African bipod firing on him.

It had started up again and was now heading eastward, *back* into the canyon that led to the crater with the mesa in its middle.

Before Schofield could even think of a response, two parallel lines of much bigger bullet-geysers erupted all around his sand-coloured bipod. They hit so close, their spray spattered his face.

This barrage of fire came from the third Penetrator helicopter, which still hovered above the X-shaped junction, turning laterally in mid-air, searching for Kevin. The black chopper's six-barrelled Vulcan cannon roared loudly as it spewed forth a long tongue of bright yellow flames.

Schofield gunned the engine of his bipod, wheeling it around to the left, *away* from the Penetrator's gunfire—but also, unfortunately, away from the rogue bipod that he was sure contained Kevin—instead taking off after the *other* South African bipod that had headed back east, toward the crater with the mesa in it.

254

The Penetrator gave chase, lowering its nose, powering forward like a charging T-rex, its thrusters igniting.

Schofield's bipod skimmed across the surface of the water, its hull barely even touching the waves, trailing the South African bipod through the winding rock-walled canyon, the shark-like Penetrator looming in the air behind it.

'Any ideas?' Book II yelled from the gunner's pod.

'Yeah!' Schofield called. 'Don't die!'

The Penetrator opened fire and two more lines of geysers hit the water all around their speeding bipod.

Schofield banked left—hard—so hard that the boat's left-hand pod lifted clear out of the water, just as a line of bullets ripped up the choppy surface beneath it.

And then, just then, two torpedoes dropped out of the bottom of the Penetrator.

Schofield saw them and his eyes widened.

'Oh, man.'

One after the other, the torpedoes splashed down into the water and a second later two identical fingers of bubbles took off after the two bipods, charging up the water-filled canyon behind them.

One torpedo immediately zeroed in on Schofield's boat.

Schofield cut right, angling for an oddly shaped boulder that jutted out from the right-hand wall of the canyon. The gently sloping boulder looked remarkably like a ramp . . .

The torpedo closed in.

Schofield's bipod whipped across the water. Book II saw what Schofield was aiming for—the boulder . . .

The bipod hit the rock ramp, just as the torpedo swung in underneath its jet engines and—

—the bipod shot up out of the water, its exposed twin hulls rocketing up the length of the rock—scratching, shrieking, screeching—and then suddenly, *whoosh!*, like a stunt car leaping up into the sky, it shot off the end of the sloping boulder, *just as* the torpedo detonated against the base of the ramp, shattering it into a thousand fragments that went showering upwards in a glorious flower-shaped formation behind the soaring bipod.

The double-hulled boat landed in the water with a splash, still moving fast.

Schofield looked forward just in time to see the South African bipod up ahead of him veering left, heading for a semi-circular tunnel burrowed into the left-hand wall of the canyon.

He took off after it, the remaining torpedo charging through the water behind him like a hungry crocodile.

The South African bipod shot into the tunnel.

A second later, Schofield's twin-hulled boat whipped into the darkness behind it.

The torpedo swung in after them.

Their headlamps blazing, the two bipods zoomed down the length of the narrow tunnel at almost a hundred miles an hour, the dark wet walls of the passageway streaking past them in a blur, like some ultra-fast indoor rollercoaster ride.

Schofield concentrated hard as he drove.

It was so *fast*!

The tunnel itself was about twenty feet wide and roughly cylindrical in shape, with its walls curving slightly as they touched the shallow water surface. About two hundred yards ahead of him, he saw a small point of light—the end of the tunnel.

Suddenly Book II yelled, 'It's closing!'

'What!'

'That other torpedo!'

Schofield spun.

The torpedo behind them was indeed moving in quickly, closing the gap fast.

He snapped to look forward—saw the water-blasting jet engines of the South African bipod five yards in front of him. *Damn it*. Since each bipod was about thirteen feet wide, the tunnel wasn't wide enough to pass.

Schofield gunned it left—but the South African bipod cut him off. Tried right. Same deal.

'What do we do?' Book II called.

'I don't—' Schofield cut himself off. 'Hang on!'

'*What?*'

'Just hold on tight!'

The torpedo weaved its way under the surface of the shallow water like a slithering snake, edging dangerously close to Schofield's stern.

Schofield hit his thrusters, pulled *closer* to the South African bipod in front of him—so that now the two sleek twin-hulled boats were whipping along at a hundred miles an hour in the tightly enclosed space *barely a foot apart.*

Schofield saw the South African driver turn quickly in his seat and see them.

'Hello!' Schofield gave the man a wave. 'Good-bye!'

And with that, just as the torpedo began to disappear underneath the stern of Schofield's boat, Schofield jammed his thrusters as far forward as they would go and yanked his steering yoke hard to the right.

His speeding bipod swung quickly right, the whole twin-hulled boat lifting completely out of the water as it ran *up* the curving right-hand wall of the tunnel. The bipod bounced so high up the wall that for a moment it was actually travelling at right angles to the earth.

The torpedo didn't care. With its original target lost, it quickly overtook Schofield's wall-skimming boat and zeroed in on the only other object in the vicinity—the South African bipod.

The explosion in the narrow confines of the tunnel was huge.

The South African bipod was blasted to bits—bits that were flung all around the tunnel, followed by a rolling, roaring fireball that filled the narrow cylindrical passageway.

Still moving fast, Schofield's twin-hulled boat swooped down off the sloping wall and blasted right through the charred remains of the South African bipod, exploding through the billowing wall of fire that now filled the tunnel before—suddenly, gloriously—it burst into the bright open space of the awaiting canyon at the end of the passageway.

Schofield eased back on the throttle and his bipod ground to a halt in the middle of this new canyon.

His face and body were soaking wet, covered in spray. Book II was the same.

He looked at this new high-walled canyon around them, trying to get a bearing on where they were, and quickly realised that this wasn't a new canyon at all—it was the same sub-canyon he had taken earlier when he and Book II had separated from Brainiac. Indeed, as he now saw, he and Book weren't far from the fork in the canyon where they had split up from Brainiac.

Schofield revved the engine, started to swing around, to continue his pursuit of the rogue South African bipod, when suddenly he heard a strange thumping noise to his right.

He snapped around.

And saw *another* helicopter—a fourth helicopter—half-obscured by the vertical wall of the canyon, hovering fifty feet above the water at the fork of the two sub-canyons.

One thing about this helicopter struck him straight away.

It wasn't a Penetrator. It was far too chunky, not nearly sleek enough.

As he saw it swing around in mid-air, Schofield recognised the chopper to be a CH-53E Super Stallion, a powerful heavy-lift transport bird like the two that usually accompanied

Marine One. The Super Stallion was renowned for its toughness and strength—with its lowerable rear loading ramp, it could hold fifty-five fully-equipped men and carry them into hell and back.

The Air Force men must have brought this Super Stallion along to carry the boy back in, as the attack-configured Penetrators only had room for three crew members.

Judging by the way it hovered at the fork of the two canyons, however, slowly turning laterally, Schofield figured that this chopper was more than just a prisoner transport—it was providing support of some kind.

Schofield spun his bipod around, headed slowly and cautiously toward the Super Stallion.

'What are you doing?' Book II asked. 'The kid is *that* way.'

'I know,' Schofield said, 'but the way I see it, we're not going to catch that boy on the water. It's time we got into the air.'

The three 7th Squadron commandos inside the Super Stallion all wore headsets. One flew the chopper while the other two spoke into microphones, speaking quickly amid the roar of the helicopter's rotor noise.

They, too, were searching for the rogue South African bipod that had slipped away after the near collision in the X-intersection.

'—Penetrator One, this is Looking Glass,' one of them said. 'There's a canyon coming up on your right, take that. It might have gone down that way—'

The other radioman said, 'Penetrator Two. Cut back to the north and check that slot canyon on your left—'

A map of the canyon system glowed green on each of the men's computer screens.

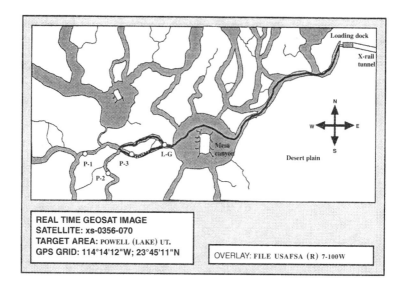

The three illuminated dots on the left—P-1, P-2 and P-3—indicated the three Penetrators prowling the canyons for the rogue bipod. The stationary dot near the mesa crater, 'L-G', depicted the Super Stallion, call-sign 'Looking Glass'. The black line indicated the path of the chase so far.

While the two radiomen continued to issue instructions, the pilot peered forward through the bubble-like canopy of the helicopter, his eyes searching the canyon in front of them.

Amid the roar of the rotor blades and the sound of their own voices in their headsets, none of the crew heard the dull *thunk!* of a Maghook hitting the underside of their mighty chopper.

Schofield's bipod sat in the water directly beneath the Super Stallion—bucking and bouncing on the churning wash generated by the helicopter's downdraft—having approached the big transport bird from behind.

A thin thread-like rope connected the bipod to the under-side of the Super Stallion fifty feet above it—the black Kevlar fibre rope of Schofield's Maghook.

And then suddenly a tiny figure whizzed up into the air

toward the chopper, reeled upward by the Maghook's internal spooler.

Schofield.

In a second, he was hanging from the Super Stallion's underbelly—fifty feet above the water's surface, right next to an emergency access hatch built into the big helicopter's floor—gripping the Maghook as it clung to the helicopter's underside by virtue of its bulbous magnetic head.

The noise was shocking up here, deafening. The windblast from the rotors made his 7th Squadron clothes press against his skin, made the Football hanging from his webbing twist and flap wildly.

Super Stallions have fully retractable landing gear, so Schofield grabbed a fat cable eyehole as a handhold. Then he hit a button on the Maghook, allowing it to unspool down to Book.

Within seconds, Book II was beside him, hanging from the Maghook on the underside of the Super Stallion.

Schofield grabbed the access hatch's pressure-release handle. 'You ready?' he yelled.

Book II nodded.

Then, with a firm twist, Schofield turned the handle and the emergency hatch above them dropped out of its slot.

The men inside the Super Stallion felt the blast of wind first.

A gale of fast-moving air rushed into the rear cabin of the Super Stallion a second before Schofield swung up through the hatch in its floor, closely followed by Book II.

They came up inside the chopper's rear troop compartment, a wide cargo hold separated from the cockpit by a small steel doorway.

The two radiomen in the cockpit both spun at once, looking back into the hold. They went for their guns.

But Schofield and Book II were already moving fast, guns up, mirroring each other's movements perfectly. One shot from Schofield and the first radioman went down. Another from Book and the second guy was history.

The chopper's pilot saw what was happening, and realised quickly that a gun wasn't his best way out of this situation.

He pushed forward on the Super Stallion's control stick, causing the entire helicopter to lurch dramatically.

Book II lost his balance immediately, and fell.

Schofield, already dancing quickly toward the cockpit, dived to the floor and slid—forward, *fast*, on his chest—toward the open cockpit door.

The pilot tried to kick the door shut and seal off the cockpit, but Schofield was too quick.

He slid head-first—rolling onto his back as he did so—sliding in through the doorway, into the cockpit, and jolting to a perfect halt inside the threshold—one hand propping open the door, the other gripping his .44 calibre Desert Eagle, aimed directly up at the bridge of the pilot's nose.

'Don't make me do it,' he said from the floor, his eyes looking up the barrel of his gun, his finger poised on the trigger.

The pilot was stunned, his mouth open. He just glared down at Schofield—on the floor, with his gun held unwaveringly in the firing position.

'Don't make me,' Schofield said again.

The pilot went for the Glock in his shoulder holster.

Blam!

Schofield put a bullet in his brain.

'Damn it,' he said, shoving the dead pilot out of his seat and taking the controls. 'I *told* you, you asshole.'

Schofield and Book's Super Stallion roared down the narrow canyonway, banking with each bend, heading for the X-intersection where all the rivercraft had nearly collided earlier.

In his mind's eye, Schofield remembered seeing the rogue bipod sneaking off down the western branch of that intersection and then disappearing off to the right, into a narrow slot canyon at the far end.

With the help of the Super Stallion's map of the canyon system, he now saw that slot canyon—it snaked its way to the north, opening onto another lake-like crater with a small mesa in it.

That was where the rogue bipod had been heading.

But what was waiting in that crater? Schofield thought.

Why were the South Africans heading there?

The Super Stallion thundered down its narrow rock-walled canyon, heading for the X-intersection, rounded a bend—

—and came face to face with one of the Air Force Penetrators.

Schofield yanked on the control stick, reining the Super Stallion to a lurching halt in mid-air.

The Penetrator was hovering above the X-intersection, turning laterally in the air, looking down each of the four rock-walled alleyways that met there. It looked like a gigantic flying shark, searching for its prey.

It saw them.

'Looking Glass, this is Penetrator Three,' a voice said sharply over Schofield's cockpit intercom. *'Got any real-time imagery from the satellite yet?'*

Schofield froze.

Shit.

'Book, quickly. Weapons check.'

The Penetrator turned in the air to face the Super Stallion.

'Looking Glass? You listening?'

Book II said, 'We got a nose-mounted Gatling gun. That's it.'

'Nothing else?'

The two helicopters faced each other, hovering above the intersection like a pair of eagles squaring off, a hundred yards apart.

'Nothing.'

'Looking Glass,' the voice on the intercom became cautious. *'Please respond immediately with your authentication code.'*

Schofield saw the Penetrator's downturned wings—saw the missiles hanging from them.

They looked like Sidewinders.

Sidewinders . . . Schofield thought.

Then, abruptly, he hit the 'TALK' button on his console. 'Penetrator gunship, this is Captain Shane Schofield, United States Marine Corps, Presidential Detachment. I am now in command of this helicopter. I've only got one word to say to you.'

'And what is that?'

'Draw,' Schofield said flatly.

Silence.

Then: *'Okay . . .'*

'What the hell are you doing?' Book II said.

Schofield didn't reply. He just kept his eyes locked on the Penetrator's wings.

A moment later, with a flash of light, an AIM-9M

Sidewinder missile blasted forward from the left-hand wing of the Penetrator.

'Oh, *shit* . . .' Book II breathed.

Schofield saw the charging missile from head-on—saw its domed nose, saw the star-shaped outline of its stabilising fins, saw the looping smoketrail issuing out behind it as it rolled through the air *heading straight for them*!

'What are you *doing*?' Book II exclaimed. 'Are you just going to sit there—?'

And then Schofield did the strangest thing.

He jammed his finger down on his control stick's trigger.

With the Sidewinder missile hurtling toward it—and only a bare second away from impact—the Super Stallion's nose-mounted Gatling gun came to life, spewing forth a line of glowing orange tracer bullets.

Schofield angled the line of laser-like bullets toward the oncoming missile, and just as the missile came within twenty yards of his helicopter—*boom!*—his bullets hit the Sidewinder *right on its forward dome*, causing it to explode in mid-air, fifteen yards short of the hovering Super Stallion.

'What the—?' Book II said.

But Schofield wasn't finished.

Now that the Sidewinder was out of the way, he swung his line of tracer bullets back up toward the Penetrator.

In the near distance, he could see the Perpetrator's two pilots fumbling to launch another missile, but it was too late.

Schofield's tracer bullets rammed into the canopy of the Penetrator—one after the other after the other—pummelling it, pounding it, causing the entire attack helicopter to recoil helplessly in the air.

Schofield's relentless stream of bullets must have gone right *through* the Penetrator's cockpit, because an instant later, one of the chopper's fuel tanks ignited and the whole attack helicopter spontaneously exploded, bursting into a billowing ball of flames before the entire flaming chopper just *dropped* out of the sky and crashed into the water below.

★

With the Penetrator out of the way, Schofield gunned his Super Stallion down the western canyonway, heading for the narrow slot canyon into which the rogue bipod had disappeared.

'What the hell did you do back there?' Book II asked.

'Huh?'

'I didn't know you could shoot down a missile with tracer bullets.'

'Only Sidewinders,' Schofield said. 'Sidewinders are heat-seekers—they use an infra-red system to lock in on their targets. But to accomplish that, the forward seeker dome on the missile has to allow infra-red radiation to *pass through* it. That means using a material *other* than plate steel. The seeker dome of a Sidewinder is actually made of a very fragile transparent plastic. It's a weak point on the missile.'

'You shot it at its weak point?'

'I did.'

'Pretty risky strategy.'

'I saw it coming. Not many people get to see a Sidewinder from head-on. It was worth taking the chance.'

'Are you always this risky?' Book II asked evenly.

Schofield turned at the question.

He paused before answering, appraised the young sergeant beside him.

'I try not to be,' he said. 'But sometimes . . . it's unavoidable.'

They came to the narrow slot canyon into which the South African bipod had fled.

The little canyon was cloaked in shadow, and it was a lot narrower than Schofield thought it would be. His Super Stallion's whizzing rotor blades only just fitted between its high rock walls.

The giant helicopter roared along the narrow canyon, moving through the shadows, before abruptly it burst out into brilliant sunshine, out into a wide crater-like lake bounded by three-hundred-foot-high vertical rock walls and with a small mesa at its northern end.

As with the other crater, the sandstorm up above the canyon system invaded this open stretch of water. The wind-hurled sand fell like rain, in slanting wave-like sheets. It assaulted Schofield's windshield, drummed against it.

'You see anything?' Schofield yelled.

'Over there!' Book II pointed off to their left, at the vertical outer wall of the crater opposite the mesa, at a point where a particularly wide canyon branched westward, away from the circular mini-lake.

There, Schofield saw a tiny rivercraft sitting on the water's surface, bucking with the medium-sized waves generated by the sandstorm.

It was the rogue South African bipod.

And it was alone.

Schofield's Super Stallion zoomed over the water-filled desert crater, flying low and fast, its rotors thumping.

Schofield stared at the bipod as they came closer.

It appeared to be stationary, as if it were lying at anchor, about twenty yards out from where the sheer rock wall of the crater plunged down into the water.

Schofield swung the Super Stallion to a halt thirty yards away from the bipod, kept it in a hovering pattern ten feet above the choppy surface of the water. Wind-hurled sand pelted the windshield.

He looked at the bipod more closely—a rope of some sort stretched down into the water beneath it.

The bipod *was* at anchor . . .

And then suddenly he saw movement.

On the bipod.

Through the veil of flying sand, he saw a pudgy-looking, bald-headed man in shirtsleeves get to his feet inside the left-hand pod, the driver's pod.

Gunther Botha.

Botha had been bent over in his pod, doing something, when Schofield's chopper had arrived under the cover of the roaring sandstorm.

In the *right-hand* section of the bipod, however, Schofield saw someone else.

It was the tiny figure of Kevin, looking very small and out of place in the fearsomely equipped gunner's pod.

Schofield felt relief wash over his body.

They'd found him.

Schofield's voice boomed out from the exterior speakers of the Super Stallion: '*Doctor Gunther Botha, we are United States Marines! You are now under arrest! Hand over the boy, and give yourself up now!*'

Botha didn't seem to care. He just hurriedly tossed something square and metallic over the side of his bipod. It splashed into the water and sank, disappearing.

What the hell is he doing? Schofield thought.

Inside the Super Stallion's cockpit, he turned to Book. 'Open the loading ramp. Then bring us around, rear-end first.'

The Super Stallion turned laterally, rotating in mid-air as its rear loading ramp folded down, opening.

The giant chopper's rear-end came round toward the stationary bipod, hovering ten feet above the water. Schofield stood on the now-open loading ramp, his Desert Eagle pistol in his hand, a hand-mike in the other, wind-blown sand flying wildly all around him.

He raised the microphone to his lips.

'*The boy, Botha,*' his amplified voice boomed.

Still Botha didn't seem to care.

Kevin, however, turned in his seat and saw Schofield, standing in the hold of the Super Stallion. A broad smile appeared across the little boy's face. He waved—a child's wave, his arm swatting rapidly from side to side.

Schofield waved back briefly.

At the moment, he was more concerned with what Botha was up to, for now he could see the fat South African virologist much more clearly.

Botha had a scuba tank strapped to his back, over his

white shirtsleeves. He hurriedly threw a full-face diving mask to Kevin and gesticulated for the little boy to put it on.

Schofield frowned. *Scuba gear?*

Whatever Botha was doing, it was time to stop him.

Schofield raised his gun and was about to fire across Botha's bow to get his attention, when suddenly there came a loud whumping noise from somewhere close above him and completely without warning, he saw the tail rotor of his Super Stallion blast out into a million pieces and *separate completely* from the rest of the chopper!

Like a tree branch snapping, the Super Stallion's tail boom broke free of the chopper's main body and dropped down into the water, causing the entire helicopter to spin wildly and veer away from the bipod.

With its tail rotor gone, the Super Stallion spun out of control—and wheeled down toward the water's surface below.

Book II wrestled with the chopper's control stick, but the Super Stallion was beyond salvation. It rolled sharply in the air, heading nose-first for the water.

In the rear cargo bay, Schofield was hurled against the side wall, somehow managed to get a grip on a canvas seat there.

The Super Stallion hit the lake.

Water flew everywhere, a gigantic whitewater splash.

The big helicopter's nose *drove* down into the water, going under for a full ten seconds before its buoyancy righted it again, and the massive chopper bobbed slowly on the surface.

Book II hit the kill switch and the chopper's engines died instantly. Its rotor blades began to slow.

Water rushed into the cargo hold.

It didn't come in through the open rear loading ramp just yet—since the ramp was designed to rest just above the water's surface in the event of a water landing—but rather it entered the crashed helicopter via the small access hatch that Schofield and Book II had used to enter it earlier.

A Super Stallion is built to stay afloat for a short while in a water crash, but since Schofield and Book had discarded the chopper's floor access hatch when they'd entered it, this Super Stallion wasn't even going to do that.

It was sinking. Fast.

Schofield ran into the cockpit. 'What the hell was that? Something hit us!'

'I know,' Book II said. He nodded out through the windshield. 'I think it was them.'

Schofield peered out through the forward windshield.

Hovering above the water in front of their sinking helicopter, partially obscured by the veil of wind-hurled sand—and flanking the anchored South African bipod—were the two remaining Air Force Penetrators.

The Super Stallion sank with frightening speed.

Water gurgled up through the access hatch, expanding outward as it rose up into the cargo hold, pulling the rear end of the chopper down into the lake.

As more water rushed into it, the helicopter dropped lower in the water. Within a minute, the rear loading ramp fell below the waterline and from that moment on, water came *flooding* in through the wide rear opening.

Up in the cockpit, Schofield and Book II were standing ankle-deep in water when abruptly the entire chopper tilted sharply skyward.

'Any risky ideas now?' Book II shouted, grabbing for a handhold.

'Not a one.'

The Super Stallion continued to sink slowly, rear-end first.

With the Football still hanging from his side, Schofield looked out through the cockpit's forward windshield.

He saw one of the Penetrators approach Gunther Botha's bipod. It hovered directly in front of the tiny rivercraft, like a gigantic menacing vulture.

Schofield saw Botha stand in his pod and face the black Air Force helicopter—waving. With his arms flailing, he looked like a tiny pathetic figure beseeching an angry bird-god.

Then, without warning, a Stinger missile shot down from

the right-hand wing of the Penetrator, trailing a dead-straight finger of white smoke.

The missile hit Botha's pod and *blasted* it out of the water.

One second Botha was there, the next he was gone, replaced by a frothing circle of ripples.

Kevin's pod, however, remained intact—severed cleanly from Botha's by the missile impact.

His pod and the cracked remains of the bipod's cross-beam just bobbed in the water under the steely gaze of the hovering Penetrator.

From his position inside the sinking Super Stallion, Schofield blanched.

They'd just killed Botha!

Holy shit.

His Super Stallion was now three-quarters underwater—its entire rear section underneath the surface. Only its dome-like glass windshield and the tip of one of its rotor blades still protruded above the waterline.

Water began to lap up against the outside of the windshield.

The entire rear cargo hold was now filled with encroaching dark-green liquid—water that wanted to rise into the cockpit, and devour the whole helicopter.

The chopper sank further.

Through the green-tinged waves slapping against the windshield, Schofield saw the Air Force Penetrator swing in above the half-destroyed bipod and lower a rescue harness down to Kevin.

'Ah, damn it,' he said aloud.

But the Super Stallion just continued to sink—down and down—and the last thing Schofield saw before the windshield was completely covered over by lapping green water, was the image of Kevin being hauled up toward the Penetrator on the harness and being pulled into the rear section of the attack helicopter's three-man cockpit.

Then the windshield was covered over completely and Schofield saw nothing but green.

★

The two Air Force Penetrators were well aware of who was inside the Super Stallion.

Their calls to 'Looking Glass' on a designated alternate frequency had gone unanswered for the last few minutes. Indeed, it was a transponder trace on the Super Stallion that had led them to this crater—where they had found Botha and the boy.

The two Penetrators hovered above the sinking Super Stallion, watching it founder, watching it drown.

Inside the lead Penetrator sat Python Willis, the commander of Charlie Unit. He gazed intently at the sinking Super Stallion, making sure it disappeared beneath the waves.

The Super Stallion's cockpit went under, followed by the tip of its rotor blade—the last remaining part of the helicopter above the waterline.

A legion of bubbles rose instantly to the surface as every ounce of air inside the sinking helicopter was replaced with water.

The two Penetrators waited.

The Super Stallion disappeared into the inky green depths of the lake, trailing multiple lines of bubbles.

Still Python Willis waited—until the bubbles stopped coming, until he was sure that there could be no air whatsoever inside the sunken helicopter.

After a few minutes, the water surface became calm.

Still the two Penetrators waited.

They lingered another ten minutes, just to be absolutely certain that nobody came up. If anyone did, they would finish them off.

Nobody came up.

At last, Python made the decision and the two Penetrators wheeled around in the air and headed back toward Area 7.

No-one could have stayed under that long, not even inside an air pocket. The air in a pocket would have gone bad by now.

No.

Shane Schofield—and whoever else was in that Super Stallion with him—was now, without a doubt, dead.

Gant, Mother, Juliet and the President were still on Level 4, in the semi-darkened observation lab. Hot Rod Hagerty and Nicholas Tate were also still with them.

'We should move,' Gant said.

'What are you thinking?' Mother asked.

'No. What are you *doing*, Sergeant Gant?' Hot Rod demanded.

'We shouldn't stay here,' Gant said.

'But this is a perfectly good hiding place.'

'We should keep moving. If they're searching for us, and we stay in the same place, they'll eventually find us. We should move at least once every twenty minutes.'

'And where exactly did you learn this?' Hagerty asked.

'It's in the training manual for Officer Candidate School,' Gant said. 'Standard evasive techniques. Surely you read it at some point in your career. Besides, there's something else I'd like to check out—'

Hagerty went red. 'I will not be spoken to like that by a *sergeant*—'

'Yes. You will,' Mother stepped up to Hagerty. At six-two, she towered over him. She nodded over at Gant: 'Because that little chickadee is smarter and cooler in a combat situation than you'll ever be. And, for your information, she ain't gonna be a sergeant for long. Soon she's gonna be an officer.

And I'll tell *you* something, I'd put my life in her hands before I put it in yours.'

Hagerty pursed his lips. 'Right. That's—'

'Colonel Hagerty,' the President said, stepping forward, 'Sergeant Gant has saved my life twice this morning—on the train downstairs and then on the platform. In both instances, she was decisive and cool-headed in a situation that would have brought many other people unstuck. I am happy to trust my safety to her judgement.'

'Fucking-A,' Mother said. 'The power of estrogen, man.'

'Sergeant Gant,' the President said. 'What are you thinking?'

Gant smiled, her sky-blue eyes gleaming.

'I'm thinking we do something about that transmitter attached to your heart, sir.'

In his sterile windowless room on the second-to-bottom floor of the Pentagon, Dave Fairfax was still hard at work decoding the intercepted telephone conversations that had come out of United States Air Force Special Area (Restricted) No. 7.

Having decrypted the incoming and outgoing messages in Afrikaans, Fairfax was pretty pleased with himself.

There was, however, still one thing that nagged at him. The two messages in English that he had found in amongst the Afrikaans messages.

He played the two messages again, listened intently.

16-JUN	19:56:09	ENGLISH – ENGLISH
VOICE 3:	Everything is in place.	*Everything is in place.*
	Confirm that it's the third.	*Confirm that it's the third.*

22-JUN	20:51:59	ENGLISH – ENGLISH
VOICE 3:	Mission is a go.	*Mission is a go.*

One thing was certain. It was the same voice on both messages.

A man's voice. American. Southern accent. Speaking slowly, deliberately.

276

Fairfax pushed his glasses up onto his nose, started typing on his keyboard.

He brought up a voice analysis program.

Then he compared the taped voice's digital signature—or 'voiceprint'—with the signatures of every other voice in the DIA's mainframe, every voice the Agency had ever secretly recorded.

Spiked displays whizzed across his screen as the program accessed the Agency's massive database of voiceprints.

And then the computer beeped:

6 MATCHES FOUND
DISPLAY ALL MATCHES?

'Yes, please,' Fairfax said as he hit the 'Y' key.
Six entries appeared on his screen:

No.	DATE	DIVISION	SOURCE FILE
1.	29-May	SPACEDIV-01	SAT-SURV (FILE 034-77A)
2.	07-Jun	SPACEDIV-01	SAT-SURV (FILE 034-77A)
3.	16-Jun	SPACEDIV-02	USAF-SA(R)07 (FILE 009-21D)
4.	22-Jun	SPACEDIV-02	USAF-SA(R)07 (FILE 009-21D)
5.	02-Jul	SPACEDIV-01	SAT-SURV (FILE 034-77A)
6.	03-Jul	SPACEDIV-01	SAT-SURV (FILE 034-77A)

Okay, Fairfax thought.

He discarded the third and the fourth entries—they were the two messages that he'd just played. Their division designator, **SPACEDIV-02**, meant his own section, Section 2.

The other four messages, however, were the property of Section 1, the main unit of Space Division located across the hall.

The source file for the Section 1 messages, **SAT-SURV**, stood for 'Satellite Surveillance'. Section 1, it seemed, had been tapping into foreign satellite transmissions lately.

Fairfax clicked on the first entry:

VOICE 1: They did the test this morning. The vaccine is operational against all previous strains. All they need now is a sample of the latest version.

Fairfax frowned. The messages in Afrikaans had also mentioned a vaccine. And a successful test.

He hit the next entry:

7-JUN 23:47:33 SATELLITE INTERCEPT (ENGLISH)

VOICE 1: Virus snatch team is en route to Changchun. Names are CAPTAIN ROBERT WU and LIEUTENANT CHET LI. Both can be trusted. As discussed, the price for delivery of the vaccine to you will be one hundred and twenty million dollars, ten million for each of the twelve men involved.

Changchun, Fairfax thought. The Chinese bio-weapons production facility.

And a hundred and twenty million dollars, to be divided among twelve men.

This was getting interesting.

Next:

2-JUL 02:21:57 SATELLITE INTERCEPT (CHINESE–ENGLISH)

VOICE 1: Copy that, Yellow Star. We'll be there.

What is this—? Fairfax thought.

Yellow Star?

But that was the . . .

He clicked on the final message:

3-JUL 04:04:42 SATELLITE INTERCEPT (ENGLISH)

VOICE 1: WU and LI have arrived back at Area 7 with the virus. Your men are with them. All the money has been accounted for. Names of my men who will need to be extracted: BENNETT, CALVERT, COLEMAN, DAYTON, FROMMER, GRAYSON, LITTLETON, MESSICK, OLIVER and myself.

Fairfax was looking at the names on the last message when suddenly the door to his subterranean office was flung open and his boss—a tall, bald bureaucrat named Eugene Wisher—stormed into the room, followed by three heavily armed military policemen. Wisher was in charge of the operation going on across the hall—the tracking of the newly launched Chinese space shuttle.

'Fairfax!' he bellowed. 'What the hell are you doing in here!'

Fairfax gulped, eyed the MPs' guns fearfully. 'Uh, wha— what are you talking about?'

'Why are you accessing intercepted transmissions from our operation?'

'Your operation?' Fairfax said.

'Yes. Our operation. Why are you downloading information from the mainframe that pertains to the classified operation going on in Section 1?'

Fairfax fell silent, deep in thought, while his boss kept yelling at him.

And suddenly it all became very, very clear.

'Oh, Christ,' he breathed.

It took some explaining—at gunpoint—but after five minutes, Dave Fairfax suddenly found himself standing in front of two DIA Assistant Directors in the operations room across the hall from his windowless office.

Monitors glowed all around the room, technicians worked at over a dozen consoles—all of it related to the tracking of the newly launched Chinese Space Shuttle, the *Yellow Star*.

'I need a personnel list for Special Area 7,' the twenty-five-year-old Fairfax said to the two high-ranking DIA chiefs standing before him.

A list came.

Fairfax looked at it. It read:

UNITED STATES AIR FORCE
SPECIAL AREA (RESTRICTED) 07
ON-SITE PERSONNEL
CLASSIFICATION: TOP SECRET

NAME	UNIT	NAME	UNIT	NAME	UNIT

COMMAND UNIT
Harper, JT (CO)

7TH SQUADRON

Alvarez, MJ	A	Dillan, ST	D	Logan, KW (MAJ)	A
Arthurs, RT	C	Doheny, FG	A	McConnell, BA	B
Atlock, FD	B	Egan, RR	B	Messick, K	E
Baines, AW	A	Fraser, MS	C	Milbourn, SK	D
Bennett, B	E	Fredericks, GH	A	Morton, IN	C
Biggs, NM	C	Frommer, SN	E	Nance, GF	D
Boland, CS	B	Gale, A	D	Nystrom, JJ	D
Boyce, LW	D	Giggs, RE	B	Oliver, PK	E
Calvert, ET	E	Golding, DK	D	Price, AL	C
Carney, LE	E	Goldman, WE	A	Rawson, MJ	C
Christian, FC	A	Grayson, SR	E	Sayles, MT	B
Coleman, GK	E	Hughes, R	A	Sommers, SR	C
Coles, M	B	Ingliss, WA	B	Stone, JK	C
Crick, DT	D	Johnson, SW	D	Taylor, AS	B
Criece, TW	A	Jones, M	D	Willis, LS	C
Davis, LR	C	Kincaid, R	B	Wolfson, HT	A
Dayton, M	E	Littleton, SO	E		

CIVILIAN STAFF

Botha, GW	MED
Franklin, HS	MED
Shaw, DE	MED

Fairfax grabbed a printout of the last message he had downloaded earlier.

3-JUL	04:04:42	SATELLITE INTERCEPT	(ENGLISH)

VOICE 1: WU and LI have arrived back at Area 7 with the virus. Your men are with them. All the money has been accounted for. Names of my men who will need to be extracted: **BENNETT, CALVERT, COLEMAN, DAYTON, FROMMER, GRAYSON, LITTLETON, MESSICK, OLIVER** and myself.

'Okay,' he pulled a fluorescent pink highlighter from the neck of his Mooks T-shirt. 'Bennett, Calvert, Coleman . . .'

He started highlighting the personnel list. When he was done, it looked like this:

UNITED STATES AIR FORCE
SPECIAL AREA (RESTRICTED) 07
ON-SITE PERSONNEL
CLASSIFICATION: TOP SECRET

NAME	UNIT	NAME	UNIT	NAME	UNIT
COMMAND UNIT					
Harper, JT (CO)					
7TH SQUADRON					
Alvarez, MJ	A	Dillan, ST	D	Logan, KW (MAJ)	A
Arthurs, RT	C	Doheny, FG	A	McConnell, BA	B
Atlock, FD	B	Egan, RR	B	Messick, K	E
Baines, AW	A	Fraser, MS	C	Milbourn, SK	D
Bennett, B	E	Fredericks, GH	A	Morton, IN	C
Biggs, NM	C	Frommer, SN	E	Nance, GF	D
Boland, CS	B	Gale, A	D	Nystrom, JJ	D
Boyce, LW	D	Giggs, RE	B	Oliver, PK	E
Calvert, ET	E	Golding, DK	D	Price, AL	C
Carney, LE	E	Goldman, WE	A	Rawson, MJ	C
Christian, FC	A	Grayson, SR	E	Sayles, MT	B
Coleman, GK	E	Hughes, R	A	Sommers, SR	C
Coles, M	B	Ingliss, WA	B	Stone, JK	C
Crick, DT	D	Johnson, SW	D	Taylor, AS	B
Criece, TW	A	Jones, M	D	Willis, LS	C
Davis, LR	C	Kincaid, R	B	Wolfson, HT	A
Dayton, AM	E	Littleton, SO	E		

CIVILIAN STAFF

Botha, GW	MED
Franklin, HS	MED
Shaw, DE	MED

'Anybody else see a pattern here?' Fairfax said.

All of the men named in the intercepted transmission were from the unit designated 'E'—or in military parlance 'Echo'.

'The only man in "E" who *isn't* mentioned,' Fairfax said, 'is this one, "Carney, LE". I can only assume that he's the man speaking on the tape.'

Fairfax turned to the two DIA chiefs standing beside him.

282

'There's a rogue unit at that base. A rogue unit that has been communicating with the Chinese government and its new space shuttle. All the men in Echo Unit.'

'—Echo Unit. Report—'

'—*This is Echo leader,*' the voice of Captain Lee 'Cobra' Carney replied.

Cobra spoke with a slow Southern drawl—measured, icy, dangerous. '*We're in the Level 3 livin' quarters. Just swept the two underground hangar levels. Nothin' there. Workin' our way down through the complex now, coverin' the stairwell as we go.*'

'—Copy that, Echo leader—'

'Sir,' another of the radio operators turned to Caesar Russell, 'Charlie Unit just arrived back from the lake. They're outside, and they have the boy.'

'Good. Losses?'

'Five.'

'Acceptable. And Botha?' Caesar asked.

'Dead.'

'Even better. Let them in through the top door.'

Gant and the others headed for the fire stairwell at the eastern end of Level 4.

'I know this isn't exactly relevant to the present situation,' Mother said as she and Gant walked side-by-side, 'but I've been meaning to ask you about your little date with the Scarecrow last Saturday. You haven't said anything about it.'

284

Gant gave Mother a crooked grin. 'Not looking for gossip, are we, Mother?'

'Why, hell yes. That's exactly what I'm looking for. Old married hags like me get off hearing about the sexual gymnastics of pretty young things like you. And I was just, you know . . . interested.'

Gant smiled sadly. 'It didn't go as well as I would have liked.'

'How do you mean?'

Gant shrugged, kept walking, gun in hand. 'He didn't kiss me. We had a great dinner at this quiet little restaurant, then we walked along the banks of the Potomac, just talking. God, we talked all evening. And then, when he dropped me home, I was hoping that he'd kiss me. But he . . . just . . . didn't. And so we stood there awkwardly and said we'd see each other later, and the date just . . . ended.'

Mother's eyes narrowed. 'Oooh, Scarecrow. I'll kick your ass . . .'

'Please don't,' Gant said as they came to the door leading to the stairwell. 'And don't tell him I told you anything.'

Mother ground her teeth. 'Mmm, okay . . .'

'In any case, I'd rather not think about it right now,' Gant said. 'We've got work to do.'

She opened the firedoor a crack, peered through it, her gun raised beside her face.

The stairwell was dark and silent.

Empty.

'Stairwell's clear,' she whispered.

She opened the door fully, took a few steps up the stairs.

Mother moved into position behind her, both of their eyes looking up the barrels of their guns.

They came to the Level 3 landing, saw the door leading into the complex's living quarters.

There was no-one here.

That's odd, Gant thought.

There were no soldiers stationed on the landing, not even a sentry left there to block their movement up through the complex.

Very odd, she thought. If she had been in charge of the opposing forces, she would be flushing every floor for the President, and *ensuring* that she blocked off the stairwell while she did so.

Obviously, the 7th Squadron operated differently.

With the stairwell unguarded, Gant and her team made swift progress upwards, came to the Level 2 hangar bay.

The Level 2 hangar—untouched, so far, by the mayhem of the day—was practically identical to the one above it, the only difference being that the collection of planes inside it was far less exotic. While the Level 1 hangar contained its pair of Stealth bombers and the SR-71 Blackbird, this one only held two AWACS surveillance aeroplanes.

Which was exactly what Gant wanted.

Two minutes later, she was inside the lower cargo hold of one of the AWACS planes, unscrewing a heavy lead panel in the floor.

The panel came free, revealing an electronics compartment—and in the middle of that compartment, secured firmly in place, was a very sturdy-looking fluorescent-orange unit, about the size of a small shoebox. The orange box appeared to be made of some superstrong material.

'What's that?' Juliet Janson asked from behind Gant.

The President answered for her. 'It's the plane's flight data recorder. The black box.'

'Doesn't look very black,' Ramrod Hagerty said sourly.

'They never are,' Gant said, extracting the small orange unit from its nook. 'It's just the name they're known by. Black boxes are nearly always painted bright orange, for better visibility in a wreck. That said, they're usually found another way—'

'Oh, *very good* . . .' the President said.

'What?' Hagerty asked. 'What?'

'Ever wondered how they find the black box so fast after an aeroplane crash?' Gant said. 'When a plane goes down, debris is spread all over the place, yet they always find the flight data recorder very quickly, usually within a few hours.'

'Yes . . .'

Gant said, 'That's because all black boxes have a battery-powered transponder inside them. That transponder emits a high-powered microwave signal, giving the box's location to crash investigators.'

'So what are you going to do with it?' Hagerty asked.

Gant called up through the hatch above her. 'Mother!'

'*Yeah?*' Mother's voice floated back.

'You found that signal yet?'

'*I'll have it in two seconds!*'

Gant gave Hagerty a look. 'I'm going to try to imperson-ate the signal coming from the President's heart.'

In the main cabin of the AWACS plane, Mother sat at a computer console.

She pulled up the screen showing the microwave signal coming into Area 7 from the low-orbit satellite. It was the same screen Brainiac had found inside the other AWACS plane earlier, depicting a twenty-five-second rebounding signature.

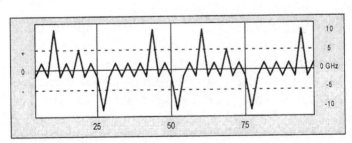

Gant came up from the cargo hold with the orange-coloured black box. She plugged a cable into a socket on its side, con-necting it to Mother's terminal. Immediately, the spike graph appeared on a small illuminated LCD screen on the black box's top.

'Okay,' Gant said to Mother, 'see that search signal, the

upward spike? I want you to set it as the "find" frequency on the black box.'

When crash investigators search for a black box, they use a radio transmitter to emit a preset microwave signal called the 'find' frequency. When the black box's transponder detects that signal, it sends out a return signal, revealing its location.

'Okay . . .' Mother said, typing. 'Done.'

'Good,' Gant said. 'Now set that rebounding frequency— the downward spike—as the return signal.'

'Okay, just a minute.'

'Will the signal strength from the black box be powerful enough to reach all the way up to the satellite?' the President asked.

'I think it'll work. They used microwave signals to talk to Armstrong on the moon, and SETI uses them to send messages into outer space.' Gant smiled. 'It's not the size that matters, it's the quality of the signal.'

'All right, done,' Mother said. She turned to Gant. 'So, Fearless Leader, what exactly *have* I just created?'

'Mother, if you've done it right, when we activate the transmitter inside this black box, we'll be mimicking the signal coming out of the President's heart.'

'So what now?' the President asked.

'Yes,' Hagerty said meanly. 'Do we just switch it on?'

'Definitely not. If we turn it on, the satellite will pick up *two* identical signals, and that might cause it to detonate the bombs. We can't risk that. No, we've just laid the groundwork. Now it's time for the hard part. Now we have to *substitute* the black box's signal for the President's.'

'And how do we do *that*?' Hagerty asked. 'Please don't tell me that you're going to perform open-heart surgery on the President of the United States with a pocket knife?'

'Do I look like MacGyver to you?' Gant asked. 'No. My theory is this: somehow Caesar Russell got that transmitter onto the President's heart . . .'

'That's right. He did it during an operation I had a few years ago,' the President said.

288

'But I'm figuring he didn't turn it on until today,' Gant said. 'The White House's scanners would have picked up an unauthorised signal as soon as it was turned on.'

'Yes, so . . .' Hagerty said.

'So,' Gant said, 'somewhere in this complex, Caesar Russell has a unit that turns the President's transmitter on and off. I'm guessing that that unit—probably just a hand-held initiate/terminate unit of some kind—is sitting in the same room as Caesar himself.'

'It is,' the President said, recalling the small unit that Caesar Russell had turned on at the very start of the challenge. 'He had it when he appeared on the television sets before, at the beginning of all this. It's red, hand-held, with a black stub antenna.'

'Right then,' Gant said. 'Now all we have to do is find his command centre.' She turned to Juliet. 'Your people have checked out this place. Any ideas?'

Juliet said, 'The main hangar. In the building overlooking the floor. There's a whole command-and-control room up there.'

'Then that's where we're going,' Gant said. 'So what we do now is simple. First, we take Caesar Russell's command centre. Then, *in between* the search signals sent down from the satellite, we use his initiate/terminate unit to turn off the transmitter attached to the President's heart, while a second later, we turn *on* the black box.'

She gave the President a wry smile. 'Like I said. Simple.'

The five remaining members of Charlie Unit were moving quickly through a low concrete tunnel, all running in a half-crouch.

Trotting along with them—and because of his height, not needing to crouch—was Kevin.

Charlie Unit had just returned from Lake Powell, after killing Botha, retrieving Kevin, and watching Schofield's chopper drown.

They had parked their two Penetrators outside and were now re-entering the complex through an entrance that connected the main facility with one of the outside hangars, an entrance known as the 'top door'.

The top door's tunnel opened onto the rear of the personnel elevator shaft, at ground level, by virtue of a foot-thick titanium door.

Charlie Unit came to the heavy silver door.

Python Willis punched in the appropriate override code. The top door was a special entrance to Area 7—if you were senior enough to know the override code, you could open it anytime, even during a lockdown.

The thick titanium door swung open—

—and Python froze.

He saw the roof of the personnel elevator parked just below his feet, sitting right there in front of him.

And standing on top of it, was Cobra Carney and four members of Echo Unit.

The other half of Echo, Python saw through the hatch in the elevator's roof, were down in the car itself.

'Jesus, Cobra,' Python said, 'you scared the shit out of me. Wasn't expecting to see you guys here—'

'Caesar told us to come get you,' Cobra drawled. 'Make sure you all got in okay.'

Python shoved Kevin forward, onto the roof of the stopped elevator. 'We lost five, but we got him.'

'Good,' Cobra said. '*Very* good.'

It was then that—through the roof hatch of the elevator— Python saw *four more men* standing in the elevator car with the Echo men.

Four Asian men.

Python frowned.

They were the four men who had been inside the decompression chamber earlier that morning—7th Squadron Captain Robert Wu and Lieutenant Chet Li, and the two Chinese lab workers. The men who had brought the latest strain of the Sinovirus back to Area 7.

'Cobra, what's going on?' Python said suddenly, looking up.

'Sorry, Python,' Cobra said.

And with that he gave a short nod to his men.

In a flash, the four members of Echo Unit on the elevator's roof raised their P-90s and unleashed a withering storm of fire on Charlie Unit.

Python Willis was hit by about a million rounds. His face and chest were turned instantly to mush. The four Charlie men behind him also dropped like flailing marionettes, one after the other, until the only figure left standing on that side of the elevator's roof was the wide-eyed and terrified Kevin.

Cobra Carney strode forward and grabbed the little boy roughly by the arm.

'Smile, kid, you're coming with me now.'

The control room overlooking the main hangar was quiet.

Boa McConnell and the four other surviving members of Bravo Unit sat slumped in the corner, looking bloodied and dirty. Two of Boa's men were seriously wounded. Colonel Jerome T. Harper—the ostensible CO of Area 7, but in reality a minion of Caesar Russell—tended to their wounds.

Another figure sat at the back of the room, shrouded in shadow—he had been sitting inside the control room for the whole morning, never uttering a word. He just watched silently.

Major Kurt Logan and the remainder of Alpha Unit were also in the control room. Logan now stood with Caesar, whispering in hushed tones. His Alpha Unit had fared little better than Bravo Unit: of his original team of ten men, including himself, there were only four left.

Caesar, however, seemed absolutely unperturbed by their losses.

'Any word from Echo Unit?'

'Cobra reports that they are now on Level 4. No sign of the President yet—'

'Damn it, *shit!*'

It was one of the other radio operators. His computer monitor had just blinked out.

There had been no warning. No dying whine.

'What is it?' the head operator asked.

'*Fuck!*' another radio man yelled as his monitor also crashed.

It spread around the control room like a virus. All around the command centre, one after the other, monitors blinked out.

'—Air-conditioning systems just went down—'

'—Water cooling system is gone—'

'What's going on?' Caesar Russell said calmly.

'—Power to the cell bay is falling rapidly—'

'The complex's power supply is crashing,' the senior operator said to Russell. 'But I don't know why . . .'

He brought up a system display screen.

S.A.(R) 07-A

SECURITY ACCESS LOG

SOURCE POWER HISTORY (3-JUL)

7-3-010223077

TIME	KEY ACTION	OPERATOR	SYSTEM RESPONSE
06:30:00	System status check	070-67	All systems operational
06:58:34	Lockdown command	105-02	Lockdown enacted
07:00:00	System status check	070-67	All systems operational (lockdown mode)
07:30:00	System status check	070-67	All systems operational (lockdown mode)
07:37:56	WARNING: Auxiliary power malfunction	System	Malfunction located at terminal 1-A2 Receiving no response from systems: TRACS; AUX SYS-1; RAD COMS-SPHERE; MBN; EXT FAN
07:38:00	WARNING: Auxiliary power capacity: 50%	System	Terminal 1-A2 not responding
08:00:15	Main power shutdown command (terminal 3-A1)	008-72	Main power disabled
08:00:18	Auxiliary power enabled	Aux System	Auxiliary power start up

08:00:19	WARNING: Auxiliary power operational. Low power protocol enabled	Aux System	Low power protocol in effect: non-essential systems disabled
08:01:02	Lockdown special release command entered (terminal 3-A1)	008-72	Door 003-V opened
08:04:34	Lockdown special release command entered (terminal 3-A1)	008-72	Door 062-W opened
08:04:55	Lockdown special release command entered (terminal 3-A1)	008-72	Door 100-W opened
08:18:00	WARNING: Auxiliary power capacity: 35%	Aux System	Terminal 1-A2 not responding
08:21:30	Security camera system shutdown command (terminal 1-A1)	008-93	SYSTEM ERROR: Security camera system already disabled per low power protocol
08:38:00	WARNING: Auxiliary power capacity: 25%	Aux System	Terminal 1-A2 not responding
08:58:00	WARNING: Auxiliary power capacity: 15%	Aux System	Terminal 1-A2 not responding
09:04:43	Lockdown special release command entered (terminal 3-A2)	077-01E	Door 62-E opened
09:08:00	WARNING: Auxiliary power capacity: 10%	Aux System	Initiate system reboot?
09:18:00	WARNING: Auxiliary power capacity: 5%	Aux System	Initiate system reboot?
09:28:00	WARNING: Auxiliary power capacity: 0%	Aux System	Commence system shutdown

'Jesus, we've been running on auxiliary power since eight o'clock!' the senior console operator said.

Colonel Harper stepped forward. 'But that should have kept us going for at least three hours, enough time to reboot the main power supply.'

While they spoke, Caesar gazed at the computer screen, at the entry:

09:04:43	Lockdown special release command entered (terminal 3-A2)	077-01E	Door 62-E opened

The '077' prefix indicated a member of the 7th Squadron. 'E' stood for Echo Unit; and '01', its leader, Cobra Carney.

Caesar's eyes narrowed. It appeared that during the last lockdown window period, Cobra Carney had opened Door 62-E—the eastern X-rail blast door down on Level 6 . . .

Jerome Harper and the radio man were still debating the power situation.

'It should have, yes,' the radio man said. 'But it appears the system only had *half* power when it kicked in, so it only lasted an hour and a half—'

The senior man's monitor blinked out. It was the last one to go.

Then, all at once, the overhead lights in the control room went out.

Caesar and the console operators were devoured by darkness.

Caesar spun, turned to look out through the windows overlooking the enormous ground-level hangar. He saw the bright halogen lights running along the length of the hangar shut off in sequence, one after the other after the other.

The hangar—and all its contents: Marine One, the destroyed cockroach towing vehicles, the blasted-open Nighthawk Two, the overhead crane system—was consumed by inky blackness.

'All systems down,' someone said in the darkness. 'The whole complex has lost power.'

Down in the AWACS plane on Level 2, Libby Gant and the others were preparing to head up through the underground base, to locate and take out Caesar Russell's control room, when without warning every single light in the subterranean hangar went out.

The gigantic hangar was plunged into darkness.

Pitch darkness.

Gant flicked on the pencil-sized flashlight attached to the barrel of her MP-10. Its thin beam illuminated her face.

'The power,' Mother whispered. 'Why would they cut the power?'

'Yeah,' Juliet said, 'surely that would only make it *harder* to find us.'

'Maybe they had no choice in the matter,' Gant said.

'What does this mean for us?' the President asked, coming up beside them.

'It doesn't change the plan,' Gant said. 'We're still going for the command centre. What we have to figure out, though, is how it affects this environment.'

At that moment, from somewhere deep within the bowels of the complex, they heard a scream—a wild scream; human, but at the same time, somehow *not* human; the terror-inspiring howl of a seriously deranged individual.

'Oh, Jesus,' Gant breathed. 'The prisoners. They're out.'

FIFTH CONFRONTATION

3 July, 0930 Hours

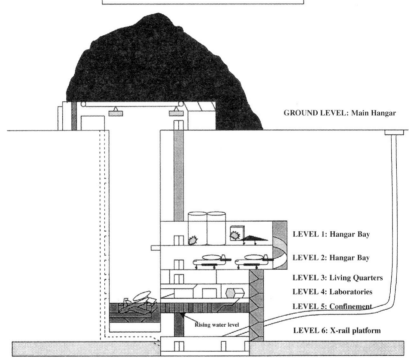

UNITED STATES AIR FORCE
SPECIAL AREA (RESTRICTION) NO.7
0930 HOURS

GROUND LEVEL: Main Hangar

LEVEL 1: Hangar Bay

LEVEL 2: Hangar Bay

LEVEL 3: Living Quarters

LEVEL 4: Laboratories

LEVEL 5: Confinement

Rising water level

LEVEL 6: X-rail platform

About ten minutes *before* the power went off at Area 7, a chunky CH-53E Super Stallion transport helicopter was sinking slowly through the aqua-green water of Lake Powell.

It made for a peculiar sight.

With its tail section completely blown apart, the chopper sank rear-end first, almost vertical, its open loading ramp swallowing water by the ton. Against the hazy green backdrop of the water all around it, it looked as if the Super Stallion was free-falling in silent ultra-slow motion.

Thin streams of bubbles weaved their way to the surface above it—the same bubbles that were being watched by the two Air Force Penetrators hovering above the lake.

Shane Schofield and Buck Riley Jnr stared out through the sinking helicopter's Lexan windshield—looking straight up.

They saw the water's surface high above them, rippling like a glass lens, fifty feet away and getting more and more distant.

Beyond the distorted lens of water they could make out the twin images of the Penetrator attack choppers hovering above the surface, waiting for them to emerge, if they dared.

In the water all around them, a bizarre yet extraordinary underwater landscape revealed itself. Giant boulders rested on the lakebed, desert trails that had once been dry land twisted and turned, there was even a giant submerged cliff that soared upward, disappearing above the water's surface. The submerged desert world appeared as a ghostly pale green.

Book II turned to Schofield. 'If you've got any more magic escape plans, now would be the time to use them.'

'Sorry,' Schofield said. 'I'm all out.'

Behind them—or rather, *below* them—water was flooding up into the cargo bay. It rose quickly through the hold, entering the helicopter via the wide-open loading ramp and any other orifice it could find.

Thankfully, the cockpit was airtight, so at seventy feet down, the still-sinking helicopter reached equilibrium—and an air pocket formed in the upturned cockpit, the same way a drinking cup submerged upside-down in a bathtub will form an air bubble.

The helicopter glided downwards until, at ninety feet, it hit the bottom.

A billowing cloud of silt exploded all around the Super Stallion as its destroyed tail section impacted against the floor of the lake and came to rest—still upright—against a massive submerged boulder.

'We haven't got much time,' Schofield said. 'This air will go bad real fast.'

'What do we do?' Book II said. 'If we stay, we die. If we swim to the surface, we die.'

'There has to be *something* . . .' Schofield said, almost to himself.

'What do you mean?'

'There has to be a *reason* . . .'

'What are you talking about?' Book II said angrily. 'A reason for what?'

Schofield spun to face him. 'A reason why Botha stopped here. In this spot. He didn't stop here for the hell of it. He had a reason to drop anchor here—'

And then Schofield saw it.

'Oh, you cunning bastard . . .' he breathed.

He was staring out over Book II's shoulder, out into the murky green haze of the underwater world.

Book II spun, and he saw it, too.

'Oh my God . . .' he whispered.

There, partially obscured by the aqua-green mist of the water, was a structure—not a boulder or a rock formation, but a distinctly *man-made* structure—a structure which looked totally out of place in the green underwater world of Lake Powell.

Schofield and Book saw a wide flat awning, a small glass-windowed office, and a wide garage door. And underneath the awning: two old-style petrol pumps.

It was a gas station.

An underwater gas station.

It was nestled up against the base of the cliff, at the point where the enormous circular crater containing the small mesa met a wide canyon stretching westward, right on the corner.

It was then that Schofield remembered what this gas station was.

It was the rest-stop petrol station that had been flooded over when Lake Powell had been created in 1963 by the damming of the Colorado River—the old 1950s-era gas station that had been built on the site of an old trading post.

'Let's move,' he said. 'Before we use up all the oxygen in here.'

'To where?' Book II asked incredulously. 'The gas station?'

'Yep,' Schofield said, looking at his watch.

It was 9:26.

Thirty-four minutes to get the Football back to the President.

'Gas stations have air pumps,' he said, 'for inflating tyres. Air that we can breathe until those Penetrators go away. Maybe when the government compensated him, the guy who owned this station just upped and left everything behind.'

'*That's* your magic escape plan? Any air left in those pumps will be forty years old. It could be rancid, or contaminated by God-only-knows what.'

'If it's air-sealed,' Schofield said, 'then some of it may still be good. And right now, we don't have any other options. I'll go first. If I find a hose, I'll signal you to come over.'

'And if you don't?'

Schofield unclipped the Football from his webbing and handed it to Book II. 'Then you'll have to come up with a magic plan of your own.'

The Super Stallion lay on the bottom of the lake, surrounded by the silent underwater world.

Abruptly, a finger of bubbles issued out from its open rear section—trailing the figure of Shane Schofield, still dressed in his black 7th Squadron battle uniform, as he entered the water from within the sunken helicopter.

Schofield hovered in the void for a moment, looked about himself, saw the gas station, but then suddenly he saw something else.

Something resting on the lake-bed directly beneath him, about three feet away.

It was a small silver Samsonite container—heavy-duty; obviously designed to protect its contents from strong impacts; about the size of two video cassettes placed side-by-side. It sat on the silty lake floor, perfectly still, weighed down by a small anchor.

It was the object Gunther Botha had tossed over the side of his bipod when Schofield and Book had interrupted him.

Schofield swam down to it, cut away the anchor with a knife, and then attached the silver container's handle to the clip on his combat webbing.

He'd look at its contents later.

Right now he had other things to do.

He headed for the underwater gas station, pulling himself through the water with long powerful strokes. He covered the distance between the Super Stallion and the gas station quickly, and soon found himself hovering in front of the ghost-like submerged structure.

His lungs began to ache. He had to find an air hose soon—

There.

Beside the open doorway of the gas station's office.

A black hose, connected to a large pressurised drum. Schofield swam for it.

He came to the hose, grabbed it and pressed down on its release valve.

The hose's nozzle sputtered to life, spewing out some pathetically small bubbles.

Not a good sign, Schofield thought.

And then, in a sudden billowing rush, a wash of big fat bubbles came bursting out of the hose.

Schofield quickly put his mouth over it and, without a second thought, breathed in the forty-year-old air.

At first, he gagged, and coughed awfully. It tasted bitter and stale, foul. But then it got cleaner and he began to breathe it in normally. The air was okay—just.

He waved to Book in the helicopter, gave him the thumbs up.

As Book swam over with the Football, Schofield pulled the air hose into the gas station's little office, so that any stray bubbles got trapped against the office's ceiling rather than rising to the lake's surface and alerting the Penetrators to their new air source.

While he did so, he looked at the submerged gas station all around him.

He was still thinking about Botha.

The South African scientist's escape plan couldn't have involved just coming to this sunken petrol station. It had to be something *more* than that . . .

Schofield looked around the gas station's office and the garage adjoining it. The whole structure was nestled up against the base of the sunken cliff.

Just then, however, through the rear window of the little office, Schofield saw something built into the base of the cliff behind the gas station.

304

A wide boarded-up doorway.

It was constructed of thick wooden beams, and it appeared to burrow *into* the cliff-face. A pair of mine-car tracks disappeared underneath the planks that sealed its entrance.

A mine.

Botha's plan was beginning to make more sense.

Thirty seconds later, Book II joined him inside the office and gulped in some air from the hose.

Another minute and Schofield leaned outside the office and saw the blurred rippling outlines of the Air Force Penetrators above the surface wheel around in the air and depart, heading back for Area 7.

As soon as they were gone, he got Book's attention and pointed at the mine entrance behind the gas station, signalling, *I'm going there. You wait here.*

Book nodded.

Schofield then flicked on the small barrel-mounted flashlight on his Desert Eagle pistol and swam out through the rear window of the office, heading for the mine entrance at the base of the cliff.

He came to the boarded-up mine, and found that some of its rotting planks had been removed—possibly recently.

He swam inside.

Darkness met him. Impenetrable underwater darkness.

The narrow beam of his flashlight revealed rough rocky walls, submerged support beams, and the pair of mine-car tracks on the floor, disappearing into the shadows.

Schofield swam quickly through the mine tunnel, guided by the beam of his flashlight.

He had to keep track of how far he had gone. There would come a time very soon when he would have to make a choice: go back to Book and get some more air from the hose, or keep going, and hope he made it to a part of the mine that wasn't filled with water.

The only thing that convinced him that he would find

such an air source was Botha. The South African scientist wouldn't have come here if he couldn't—

Suddenly Schofield saw a narrow vertical shaft branching off his tunnel. A rung-ladder ran up its length.

He swam over to the shaft, pointed his flashlight up into it. The shaft went both up and down, disappearing into blackness in both directions. It was an access shaft of some sort, allowing quick and easy movement to all levels of the mine.

Schofield was running out of air.

He did the math.

The lake was about ninety feet deep here. Hence, ninety feet up that rung-ladder, the water should level out.

Screw it.

It was the only option.

He turned back to get Book.

Two minutes later, he returned to the mine tunnel, this time with Book II—and the Football—beside him, plus a new lungful of air.

They headed straight for the vertical access shaft, used its rung-ladder to pull themselves up it.

The shaft was a tight cylinder, with earthen doorways opening off it every ten feet or so. Climbing it was like climbing up a very narrow sewer pipe.

Schofield led the way, moving quickly, counting the rungs as he climbed, calculating one foot for every rung.

At fifty rungs, his lungs began to burn.

At seventy, he felt bile crawling up the back of his throat.

At ninety, he still saw no sign of the surface, and he started to worry that he had got it all wrong, that he had made a fatal mistake, that this was the end, that he was about to black out—

—then suddenly, gloriously, Schofield's head exploded out of the water into beautiful cool air.

He immediately swung his body to the side to allow Book II to surface next to him. Book burst out of the water and both of them gulped in the fresh air as they hung from the ladder in the tight vertical well.

The shaft still rose into darkness above them—only now it was no longer filled with water.

Once he had regained his breath, Schofield climbed up out of the water and stepped through the nearest earthen doorway.

He emerged inside a wide flat-floored cavern, an old administration chamber for the mine. What he saw *inside* the chamber, however, stopped him cold.

He saw boxes of provisions—food, water, gas cookers, powdered milk—hundreds of boxes.

Hundreds and hundreds of boxes.

A dozen fold-out cots lined the walls. A table covered with fake passports and drivers' licences stood in one corner.

It's a camp, Schofield thought. *A base camp.*

With enough food to last for weeks, months even—for however long it would take for the United States government to *stop* searching Lake Powell for the men who had stolen the Sinovirus and its prized vaccine source: Kevin.

Then, once the coast was clear, Botha and his men would leave the lake and make their way back to their homeland at their leisure.

Schofield looked at the stacks of boxes. Whoever had done this had been bringing stuff here for a *long* time.

'Geez.' Book II joined Schofield in the chamber. 'Somebody came prepared.'

Schofield looked at his watch.

9:31 a.m.

'Come on. We've got twenty-nine minutes to get this briefcase back to the President,' Schofield said. 'I say we go for the surface, and see if there's a way to get back to Area 7.'

Schofield and Book II climbed.

As fast as they could. Up the vertical access shaft. Schofield with Botha's small Samsonite container. Book II with the Football.

Within a minute, they reached the top of the ladder and stepped up into a wide aluminium building of some sort, kind of like an oversized shed.

A set of mine-car tracks began over on the far side of the shed, disappearing into the earth. They were flanked by a collection of rusty loading trays and old conveyor belts. Everything was covered in dust and cobwebs.

Schofield and Book raced for the external door, kicked it open.

Brilliant sunlight assaulted their eyes, wind-blown sand blasted their faces. The sandstorm was still raging.

The two tiny figures of Schofield and Book II stepped out of the mine shed . . .

. . . and they found themselves standing on a gigantic flat-topped desert peninsula that stretched out into Lake Powell. They looked like ants against the magnificent Utah landscape—the magnitude of the earth around them dwarfing even the large aluminium shed from which they had emerged.

Strangely, though, there was *another* structure on this vast flat-topped peninsula. It stood a bare fifty yards away from the mine shed: a small farmhouse, with a barn attached to its side.

Schofield and Book ran for it through the storm-tossed sand.

The letterbox at the gate read: 'HOEG'.

Schofield bolted past it, into the front yard.

He came to the side of the farmhouse, crouched underneath a window, peered inside, just as the wall beside him exploded with automatic gunfire. He spun to see a man dressed in denim overalls come charging around the corner of the farmhouse with an AK-47 assault rifle in his hands.

Blam!

Another shot rang out above the sandstorm and the farmer dropped to the dusty ground, dead.

Book II appeared at Schofield's side, his M9 pistol smoking.

'What the hell is going on here?' he yelled.

'I'm guessing,' Schofield said, 'that if we live through this, we'll find that Mr Hoeg is a friend of Gunther Botha's. Come on.'

Schofield ran for the barn, threw open its doors, hoping against hope that he would find some kind of transportation inside it . . .

'Well, it's about time we had a bit of luck,' he said. 'Thank you, God. We deserved a break.'

Standing there before him—glistening like a new car in a showroom—was a vehicle common to the farms in these parts: a beautiful lime-green biplane, a cropduster.

Three minutes later, Schofield and Book were shooting through the sky, soaring high over the snake-like canyons of Lake Powell.

It was 9:38 a.m.

This is going to be close, Schofield thought.

The plane was a Tiger Moth—an old World War II

biplane often used for cropdusting in the dry south-west. It had two parallel wings, one above the fuselage and one below, that were joined by vertical struts and criss-crossing wires. Two spindly landing wheels stretched down from the forward end of its body, like the elongated legs of a mosquito, and an insecticide sprayer was attached to its tail.

Like most biplanes, it was a two-seater—the pilot sitting in the back seat, the co-pilot up front.

And it was a good plane too, well looked after. Mr Hoeg, it seemed, in addition to being a goddamned spy, was obviously an aeroplane enthusiast.

'What do you think?' Book said into his flight helmet's microphone. 'Do we go for the X-rail?'

'Not now,' Schofield replied. 'There's not enough time. We head straight for Area 7. For the Emergency Exit Vent.'

Dave Fairfax's heart was racing.

This had turned into quite an eventful day.

After he'd heard Dave's assessment of the situation at Area 7 and the presence of a rogue unit there, the DIA assistant director in charge of surveilling the Chinese space shuttle had ordered a blanket tap of a one-hundred-mile circle surrounding Areas 7 and 8. Now, *any* signal coming out of that zone would be picked up by the DIA's surveillance satellites.

Impressed by Fairfax's work on the matter thus far, the assistant director also gave the young cryptanalyst free rein to further pursue the case. 'Do whatever you have to, young man,' he'd said. 'You report directly to me now.'

Fairfax, however, was still puzzled.

Perhaps he was just excited, but something still nagged at him. The pieces still didn't quite add up.

The Chinese had a shuttle up in space, communicating with a rogue unit at a US Air Force base.

Okay.

So there was something at this base that the Chinese wanted. Fairfax guessed it was the virus vaccine that kept getting mentioned in all the decoded messages.

Okay . . .

And the shuttle was the best way to communicate directly with the men on the ground.

No.

That wasn't right. The Chinese could use any of a dozen different satellites to communicate with men on the ground. You didn't need a whole shuttle to do that.

But what if the shuttle had another purpose . . .

Fairfax turned to one of the Air Force liaison people the DIA had called in. 'What sort of hardware does the Air Force keep at Area 7?'

The Air Force guy shrugged. 'Couple of Stealths, an SR-71 Blackbird, a few AWACS birds. Apart from that, it's mainly used as a biological facility.'

'What about the other complex then? Area 8?'

The Air Force man's eyes narrowed. 'That's another story altogether.'

'Hey. This is need-to-know. Believe me, I *really* need to know.'

The Air Force man hesitated for a moment.

Then he said, 'Area 8 contains two working prototypes of the X-38 space shuttle. It's a satellite killer—a smaller, sleeker version of the standard shuttle that gets launched off the back of a high-flying 747.'

'A satellite killer?'

'Carries special zero-gravity AMRAAM missiles on its wings. It's designed for a quick launch and short target-oriented missions: flying up into a low-earth orbit, knocking out enemy spy satellites or space stations, then coming home.'

'How many people can it hold?' Fairfax asked.

The Air Force man frowned. 'Three command crew. Maybe ten or twelve in the weapons hold, at the very most. Why?'

Now Fairfax was thinking fast.

'Oh, no way . . .' he breathed. 'No *way*!'

He lunged for a nearby printout.

It was the printout of the last message he had decoded, the same one he had used to reveal the men of Echo Unit as traitors. It read:

VOICE 1:   WU and LI have arrived back at Area 7 with the virus. Your men are
           with them. All the money has been accounted for. Names of my men
           who will need to be extracted: BENNETT, CALVERT, COLEMAN,
           DAYTON, FROMMER, GRAYSON, LITTLETON, MESSICK, OLIVER,
           and myself.

Fairfax read the line: 'Names of my men who will need to be extracted.'

'Extracted . . .' he said aloud.

'What are you thinking?' the Air Force liaison man asked.

Fairfax was in a world of his own now. He saw it all clearly.

'If you wanted to get a top-secret vaccine out of a top-secret Air Force base in the middle of the US desert, how would you do it? You couldn't fly it out, because the distance is too far. You'd be shot down before you even made it to California. Same for an overland extraction. You'd never make it to the border before we caught you. By sea? Same problem. But these Chinese bastards have figured it out.'

'What do you mean?'

'You don't get something out of America by going north, south, east or west,' Fairfax said. 'You get it out by going *up*. Into space.'

Schofield looked at his watch.

9:47 a.m.

Thirteen minutes to get the Football to the President.

He and Book II had been flying for several minutes now, soaring over the desert landscape in their gaudy lime-green biplane at a swift 190 miles an hour.

In the distance ahead of them—rising up out of the flat desert plain—they could just make out the low mountain, the runway, and the small cluster of buildings that was Area 7.

Immediately after they had taken off, Schofield had taken the opportunity to open the silver Samsonite container that he had found on the lake floor.

Inside it, he saw twelve shiny glass ampoules, sitting in foam-lined pockets. Each tiny glass bulb was filled with a strange blue liquid. A white stick-on label on each ampoule read:

I.V. VACCINATION AMPOULE

Measured dose: 55 ml

Tested against SV strain V.9.1

Certified: 3/7 05:24:33

Schofield's eyes widened.

It was a field vaccination kit—measured doses of the

314

vaccine that Kevin's genetically-constructed blood had provided, doses that could be administered by syringe. And created only this morning.

It was Gunther Botha's masterwork.

The antidote to the latest strain of the Sinovirus.

Schofield stuffed six of the little glass ampoules into the thigh pocket of his 7th Squadron fatigues. They might come in handy later.

He tapped Book II on the shoulder, handed him the other six. 'Just in case you catch a cold.'

Still sitting in the forward seat of the biplane, for the whole trip thus far Book II had been staring silently forward.

He took the ampoules Schofield offered him, pocketed them in his stolen 7th Squadron uniform. Then he just resumed his brooding forward gaze.

'Why don't you like me?' Schofield asked suddenly, speaking into his helmet mike.

Book II's head cocked to the side.

A moment later, the young sergeant's voice came through Schofield's helmet. 'There's something I've been wanting to ask you for a long time, Captain.' His voice was low, cold.

'What's that?'

'My father was on that mission to Antarctica with you. But he never came back. How did he die?'

Schofield fell silent.

Book II's father—Buck Riley Snr, the original 'Book' Riley—had died an horrific death during that terrible mission to Wilkes Ice Station. A murderous British SAS commander named Trevor Barnaby had fed him, live, to a pool of ferocious killer whales.

'He was captured by the enemy. And they killed him.'

'How?'

'You don't want to know.'

'*How?*'

Schofield shut his eyes. 'They hung him upside-down over a pool of killer whales and lowered him in.'

'The Marine Corps never tells you how,' Book II said softly, his voice tinny over the radio. 'They just send you a letter, telling you what a patriot your dad was, and inform-ing you that he was killed in action. Do you know, Captain, what happened to my family after my father died?'

Schofield bit his lip. 'No. I don't.'

'My mother used to live on the base at Camp Lejeune, North Carolina. I was in basic training at Parris Island. You know what happens to a Marine's wife when her husband is killed in action, Captain?'

Schofield knew. But he said nothing.

'She gets moved off the base. Seems the wives of living soldiers don't like the presence of newly single widows on the base—widows who might go stealing *their* husbands.

'So my mother, after losing her husband, got moved out of her home. She tried to start over, tried to be strong, but it didn't work. Three months after she was moved off the base, they found her in the bathroom of her new shoe-box apartment. She'd taken a whole bottle of sleeping pills.'

Book II turned in his seat, looked Schofield straight in the eye.

'That's why I was asking you about using risky strategies before. This isn't a *game*, you know. When someone dies, there are consequences. My father is dead, and my mother killed herself because she couldn't live without him. I just wanted to make sure my father didn't die because of some high-risk tactical manoeuvre of yours.'

Schofield was silent.

He'd never really known Book II's mother.

Book Snr hadn't really socialised with his fellow Marines, preferring to spend his downtime with his family. Sure, Schofield had met Paula Riley at the odd lunch or dinner, but he'd never really got to know her. He'd heard about her death—and at the time he'd wished that he'd done more to help her.

'Your father was the bravest man I have ever known,' Schofield said. 'He died saving another person's life. A little girl fell out of a hovercraft and he dived out after her, shielded her from the fall. That's how they caught him.

316

Then they took him back to the ice station and killed him. I tried to get back in time, but I . . . I didn't make it.'

'I thought you said you'd never lost to a countdown.'

Schofield said nothing.

'He talked about you, you know,' Book II said. 'Said you were one of the finest commanders he'd ever served under. Said he loved you like his own son, like me. I don't apologise for being a little cold toward you, Captain. I just had to get your measure, make my mind up for myself.'

'And your decision?'

'I'm still making up my mind.'

The plane swooped down toward the desert floor.

It was 9:51 when the lime-green Tiger Moth touched down on the dusty desert plain, kicking up a cloud of sand behind it, in the midst of the raging sandstorm.

As soon as the biplane skidded to a halt Schofield and Book II were out of it—Schofield holding the Football and his Desert Eagle pistol, Book with two nickel-plated M9s—charging toward the trench carved into the earth that housed the entrance to the Emergency Exit Vent.

Bodies lay everywhere, half-covered in sand.

Nine Secret Service people, all dressed in suits. And all dead. Members of Advance Team 2.

Four dead Marines littered the ground as well. All in full dress uniform. Colt Hendricks and the men of Nighthawk Three, who had come out here to check on the Escape Vent.

Christ, Schofield thought as he and Book II hurdled the bodies, heading for the Vent's entrance.

All this death . . . and all of it would have consequences.

9:52 a.m.

Schofield and Book hit the entrance to the Emergency Exit Vent on the fly—it was still open from the Reccondos' entry before—and entered a narrow concrete tunnel and the cool shade of the Area 7 complex.

They came to a rung ladder that stretched down into

318

darkness—grabbed it and slid down it for a full *five hundred feet*. There were no lights here, so they slid by the light of Schofield's small barrel-mounted flashlight. Armed with his two ornamental pistols, Book II didn't have a flashlight.

9:53 a.m.

They hit the bottom, and saw a long one-man-wide concrete tunnel stretching away from them, gradually sloping downward—again, no lights.

They took off down it, running hard.

Schofield spoke into his Secret Service wrist mike as he ran: 'Fox! Fox! Can you read me? We're back! We're back inside the complex!'

His earpiece fizzled and crackled.

No reply.

Maybe Secret Service radios weren't designed to withstand long underwater swims.

9:54.

After several hundred yards of running down the ultra-narrow passageway, they burst out through the Emergency Exit Vent's door on Level 6, and found themselves standing on the northern tracks of the X-rail station.

The underground station was pitch-black.

Total darkness.

Frightening.

By the beam of his gunlight, Schofield could make out a score of dead bodies, plus a charred, blasted-open section in the middle of the central platform—the spot where Elvis's RDX grenade had gone off earlier.

'The stairs,' he said, pointing his beam at the door leading to the firestairs on their left. They leapt up onto the platform, charged for the door.

'Fox! Fox! Can you read me?'

Fizzle. Crackle.

They came to the stairwell door. Schofield threw it open—

—and immediately heard the rapid *clang-clang-clang* of more than a dozen pairs of combat boots booming down the stairs . . . and getting louder.

'Quickly, this way,' he said, diving down onto the tracks

on the southern side of the platform, taking cover underneath the struts of the small X-rail maintenance vehicle sitting there.

Schofield killed his flashlight as Book II landed on the tracks beside him—not a second before the stairwell door burst open and Cobra Carney and the men of Echo Unit came charging out of it, a gaggle of wobbling flashlight beams moving quickly through the darkness.

Schofield immediately saw Kevin among them, surrounded by four men of Asian extraction.

'What is *this*?' Book II whispered.

Schofield stared at the four men flanking Kevin.

They were the four men he had seen inside the decompression chamber earlier, the ones who had brought the Sinovirus back from China.

His mind raced.

What was going on?

Kevin had only just been returned to Area 7 on the Penetrators. Yet now he was being moved again. Had Caesar instructed this team of commandos to take him to another, more secure location?

And yet again the question nagged Schofield: *What did Caesar Russell care for Kevin? Wasn't he after the President?*

Cobra and his men leapt down onto the tracks on the other side of the platform, moving with purpose.

It was then—by the light of Echo Unit's flashlights—that Schofield saw that the blast doors sealing the X-rail tunnel on the other side of the platform were *open*. They were the doors that sealed off the tunnel that led to Area 8.

Cobra and his men, with Kevin and the four Asian men among them, disappeared inside the eastern tunnel, looking behind themselves as they went.

Looking behind themselves . . . Schofield thought.

And then he saw Cobra Carney take one last anxious glance over his shoulder before he entered the tunnel, and suddenly Schofield knew.

These men were *stealing* Kevin . . . *from Caesar*.

★

Up in the darkened hangar on Level 2, Gant looked nervously at her watch.

9:55 a.m.

Five minutes until the President had to place his palm on the Football's analyser plate.

And still no word from Scarecrow.

Shit.

If he didn't come back soon, this show was over.

Gant and Mother—with Juliet, the President, Hagerty and Tate—had left the AWACS plane on Level 2, and guided by the flashlights on their gunbarrels, had made their way across the underground hangar toward the wide aircraft elevator shaft.

Still carrying the black box that she had pilfered from the AWACS's belly, Gant was heading for Caesar Russell's command centre up on ground level to carry out her plan.

But if Schofield didn't get back with the Football soon, any plan she had would become academic.

The complex was eerily silent.

When combined with the pitch darkness that now shrouded the underground facility, it made for a very haunting atmosphere.

For a moment, Gant thought she heard her earpiece crackle: ' —ox? —ead me?'

Juliet heard it, too. 'Did you hear that—?'

And then so suddenly that it made them all jump, a gunshot echoed up through the elevator shaft.

Loud and booming.

The blast of a pump-action shotgun.

What followed the gunshot, however, was infinitely more terrifying.

A cackle of laughter.

An *insane* cackle that floated up the shaft, cutting through the air like a scythe.

'Nah-ha-*haaaaaaaah! Hellooooo* everybody! *We're coming to get you!'*

This was followed by a man's voice howling like a wolf. 'Arrooooo!'

Even Mother gulped. 'The prisoners . . .'

'They must have found the arms cabinet down in the cell bay,' Juliet said.

Abruptly, a loud mechanical clanking noise reverberated up through the elevator shaft.

Gant looked out over the edge.

The giant aircraft elevator platform lay at the bottom of the shaft on Level 5, the remains of the destroyed AWACS plane on its back half-submerged in a wide body of water.

At various places on the elevator platform, Gant saw torches—flaming torches, about twenty of them—moving all around, flickering in the darkness. Torches held aloft by men.

The escaped prisoners.

'How many do you see?' Juliet asked.

'I don't know,' Gant said. 'Thirty-five, forty. Why, how many are there?'

'Forty-two.'

'Oh, perfect.'

Then, abruptly, with a great groaning lurch, the elevator platform lifted up out of the lake at the base of the shaft, dripping water.

'I thought the power . . .' Mother began.

Juliet shook her head. 'It has a stand-alone hydraulic engine, for use in a power blackout like this.'

The elevator lumbered up the shaft, its massive form moving steadily through the darkness.

'Quickly. Away from the edge.' Gant pushed the President back behind the landing gear of one of the AWACS planes nearby. She and Mother and Juliet clicked off their barrel-mounted flashlights.

The gigantic elevator platform rumbled past the open doorway of Level 2, continued slowly upward. As it did so, Gant peered around the landing gear of the AWACS.

The scene looked like something out of a horror movie.

They were standing on the rising elevator platform— holding flaming torches above their heads; shotguns and pistols in their spare hands—and they howled like animals, whooping it up, their shrill calls grating like fingernails on a chalkboard in the dark silence of the complex.

The prisoners from the Level 5 cell block.

Half of them were not wearing shirts—their bare chests shone in the firelight of their torches. Others wore bandannas wrapped around their heads and biceps.

All of them, however, wore soaking-wet trousers, caused by the rising water on Level 5.

Then the elevator rose out of Gant's view, and she emerged from her hiding spot to watch its underside climb and climb until it arrived at the main hangar with an ominous, thunderous boom.

Caesar Russell strode purposefully across the control room overlooking the main hangar.

He had just seen the aircraft elevator platform—with its cargo of howling and shotgun-firing prisoners—rise into view. No sooner had it stopped than prisoners bolted off it, scattering in every direction.

'Get on the hand-helds,' Caesar ordered coolly. 'Tell Charlie to wait at the top door and prepare for evacuation to the secondary command post. We'll come to them. Where's Echo?'

'I can't raise them, sir,' the nearest radio man replied.

'Never mind. We'll contact them later. Let's go.'

Everyone started moving. Logan and his three Alpha men. Boa McConnell and his four Bravo men.

Caesar used a keypad to unlock a small pressure-door set into the northern wall of the control room, hurled it open.

A smooth concrete passageway stretched away from him, sloping down and to the left, where it would ultimately connect with the top door's passageway.

The three Alpha men led the way. They charged into the passageway, guns first. Caesar himself went next, followed by Logan.

Colonel Jerome Harper was next in line, but he never got the chance.

For just as Logan disappeared inside the passageway's entrance, the regular door on the *other* side of the control room flew open, revealing five shotgun-toting prisoners!

Boom!

An entire console was blasted to pieces.

In the escape passageway, Logan spun—and saw the intruders, and realised that the others weren't going to make it into the tunnel—and with a look to Harper, he made the call and slammed the escape door shut behind him, sealing off the passageway, sealing Harper and the remaining Air Force men inside the control room.

Eleven men in total were left behind: Harper, Boa McConnell, Boa's four Bravo Unit men, the four radio operators, and the unseen man who had been observing the morning's events from the shadows.

All were left in the control room, at the mercy of the murderous prisoners.

Down in the Level 6 X-rail station, Schofield and Book II hurried out from their hiding spot underneath the compact maintenance vehicle, leapt up onto the platform and dashed for the door to the firestairs.

9:56.

Schofield yanked open the door and instantly heard shotgun fire echoing down the stairwell, followed by a loud '*Arroooo!*'

He shut the door quickly.

'Well, it's official,' he said. 'We have just arrived in hell.'

'Four minutes to find the President,' Book II said.

'I know. I know,' Schofield looked about himself. 'But to do that we have to get up into the complex somehow.'

He stared out into the darkness of the underground railway station.

'Quickly, this way,' he started racing down the platform.

'What?' Book II said, chasing after him.

'There's another way up into the complex. Those 7th Squadron guys used it before—the air vent at the other end of the platform!'

9:57.

The two of them reached the air vent.

Schofield tried his mike again, hoping he hadn't busted it during that swim through Lake Powell.

'Fox! Fox! Can you read me?'

Pop. Fizz. Nothing.

He and Book clambered into the air vent, hurried down its length, their boots reverberating with every step.

They came to the base of the vent's four-hundred-foot-tall vertical shaft.

'Whoa,' Book II said, looking up the shaft. It disappeared into black infinity.

9:58.

Schofield said, 'Quickly, up the air vent. We use the cross-vents to reach the aircraft elevator shaft and then we cut across the platform and see if we can find them.'

Schofield fired his Maghook up into the darkened air vent, delaying the activation of its magnet. The grappling hook boomed up the shaft, flying fast, before Schofield initiated its magnetic charge and immediately—*whump!*—the hook snapped left in mid-air, dragged sideways by its powerful magnetic pull, and attached itself to the vertical wall of the vent.

9:58:20.

Schofield went first, whizzing up into the shaft on the Maghook's rope. Book II came up behind him.

9:58:40.

They hurried into the nearest horizontal cross-vent, charged down it, the Football flailing in Schofield's spare hand.

9:58:50.

They came to the enormous aircraft elevator shaft. It yawned before them, shrouded in black. The only light: some orange firelight way up at the top of the shaft winking through the tiny square aperture that usually contained the mini-elevator. The main platform, it seemed, was right up at ground level, up in the hangar there.

Schofield and Book II stood at the mouth of the cross-vent. They were on Level 3.

Schofield brought his mike to his lips.

'Fox! Fox! Where are you!'

326

'*Hey!*' a familiar female voice echoed down through the shaft.

Schofield snapped to look up, brought his gunlight around.

And saw a small white spot—the beam of another barrel-mounted flashlight—blinking back at him *from the other side of the shaft,* but from one level above, from the massive hangar doorway of Level 2.

And above the flashlight, in the glow of its beam, Schofield saw the very anxious face of Libby Gant.

9:59:00.

'Fox!'

'*Scarecrow!*'

Gant's voice came through Schofield's earpiece loud and clear now. The water damage must have only affected its range.

'Damn it!' Schofield said. 'I thought the elevator platform would be here!'

'*The prisoners took it up to the main hangar,*' Gant said.

9:59:05

9:59:06

'*Jesus, Scarecrow. What do we do? We only have a minute left . . .*'

Schofield was thinking the same thing.

Sixty seconds.

Not enough time to go down to the bottom of the shaft, swim across, and come back up again. And not enough time to shuffle hand-over-hand around the walls of the shaft, either. And they couldn't swing across on a Maghook—it was too far.

Damn, he thought.

Damn-damn-damn-damn-damn-damn-damn-damn.

'*What about a Harbour Bridge?*' Mother's voice came in over Schofield's earpiece.

The 'Harbour Bridge' was a legendary Maghook trick. Two people fired two oppositely-charged Maghooks in such a way that the two hooks hit in mid-air and stuck together.

It was named after the Sydney Harbour Bridge, the famous Australian landmark that was built from opposite sides of Sydney Harbour, two separate arcs that ultimately met in the middle. Schofield had seen a number of Marines try it. None of them had succeeded.

'No,' he said, 'the Harbour Bridge is impossible. I've never seen anyone hit another Maghook in mid-flight. But maybe . . .'

9:59:09

9:59:10

He looked over at the President and Gant standing in the doorway to Level 2, gauged the distance.

Then he looked up—and saw the darkened underside of the aircraft elevator platform, way up at the top of the shaft.

Mother's suggestion, however, had given him an idea.

Maybe with two Maghooks they could . . .

'Fox! Quickly!' he said. 'Where is the mini-elevator?'

'Where we left it before, up on Level 1,' Gant said.

'Go up to Level 1. Get on it. Take it up the shaft and stop it a hundred feet below the main elevator platform. Go! *Now!'*

Gant knew not to argue. There was no time. She grabbed the President and dashed out of Schofield's sight.

9:59:14

9:59:15

Schofield dashed past Book II, heading back along the horizontal cross-vent to the main vent.

He came to the vertical ventilation shaft and without even a blink, fired his Maghook up into it again.

This time he waited until the Maghook had played out its entire one hundred and fifty feet of rope before initiating the grappling hook's magnetic pull.

As before, the Maghook's powerful magnetic charge yanked the upwardly-flying hook sideways in mid-air, and it thunked hard against the metal wall of the vent, and held fast.

9:59:22

9:59:23

328

Schofield whizzed up the shaft again.

This time Book II didn't go with him—Schofield didn't have the time to send the Maghook back down for him. He'd have to do this alone, and besides, he needed the Maghook . . .

Schofield shot up the shaft on the Maghook's rope, the air vent's close steel walls rushing past him on all four sides. He stopped the hook's reeling mechanism as he came to another cross-vent three levels up—but still a hundred feet below the main hangar. He charged into the cross-vent.

9:59:29

9:59:30

Came to the aircraft elevator shaft again. The underside of the giant elevator platform loomed closer now, only a hundred feet above him. He could hear the gunshot blasts and catcalls of the prisoners up in the hangar and wondered for the briefest of moments what on earth they were doing up there.

9:59:34

9:59:35

And then, by the light of his barrel-mounted flashlight, he saw the mini-elevator whizzing up the concrete wall on the other side of the massive elevator shaft. The small figures of Gant, Juliet, Mother and the President were on it.

9:59:37

9:59:38

As the mini-elevator drew level with him, Schofield said, 'Okay! Stop there!'

The mini-elevator jolted to a halt, now diagonally opposite Schofield but separated from him by a sheer concrete chasm two hundred feet wide.

And so they faced each other, from opposite sides of the enormous shaft.

9:59:40

'Okay, Fox,' Schofield said into his radio. 'I want you to fire your Maghook into the underside of the elevator platform.'

'But it's not long enough to swing across on . . .'

'I know. But *two* Maghooks will be,' Schofield said. 'Try

and hit the platform about a quarter of the way across. I'll do the same from this side.'

9:59:42

Schofield fired his Maghook. With a loud, puncture-like whump, the hook flew into the air, flying diagonally up into the shaft.

And then—*clunk!*—the magnetic head of the hook affixed itself to the underside of the elevator platform.

9:59:43

Clunk! A similar noise came from the other side of the shaft. Gant had done the same with her Maghook.

9:59:45

9:59:46

Schofield held his Maghook with one hand. Then he opened the Football, revealing the countdown timer inside it—00:00:14 . . . 00:00:13—and held it by its handle, *folded open*.

'Okay, Fox,' he said into his mike. 'Now give the rope to the President. We've got twelve seconds now, so we'll only get one shot at this.'

'*Oh, you have got to be kidding,*' Mother's voice said.

On the other side of the shaft, Gant gave the Maghook's launcher to the President of the United States. 'Good luck, sir.'

Now, Schofield and the President stood on opposite sides of the great concrete elevator shaft, holding onto the diagonally-stretched ropes of their respective Maghooks, looking like a pair of trapeze artists about to perform their act.

9:59:49

9:59:50

'Go!' Schofield said.

And they swung.

Out over the shaft.

Two tiny figures, on two equally tiny thread-like ropes.

Indeed, as the two of them swung in mirroring pendulum-like arcs, they *did* look like trapeze artists—swinging toward each other, aiming to meet in the middle, Schofield holding out the open briefcase, the President reaching forward with his outstretched hand.

9:59:52

9:59:53

Schofield reached the base of his arc, started coming up.

In the dim light, he saw the President swooping in toward him, a look of sheer terror plastered across his face. But the chief executive swung well, gripping his rope tightly, reaching forward with his right hand.

9:59:54

9:59:55

And they came close, rising in their pendulum motions, reaching the extremities of their arcs . . .

9:59:56

9:59:57

. . . and, four hundred feet above the base of the elevator shaft, swinging in near total darkness, *they came together*, and the President pressed his outstretched palm against the analyser plate in Schofield's hand.

Beep!

The timer on the Football instantly reset itself.

00:00:02 became 90:00:00 and the clock immediately began counting down once more.

As for Schofield and the President, having briefly shared the same space of air four hundred feet above the world, they now parted, swooping back toward their respective starting points.

The President arrived back at the mini-elevator platform, where he was caught by Gant, Mother and Juliet.

On the other side of the elevator shaft, Schofield swung back to his cross-vent.

He landed lightly on the edge of the tunnel, breathing deeply with relief, the stainless-steel Football hanging open in his hand.

They'd done it. At least for another ninety minutes. Now all he had to do was get himself and Book over to the President. Then they'd be back in business.

Schofield reeled in his Maghook, then turned to head back down the cross-vent to get Book—

Shuck-shuck.

Three men were blocking his way—men wearing blue jeans but no shirts. They also brandished pump-action Remingtons and they variously had tattooed chests, bulging biceps, or no front teeth.

'Reach for the sky, pardner,' one of the shotgun-toting prisoners said.

Caesar Russell charged through the low concrete escape tunnel.

The three remaining men from Alpha Unit ran in front of him. Kurt Logan hurried along behind.

They'd just left Harper and the others in the control room to be captured by the escaped inmates, and were now bolting down the escape passageway, racing for the point where it met the top door exit.

They rounded a bend, came to a heavy steel door half-buried in concrete, keyed the code. The door opened.

The top door's exit tunnel appeared before them, heading right and left.

To the right—freedom, via the exit that opened onto one of the exterior hangars here at Area 7.

To the left, around a bend, the regular elevator shaft, and . . .

. . . something else.

Caesar froze.

He saw a combat boot protruding around the corner that led to the regular elevator shaft.

The black combat boot of a dead commando.

Caesar stepped closer.

And saw that the boot belonged to the horribly bloodied body of Python Willis—the commanding officer of Charlie

Unit, the 7th Squadron unit that had been bringing Kevin back to Area 7.

Caesar's face darkened.

Charlie Unit lay dead before him. And Kevin was nowhere to be seen.

Then Caesar saw the mark on the wall next to Python Willis's dead fingers, a symbol scrawled in blood, a final gesture from Charlie Unit's commander before he'd died.

A single capital 'E'.

Caesar just stared at it, pursing his lips.

Logan came up beside him. 'What is it?'

'Let's get to the secondary command post,' Caesar said flatly. 'And when we get there, I want you to find out what's happened to Echo Unit.'

Shane Schofield emerged from the air vent hatch underneath Marine One, flanked by the four heavily-armed prisoners. He no longer carried the Football. One of his captors now held it like a new toy.

As he slid out from underneath the Presidential heli-copter, he thought he heard clapping and shouting . . .

. . . and then suddenly—*boom!*—a gunshot made him start. The shot was quickly followed by a loud roar of approval.

Then another booming gunshot—and more cheers and applause.

Schofield felt his blood run cold.

What the hell was he walking into?

He emerged from beneath Marine One and immediately saw about thirty prisoners, their backs to him, gathered around the central aircraft elevator platform.

In the time since his capture in the air vent down below, the massive platform—with the tangled remains of the destroyed AWACS plane still on it—had been lowered about ten feet below the floorline of the hangar and halted, so that now it formed a gigantic square-shaped pit in the centre of the hangar.

334

The mob of inmates was crowded around the makeshift pit, looking intently down into it like gamblers at a cock-fight, shaking their fists, shouting and cat-calling. One shaggy-looking individual was screaming, 'Run, little man! Run! Run! *Ha-haaaaa!*'

They were the most motley crew Schofield had ever seen.

Their angry faces were covered in scars and tattoos. Each prisoner's uniform had been tailored to his own personal tastes—some had ripped off their shirtsleeves and turned them into headbands, others wore their shirts open, others still, wore no shirts at all.

Schofield was marched over to the edge of the pit. He looked down into it.

Amid the maze of AWACS plane pieces that littered the square concrete hole, he saw two blue-uniformed Air Force men—young men and, judging by their perfectly pressed uniforms, office bunnies, radio operators probably—running like frightened animals.

In the pit with them were five burly inmates—all armed with shotguns—prowling through the maze, *hunting* the two hapless radio operators.

Schofield saw the bodies of two more radio men lying in pools of blood in separate corners of the pit: the cause of the cheers he had heard moments before.

It was then, however, that to Schofield's horror, a small band of prisoners emerged from the *other* side of the hangar.

In the midst of this new group of inmates, Schofield saw Gant, Mother, Juliet . . . and the President of the United States.

'Tell me this isn't happening,' he breathed to himself.

Down in the darkness of the Level 1 hangar, Nicholas Tate III, Domestic Policy Adviser to the President of the United States, gazed nervously up into the elevator shaft.

The President and his three female protectors hadn't returned from their trip up the shaft on the detachable mini-elevator, and now Tate was worried.

'Do you think the inmates got them?' he asked Hot Rod Hagerty.

They could hear the shouts and gunshots from up in the main hangar. It was like standing outside a stadium during a football match.

'I hope not,' Hagerty whispered.

Tate continued to stare up into the shaft, a thousand thoughts flickering through his mind, most of them relating to his own self-preservation. A minute passed.

'So what do you think we should do?' he said at last, without turning around.

There was no reply.

Tate frowned, spun around. 'I said—' He froze.

Hagerty was nowhere to be seen.

The Level 1 hangar stretched away from him, shrouded in darkness, the only presence, the shadows of the gigantic planes inside it.

Tate's face went blank.

Hagerty was gone.

Vanished—silently, *instantly*—in the space of a single minute.

It was as if he'd just been erased from existence.

A lightning bolt of fear shot through Nicholas Tate. Now he was alone, *down here*, in a locked-down facility filled with treacherous Air Force commandos and the nastiest collection of murderers known to man.

And then he saw it.

Saw a glint of light on the floor a few yards away from him, at the spot where he had last seen Hagerty standing. He went over to it, picked it up.

It was a ring.

A gold officer's ring.

Hagerty's graduation ring from Annapolis.

The last two radio operators didn't last long.

As the final shots rang out from within the pit, Schofield and Gant were shoved together, the others beside them.

'Hey there,' Gant said.

'Hi,' Schofield said.

After Schofield and the President's daring trapeze act, Gant and her team hadn't fared any better than Schofield had.

No sooner had the President swung back onto the mini-elevator than the little platform had jolted suddenly and whizzed up the shaft—called by someone up in the main hangar.

They had risen up into the hangar and found themselves in the middle of a whole new nightmare.

The prisoners—the former test subjects for Gunther Botha's vaccine—were now in charge of Area 7.

Although there was no way she could have hidden their meagre supply of guns, Gant did manage to hide her Maghook on their short ride up the shaft. It now lay clinging magnetically to the *underside* of the detachable mini-elevator.

Unfortunately, when the little platform had arrived up in the ground-level hangar—rising up through the matching square hole in the corner of the main platform—Gant had still had the black box from the AWACS plane in her possession.

But she hadn't wanted to alert any of the prisoners to its significance, so she'd placed it on the floor of the mini-elevator, and as soon as the platform had come flush against the floor of the main hangar, she'd 'accidentally' kicked it clear, sending it tumbling out onto the hangar floor, a short way from the elevator shaft.

With the hunt in the pit now over, the prisoners gathered around the aircraft elevator shaft turned their attention to the President and his guardians.

An older prisoner stepped out of the larger group of inmates, a shotgun held lazily in his hand.

He was a very distinctive-looking individual.

He appeared to be about fifty, and judging from the confidence of his stride, he clearly had the respect of the group. Although the top of his head was bald, long grey-black hair flowed down from its sides, growing past his shoulders. A narrow angular nose, pale white skin, and hollow bloodless cheeks completed his very Gothic appearance.

'Come into my parlour, said the spider to the fly,' the long-haired man said as he stepped in front of the President. He had a soft silky voice, menacing in its slow articulation.

'Good morning, Mister President,' he said pleasantly. 'How nice of you to join us. Remember me?'

The President said nothing.

'But of course you do,' the prisoner said. 'I'm an 18-84. In one way or another, you've met all nine of the people who during your presidency have been convicted under Title 18, Part I, Chapter 84 of the United States Code. It's that part of the Code that prohibits ordinary Americans from attempting to assassinate their President.

'Grimshaw, Seth Grimshaw,' the long-haired prisoner said, offering his hand. 'We met in February, just a couple of weeks after you became President, as you were leaving the Bonaventure Hotel in LA via its underground kitchen. I was the one who tried to put a bullet in your skull.'

The President said nothing.

And he didn't take Grimshaw's proffered hand.

'You managed to keep that whole incident quiet,' Grimshaw said. 'Very impressive. Especially since all someone like me really wants is publicity. And besides, it's not wise to scare the nation, is it? Better to keep the ignorant masses unaware of these troublesome little attempts on your life. As they say, ignorance is bliss.'

The President said nothing.

Grimshaw looked him up and down, cast a bemused eye over the black combat clothing that the Chief Executive now wore. The President, Juliet and Schofield were all still dressed in their black 7th Squadron combat attire. Gant and Mother, on the other hand, still wore their formal—but now very dirty—Marine dress uniforms.

Grimshaw smiled, a thin, satisfied smile.

Then he strolled over to the inmate holding the Football and took the silver briefcase from him. He opened it, then glanced from its countdown display screen to the President.

'It would appear that my recently liberated associates and I have intruded upon something rather interesting. A game of cat-and-mouse, it would seem, judging by your clothes and the way you unceremoniously scampered through my cell block earlier.' He clucked his tongue reproachfully. 'Really, Mister President, I must say, this is not at all presidential. Not at all.'

Grimshaw's eyes narrowed.

'But who am I to stop such an imaginative spectacle? The President and his loyal bodyguards versus the treacherous military–industrial complex.' Grimshaw turned. 'Goliath. Bring the other captives over here.'

At that moment, an extraordinarily large prisoner— Goliath, Schofield guessed—stepped out from behind Grimshaw and headed off in the direction of the hangar's internal building. He was an absolute *giant* of a man, with massive tree-trunk-sized biceps and a squared-off head reminiscent of Frankenstein's monster. He even had a flat square bulge that protruded from his forehead—the signature mark, Schofield knew, of someone who'd had a steel plate inserted in his skull. Goliath carried a P-90 assault rifle in one massive fist and Schofield's Maghook in the other.

He returned moments later.

Behind him came the seven Air Force men who—along with the four unfortunate radio operators—had been captured inside the control room earlier:

Colonel Jerome T. Harper.

Boa McConnell and his four Bravo Unit men, two of whom were badly wounded.

And the lone individual who had been observing the morning's events from the shadows of Caesar Russell's control room.

Schofield recognised him instantly.

So did the President.

'Webster . . .' he said softly.

Warrant Officer Carl Webster, the official guardian of the Football, stood with the Air Force people, looking *very* uncomfortable. Beneath his thick hairy eyebrows, his eyes darted left and right, as if searching for an escape.

'You cocksucking little bastard,' Mother said. '*You* gave the Football to Russell. You sold out the President.'

Webster said nothing.

Schofield watched him. He had wondered whether Webster had been abducted by the 7th Squadron earlier that morning. More than anything else, Caesar Russell had needed the Football to carry out his presidential challenge, and Schofield had speculated as to how he had obtained it from Webster.

Quite clearly, force hadn't been necessary—the blood on the Football's handcuffs had obviously been a ruse. Webster, it seemed, had been bought long before the President had arrived at Area 7.

'Now, now, children,' Seth Grimshaw said, waving the Football in his hand. 'Save your strength. You'll be able to settle all your scores in a moment. But first'—he turned to the Air Force colonel, Harper—'I have a question that needs answering. The exit to this facility. Where is it?'

'There is no exit,' Harper lied. 'The facility is in lock-down. You can't get out.'

Grimshaw raised his shotgun, pointed it at Harper's face, shucked the pump action. 'Perhaps I'm not being specific enough.'

He then turned and fired two booming shots into the two injured Bravo Unit men standing next to Harper. They were blasted off their feet.

Grimshaw turned the gun back to Harper, raised his eyebrows expectantly.

Harper's face went white. He nodded over at the regular elevator: 'There's a door that branches off the personnel elevator shaft. We call it the top door. It leads outside. Keypad code is 5564771.'

'Thank you, Colonel, you really are too kind,' Grimshaw said. 'Now then, we must let you children finish what you've started. As I'm sure you'll understand, once we depart this dreadful place, we can't allow any of *you* to leave it alive. But as a final gesture of goodwill, I am going to offer you all one last favour—albeit one that is more for my entertainment than yours.

'I am going to give you all one last chance to kill each other. Five against five. In the killing pit. So at least the winner will die knowing who won your impromptu civil war.' He turned to Goliath. 'Put the Air Force people in here. Start the President's little posse on the other side.'

Schofield and the others were marched at gunpoint to the far side of the pit, the eastern side.

The five remaining Air Force men—Jerome Harper, Boa McConnell, the last two men from Bravo Unit, and the traitor, Warrant Officer Webster—stood directly opposite them, separated by the two-hundred-foot-wide sunken aircraft elevator platform.

'Let the battle begin,' Seth Grimshaw bared his teeth. 'To the *death*.'

Schofield dropped down into the pit and immediately found himself confronted by a twisted metal maze—the enormous broken pieces of the smashed AWACS plane.

The Boeing 707's wings lay at all angles, snapped and broken and still dripping with water. Its gigantic barrel-like jet engines stood on their ends. And in the very centre of the pit—easily the largest single piece of the destroyed plane—stood the AWACS's horribly broken fuselage. Long and cylindrical, it lay diagonally across the pit, nose down, like a massive dead bird.

The darkness of the main hangar didn't help things.

The only light was the firelight from the inmates' torches—they cast long shadows down into the maze, turning it into a dark metal forest where you couldn't see more than a few feet in front of your face.

How the hell did we get into this? Schofield thought.

He and the others stood on the eastern side of the pit, up against its solid concrete wall, not sure what to do.

Abruptly, a shotgun round blasted into the wall above Schofield's head.

Seth Grimshaw called: 'The two teams will engage each other immediately! If you do not begin eliminating one another soon, we will start eliminating you from up here!'

'Christ . . .' Juliet Janson gasped.

342

Schofield turned to face his group. 'Okay, we don't have much time, so listen up. Not only do we have to survive this, but we have to find a way out of here afterwards.'

'The mini-elevator,' Gant nodded to their right, to the north-eastern corner of the pit where the detachable mini-platform now lay flush against the pit's floor, albeit covered by five armed prisoners.

'We're going to need a diversion,' Schofield said, 'something to—'

The flying piece of metal nearly took his head clean off.

Schofield saw it at the very last second and on a reflex, he ducked, just as the jagged piece of steel slammed like an axe into the concrete wall behind him.

He spun, searching for the source of the projectile—and he saw it in the shapes of the two commandos from Bravo Unit, bursting out of the darkness, hurdling the pieces of broken plane, each man holding a length of jagged metal like a sword, and charging at Schofield's group at speed!

'Scatter!' Schofield yelled as the first commando came storming toward him, swinging down hard with his 'sword'.

Schofield blocked the blow by grabbing the man's downward-moving wrist, while Gant engaged the other commando.

'*Go!*' Schofield yelled to Juliet, Mother and the President. 'Get out of here!'

Juliet and the President dashed off into the darkness. But Mother hesitated.

Schofield saw her. 'Go! Stay with the President!'

The prisoners cheered with delight as over by the eastern wall of the pit, Schofield fought with the first 7th Squadron commando, while behind him, Gant grappled with the second Bravo Unit man.

The President and Juliet—with Mother a short distance behind them—dashed north through the darkened maze, heading for the mini-elevator at the north-eastern corner.

From above them, however, the chanting prisoners saw what Juliet and the President and Mother could not: three figures closing in on them from their left, moving quickly along the northern wall of the pit—Jerome Harper, Carl Webster, and co-ordinating the assault, Captain Boa McConnell.

Schofield and Gant stood back-to-back, fighting their own separate battles.

Gant had taken up a length of piping from the floor, and was now wielding it like a quarterstaff against the blows of her Bravo Unit commando.

The Bravo man swung his piece of steel viciously, two-fisted, but Gant parried well, holding her length of pipe sideways, blocking the blow.

'How you doing back there?' Schofield asked, between blows with his own enemy.

'Just . . . frigging . . . dandy,' Gant said, gritting her teeth.

'We have to get to the President.'

'I know,' Gant said, 'but first . . . I have to . . . save your ass.'

She glanced over her shoulder at him and smiled, and in a fleeting instant, she saw his opponent move in for another blow and she shouted, 'Scarecrow! *Duck!*'

Schofield dropped like a stone.

His opponent's sword swooshed over his head, and the man overbalanced, and stumbled right toward Gant.

Gant was waiting.

Turning her attention from her own assailant for the briefest of moments, she swung her length of pipe hard, baseball-style.

Shwack!

The sound of her pipe hitting the Bravo Unit man's head was absolutely sickening. The commando collapsed in a heap just as Gant spun again—pirouetting like a ballet dancer—returning just in time to block the next blow from her own attacker.

344

'Scarecrow! Go!' she yelled. 'Get to the President!'

And with a final look at her, Schofield dashed off into the darkened wreckage.

About twenty yards to the north of Schofield and Gant, Juliet Janson and the President were running hard, weaving their way through the debris-littered maze, heading for the north-eastern corner, but unaware of the three men closing in on them from the left.

They went for Juliet first.

Two figures came bursting out of the darkness, from behind the destroyed rear-end of the AWACS plane—Boa McConnell and Warrant Officer Carl Webster. They crash-tackled Juliet hard, hurling her to the floor.

The President spun to see her hit the floor, held down by Boa and Webster. Then he turned again, and saw Colonel Jerome Harper, standing amid the AWACS wreckage, watching from a distance.

The President was hurrying to help Juliet when—*whoosh*—a large blurring shape came exploding out of the nearby wreckage, missing him by inches.

Mother.

Flying through the air, out of the darkness, linebacker-style. *Crunchhhh!*

She shoulder-charged Boa McConnell so hard that she almost snapped his neck. The 7th Squadron commander was thrown off Juliet's body, visibly dazed.

Carl Webster was momentarily startled by the sudden loss of his fellow attacker, and he turned to see what had happened—

—just in time to receive a powerful punch from Mother.

Even though he was a bulky man, Webster was thrown right off Juliet by the blow and went crashing into a collection of plane pieces. Without a pause, he snatched up a wicked-looking four-foot strip of metal and brandished it at Mother.

Mother growled.

Webster charged.

The fight was as brutal as they come.

They couldn't have been more evenly matched—both were experienced in hand-to-hand combat, both were over six feet tall, and they both weighed in at over two hundred pounds.

Webster roared as he swung his makeshift metal sword. Mother ducked, then quickly grabbed a busted piece of the AWACS's wing-flap to use as a shield. Webster's blows clanged down against her shield as he forced her back toward the battered wing of the plane.

As she danced backwards, staving off Webster's slashes, Mother bent down and scooped up a jagged sword of her own.

She tried to strike back, but Webster had all the momentum. He swung again, cutting deep into her shoulder, tearing open the sleeve of her dress coat, drawing blood.

'Arrgh!' Mother shouted, dropping her shield, fending off the next three blows with only her sword.

Damn it, all she needed was one opening, one chance . . .

'Why did you betray the President!' she yelled as she stumbled backwards, trying to distract him.

'There comes a time when a man has to make a decision, Mother!' the Army warrant officer barked back, yelling between blows. 'When he has to choose a side! I have fought for this country! I have had friends who died for it, only to be *fucked over* later by politicians like him! So when the opportunity arose, I decided that I was no longer going to stand by and watch yet another two-bit, whore-banging, draft-dodging *fuck* drive this country into the ground!'

Webster swung—a lusty, sideways swipe.

Mother jumped backwards, avoiding the blow, leaping up onto the wing of the plane, so that she was now three feet off the ground.

But the wing wobbled slightly under her weight, and she lost her balance for a split second and Webster slashed viciously with his sword—once again slicing sideways— aiming for her now-exposed ankles, way too fast for her to block in time.

And the vicious blow hit home—

Clang!!!

Webster's weapon-hand vibrated monstrously as his jagged metal sword slammed into Mother's dress-uniformed pants leg, just below the knee.

Webster blanched.

'*What*—?'

Mother smiled.

He'd hit her prosthetic lower leg—her *titanium-alloy* prosthetic lower leg!

Seeing her opponent's confusion, Mother took her one and only opportunity, and swung her own makeshift sword with all her might.

Slash!

A fountain of blood sprayed out from Webster's throat as Mother's blade sliced across his neck, severing his carotid artery.

Webster's blade fell from his hand, and he dropped to his knees, clutching his bleeding throat. He held his hands out in front of him, gazing at the blood on them in disbelief. Then he took one final horrified look up at Mother, after which he fell face-first into a pool of his own blood.

The crowd of inmates roared with delight.

By now, the assembled mob—Seth Grimshaw included—had moved around to the northern side of the pit in an effort to find better spectating positions.

Some of them had started cheering for the President, a happily deranged chant in the tradition of American Olympic supporters: 'U–S–A! U–S–A!'

On the eastern side of the pit, Gant was still engaged in the fight of her life.

Her 7th Squadron opponent's sword-like length of steel clanged against her own quarterstaff pipe.

They fought amid the wreckage, trading blows, the Bravo Unit commando driving her backwards. As he did so, he began to smile with every raging swing. Clearly, he felt he had the edge.

And so he swung harder, but as Gant saw, this only served to wear him out more with every blow.

So she feigned fatigue, staggered backwards, 'desperately' fended off his swings.

And then her assailant swung—a lunging sloppy effort, the swipe of a tiring man—and quick as a flash, belying her apparent fatigue, Gant ducked beneath the blow and launched herself upward, thrusting her pipe forward—end-first—ramming its solid tip right into the throat of her stunned opponent, crushing his Adam's Apple, ramming it two inches back into his windpipe, stopping him dead in his tracks.

The man's eyes went instantly wide with disbelief. He wobbled unsteadily, wheezing, choking. He may have been standing up, but he was already dead. Staring stupidly at Gant, he crumpled to the ground.

The crowd of prisoners was oddly silent—stunned, it seemed, by Gant's lightning-fast death blow.

Then they *roared* their approval. Wolf whistles rained down on Gant. Claps and cheers.

'Whoa, baby!'

'Now *that* is what I call a *woman!*'

At the northern end of the pit, the President slid to the ground beside Juliet Janson, hauled her up, but when they both got to their feet, they froze.

Before them, standing next to one of the upturned engines of the AWACS plane—alone but closer now—stood Colonel Jerome T. Harper.

On the ground to his left, lying on the floor, was Boa McConnell. He was groaning painfully, still reeling from Mother's crunching shoulder-tackle earlier.

The hoots and hollers from the prisoners enveloped them.

'Come on, Mister Prez! Get some blood on your hands! *Kill the fucker!*'

'Eat shit, Harper!'

'U–S–A! U–S–A!'

Harper knew the score. All his men were either dead or useless.

And yet still he seemed strangely confident . . .

It was then that he pulled something out of his pocket.

It looked like a hi-tech grenade of some sort—a small pressurised cylindrical canister with a nozzle on its top and a vertical clear-glass window on its side.

Through the narrow glass window, the President could see the contents of the grenade very clearly.

It was filled with a mustard-yellow liquid.

'Oh, Jesus . . .' he breathed.

It was a biological grenade.

A *Chinese* biological grenade.

A pressure-sealed explosive charge filled with the Sinovirus.

An evil grin cracked Harper's face.

'I was hoping it wouldn't come to this,' he said. 'But fortunately for me, like every Air Force man at this complex, I have already been immunised against the Sinovirus. The same, however, cannot be said for you or your brave Marine guardians.'

Then, without so much as a blink, Harper pulled the pin on the Sinovirus grenade.

Harper didn't see him until it was too late.

As he pulled the pin on the grenade, all he saw was a flashing blur of movement from the wreckage to his immediate left.

The next thing he knew, Shane Schofield was standing beside him, emerging from the darkness, swinging a length of piping upward like a baseball bat.

The pipe struck Harper on the underside of his wrist, causing the Sinovirus grenade to fly out of his hand and go soaring upwards.

The live biological grenade flew up into the air.

It flew in a kind of bizarre slow motion, tumbling end-over-end, high above the northern half of the pit.

Schofield watched it, eyes wide.

The prisoners watched it, mouths agape.

The President watched it, awestruck.

Harper watched it, an evil grin forming on his face.

One, one-thousand . . .

Two, one-thousand . . .

Three . . .

At that moment, at the height of its arc, about thirty feet above the floor of pit—directly above its northernmost section—the Sinovirus grenade went off.

★

In the firelight of the prisoners' torches, the aerosol explosion of the grenade inside the hangar was almost beautiful.

It looked like the blast of a water-filled firecracker—a giant star-shaped burst of mist—with multiple fingers of watery yellow particles shooting outwards from a central point, showering laterally, fanning out like a giant umbrella over the sunken aircraft elevator platform, orange firelight glinting off every single particle.

And then in wondrous slow motion, the whole misty cloud began to *fall*, first at its extremities, then in its centre, down over the pit.

Like slow-falling snow, the Sinovirus particles descended.

Since it had detonated above the floor-line of the hangar, the yellow mist hit the prisoners standing on the rim first.

Their reaction was as sudden as it was violent.

Most of them doubled over where they stood, started hacking, vomiting. Some fell to their knees, dropping their flaming torches, others lapsed instantly into involuntary fits.

Within a minute, all but two were on the floor, writhing in agony, screaming as their insides began to liquefy.

Seth Grimshaw was one of the two.

Along with Goliath, he stood unaffected by the falling yellow mist, while everyone around him lay dying.

Although only they and the now-dead Gunther Botha knew it, Grimshaw and Goliath had been the original test subjects for the vaccine against the Sinovirus the previous afternoon.

Unlike the others, they had Kevin's vaccine coursing through their veins.

They were immune.

The yellow mist fell through the darkness.

It was now about fifteen feet above the lowered elevator platform—five feet above the rim—and still falling steadily.

Alone on the eastern side of the pit, Libby Gant had seen

the grenade detonate, had seen the spectacular aerosol explosion high above the pit. She didn't have to be a rocket scientist to guess what it was.

A biological agent.

The Sinovirus.

Move!

Gant spun. She was standing right next to the eastern wall of the pit, ten feet below the rim. The rim itself was now empty, all the inmates having moved around to the northern side earlier.

Gant didn't waste a second.

She was still wearing her full dress uniform, which meant she had no gas-mask—so she definitely didn't want to be here when the Sinovirus descended into the pit.

The particles were fourteen feet off the floor.

And falling . . .

Gant pushed one of the AWACS plane's big black tyres up against the concrete wall, jumped up onto it, hauled herself out of the ten-foot-deep pit.

She rolled up onto the hangar's floor, careful to stay low, beneath the layer of descending Sinovirus particles.

She saw the hangar's internal building about twenty yards away from her, saw the slanted observation windows of its upper level.

The control room, she thought. *Caesar's command centre.*

Staying low but moving fast, Gant hurried for the doorway at the base of the internal building.

The yellow haze continued to fall.

Having consumed the prisoners on the northern edge of the pit, its particles now dipped below the rim, *drifting down into the pit itself.*

Schofield looked anxiously about himself.

In the pandemonium of the grenade blast and the ensuing wails of the dying prisoners—as they fell, they dropped their torches, plunging the pit into even thicker darkness—he had lost sight of Jerome Harper.

After the blast, Harper had dashed off into the darkened forest of the AWACS wreckage, disappearing. Schofield didn't like the idea of him lurking somewhere in the area.

But right now, he had other things to worry about.

The mist was now *inside* the pit—nine feet off the floor—and still falling.

He looked over at the President and Juliet.

Like him, they were still wearing their stolen 7th Squadron uniforms—complete with ERG-6 half-face gas-masks wrapped around their necks.

'Captain! Your gas-mask! Put it on!' the President yelled, pulling on his own mask. 'If you breathe the virus into your lungs directly, it'll kill you in seconds! With the mask on, it's a lot slower!'

Schofield lifted his mask over his face.

Juliet, however, yanked her mask up and over her head and threw it over to Mother, just back from her fight with Webster. Unlike the other three, Mother was still dressed in her mask-less full dress uniform.

'But what about you—?' she said.

Juliet indicated her Eurasian features. 'Asian blood, remember. It won't hurt me. But it'll kill you if you don't put that on!'

'Thanks!' Mother said as she clamped the mask over her nose and mouth.

'Quickly!' Schofield said. 'This way!'

Gas-mask on, he charged into the darkened maze of wreckage, heading for the north-eastern corner, for the mini-elevator parked there.

The others took off after him, racing into the darkness.

After several seconds of running, Schofield came to the mini-elevator, lying flush against the floor in the corner of the pit.

A flaming torch lay on it. One of the dying prisoners up on the rim must have dropped it into the pit when the virus had struck him down.

Schofield snatched it up and turned to see the President and Mother arrive at his side.

It was only then that any of them noticed.

No Juliet.

Juliet Janson lay sprawled on the ground back near the AWACS's fuselage.

Just as she had been about to charge into the maze after Schofield and the others, a strong hand had appeared from completely out of nowhere and grabbed her ankle, causing her to trip and fall.

The hand belonged to Boa McConnell, lying spread-eagled on the floor, still dazed from Mother's tackle earlier, but alert enough to recognise one of his enemies.

Now, he held onto Juliet's ankle, refusing to let go.

Juliet struggled.

Boa extracted a long K-Bar knife from his boot, raised it. Juliet's eyes went wide as he made to plunge the knife into her ankle . . .

Blam! McConnell's head exploded like a burst balloon, shot from somewhere above them. He flopped to the floor, dead.

Juliet scrambled away from the body. She looked upward, searching the darkness for the source of the gun-shot.

She found it in the shape of a flaming torch over on the southern side of the pit, being waved from side to side, accompanied by a voice that called: 'Janson! Agent Janson!'

Juliet squinted to see the owner of the torch.

In the flickering glow of the torch's flames, she could just make out the man holding it—a man in 7th Squadron cloth-ing brandishing a nickel-plated pistol in his spare hand.

Book II.

'Janson! Where are you?' Schofield said into his radio mike, as he waited impatiently on the detachable mini-elevator.

Book II's voice answered him. *'Scarecrow, it's Book. I've got Janson. You get out of here.'*

'Thanks, Book. Fox, you still alive?'

No reply.

Schofield's whole body froze.

And then: *'I'm here, Scarecrow.'*

He started breathing again. 'Where are you?'

'I'm inside the building at the eastern end of the hangar. Get the President out of here. Don't worry about me.'

'All right . . .' Schofield said. 'Listen, I have to get to Area 8. The bad guys have taken Kevin there. I'm going to take the President with me. Rendezvous with us there when you—oh, shit!'

'What is it?'

'The Football. It's still up in the hangar somewhere. Grimshaw had it.'

'Leave that to me,' Gant said. *'You just get the President out of here. I'll meet you at Area 8 as soon as I can.'*

'Thanks,' Schofield said. 'And Fox . . .'

'Yeah?'

'You be careful.'

There was a pause at the other end. *'You too, Scarecrow.'*

And with that Schofield pressed a button and the mini-elevator whizzed him, Mother and the President swiftly down the shaft.

As they descended quickly, Mother touched Schofield on the shoulder, spoke through her gas-mask.

'Area 8?'

Schofield turned to face her. 'That's right.'

No matter how he looked at it, his mind kept coming back to the same image: the image of the 7th Squadron unit down on the Level 6 platform taking Kevin into the X-rail tunnel, heading for Area 8.

Kevin . . .

The little boy was at the centre of all of this.

Schofield said, 'I want to find out what this whole thing has been about. But to do that, I need two things.'

'What?'

He indicated the President. 'First: *him*.'

'And second?'

'Kevin,' Schofield said firmly. 'Which is why we have to get to Area 8 fast.'

Caesar Russell, Kurt Logan and the three surviving commandos from Logan's Alpha Unit charged across the
runway of Area 7 in the glare of the blazing desert sun,
raced into the four-storey airfield control tower that stood
about a hundred yards from the main complex.

Having emerged from the top door exit inside a small side
hangar, they'd made their way to the tower, which doubled
as the base's secondary control room.

They hurried into the tower's command centre—it was a
replica of the one inside Area 7—and started flicking
switches. Television monitors came to life. Console lights
flicked on.

Caesar said, 'Get me a fix on Echo Unit's personnel
locators.'

It didn't take long for Logan to find Echo. Every 7th
Squadron member had an electronic locator surgically
implanted beneath the skin on his wrist.

'They're on the X-rail. Arriving at Area 8 right now.'

'Fire up the Penetrators,' Caesar said. 'We're going to
Area 8.'

Down on Level 1 of the underground complex, Nicholas
Tate was wandering around in a terrified daze.

After the sudden and mysterious disappearance of Hot Rod Hagerty, he didn't know what to do.

Flashlight in hand, he walked absently to the far end of the darkened hangar, searching for Hagerty. But he stopped twenty yards short of the ramp there when he saw something emerging from it. Already somewhat muddled, now his mind reeled at the sight that met him.

It was almost surreal.

A family of bears—yes, *bears*—stepped out from the ramp and onto the floor of Level 1.

One gigantic male, a smaller female, and three awkward-looking little cubs ambled out onto the hangar floor. They were all hunched forward, padding along on all fours, sniffing the petrol-soaked air all around them.

Tate wobbled unsteadily.

Then he turned and ran back toward the main elevator shaft.

The detached mini-elevator whipped down the aircraft elevator shaft in near total darkness, with Schofield, Mother and the President on its back, the orange glow from Schofield's torch the only light.

As they descended, Schofield yanked a couple of Gunther Botha's glass ampoules from his thigh pocket—the small glass bulbs containing the antidote to the Sinovirus.

He turned to the President, spoke through his gas-mask: 'How long do we have?'

'Half an hour till the first symptoms set in,' the President said, 'when it invades the body through the skin. Dermal infection is slower than direct inhalation. That antidote, however, will neutralise the virus in its tracks.'

Schofield handed a glass bulb to both Mother and the President, then pulled out another one for himself. 'We need to find some hypodermic needles before we head to Area 8,' he said.

They rode the mini-elevator down to Level 1.

When they arrived there, however, they were met by

Nicholas Tate, bursting forth from the darkness wide-eyed and alarmed. He stepped straight *onto* the mini-elevator.

'I . . . er . . . don't think you want to go that way,' he said.

'Why not?' Schofield asked.

'*Bears*,' Tate said dramatically.

Schofield frowned, looked to the President. Clearly, Tate had lost it.

'Where's Ramrod?' Mother asked.

'Gone,' Tate said. 'Just—*poof*—disappeared. One minute he was standing here behind me, the next he was just *missing*. All he left was this.'

Tate held up Hagerty's Annapolis graduation ring.

Schofield didn't get it.

The President did.

'Oh, *Jesus*,' he said. 'He's out.'

'Who's out?' Mother asked.

'There's only one person in this complex who is known to leave a person's jewellery at the site of an abduction,' the President said. 'The serial killer, Lucifer Leary.'

'The Surgeon of Phoenix . . .' Schofield whispered, recalling the name and the horror that went along with it.

'Oh, super,' Mother spat. 'Just what we need. *Another* fucking wacko running around this place.'

The President turned to Schofield. 'Captain, we don't have time for this. If Caesar Russell's got that boy . . .'

Schofield bit his lip. He didn't like leaving anybody behind, even Ramrod Hagerty.

'Captain,' the President said, his face hard, 'as I said earlier this morning, sometimes in this job I have to make difficult decisions—and I'm going to make one now. If he's still alive, Colonel Hagerty is going to have to look after himself. We can't spend the next hour searching this facility for him. There's something bigger at stake here. Much bigger. We have to get that boy back.'

They took the mini-elevator to the second underground hangar, Level 2, and—now accompanied by the confused

Nicholas Tate—dashed down its length.

Thankfully, there were no bears in this hangar.

They hit the fire stairwell at a run and rushed down it, guided by the light of Schofield's flaming torch. Since they had come direct from their fight in the pit, they had no weapons, no flashlights, no nothing.

They came to the bottom of the stairwell, and the door to Level 6.

Cautiously, Schofield opened it.

The Level 6 X-rail platform was completely dark.

No sound. No sign of life.

Schofield edged out onto the platform. Dark shapes littered the area—bodies from the three separate gunfights that had taken place down there over the course of the morning, the charred remains of Elvis's RDX explosion.

Schofield and Mother ran straight over to the bodies of some Bravo Unit men. They grabbed a P-90 assault rifle each, plus SIG-Sauer pistols. Schofield even found a first-aid field kit on one of the men which contained four plastic-wrapped hypodermic needles.

Perfect.

He tossed a SIG to the President, but didn't offer a gun to the unstable Tate.

'This way,' he said.

He hurried along the platform, heading for the X-rail engine that sat on the northern tracks of the underground railway station, pointing toward the open tunnel that led to Area 8.

Up in the main hangar, Book II was pulling Juliet Janson out of the ten-foot-deep pit that was the aircraft elevator platform. He was wearing his uniform's ERG-6 gas-mask.

A thin residual mist hung over the area, the lingering cloud of the Sinovirus.

Juliet came out of the pit, and with a shout, she saw them: Seth Grimshaw and the giant Goliath disappearing inside the personnel elevator. And Grimshaw was still holding the Football.

'Over there!' she pointed. 'They're going for the exit in the elevator shaft. That Air Force guy Harper gave Grimshaw the exit code.'

'Do you know the code?' Book II asked.

'Do I ever,' Juliet leapt to her feet. 'I was there when Harper said it. Come on.'

Libby Gant was on her own.

She was standing in a dark hallway inside the command building at the eastern end of the hangar, at the base of a set of stairs—unarmed but alert as hell.

In the hangar outside, the Sinovirus was loose, and she didn't have a gas-mask.

Okay, she thought, *surely in a facility like this, there would*

362

have to be some—

She found them in a cupboard underneath the stairs: biohazard suits. Great big yellow Chemturions—with large, baggy plastic helmets, balloon-like yellow coveralls, and self-contained air-packs.

In the same cupboard, Gant also found a chunky Maglite flashlight. Very handy.

She slipped into one of the Chemturion suits as fast as she could, pulling its Ziploc zipper shut, turning on its self-contained air-supply. The suit immediately inflated and she started hearing her own breathing as a Darth Vader-like wheeze.

Now safe from the Sinovirus, she had something else she wanted to do.

She recalled her previous plan: find Caesar Russell's command centre—get the initiate/terminate unit that he'd used to start the transmitter on the President's heart—then use the black box that she'd taken from the AWACS plane earlier to impersonate the President's radio signal.

The black box.

So far as she knew, it was still on the floor of the main hangar, in the spot where she had kicked it away from the mini-elevator.

She decided to search the command centre for the I/T unit first. Then she'd go back for the black box.

Guided by the light of her newfound flashlight, she climbed the stairs, came to the command room's doorway.

The door was ajar.

Slowly, Gant pushed it open, to reveal a very battered-looking room.

It looked like a war had been fought in there.

The room's plasterboard walls were shredded with bullet holes. The slanted windows overlooking the main hangar were cracked or completely shattered. Several computer consoles bore fat round holes in their monitors. Others just sat there blank, lacking a power source.

Dressed in her yellow biohazard suit, Gant entered the room, stepping over a pair of dead 7th Squadron men lying

363

all shot up on the floor. Their weapons were gone, presumably taken by the inmates who had stormed through here.

Through the faceplate of her airtight suit, Gant's eyes swept the control room, searching for the—

Yes.

It was sitting on top of one of the computer monitors and it was just as the President had described it: a small red hand-held unit, with a black stub antenna sticking out of its top.

The initiate/terminate unit.

Gant picked it up, examined it. It looked like a miniature mobile phone.

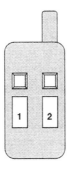

She saw two switches on its face. Beneath each switch was a crude length of tape marked with a handwritten '1' and '2'.

Gant frowned. *Why would Caesar need . . . ?*

She shook the thought away, stuffed the I/T unit into the chest pocket of her biohazard suit.

As she did so, she peered out over the darkened hangar to see if she could spot the black box down by the pit.

The vast hangar floor stretched away from her, veiled by the unearthly mist of the Sinovirus.

Except for the flickering flames of the prisoners' discarded torches, nothing moved.

The area was awash with irregularly-shaped objects: slumped bodies, Marine One, a crashed cockroach, one battered helicopter, even Bravo Unit's busted-open barricade of crates and boxes.

Gant's flashlight had a powerful beam, and in the middle of some bodies and debris on the near side of the pit, it illuminated the bright-orange outline of the AWACS's black box.

Excellent . . .

Gant made to leave, when abruptly, a glint of pale-blue light caught her eye.

She paused. It seemed that not *every* monitor in the control room had been shot or lost power.

Hidden underneath a fallen piece of shredded plasterboard, a lone screen was still glowing.

Gant frowned.

The complex's power was out—which meant this system must be operating on an independent power source. Which meant it must be pretty important . . .

She lifted the broken piece of wall off the screen. The screen read:

LOCKDOWN PROTOCOL S.A.(R) 7-A
FAILSAFE SYSTEM HISTORY
7-3-468201103

TIME	KEY ACTION	SYSTEM RESPONSE
0658	AUTHORIZED LOCKDOWN INITIATE CODE ENTERED	LOCKDOWN PROTOCOL ENABLED
0801	AUTHORIZED LOCKDOWN EXTENSION CODE ENTERED	LOCKDOWN PROTOCOL CONTINUED
0900	AUTHORIZED LOCKDOWN EXTENSION CODE ENTERED	LOCKDOWN PROTOCOL CONTINUED
1005	NO AUTHORIZED CODE ENTERED	FACILITY SELF-DESTRUCT MECHANISM ARMED
1005	****************************WARNING**************************** EMERGENCY PROTOCOL ACTIVATED. IF YOU DO NOT ENTER AN AUTHORIZED LOCKDOWN EXTENSION OR TERMINATION CODE BY 1105 HOURS, FACILITY SELF-DESTRUCT SEQUENCE WILL BE ACTIVATED. SELF-DESTRUCT SEQUENCE DURATION: 10:00 MINUTES. ****************************WARNING****************************	

Gant's eyes went wide.

Facility self-destruct sequence . . .

No wonder this system operated on an independent power source.

But for whatever reason—presumably the sudden intrusion of the inmates—Caesar Russell's people had failed to enter the appropriate lockdown extension code during the window period after 10:00 a.m.

So now, if no-one entered an extension or termination code before 11:05 a.m., Area 7's self-destruct sequence would begin—a ten-minute procedure that would culminate in the hundred-megaton thermonuclear warhead buried in the earth beneath the complex going off.

'Holy mother of God . . .' Gant breathed. She looked at her watch.

It was 10:15 a.m.

She turned to go—

—at the same moment as a long length of steel piping crashed down against the back of her suit-hooded head.

Gant dropped to the floor, out cold.

She never saw her attacker.

Never saw him heft her onto his shoulder.

Never saw him carry her out of the control room.

The X-rail train boomed through the tunnel system, rocketing along on its quartet of tracks at tremendous speed, heading toward Area 8.

It wouldn't be a long trip. At two hundred miles per hour, they'd cover the twenty miles in about six minutes.

Although he didn't know exactly where Echo Unit was going with Kevin, Schofield at least knew they had come this way.

It was better than nothing.

Having set the train's autopilot, he walked back into the main cabin and sat down with Mother and the President. Nick Tate was off at the other end of the carriage, still somewhat out of it, staring with great concentration at the buttons on his cellular phone.

Schofield sat down. As he did so, he pulled out his newfound syringe and the antidote to the Sinovirus, and set about injecting himself with it. Mother and the President did the same.

As he jabbed the needle into his arm, Schofield looked up at the President. 'Now, sir, if you don't mind, would you *please* tell me what the hell is going on at this base.'

★

The President pursed his lips.

'You could start,' Schofield prompted, 'with why an Air Force Lieutenant General wants to kill you in front of the nation. Then you could tell me why he *also* wants to keep his hands on a genetically-engineered boy who is the vaccine to an ethnic bullet.'

The President bowed his head, and nodded.

Then he said, 'Technically, Caesar Russell is no longer a lieutenant general in the Air Force. Technically, he is *dead*. On the twentieth of January this year, the day of my inauguration, Charles Samson Russell was executed by lethal injection at Terre Haute Federal Penitentiary for the crime of high treason.'

'What he *wants*,' the President said, 'is what he wanted before he was executed. To radically change the face of this country. Forever. And the two things he needs to do to effect that are: one, kill me, in a highly visible, highly embarrassing way. And two, to retain control of the Sinovirus vaccine.

'To understand why he's doing this, however, you have to understand Russell's history, in particular his links with a clandestine Air Force society known as the Brotherhood.'

'Yes . . .' Schofield said cautiously.

The President leaned forward. 'Over the past thirty years, various Congressional Armed Services Committees have heard about the existence of certain *undesirable* societies within the branches of our armed forces; informal underground organisations with less-than-acceptable common interests. Hate societies.'

'For example?'

'In the eighties there was a secret group of men in the Army known as the Bitch Killers. They opposed the presence of women in the Army, so they engaged in activities to drive them out of the service. More than eighteen sexual assaults in the Army were attributed to members of this group, even if actual proof was difficult to establish. The extent of its membership was never fully ascertained, but then, that's the problem with these sorts of societies: there is *never* any physical proof of their existence. They're like ghosts, existing in non-tangible ways—a knowing look during a salute, a nod in a hallway, a subtle promotion over a non-member.'

Schofield was silent.

While he had never been approached by anyone linked with such a group in his career, he had heard of them. They were like hardcore college fraternities, small groups with their own secret handshakes, their own 'codes', their own disgusting initiation ceremonies. For officers, they started at places like West Point and Annapolis; for enlisted men, at training camps around the country.

The President said, 'They form for various reasons: some have religious skews—for example, anti-Semitic groups like the old 'Jewboy League' in the Navy. Or the sexist ones, like the Bitch Killers. The formation of groups like this in high-risk occupations is well-documented—even police forces like the L.A.P.D. are known to have secret hate societies within their ranks.

'But in terms of sheer violence, the worst groups were always the racist societies. There used to be one in every service. In the Navy, it was the Order of White America. In the Army, the Black Death. In the Air Force, it was a group known only as the Brotherhood. All three displayed a particular hostility toward black Americans in their ranks.

'But the thing is,' the President said, 'they were all thought to have been wiped out during a Department of Defence-initiated purge in the late 1980s. Now while we haven't heard about a resurgence of racist elements in either the Army or the Navy, it was discovered recently that the Brotherhood is indeed alive and well, and one of its key figures was none other than General Charles "Caesar" Russell.'

Schofield said nothing.

The President shifted in his seat. 'Charles Russell was tried and convicted for ordering the murder of two Navy admirals, advisers to the Joint Chiefs of Staff. Turned out, Russell had approached them shortly after my announcement to run for President and asked them to join him in some kind of treasonable endeavour that would change

America forever. The only details he told them were that the plan would involve the removal of the President, and that it would rid America of its "human waste products". The two admirals refused his offer, so Caesar had them eliminated. What he didn't know was that one of those admirals had secretly taped his offer and tipped off the FBI and the Secret Service.

'Russell was arrested and tried for murder and treason. Since it was a military proceeding, the trial was held immediately, albeit in closed session. During the case the question as to what America's "human waste products" actually were was debated at length. Equivocal evidence was brought that Russell was a member of the Brotherhood—a secret cabal of high-ranking USAF officers, mainly from the Southern belt, who intentionally hinder the rise of black Americans through the ranks of the Air Force. It didn't help that the military prosecutor was black, but in any case the issue was never resolved. On the basis of the taped evidence, Russell was found guilty and sentenced to death. When he decided not to lodge any appeals whatsoever, his execution was fast-tracked—and he was "executed" in January of this year. And that was that. Or so we thought.'

Schofield said, 'I get the feeling that you knew what Caesar was planning, even if it didn't come out in the court case.'

The President nodded.

'Over the past ten years, Caesar Russell has been in charge of every major United States Air Force base between Florida and Nevada. The 20th at Warren in Wyoming, which looks after our ICBM stockpile. Space Warfare at Falcon, Colorado, which controls defence satellites and space missions. Area 7, of course. Hell, he even spent a year at AFSOC at Hurlbut Field in Florida, supervising the Air Force's crack special ops teams, including the 7th Squadron. He has loyal followers at each of those bases, senior officers who owe their positions to him, a small but powerful clique of base-commanders who we now suspect are also members of the Brotherhood.

'What Russell also knows, however, is what's inside every one of our most secret bases. He knew of the Sinovirus from its earliest development phases, knew of its potential uses, and he knew of our response to it—a genetically-constructed virus-resistant human being— right from the very beginning.

'The thing is, Charles Russell is smart, very smart. He thought of *other* possibilities for the one person in the world in possession of the ultimate ethnic bullet and its vaccine. Judging by this transmitter attached to my heart, it looks like he's been planning a revolution for some time now, but it's only the advent of the Sinovirus that makes it totally perfect for him.'

'How so?'

'Because Caesar Russell wants to take America back to its pre-Civil War state,' the President said simply.

There was a silence.

'Did you hear the names of the cities he's put his plasma bombs in? Fourteen devices, in fourteen airports, all around the country. Not true. They're not placed *all* around the country. They're only placed in *northern* cities. New York, Washington DC, Chicago, LA, San Francisco, Seattle. The farthest south those bombs get is St Louis. No Atlanta, no Houston, no Miami even. Nothing below the Tennessee– Kentucky state line.'

'Why those cities, then?' Schofield asked slowly.

The President said, 'Because they represent the North, the liberals, the dandies of America who talk a lot, produce nothing, and yet consume everything. And Caesar wants an America *without the North.*

'For with the Sinovirus and its cure in his possession, he will have what's left of the nation at his mercy. Every man, woman and child—black and white—will owe their life to him and his precious vaccine.'

The President winced.

'I imagine the black population would be eliminated first, with the vaccine being administered only to white Americans. Considering Caesar's racist tendencies, I assume it was the black population he was talking about when he mentioned "human waste products".

'But remember what I said before: he has to do two things to get what he wants: he has to have Kevin in his possession, *and he also has to kill me.* For no revolution—no true revolution—can take place without the visible and humiliating destruction of the previous regime. The execution of Louis XVI and Marie Antoinette in France; the imprisonment of the Czar in Russia in 1918; Hitler's complete "Nazification" of Germany in the thirties.

'Anybody can kill a President, if they are determined enough. A revolutionary, however, has to do it *in front of the people he desires to rule*—showing them that the previous ruling system no longer deserves their respect.

'And don't be mistaken, Caesar Russell isn't doing this in front of America. He's doing it in front of the most extreme elements of America—the Timothy McVeighs of the country; the poor, the angry, the disenfranchised, the white supremacists, the white trash, the anti-federal militias—those parts of the nation, located mainly in the southern states, that wouldn't give two shits if the cappuccino-drinking liberals in New York, Chicago and San Francisco were blasted off the face of the earth.'

'But the country would be decimated . . .' Schofield said. 'Why would he want to rule a destroyed country?'

'Yes, but you see, Caesar doesn't see it that way,' the President said. 'To his mind, the country wouldn't be destroyed. It would merely be purified, renewed, *cleansed*. It would be a new beginning. The southern city centres would be intact. The Mid-West would still be largely intact, able to provide sustenance.'

Schofield asked, 'What about the other armed forces? What would he do about them?'

'Captain, as you would well know, the US Air Force receives more funding than all the other armed services combined. Sure, it may have only 385,000 personnel, but it has more missiles and strike capability than all the other services combined. If, by virtue of the Brotherhood and his previous commands, Caesar has even a *fiftieth* of the Air Force behind him, he could scramble his bombers and take out every key Army and Navy installation in this country—plus every Air Force base that was not allied with him—before they could even raise a small counter-offensive effort.

'Foreign defence would be the same. With its stealth bombers, strike fighters and a stockpile of nuclear missiles greater than that of any other *country* in the world, Caesar's new Air Force, acting alone, would be more than capable of handling any hostile foreign incursion.

'Captain, make no mistake, to Caesar's warped mind, this scenario would be perfect: America would be isolationist once again, completely self-sufficient, and governed by an absolutely lily-white regime. Back to its pre-Civil War state.'

'Mother*fucker* . . .' Mother breathed.

Schofield frowned.

'Okay, then,' he said, 'so what if Russell *can't* pull this off? What if he fails? Surely he isn't just going to accept defeat and walk away. I can't see him simply disarming his bombs if he loses and saying, "Oh well, I was wrong, you win."'

'No,' the President said seriously. 'That worries me, too. Because if by some miracle we do survive all this, the question becomes: what has Caesar got in store for us then?'

After prising apart the personnel elevator's exterior doors, Book II and Juliet Janson came to the 'top door' exit.

Juliet entered the code Harper had revealed earlier: 5564771.

With a sharp hiss, the heavy titanium door opened.

They raced down the concrete corridor beyond it, each holding one of Book's pistols.

They ran for about forty yards before, abruptly, they burst through another door and found themselves standing inside an ordinary-looking aircraft hangar. Shafts of brilliant sunlight slanted in through the hangar's wide-open doors. The hangar was completely empty: no planes, no cars, no—

Goliath must have been waiting behind the door.

Juliet stepped out first, only to feel the barrel of a P-90 press up against the side of her head.

'Bang-bang, you're dead,' Goliath said oafishly.

He squeezed the trigger *just as* Book II—whom Goliath hadn't seen yet—lunged forward and with lightning speed swiped back the P-90's charging handle, *ejecting* the round that was in its chamber.

Click!

The gun against Juliet's head fired nothing.

'Wha—?' Goliath snapped to look at Book II.

And then everything happened very fast.

In one movement, Juliet grabbed the barrel of Goliath's P-90 and whipped up her own gun, at the same moment as Goliath's *other* enormous fist—which still held Schofield's Maghook—came rushing at her face. The Maghook hit Juliet on the side of the head, and she and the P-90 went sprawling to the floor. Juliet hit the ground hard. The P-90 clattered away.

Book raised his Beretta—but not fast enough. Goliath caught his gunhand . . . and growled at him.

Now the two men were holding the same gun.

Goliath thrust his Frankensteinian chin right up close to Book II's face as he began depressing Book's own trigger finger.

Blam!-Blam!-Blam!-Blam!-Blam!-Blam!-Blam!-Blam!

As the gun boomed, Goliath brought it round in a wide arc, angling it so that in a few shots' time, it would be pointed at Book's head.

It was like an arm wrestle.

Book II tried with all his might to stop the movement of the gun, but Goliath was far too strong.

Blam!-Blam!-Blam!

The gun was now pointed at Book's left arm—

Blam!

Book's left bicep exploded. Blood sprayed all over his head. He roared with pain.

Then before he knew it, the gunbarrel was pointing directly at his face and—

Click.

Out of ammo.

'That's better,' Goliath grinned. 'Now we can have a fair fight.'

He discarded the gun and—one-handed—grabbed Book by the throat and thrust him up against the wall.

Book's feet dangled twelve inches off the ground.

He struggled uselessly in Goliath's grip, his wounded arm burning. He let fly with a weak punch that hit Goliath square on the forehead.

The big man didn't even seem to feel the blow. Indeed, Book's fist seemed to just bounce off his skull.

Goliath chuckled stupidly. 'Steel plate. May not make me too bright, but it sure makes me tough.'

Goliath brought up the Maghook in his spare hand, so that it was now pointed at Book's eyes.

'What about you, soldier boy? How strong is your skull? You think this little hook-gun could crush it? What do you say we find out . . .'

He pressed the Maghook's cold magnetic head up against Book II's nose.

Book, held up by his neck, grabbed the Maghook with both hands, and despite his wounded arm, pushed it back toward Goliath. The Maghook went vertical, but then to Book's horror, it started to come *back* toward his face. Goliath was going to win this arm wrestle, too.

Then suddenly Book saw the way out.

'Aw, what the hell,' he said.

And so he reached forward, gripped the Maghook's launcher and pressed the button marked 'M' on it, initiating the grappling hook's powerful magnetic charge.

The response was instantaneous.

The lights on the Maghook's magnetic head burst to life, and the now-charged head began searching for a metallic source nearby.

It found it in the steel plate inside Goliath's forehead.

With a powerful *thud!* the Maghook lodged itself against the big man's brow. It stuck hard, as if it were being *sucked* against the prisoner's very skin.

Goliath roared with rage, tried to extract the Maghook from his forehead, in doing so, releasing Book.

Book II dropped to the floor, gasping, clutching the ragged red hole in his bicep.

Goliath was spinning around, wrestling like an idiot with the Maghook attached to his face.

Book II kept his distance, at least until the staggering Goliath had his back to the wall. Then Book just stepped forward, grabbed the handgrip of the Maghook with his good hand and, without mercy, pulled the trigger.

The Maghook discharged with a gaseous *whump!* and

Goliath's head was sent thundering backwards—his neck snapping almost ninety degrees the wrong way—his skull smashing against the wall behind him, creating a basketball-sized crater in the concrete. For his part, Book II was hurled several yards in the other direction, care of Newton's Third Law.

Still, he fared far better than Goliath. The gigantic prisoner now slid slowly to the floor, his eyes wide with shock and his head cracked open like an egg, a foul soup of blood and brains oozing out of it.

While Book II had been fighting with Goliath, the still-dazed Juliet had been trying to regather her pistol from the floor nearby.

When at last she got it and stood up, she stopped dead.

He was just standing there. Twenty yards away. On the other side of the hangar—Seth Grimshaw.

'I remember you now,' Grimshaw said, stepping forward.

Janson said nothing, just stared at him. She saw that he was still holding the Football . . . and a P-90 assault rifle, held low, one-handed, aimed right at her.

'You were at the Bonaventure when I tried to take out His Majesty,' Grimshaw said. 'You're U-triple-S. One of those chirpy little fucks who think that throwing their bodies in front of a corrupt President is in some way *honourable*.'

Janson said nothing.

She held her nickel Beretta by her side, down by her thigh.

Grimshaw had his rifle levelled at her. He smiled.

'Try and stop this.' He began to squeeze the trigger on his P-90.

Janson was ice-cool. She had one chance, and she knew it. Like all members of the Secret Service, she was an expert marksman. Grimshaw, on the other hand—like nearly all criminals—was shooting from the hip. The Secret Service had actually done probability scales on this sort of thing: in all likelihood, Grimshaw would miss with at least his first three shots.

Taking into account the time it would take for her to raise her own gun, Janson would have to hit him with her first.

Back the odds, she told herself. *Back the odds.*

And so as Grimshaw pulled his trigger, she whipped up her pistol.

She brought it up fast, superfast, and fired . . . *at exactly the same time as* Grimshaw loosed three short rounds himself.

The odds, it seemed, were wrong.

Both shooters fell—like mirror images—snapping backwards on opposite sides of the hangar, dropping to the ground in identical splashes of blood.

Janson lay on her back on the shiny polished floor of the hangar—gasping, breathing fast, looking up at the ceiling— a bloody red hole in her left shoulder.

Grimshaw, on the other hand, didn't move.

Didn't move at all.

He lay completely still, on his back.

Although Janson didn't know it yet, her single bullet had punctured the bridge of Grimshaw's nose, breaking it, creating a foul blood-splattered hole in his face. The exit wound that had blasted out the *back* of his head, however, was twice as big.

Seth Grimshaw was dead.

And the Football lay neatly at his side.

The X-rail train shot through the tunnel system.

After his talk with the President, Schofield had moved into the driver's compartment. They'd be arriving at Area 8 in a couple of minutes, and he wanted a short moment's peace.

With a soft shooshing sound, the compartment's sliding door opened and Mother entered.

'How you doing?' she said as she sat down beside him.

'To be honest,' he said, 'when I woke up this morning, I didn't think the day would turn out like this.'

'Scarecrow, why didn't you kiss her?' Mother asked suddenly.

'What? Kiss who?'

'Fox. When you took her out to dinner and dropped her home. Why didn't you kiss her?'

Schofield sighed. 'You'll never make it in the diplomatic corps, Mother.'

'Blow me. If I'm going to die today, I'm sure as hell not going to die wondering. Why didn't you kiss her? She wanted you to.'

'She did? Ah, damn it.'

'So why didn't you?'

'Because I . . .' he paused. 'I guess I got scared.'

'Scarecrow. What the *fuck* are you talking about? What were you afraid of? The girl is crazy about you.'

'And I'm crazy about her, too. I have been for a long time. Do you remember when she joined the unit, when the selection committee put on that barbecue at the base in Hawaii? I knew it then—as soon as I saw her—but back then I figured she could never be interested in me, not with these . . . things.'

He touched the twin scars running vertically down his eyelids.

He snuffed a laugh. 'I didn't talk much at that lunch. I even think she caught me staring off into space at one point. I wonder if she knows I was thinking about *her*.'

'Scarecrow,' Mother said. 'You and I both know Fox can see beyond your eyes.'

'See, that's the thing. I know that,' Schofield said. 'I know that. I just don't know what I was thinking last week. We were finally going out on a date. We'd got along so well all night. Everything was going great. And then we arrived at her front door and suddenly I didn't want to screw everything up by doing the wrong thing . . . and well, I don't know . . . I guess . . . I guess I just froze up.'

Mother started nodding sagely—then she burst out laughing.

'I'm glad you think this is funny,' Schofield said.

Mother kept laughing, clapped a hand on his shoulder. 'Scarecrow, you know, every now and then, it's nice to see that you're human. You can leap off ice cliffs and swing across giant elevator shafts, but you still freeze up when it comes to kissing the girl. You're beautiful.'

'Thanks,' Schofield said.

Mother stood up to go.

'Just promise me this,' she said kindly. 'When you see Fox next, kiss the fucking girl, will you!'

While Schofield, Mother and the President were shooting through the X-rail tunnel *under* the desert floor toward Area 8, Caesar Russell and his four remaining 7th Squadron men were zooming through the air *above* the desert in their two Penetrator attack choppers, heading in the same direction, a few minutes ahead of the X-rail train.

The small cluster of buildings that was Area 8 rose up out of the sandy landscape in front of the two helicopters.

Area 8 was essentially a smaller version of Area 7: two box-shaped hangars and a three-storey airfield control tower sat alongside the facility's black bitumen runway, complete with its sand-covered extensions that Schofield had observed earlier that day.

As the two Penetrators approached it, Caesar saw the gigantic doors to one of the complex's hangars suddenly part in the middle, and open.

It took the doors a long while to open fully, but once they had, Caesar's jaw dropped.

One of the most amazing-looking flying objects known to man rolled slowly out of the hangar.

Truth be told, what Caesar saw was actually *two* flying objects. The first was a massive Boeing 747 jumbo jet, painted in glistening silver. The jumbo, with its imperious nose and outstretched swan-like wings, edged out from the shadows of the hangar.

It was, however, the smaller aircraft mounted on the *back* of the 747 that seized Caesar's attention.

It looked incredible.

Its paint scheme was like that of NASA's regular space shuttles: mainly white, with the American flag and 'UNITED STATES' written in bold lettering on its side, and with the distinctive black-painted nose and underbelly.

But this was no ordinary space shuttle.

It was the X-38.

One of two sleek mini-shuttles purpose-built by the United States Air Force for the tasks of satellite killing and, where necessary, the boarding, takeover or destruction of foreign space stations.

In shape, it was similar to the standard shuttles—delta planform, with flat triangular wings, a high aerodynamic tail, and three conical thrusters on its rear end—but it was smaller, much more compact. For where *Atlantis* and her sister shuttles were heavy long-haul vehicles designed for ferrying bulky satellites into space, this was the sports version, designed for blasting them out of existence.

Four specially designed zero-gravity AMRAAM missiles hung from its wings, on the outside of two enormous Pegasus II booster rockets—massive cylindrical thrusters filled to the brim with liquid oxygen—that were attached to the underbelly of the bird.

What a lot of people don't realise is that many of today's space flights are conducted with what is essentially late 1960s technology. Saturn V and Titan II boosters were used in the original US–Soviet space race in the sixties.

The X-38, however, with its 747 launch-platform and its stunning Pegasus II boosters, is the first orbiter to truly bring space flight into the 21st century.

Its specially-configured 747 launcher—fitted with new extra-powerful Pratt & Whitney turbofan engines, enhanced pressurisation systems and extra radiation protection for the pilots—can carry the X-38 to a release height of around 67,000 feet, 24,000 feet higher than a commercial jumbo can fly. Air-launch saves the shuttle one-third of its first-stage power/lift ratio.

Then the Pegasus II boosters kick in.

More powerful than Titan III by a whole order of magnitude, the boosters provide enough lift after the high-altitude launch to carry the shuttle into a low-earth orbit. Once expended, they are jettisoned from the shuttle. The X-38—now in a stationary orbit about two hundred and ten miles above the earth—can then manoeuvre freely in space, killing enemy satellites at will, and co-ordinate its landing, all under its own power.

Caesar Russell gazed at the mini-shuttle.

It was absolutely magnificent.

He turned to Kurt Logan. 'That shuttle cannot be allowed to get off the—'

He didn't get to finish the sentence, for at that moment—completely without warning—five Stinger missiles came rocketing out from the darkened hangar behind the silver 747, swooping in a wide arc around its wings before rising sharply into the air, heading straight for Caesar's two Penetrators.

Echo Unit had seen them.

The underground X-rail station of Area 8 was identical to the one at Area 7: two tracks on either side of an elongated central platform, with an elevator sunk into the northern track's wall.

After about seven minutes of superfast travel, Schofield's X-railcar zoomed into the station, bursting into the white fluorescent light of Area 8. The bullet-shaped engine decelerated quickly, stopped on a dime.

Its doors hissed open and Schofield, Mother and the President of the United States came charging out of it, heading straight for the elevator set into the northern wall. Trailing behind them—looking completely lost and now holding his cell phone to his ear—was Nicholas Tate III.

Schofield hit the elevator's call button.

As he waited for the lift to arrive, he noticed Tate for the first time. The White House suit was clearly rattled, freaked out by the morning's events. But it was only then that Schofield realised that Tate was *speaking* into his cell phone.

'*No,*' Tate said irritably into the phone, 'I want to know who *you* are! *You* have interrupted *my* phone call to *my* stockbroker. Identify yourself.'

'What on earth are you doing?' Schofield asked.

Tate frowned, spoke very seriously—in doing so, indicating that he had gone completely bonkers. 'Well, I *was* calling my broker. I figured by the way things are going today, I'd sell off my US dollars. So, after we got out of that train tunnel, I called him up, but no sooner do I get him on the line than this *asshole* cuts across the connection.'

Schofield snatched the phone from Tate's hand.

'*Hey!*'

Schofield spoke into it. 'This is Captain Shane M. Schofield, United States Marine Corps, Presidential Detachment, serial number 358-6279. Who is this?'

A voice came through the phone: '*This is David Fairfax of the Defense Intelligence Agency. I'm speaking from a monitoring station in DC. We have been scanning all transmissions emanating from two Air Force bases in the Utah desert. We believe that there may be a rogue Air Force unit at one of those bases and that the President's life may be in danger. I just enacted an emergency breakthrough on your friend's telephone call.*'

'Believe me, you don't know the half of it, Mister Fairfax,' Schofield said.

'*Is the President safe?*'

'He's right here.' Schofield held the phone out for the President.

The President spoke into it: 'This is the President of the United States. Captain Schofield is with me.'

Schofield added, 'And we are currently in pursuit of that rogue Air Force unit you just mentioned. Tell me everything you know about it—'

Just then, the elevator pinged.

'Hold on.' Schofield raised his P-90 toward the elevator.

The doors opened . . .

. . . revealing horribly blood-splattered walls and a particularly grisly sight.

The gunned-down bodies of three dead Air Force men lay strewn about the elevator—no doubt members of the skeleton crew stationed at Area 8.

'I think we got a fresh trail,' Mother said.

They hurried into the lift.

Tate stayed behind, determined not to go near any more danger. The President, however, insisted on going with Schofield and Mother.

'But, sir—' Schofield began.

'Captain. If I'm going to die today as the representative of this country, I'm not going to do it cowering in some corner, waiting to be found. It's time to stand up and be counted. And besides, it looks like you could do with some numbers.'

Schofield nodded. 'If you say so, sir. Just stay close and shoot straight.'

The elevator doors closed and Schofield hit the button for ground level.

Then he brought Tate's cell phone back to his ear.

'Okay, Mister Fairfax. Twenty-five words or less. Tell me everything you know about this rogue Air Force unit.'

In his subterranean room in Washington, Dave Fairfax sat up straighter in his chair.

Events had just got a lot more real.

First, he had picked up the cell phone call coming out of Area 8. Then he had cut across the line—interrupting some moron—and now he was speaking to this Schofield character, a Marine on the President's helicopter detail. As soon as he had heard it, Fairfax had punched Schofield's serial number into his computer. Now he had Schofield's complete military history—including his current posting on Marine One—right in front of him.

'Okay,' Fairfax said into his headset mike. 'As I said, I'm DIA, and recently I've been decoding a set of unauthorised transmissions coming out of those bases. Now, first of all, we think a team of former South African Reccondos are heading there—'

'Don't mind them. Killed them already,' Schofield's voice said. *'The rogue unit. Tell me about the rogue unit.'*

'Oh . . . okay,' Fairfax said. 'By our reckoning, the rogue unit is one of the five 7th Squadron units guarding the Area 7 complex: the unit designated "Echo" . . .'

At Area 8, the elevator whizzed up the shaft.

Fairfax's voice came through the cell phone. ' . . . *We believe that this unit is aiding Chinese agents in an attempt to steal a biological vaccine that was being developed at Area 7.*'

Schofield said, 'Do you have any idea how they're going to get the vaccine out of America?'

'*Uh, yeah . . . yeah I do,*' Fairfax's voice said. '*But you might not believe it . . .*'

'I'll believe just about anything, Mister Fairfax. Try me.'

'*Okay . . . I believe they're going to load the vaccine onto a satellite-killer shuttle based at Area 8 and fly it up into a low orbit where they will rendezvous with the Chinese space shuttle that launched last week. They will then transfer both themselves and the vaccine onto the Chinese shuttle and land it back inside Chinese territory where we can't get to it or them . . .*'

'Son of a bitch,' Schofield breathed.

'*I know it sounds crazy, but . . .*'

' . . . but it's the only way to get something out of the United States,' Schofield said. 'We could stop any other extraction method—car, plane, boat. But if they went up into space, we'd never be able to follow them. They'd be home by the time we got a chase shuttle onto the pad at Canaveral.'

'*Exactly.*'

'Thanks, Mister Fairfax. Call the Marines and the Army, and get them to mobilise whatever air-capable units they have—Harriers, choppers, anything—and send them directly to Areas 7 and 8. *Do not use the Air Force.* Repeat: *Do not use the Air Force.* Until further notification, treat all Air Force personnel as suspicious.'

As he spoke, Schofield saw the illuminated numbers on the elevator ticking upward: 'SL-3 . . . SL-2 . . .'

'As for us,' Schofield said, 'we have to go now.'

'*What are you going to do? What about the President?*'

'SL-1' became 'G' and suddenly Schofield heard muffled gunfire beyond the elevator doors.

Ping!

The elevator had reached the ground floor.

'We're going after the vaccine,' he said. 'Call you later.'
And he hung up.
A second later, the elevator's doors opened—

SIXTH CONFRONTATION

3 July, 1023 Hours

—and suddenly Schofield and the others entered a whole new ball game.

In the main hangar of Area 8, a fierce gun-battle was already underway.

Explosions boomed, gunfire roared.

Shafts of sunlight streamed in through the hangar's gigantic open doors. About fifty yards away from the elevator, filling the open doorway—partially blocking the incoming sun—was the bird-like rear-end of a silver Boeing 747.

'Son of a bitch,' Schofield breathed as he saw the streamlined space shuttle mounted on the 747's back.

Gunfire rang out from over by the hangar doors.

Five black-clad 7th Squadron commandos—the treacherous men from Echo Unit, Schofield guessed—were taking cover behind the doors, firing their P-90s at something *outside* the hangar.

'This way,' Schofield said, hurrying out of the elevator. The three of them skirted around a Humvee and a pair of cockroach towing vehicles until they could see what lay beyond the hangar doors: two black Penetrator helicopters, hovering low over the tarmac outside the hangar, *blocking the way* of the shuttle-carrying 747.

The six-barrelled Vulcan mini-guns mounted underneath the noses of the two Penetrators were raining down a storm of bullets on the Echo Unit men in the hangar—pinning them down, preventing them from dashing across the twenty yards of open ground to the wheeled stairway that led onto the 747.

Missiles lanced out from the wing-stubs of the Penetrators, zeroing in on the 747. But the jumbo must have been using the latest electromagnetic countermeasures, because the missiles never got near them—they just went berserk as soon as they got close to the big plane, rolling through the air away from it, before slamming into the ground and detonating in showers of concrete and sand.

Even the onslaught of flashing orange tracer bullets from the helicopters just veered *away* from the body of the giant jumbo, as if some invisible magnetic shield prevented them coming near it.

From his position behind the cockroach, Schofield recognised two of the men seated inside one of the helicopters: Caesar Russell and Kurt Logan.

I'll bet Caesar's not happy with Echo, he thought.

Caesar and Logan must have arrived only moments earlier—just as the men of Echo had been boarding their escape plane. Caesar's choppers, it seemed, must have opened fire before all the Echo men had been able to get on the plane, before they'd been able to get away with Kevin.

Kevin . . .

Schofield scanned the battlefield. He couldn't see the little boy anywhere.

He must already be on board the plane . . .

And then without warning the 747 powered up, its four massive jet engines blasting air everywhere, sending any loose objects tumbling across the hangar.

The plane started moving forward—away from the hangar, out onto the runway—*toward* the two black Penetrators. Its wheeled staircase clattered to the ground behind it.

It was a good tactic.

The Penetrators knew that they stood no chance against the weight of the rolling 747, so they split like a pair of frightened pigeons, moving out of the way of the massive jumbo.

It was then that Schofield saw an Echo man standing in the open side door of the 747, saw him wave to his men still in the hangar and then toss a thin rope ladder from the doorway. The rope ladder hung from the small doorway, swaying beneath the rolling plane.

At that same moment, movement near the *hangar's* entry caught his eye and he spun, and saw the five Echo men at the hangar door dash for the Humvee parked near his cockroach.

They were going to try to board the 747 . . .

. . . *while it was moving*!

As soon as the Echo men moved, a withering burst of tracer fire from the Penetrators outside flooded in through the hangar's open doorway, shredding the ground at their feet.

Two of the men fell, hit, their bodies erupting in a thousand explosions of red. The other three made it to the Humvee, clambered inside, started her up. The big car peeled off the mark, turning in a wide circle—

Shoooooom!

A missile rocketed in through the open hangar doors, heading straight for the skidding Humvee.

The Humvee's life was short.

The missile hit it square on the nose—so hard that the wide-bodied jeep was sent flailing back across the slippery hangar floor, before it slammed against a wall and filled with light and blasted outwards in a shower of metal.

'Holy exploding Humvees, Batman!' Mother said.

'Quickly!' Schofield said. 'This way!'

'What are we doing?' the President asked.

Schofield pointed at the moving jumbo outside. 'We're getting on that plane.'

As with many desert bases, Area 8's elongated runway was roughly L-shaped, with the shorter arm of the 'L' meeting the open doorway of the complex's main hangar.

Aircraft took off and landed on the longer arm of the 'L' but to get out to that runway, all planes had to taxi along the shorter strip first. While the main runway was over five thousand yards long, the shorter runway—or taxiway—was only about four hundred yards in length.

The silver 747—with the glistening white X-38 space shuttle on its back—rumbled along the taxiway, flanked by the two black Air Force Penetrators.

Windblown sand whistled all around it, the brutal desert sun glinted off its sides.

The big jumbo had reached the halfway point of the taxiway when a speeding vehicle came blasting out of the main hangar behind it.

It was a cockroach.

One of the white flat-bodied towing vehicles that had been parked inside the hangar. Looking like a brick with wheels, it thundered along the taxiway, *chasing after* the big plane.

In the cramped driver's compartment of the cock-roach, Mother drove. Schofield and the President shared the passenger seat.

'Come on, Mother, pick it up!' Schofield urged. 'We've got to catch it before it gets to the main runway! Once it gets there and starts on its flight run, we're screwed.'

Mother jammed the cockroach into third, its highest gear. The towing vehicle's V8 engine roared as it leapt forward, accelerating through the shimmering desert heat.

The cockroach whipped across the taxiway, closed in on the shuttle-carrying 747.

The Penetrators opened fire on it, but Schofield kicked open the passenger-side window and unleashed a burst from *both* his and Mother's P-90 assault rifles, hitting the nose-mounted Vulcan cannon on one of the Penetrators, causing it to bank away. But the other chopper kept firing hard, kicking up sparks all around the speeding cockroach.

'Mother! Get us under the plane! We need its counter-measures!'

Mother hit the gas and the cockroach surged forward, hit

its top speed. It reeled in the lumbering 747—inch by painful inch—until at last the speeding towing vehicle sped underneath the silver jumbo's high tail section.

It was like entering an air bubble.

The bullets from the second Penetrator no longer hit the ground all around them. The fireworks display of their impact sparks ended abruptly.

The cockroach kept rushing forward—now speeding along in the shadow of the shuttle-carrying 747—pushing past its rear landing gear while still remaining in the shelter of its massive body.

The cockroach weaved under the left-hand wing of the 747, the tarmac rushing by beneath it, heading for the rope ladder that dangled from the plane's still-open left-hand door.

The cockroach came to the rope ladder—

—just as the entire 747 abruptly swung right.

'God damn it!' Mother yelled as the cockroach swung out from the shelter of the jumbo into glaring sunlight.

'It's turning onto the main runway!' Schofield shouted.

Like a giant, slow-moving bird, the silver 747—with the X-38 shuttle on its back—turned onto Area 8's elongated runway.

'Get to that ladder, Mother!' Schofield called.

Mother gunned it, yanked the steering wheel hard-right, directing the cockroach—now momentarily deprived of the jumbo's electromagnetic protection—back in toward the flailing rope ladder, but not before one of the Penetrators swung quickly around in front of the turning 747 and opened fire.

A devastating line of tracer bullets impacted against the tarmac in front of the cockroach, kicking up sparks that ricocheted everywhere.

Several bullets smacked against the cockroach's windscreen, cracking it. Many more, however, bounced up *underneath* the towing vehicle's speeding front bumper and impacted against the underside of the cockroach—three of them hitting the vehicle's steering column.

The response was instantaneous.

The steering wheel in Mother's hands went haywire.

The cockroach fishtailed wildly, lurching sideways as it sped along the runway under the wing of the 747, swinging left and right.

Mother had to use all her strength just to keep a grip on the steering wheel, to keep the cockroach under control.

The 747 finished its turn, began to straighten up.

The runway in front of it stretched away into the distance—a long, straight ribbon of black that disappeared into the shimmering desert horizon.

'Mother . . . !' Schofield yelled.

'I know!' Mother shouted. 'You go! Get up on the roof! I'll bring us under the ladder! And take the Prez here with you!'

'But what about you—?'

'Scarecrow! In about twelve seconds, that jumbo is going to take off and if *you* aren't on it, we lose that kid! I have to stay at the wheel of this thing, otherwise it'll spin out!'

'But those Penetrators will kill you once we're gone . . . !'

'That's why you have to take *him* with you!' Mother said nodding at the President. 'Don't mind me, Scarecrow. You know it'll take more than a bunch of Air Force cocksuckers to get rid of *me*.'

Schofield wasn't so sure.

But he saw the look in her eye, and he knew that she was prepared to keep driving the cockroach—to her almost certain death—so long as he and the President got on board that plane.

He turned to the President. 'Come on. You're coming with me.'

The cockroach raced alongside the 747, once again shielded by its electronic countermeasures, swung in underneath its forward left-hand entry door—the door from which the rope ladder dangled.

The two tiny figures of Schofield and the President—still dressed in their black combat uniforms—climbed up onto the roof of the speeding towing vehicle. Conveniently, their

7th Squadron uniforms came with protective goggles, so they put them on to protect their eyes against the storm of sand blowing all around them.

Down in the driver's compartment, Mother continued to grapple with the steering wheel of the cockroach, trying with all her might to keep the rampaging vehicle on a straight course.

On the roof of the cockroach—in the face of the battering wind—Schofield reached for the flailing rope ladder. It fluttered and swayed just out of his reach—

Then suddenly a deafening *roar* filled his ears.

The 747's four wing-mounted jet engines were coming to life.

Schofield's blood ran cold.

The plane was powering up for take-off, starting its run down the airstrip. Any second now, it would accelerate considerably and pull away from the cockroach.

The rope ladder continued to flutter in the raging wind, a few feet in front of the speeding cockroach. Billowing clouds of sand flew everywhere.

Schofield turned to the President and yelled: 'Okay! I grab the ladder! You grab me!'

'What!'

'You'll understand!'

And with that, Schofield charged across the flat roof of the cockroach and leapt off its forward edge . . .

. . . and flew through the air, reaching up with his outstretched arms . . .

. . . *and caught the bottom rung of the dangling rope ladder.*

He waved for the President to follow. '*Now you grab me!*'

With a doubtful shake of his head, the President said, 'Okay . . .'

And he ran forward and jumped—

—just as the silver 747 shot forward, its engines engaging.

The President flew through the short space of air in front of the speeding cockroach before his body *slammed* into Schofield's, and he threw his arms around the young captain's waist, clasping his hips tightly while Schofield himself held on grimly to the bottom rung of the rope ladder with both of his hands!

Mother's cockroach instantly peeled away behind them, unable to keep up. The two Penetrators also gave up the chase, wheeling to a halt in mid-air above the runway.

Hanging from the rope ladder—and travelling at close to a hundred miles an hour, with the wind whipping all around him and the President of the United States hanging from his waist—Schofield watched in horror as one of the Penetrators loosed a missile at Mother's now-unprotected cockroach.

The missile hit the cockroach's tail and detonated hard, lifting the rear end of the still-speeding towing vehicle a clear five feet off the ground.

With the missile impact, the cockroach fishtailed wildly—and shot off the runway, onto the sand, kicking up an enormous billowing dustcloud—and then it flipped— and tumbled—and rolled—once, twice, three times—before it came to a thumping crashing crushing halt, right on its cockpit, surrounded by falling sand.

And as he hung from the doorway of the accelerating 747, Schofield could only stare at the dust-covered wreck and pray that Mother had died quickly.

But right now he had other things to do.

The 747 continued to rush down the runway.

As it did so, the two tiny figures of Schofield and the President could be seen dangling from its forward left-hand doorway.

The 747 picked up speed. With the extra weight of the X-38 on its back, it required an unusually long take-off run.

Wind whipped all around Schofield and the President as they hung from the rope ladder.

'You go first!' Schofield yelled. 'Climb up my body and then go up the ladder!'

The President did as he was told.

With the runway rushing by beneath them, he first climbed up Schofield's body, using his combat webbing for hand and footholds. Then he stepped off Schofield's shoulders onto the rope ladder itself and began to climb it.

As soon as the President was on the ladder, Schofield began to haul himself up, using only his arms.

The ground continued to whip by beneath them as they ascended the rope ladder, the wind slamming into their bodies.

And then, all of a sudden, as they reached the doorway at the top of the ladder, the speeding runway beneath them just dropped away—dropped dramatically away—and receded rapidly into obscurity.

Schofield swallowed.

They were now in the air.

Caesar Russell's helicopter landed softly on the runway far beneath the rising 747, twenty yards away from Mother's crashed cockroach.

Caesar stepped out of the chopper and just gazed up after the plane.

Kurt Logan walked over to the torpedoed cockroach. It was a battered, tangled wreck. Mangled steel lay everywhere.

Its driver's compartment was completely flattened, its windshield and roof struts bent shockingly inward. It looked like an aluminium can that had been crumpled flat.

And then he saw the body. It lay face-down in the sand in front of the smashed towing vehicle—twisted and broken. Only the torso and limbs were visible, the head was not. Mother's head lay somewhere underneath the cockroach's lowered front bumper, crushed flat against the ground. Her left pants leg ended abruptly at the knee—her lower leg wrenched off by the force of the impact.

Logan returned to Russell's side. Caesar hadn't taken his eyes off the rising silver plane.

'Echo has the boy,' Logan said. 'And the Marines have the President.'

'Yes,' Caesar said, staring up at the fleeing jumbo. 'Yes. So now, regrettably, we move to the alternate plan. Which means we head back to Area 7.'

The President landed with a heavy thump inside the open doorway of the 747, absolutely breathless.

Schofield followed a few seconds later, also breathing hard. He managed to stagger to his knees and pull the door shut behind him. It sealed with a loud *whump!*

Both men were lying on the floor, still wearing their

protective goggles, when one of the pilots of the 747—a commando from Echo Unit—came down the stairwell from the upper deck.

The pilot was wearing a baggy bright-orange flight-suit which Schofield immediately recognised as a pressure suit.

Pressure suits were mandatory on all high-altitude or low-orbital flights. Although baggy on the outside, they were actually quite figure-hugging on the inside, with elasticised cuffs that ran down the wearer's arms and legs. The cuffs squeezed its wearer's limbs to regulate bloodflow through the body and to stop blood draining from the head.

This man's suit had a metal ring around its neck, to which could be attached a space-flight helmet, and a plug-in hose socket on its waist, to which one connected a life-support unit.

'Ah, you made it,' the Echo pilot said as he approached them, obviously not seeing beyond their 7th Squadron outfits and filthy sand-covered goggles. 'Sorry, but we couldn't wait for you any longer. Cobra made the call. Come on, it's only Coleman and me left. Everyone else is already up in the shutt—'

Smack!

Schofield stood quickly and punched him hard in the face, dropping him with one hit.

'Apology not accepted,' Schofield said. Then he turned to the President. 'Wait here.'

'Okay,' the Chief Executive replied quickly.

The 747 soared into the sky. Inside it, the world was tilted crazily, at an almost 45-degree angle.

Schofield hurried up the stairs that led to the 747's upper deck and cockpit. He held his P-90 poised in front of him, searching for the second pilot, the man named Coleman.

He found him as he was emerging from the cockpit. Another sharp blow later—this time with the butt of his P-90—and Coleman was also out cold.

Schofield rushed into the empty cockpit, scanned it quickly.

He'd been hoping to seize the controls and bring the plane down . . .

No dice.

A screen on the cockpit's display revealed that the plane was flying on autopilot, and heading for an altitude of 67,000 feet—the height at which the 747 would release the space shuttle on its back.

At the bottom of the screen, however, were the words:

AUTOPILOT ENGAGED.
TO DISABLE AUTOPILOT OR ALTER SET COURSE
ENTER AUTHORIZATION CODE.

Authorization code? Schofield thought.
Shit.

He couldn't switch off the autopilot. Which meant he couldn't bring the plane down . . .

So what *could* he do?

He looked about himself, saw the clouds outside, saw the unconscious body of the pilot named Coleman lying on the floor just outside the cockpit.

And as his eyes fell on the pilot's body, he got an idea.

Schofield came back down to the President, hauling the unconscious Coleman on his shoulder.

He nodded toward the other knocked-out pilot at the President's feet. 'Put on his flight-suit,' Schofield said as he dropped Coleman's body to the floor and started undressing it.

Within minutes, Schofield and the President were wearing the two pilots' bright-orange pressure suits—with SIG-Sauer pistols concealed in their thigh pockets.

'Where to now?' the President asked.

Schofield gave him a serious look. 'Where no man has gone before.'

The X-38 space shuttle was connected to the launch jumbo by a cylindrical umbilical. Half a dozen titanium struts actually mounted the shuttle onto the back of the 747, but it was the umbilical that allowed human access to and from the spacecraft.

Basically, the umbilical looked like a long vertical tube that stretched upward from the back of the jumbo into the underside of the shuttle. Its entrance was at the mid-point of the jumbo, halfway along its lower deck.

Schofield and the President hurried toward it.

On the way, they found gear that had been waiting for the two Echo Unit pilots: two white briefcase-like life-support systems—small self-contained air-conditioners just like those carried by the shuttle astronauts—and a pair of spherical gold-tinted space helmets that clicked onto the neck-rings of their pressure suits.

The reflective gold tint of the helmets' dome-shaped visors—a feature designed to protect the wearer from the brutal quantities of ultra-violet radiation one experiences at extremely high altitudes—completely hid their faces.

They came to the umbilical's entrance: a tubular vertical tunnel that disappeared into the ceiling. A thin steel ladder rose up through its core.

Now dressed completely in his space suit, his face hidden by his reflective gold visor, Schofield peered up into it.

At the top end of the tube, about thirty yards straight up, he could see the illuminated interior of the X-38 shuttle.

He turned to the President and signalled with his finger: *up*.

They climbed the ladder slowly, weighed down by their cumbersome space suits and life-support briefcases.

After about a minute of climbing, Schofield's helmeted head rose up through a circular hatch in the floor of the shuttle.

Schofield froze.

The rear cargo compartment of the space shuttle looked like the interior of a high-tech bus.

It was only a small space, compact, designed to hold anything from men to weapons to small satellites. It had pristine white walls that were lined with life-support sockets, keypads and tie-down equipment studs. At the moment, however, the cabin was in personnel-carrying mode: about a dozen heavy-looking flight seats faced forward, grouped in pairs.

And strapped into those seats, Schofield saw, were the men of Echo Unit and their Chinese conspirators.

There were five of them inside the cargo cabin, and they all wore identical space suits—gold-tinted helmets and baggy orange pressure suits with small US flags sewn onto the shoulders.

How ironic, Schofield thought.

They were also strapped tightly into their flight seats, in readiness for the high-G transit into orbit.

Through the cockpit door at the front of the cargo compartment, he saw three more space-suited individuals—the shuttle's flight team. Beyond them he could see the clear open sky.

As he stood there, sticking half out of the shuttle's floor hatch, Schofield felt his adrenalin surge.

He knew that their reflective gold helmets prevented him and the President from being recognised. But still he felt self-conscious, certain that he looked like an impostor stepping into the heart of enemy territory.

Near the front end of the compartment, there were several empty seats—waiting, presumably, for the two 747 pilots, and the five Echo commandos who had been cut off down in the hangar.

Slowly, Schofield raised himself up and out of the umbilical tunnel.

No-one paid him any special attention.

He searched the cabin for Kevin, and at first, to his horror, *didn't* see him.

No . . .

But then he noticed that one of the five space-suited figures seated inside the cabin didn't quite seem to fill out his oversized suit.

In fact, it looked almost comical. The suit's gloved arms

hung limply on this figure, its booted leggings dangled clumsily to the floor. It appeared that the wearer of this suit was *way too small* for it . . .

It had to be.

Rather than bunching up the space suit to allow Kevin's hands to reach into its gloves, the Echo men had made sure that the little boy was receiving the full benefit of the pressure suit's blood-regulating cuffs, even if that meant he looked like Charlie Chaplin wearing an oversized outfit.

All right, Schofield thought as he stepped out of the umbilical's hatch. *How am I going to do this?*

Why not just grab Kevin before anyone has a chance to unbuckle themselves, then dive down into the umbilical and get back into the 747 and—

Just then a hand seized Schofield's arm, and a voice exploded in his ear.

'*Yo, Coleman.*'

It was one of the shuttle's pilots, faceless behind his gold visor. He had stepped back into the personnel cabin and grabbed Schofield's arm. His tinny voice came in over Schofield's helmet intercom.

'*Just you two? What happened to the others?*'

Schofield just shook his head sadly.

'*Aw, well,*' the faceless astronaut said. He pointed with two fingers to a pair of flight seats close to the cockpit door. '*Take a seat and strap in.*'

Then, with casual efficiency, the astronaut crouched down, helped the President out of the umbilical, and shut the entry hatch behind him!

Then he just strode forward to the cockpit, speaking into his intercom as he did so: '*All personnel, prepare for separation from the launch vehicle in thirty seconds.*'

The cockpit door slid firmly shut behind the pilot, sealing it off, and Schofield was left standing in the middle of the cabin, staring at the closed pressure hatch in the floor beneath him.

Holy shit . . .

They were about to go into orbit.

With the President behind him, Schofield made his way forward, to two empty seats near the cockpit door.

As he did so, he observed how the Echo men had attached themselves to the shuttle's centralised life-support system and strapped themselves into their seats.

He arrived at his seat, and plugged a secondary hose from his life-support briefcase into a socket in the seat's arm. Then he sat down and started securing his seat-harness.

The President, watching him, did the same, strapping himself into a seat on the other side of the central aisle.

Once he was safely secured, Schofield turned to look about himself.

Across the aisle from him, in the seat directly behind the President, he saw the lopsided figure of Kevin, looking very awkward in his oversized space suit.

It was then that a strange thing happened.

Kevin waved at him.

Waved at him.

It was a rapid side-to-side wave which made the little boy's over-long sleeve flap stupidly in the air.

Schofield frowned, did a double take.

He was wearing his opaque gold-tinted space helmet. There was no way Kevin could see his face.

Did Kevin know who he was?

How *could* Kevin know who he was?

Schofield dismissed the thought as stupid. Kevin must have just been waving at all of the astronauts.

He turned to check on the President—saw him draw his seatbelts tightly across his chest. The President seemed to take a long, deep breath. Schofield knew how he felt.

Suddenly, voices came in over their helmet intercoms.

'Booster ignition standing by . . .'

'Approaching launch height . . .'

'Umbilical release in three . . . two . . . one . . . mark.'

There came a loud clunking noise from beneath the shuttle, and abruptly, the whole spacecraft rose slightly in the air, felt lighter.

'Umbilical has separated . . . we are clear of the launch vehicle . . .'

There came a soft chuckle. Then Cobra Carney's voice: *'Burn it.'*

'Certainly, sir. Prepare to engage Pegasus boosters . . . Ignition in three . . .'

The shuttle beneath Schofield began to rumble ominously.

' . . . two . . .'

He waited in tense anticipation.

' . . . one . . . mark.'

It looked like someone had ignited a flamethrower.

When the X-38's Pegasus boosters fired, the space shuttle was positioned slightly above its abandoned 747 launch vehicle—its gigantic boosters pointed *directly at* the silver jumbo beneath it.

The boosters ignited, bright as magnesium flares. Two incredibly long tongues of white-hot fire blasted out from the twin cylindrical boosters on the underside of the X-38.

The two lances of fire shot like lightning bolts straight into the 747, severing it in the middle, cutting through it like a pair of blowtorches.

The 747 just snapped in half under the weight of the fiery blast, its back broken in an instant. The fuel inside its wings ignited immediately, and a split-second later, the whole gigantic plane just exploded, showering the sky with a thousand pieces of smoke-trailing debris.

Schofield never saw the 747 get destroyed. He was in a whole new world now.

The blast of the boosters igniting was like nothing he had ever heard.

It was *loud*. Booming. All-consuming.

It had been like the sound of a jet engine thundering to life—only multiplied by a thousand.

Now the shuttle tilted sharply upwards and *rocketed* forward.

Schofield was thrust back into his seat by the G-force. The whole cabin began to shake and shudder. He felt his cheeks flatten, press back against his face. He clenched his teeth.

Apart from the closed cockpit door, the only visible link between the flight deck and the rear cargo compartment was a five-inch-thick window set into the cockpit's back wall.

Through this window, Schofield could see right through to the forward windshield of the shuttle—through which he could actually see the sky turning purple as they rose higher.

For a few minutes the shuttle soared upward, its massive boosters lifting it high into the sky. Then, abruptly, over the roar of the rockets, the flight team's voices returned:

'Prepare to jettison boosters and switch over to self-contained power . . .'

'Copy that.'

'Stand by for booster release. In three . . . two . . . one . . . mark.'

Kerchunk!

Schofield felt the weight of the enormous booster rockets drop away from the rising shuttle.

He looked over at the President—the Chief Executive was gripping his armrests tightly. As far as Schofield was concerned, that was actually a good sign. It meant that the President hadn't passed out.

The X-38 rose into the sky. The shuddering and shaking had stopped now and the ride became smoother, quieter, almost as if the X-38 was floating on air.

The respite gave Schofield a chance to take in his surroundings more closely.

The first thing he saw was a keypad next to the cockpit door—a locking mechanism, presumably for use in emergencies, like when cabin pressure was lost.

Schofield also examined his space suit. There was a small unit sewn into the sleeve of his left forearm which appeared to control his helmet intercom. At the moment, the unit's display screen indicated that he was currently on channel '05'.

He looked over at the President, surreptitiously tapped his wrist unit, then held up three fingers: *Switch to channel three.*

The President nodded. A few seconds later, Schofield said, 'Can you hear me?'

'*Yes. What's the plan?*'

'We sit tight. And we wait for a chance to take over this bird.'

The shuttle flew higher.

As it did so, the view outside its forward windshield gradually changed. The sky transformed from cloudy purple to ominous black.

And then abruptly, as though a veil had been lifted, Schofield found himself looking at a glorious galaxy of stars, and beneath the starfield—glowing like an opal against the jet-black sky—the wide elliptical expanse of the Earth, curving downward at both extremities, stretching away into the distance like some unbelievably gigantic luminescent orb, so absolutely *immense* in its size that it was almost too large to comprehend.

It was breathtaking.

They weren't far up, almost exactly at the dividing line between space and the outer atmosphere, about two hundred miles.

The Earth itself—curved and massive and dazzling—filled almost three-quarters of Schofield's field of vision.

He stared at the sight, at the glowing turquoise planet hovering in front of the universe. Then he turned his gaze to the starfield above the planet. It was so clear up here, the starry sky so endless.

And then, one of the stars began to move.

Schofield blinked, looked again.

One of the stars was definitely moving.

'Holy *Christ* . . .' he breathed.

It wasn't a star at all.

It was a shuttle, a space shuttle, all but identical in shape and size to the regular American models.

It soared effortlessly in the weightlessness of space, cutting a dead-straight line toward them. The red and yellow flag on its tail was unmistakable.

It was the Chinese space shuttle.

Schofield flicked back to channel 05 in time to hear Cobra's voice say: '*Yellow Star, this is Fleeing Eagle, I have visual on you now. We are reducing thrust to begin parking orbit. You may commence your approach in thirty seconds.*'

Just then, the cockpit door slid open and two of the X-38's pilots emerged.

Schofield snapped to look up.

Now that they were in low orbit, they could move around the cabin. It was zero gravity, so they stepped lightly, using hand-grips attached to the ceiling to move around.

Both pilots still wore their gold-tinted helmets, still carried their briefcase-like life-support units at their sides. They strode past Schofield and the President, heading aft to prepare for the docking with the Chinese shuttle.

A couple of the other space-suited men in the cargo hold

also began unbuckling their seatbelts, getting up to help with the transfer.

Schofield saw the chance, tuned to channel 03.

'Okay,' he turned to the President. 'This is it. Follow me.'

As casually as he could make it look, Schofield reconnected his air-hose to his life-support briefcase and began unbuckling his seatbelts.

The President did the same.

As his belts came free, Schofield felt the weightlessness take hold of him. He gripped a ceiling handhold and before anyone could stop him—or even ask him what he was doing—he casually stepped over to Kevin and began re-attaching the boy's life-support briefcase and disengaging him from his seat.

A couple of the faceless Echo astronauts looked over, curious.

Schofield gestured to the cockpit—*Wanna have a look?*

Kevin nodded.

The Echo men went back to their work.

With the President in tow behind him—holding onto the ceiling handholds—Schofield led Kevin forward, into the shuttle's cockpit.

The view from the cockpit was even more incredible.

Through the panoramic forward windshield, the Earth looked amazing, stretching away from them like an enormous aqua-blue convex lens.

The last remaining pilot in the cockpit turned in his seat as they entered.

Over to channel 05: 'Just thought we'd come up and see the view,' Schofield said, coughing through his voice to mask it.

'Not bad, huh? Just be sure to keep your visors on. Radiation's a killer, and the sun is almost blinding.'

Schofield put Kevin in the empty co-pilot's seat. Then he turned to the President, clicked back to channel 03.

'You unbuckle his seatbelts, then use them to secure his arms. I'll take care of his life-support hose.'

'Huh—how? When?'

'After I do this . . .' Schofield said.

And with that he leaned forward, grabbed the pilot's gold-tinted visor, and wrenched it open.

'*Argh!*' the pilot roared, as raw white sunlight assaulted his eyes. Underneath his gold-tinted visor was a clear glass bubble that afforded no protection against the pure sunlight.

Schofield then ripped the man's life-support system out of its wall socket, while at the same time, the President unclasped his seatbelts and quickly looped them *behind* the man's flight seat, pinning his arms firmly to his sides.

Deprived of his life-support—and now tied to his own seat—the pilot started to gasp desperately for air.

Schofield dived for the cockpit door, slammed his fist down on a switch next to the entryway. The door slid quickly shut, enclosing the three of them inside the cockpit.

The President spun, 'So what—?'

But Schofield was still moving.

He knew he had about three seconds before someone re-opened the cockpit door from the rear cargo compartment.

There was a keypad next to the door, identical to the one on the other side.

Schofield rushed over to it.

Apart from the usual numbered keys and open/close switches, there was one long red rectangular button on the panel, concealed behind a clear-plastic safety casing. It read:

EMERGENCY USE ONLY:
COCKPIT SECURITY LOCK

Schofield flipped open the safety casing and hit the big red button.

Immediately—*thunk-thunk-thunk-thunk-thunk!*—the door's five emergency dead-bolts locked into place, sealing off the cockpit like a bank vault.

A second later, Schofield heard a weak thumping noise coming from the other side: the sound of the Echo men hammering angrily on the door.

412

Reflective gold helmets peered in through the five-inch-thick window in the dividing wall, waving furious fists.

Schofield didn't care.

This shuttle was now his.

He leaned over Kevin in the co-pilot's seat, the Earth and the stars laid out before him.

In addition to the view, he was confronted by another intimidating sight: the X-38's flight console—a collection of about a million tiny switches, lights, buttons and monitors. It looked like the cockpit of a jumbo jet . . . only *more* complex.

The President took the rear navigator's seat, lifting Kevin onto his lap.

'So, what now?' he asked. 'Don't tell me you know how to fly a space shuttle, too, Captain.'

'Unfortunately not,' Schofield said. He turned to face the bound and still-gagging shuttle pilot. 'But he does.'

Schofield pulled his SIG-Sauer from his thigh pocket and held it to the choking pilot's visor. The President re-attached the man's life-support hose. The pilot stopped gasping as Schofield flicked his intercom to channel 03.

'I need you to help me bring this thing back down to earth,' Schofield said.

'*Fuck you . . .*' the pilot said.

'Hmm,' Schofield said. He then nodded to the President, who yanked the pilot's life-support hose out of its socket again. The Echo Unit pilot immediately resumed his gagging.

Schofield tried again. 'How about I put this another way: either you tell me how to pilot this thing safely back to Utah, or I do it without your help. Now, given the way I fly, either we'll burn up on re-entry or crash into a friggin' mountain. Either way, we die. So, the way I see it, you either tell me how to do it, or you get killed watching me try.'

The President re-attached the pilot's life-support hose. The bound man's face was almost blue.

'*Okay,*' he breathed. '*Okay . . .*'

'Great,' Schofield said, 'Now, the first thing I need is—'

He cut himself off as illuminated green words scrolled out rapidly across the cockpit's transparent Heads-Up Display, or HUD, in the windshield:

FLEEING EAGLE, THIS IS YELLOW STAR.
YOU HAVE ALTERED COURSE.
PLEASE REALIGN TO VECTOR THREE-ZERO-ZERO.

Schofield stared at the words on the HUD. They seemed to hover in the air in front of the starfield.

Then, beyond the transparent display, he saw the Chinese space shuttle, much closer now.

It glided slowly and effortlessly through the void toward his ship, about three hundred yards away and closing quickly.

FLEEING EAGLE, PLEASE CONFIRM.

'Please confirm . . .' Schofield muttered as he scanned the cockpit's enormous array of switches and found the weapons section. 'Confirm *this*.'

He flipped open a safety casing to reveal two red buttons marked 'MSSLE LNCH'.

'This is for Mother,' he said as he jammed his fingers down on both buttons.

The two shuttles faced each other in space—hovering above the outer atmosphere, lit from below by the brilliant reflected light of the world—the compact X-38 and the much larger Chinese shuttle.

And then suddenly, twin bolts of white shot out from the wings of the X-38—two missiles, sleek zero-gravity AMRAAMs. They blasted off their wing-mounts and rocketed through the vacuum between the two shuttles.

The missiles moved unbelievably fast, converging on the Chinese shuttle like a pair of giant winged needles.

They left no smoketrails in their wakes. No puffs of flame or fire, for nothing survives in a vacuum. Their tail thrusters simply glowed orange against the black star-filled sky.

There was nothing the Chinese space shuttle could do. There were, quite simply, no defensive measures it could employ up here.

The two AMRAAMs slammed into the Chinese ship at exactly the same time—one hitting it in the middle, the other in the nose.

The shuttle just *cracked*.

There was an instantaneous flash of blinding white light and the Chinese shuttle spontaneously blew out into pieces which, after the initial blast, just radiated outwards in a kind of accentuated slow motion.

The *Yellow Star* would not be returning to Earth.

The Echo men were still hammering on the cockpit door as, under the instructions of the tied-up pilot, Schofield enabled the X-38's automated re-entry procedures.

There was nothing the men from Echo Unit could do.

The cockpit door was three-inch-thick titanium. And firing a gun through the five-inch-thick glass window didn't look like a clever option

Indeed, as the X-38 began its controlled descent out of its orbit, hit the atmosphere and engaged its heat-shields against the 4,000°F temperatures outside, they could only strap themselves back into their seats and hang on.

The shuttle rocketed downward under the autopilot. As it did so, Schofield watched the starfield above them slowly fade away, replaced by a hazy purple aura, before suddenly, brilliantly, they burst down into dazzling blue sky.

The orbiting X-38 had travelled eastward—but because it hadn't actually been up that long, only about halfway across Colorado. Looking down, and facing *west* now, Schofield saw steel-grey mountains and lush green valleys. Beyond them, on the curved horizon, he could see the sandy-yellow Utah desert.

He looked at his watch.

10:36 a.m.

They hadn't been in orbit long at all. About twelve minutes, in fact. Now, gliding downward at supersonic speed, they'd be back in Utah in only a couple more.

Suddenly, the heads-up display came to life:

SOURCE AIRFIELD BEACON DETECTED
AIRFIELD IDENTIFIED AS UNITED STATES AIR FORCE
SPECIAL AREA (RESTRICTED) 08
PROCEEDING TO SOURCE AIRFIELD

Area 8, Schofield thought.

No.

He didn't want to go there.

So far as he could see, the only way to end this challenge once and for all was to get away from these bases with the President *and* the Football.

But to do that, they needed the Football.

And the Football—whose interminable countdown still needed to be satisfied by 11:30—was last seen at Area 7, in the hands of Seth Grimshaw.

Schofield turned to his captive shuttle pilot. 'We need to get to Area 7.'

The X-38 descended rapidly, shooting westward, blasting over the barren Utah desert.

It flew down toward Area 8, roaring through the air, but as it came close, Schofield disengaged the autopilot and, now flying the shuttle manually like a regular plane, he allowed the shuttle to overshoot the base.

They covered the twenty miles to Area 7 in less than a minute, and very soon, he saw the low mountain and the cluster of hangars and buildings, and the elongated runway in the sand. In the far distance, on the horizon, he saw the wide expanse of Lake Powell, with its twisting network of water-filled canyons.

He aimed for the runway, sweeping in low over the buildings of Area 7. It ran from east to west, so he was coming straight for it.

The X-38 boomed over the Area 7 complex, shaking its walls, before touching down perfectly on its black bitumen runway.

But it came in fast—very fast.

Which was why Schofield didn't see the two black Penetrator helicopters sitting silently next to Area 7's hangars.

Didn't see one of them immediately power up and rise into the air as soon as his tyres had hit the tarmac.

The X-38 rocketed down the desert runway, its tyres smoking.

Schofield tried to rein in the speeding spacecraft, releasing a brake-parachute which fluttered to life behind it. The shuttle began to slow.

When at last it had lost all its momentum, Schofield flicked some switches, prepared to take her back to the main hangar.

He never even got to turn the shuttle around.

For at the very moment that he brought it to a halt, he saw the Penetrator helicopter swing menacingly into place in front of him, hovering above the runway like an evil bird of prey.

The space shuttle and the winged attack helicopter squared off like a pair of gunslingers on a Wild West street—the shuttle on the runway, the Penetrator floating in the air in front of it.

Inside the shuttle's cockpit, Schofield yanked off his helmet. The President did the same.

'Shit. What do we—?' the President asked.

Bang!

The cockpit door shuddered.

The men of Echo Unit were out of their seats and were once again pounding on it.

Then suddenly the voice of the Penetrator's pilot came in

over the radio. It was one of Caesar Russell's 7th Squadron men.

'*X-38, this is Air Force Penetrator. Be advised, we have missile lock on you. Release the boy now.*'

Schofield spun to look at Kevin, thinking fast.

The world was closing in on them—the Penetrator outside, the Echo men inside, missile lock . . .

And then he saw the compartment sunk into the wall beyond Kevin's seat.

He turned to the President. 'Sir, could you help Kevin get his suit off, please.'

The President did so while Schofield hit the 'TALK' button. 'Air Force Penetrator, what are your intentions?'

As he spoke, Schofield climbed over to the wall compartment and yanked it open.

A sign on its door panel read: SURVIVAL KIT.

The Echo men continued to pound on the cockpit door.

'*If you release the boy,*' the Penetrator pilot said, '*we leave you in peace.*'

'Yeah, right,' Schofield muttered.

He was foraging frantically through the shuttle's survival compartment. 'Come on,' he breathed, 'there *has* to be one in here. There always is . . .'

Into his mike, however, he said, 'And if we don't release the boy?'

'*Then we might just have to cut our losses and kill you all.*'

It was then that Schofield found what he was looking for inside the compartment: a two-foot-long cylindrical metal tube that looked like a—

He grabbed it, snapped to look up—and found himself looking out through the five-inch-thick glass window that opened onto the rear section of the shuttle. On the other side of the glass, aimed right at his face, was a *pistol*, held by one of the Echo men!

With a flash of white light—and a silent *bang*—the pistol fired.

Schofield shut his eyes, waited for the bullet to crash through the glass and enter his head.

But the glass was too thick. The bullet just scratched the surface and pinged away.

Schofield breathed again, raced back to his seat.

'Air Force Penetrator,' he said as he climbed back into his flight seat and started doing up his seatbelts. 'All right. All right. Listen. I also have the President here.' As he spoke, he indicated for the President to undo his belts.

'*The President . . .*'

'That's right. I'm going to send him out with the boy. I'm sure you won't mind that. Now, I have your word, you won't fire on us if we send them out?'

'*That's right.*'

'Okay,' Schofield said to Kevin and the President. 'When I release the hatch, I want you two to get as far away from this shuttle as you can. All right?'

'Right,' Kevin said.

'Right,' the President nodded. 'But what about you?'

Schofield pulled the hatch release lever.

With a sharp *snap-whoosh!* a small section of the shuttle's ceiling—the part directly above the tied-up shuttle pilot— went catapulting high into the air, flying end over end.

A wide square of blue sky opened over the pilot.

'Just get as far away from this shuttle as you can,' Schofield said. 'I'll be joining you in a minute. I just have a helicopter to kill.'

In the shimmering desert heat, two tiny figures emerged from the shuttle's cockpit hatch.

The President and Kevin.

The President still wore his orange flight suit, only now he was helmetless. Kevin just wore the regular clothes he'd been wearing underneath his oversized space suit.

The Penetrator loomed above them, its rotor wash shaking the air.

A plastic rope-ladder hung down from the shuttle's roof. It had unrolled automatically when the escape hatch had been jettisoned.

The President and Kevin descended the ladder quickly, under the watchful eye of the Penetrator's three crew members.

Then their feet touched the burning-hot tarmac and they hurried away from the shuttle.

Meanwhile, inside the shuttle's cockpit, Schofield was positioning the metal tube on his lap, waiting tensely for Kevin and the President to get clear.

He exchanged a glance with the still-bound shuttle pilot. 'What're you looking at?' he said—

Zzzzzzzzz!

Without warning, a spray of brilliant orange sparks exploded out from the door behind him.

Holy . . .

The Echo men were using *a blowtorch* to cut through the door!

Must wait for the President and the boy to get clear . . .

And then the Penetrator pilot's voice came through. *'Thank you, X-38. I'm sorry for misleading you, but unfortunately you must now be destroyed. Goodnight.'*

Instantly, a Sidewinder missile shot out from the right-hand wing-stub of the Penetrator, a smoketrail looping through the air behind it. It zoomed downwards, heading straight for the space shuttle's windshield.

The blowtorch's sparks sprayed into the cockpit from behind.

Screw it, Schofield thought. *Time to blow this joint.*

And with that, he yanked on the ejection lever beside his seat.

Like a New Year's Eve firecracker shooting up into the sky, Shane Schofield rocketed up into the air above the grounded space shuttle, sitting on his flight seat.

He carved a perfectly straight vertical path into the air, in the process creating a bizarre triangle between himself, the space shuttle and the Penetrator helicopter.

And then everything happened at once.

First, the Penetrator's missile *slammed* into the X-38 beneath Schofield, causing it and the Echo men inside it to explode in a billowing blasting fireball.

For his part, Schofield shot high into the air above the flaming explosion, reaching the zenith of his flight path just as he drew level with the Penetrator's shocked crew.

It was only then that the chopper's three crew members saw Schofield heft the cylindrical tube from the shuttle's survival kit onto his shoulder—*as he flew upwards on the ejection seat.*

Only it wasn't just any old tube.

It was a rocket launcher.

A compact M-72 single-shot disposable rocket launcher, supplied in the survival kit for astronauts who crash-landed in enemy territory and needed some lightweight but heavy-hitting firepower.

Hovering in the air in his ejection seat, high above the billowing fireball that had been the X-38, Schofield jammed his finger down on the rocket launcher's trigger.

Instantly, a streamlined warhead *shoomed* out from the M-72 on his shoulder, streaking through the air at phenomenal speed, heading straight for the Penetrator's cockpit.

The warhead smashed through the helicopter's glass windshield and detonated violently. The walls of the attack helicopter blasted outwards, the chopper just disintegrating in mid-air.

It dropped out of the sky—a blazing, flaming wreck, trailing a plume of thick black smoke—and crashed down against the tarmac, shattering into pieces.

The final episode of the sequence was the inflating of Schofield's parachute.

It blossomed to life above his ejection seat, lifting him out of it. Then the parachute carried him safely back down to earth, landing him gently on the runway a short way from the twin flaming ruins of the space shuttle and the Penetrator.

The President and Kevin rushed up to him.

'That was *so* cool!' Kevin gasped.

'Yes. Remind me never to point a loaded weapon at you,' the President said.

Schofield discarded his parachute, gazed back down the runway toward the buildings of Area 7.

Area 7 . . .

Strangely, the first thing he thought about was not the Football nor the fate of the country.

It was Libby Gant.

He'd last seen her during their battle in the pit, when Colonel Harper's Sinovirus grenade had gone off and they'd been separated.

But then he saw the helicopter.

Saw the *second* Penetrator—Caesar and Logan's Penetrator—sitting empty and abandoned outside the main hangar complex.

'Caesar came back to Area 7 . . .' Schofield said aloud. 'Why would he do that?'

It was then that he saw a figure emerge from the base of the airfield's control tower, waving one arm weakly.

It was Book II.

Schofield, Kevin and the President met Book at the base of the tower.

Book II looked pale, weary. He wore a thick bandage over a wound on his left bicep; the rest of the arm was held in a makeshift sling.

'Scarecrow. Quick,' he said, obviously still in pain. 'You better come and see this. *Now.*'

As they climbed the stairs of the control tower, Schofield said, 'When did Caesar come back to Area 7?'

'They landed only a few minutes before you did. They *were* all heading for that top door entrance when you guys arrived. I was looking after Janson up in the tower, and we saw the whole ejection-seat thing. Caesar and Logan watched it from the hangar entrance, but when you blasted their boys to kingdom come, they headed straight inside the complex again.'

'Caesar went back inside the complex . . . Why?' Schofield said, thinking hard. Then he looked up. 'Any word from Gant?'

'No,' Book II said. 'I figured she was with you.'

'We got separated when that Sinovirus grenade went off before. She must still be inside the complex.'

They arrived at the top level of the tower. Juliet Janson lay slumped on a chair, a bandage over her bullet-wounded shoulder, alive but very pale.

Beside her, lay the Football.

'So what did you want me to see?' Schofield asked Book.

'This,' Book II said, indicating one particular computer screen. It was flashing:

```
*******************************WARNING*********************************
EMERGENCY PROTOCOL ACTIVATED.
IF YOU DO NOT ENTER AN AUTHORIZED LOCKDOWN EXTENSION
OR TERMINATION CODE BY 1105 HOURS, FACILITY
SELF-DESTRUCT SEQUENCE WILL BE ACTIVATED.
SELF-DESTRUCT SEQUENCE DURATION: 10:00 MINUTES.
*******************************WARNING*********************************
```

Schofield looked at his watch.

It was 10:43.

Twenty-two minutes till the complex's thermonuclear self-destruct mechanism was set in motion.

And they'd had no word from Gant . . .

Shit.

'There's another thing,' Book II said. 'We've managed to get the generators back on line, but the power's still very low. We've been able to get a couple of systems back on, some light systems, a few communication lines and the internal broadcast system.'

'And . . . ?'

'Have a look at this.'

Book II hit a switch, and one of the console monitors blinked to life.

On it, Schofield saw the image of the control room overlooking the main hangar.

And standing inside the heavily battered room, looking directly into the camera as he had done on several occasions earlier that morning, was Caesar Russell.

Russell grinned at the camera.

When he spoke, his voice boomed out from the tower's speakers.

'Greetings, Mister President, people of America. I know it's

*a little early for my hourly update, but since, alas, it appears
that my race has been run, I'm sure you won't mind an early
commentary.*

'*My men are vanquished, my cause lost. I would commend the
President and his brave bodyguards for their efforts, but such is
not my way. I merely leave you all with a parting comment: this
country can never be the same, not after today . . .*'

Then Caesar did something that made Schofield's blood
completely freeze.

He pulled open the front of his combat fatigues, revealing his chest.

Schofield's jaw dropped. 'Oh no . . .'

There, on Russell's chest, was a long vertical scar, right
over his heart—the scar of a man who had had heart surgery
sometime in the past.

Caesar grinned, an evil, maniacal, completely *insane* grin.

'*Cross my heart,*' he said, '*and hope to die.*'

'What?' the President said. 'I don't get it.'

Schofield was silent.

He got it.

He snatched a piece of paper from his pocket. It was the
printout he'd got Brainiac to produce inside the AWACS
plane right at the very start of all this—when he'd needed to
know if there really was a radio transmitter planted on the
President's heart.

Schofield scanned the printout. It still had the circles
Brainiac had drawn on it before:

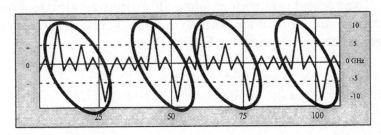

He recalled Brainiac's earlier explanation.

'It's a standard rebounding signature. The satellite sends down a search signal—they're the tall spikes on the positive side—and then, soon after, the receiver on the ground, the President, bounces that signal back. Those are the deep spikes on the negative side.

'Search and return. Interference aside, the rebounding signature seems to repeat itself once every twenty-five seconds.'

'Interference aside . . .' Schofield said as he stared at the printout.

'Only there is no interference. There are *two separate signals.* The satellite needs to pick up two signals . . .' He grabbed a nearby pen and joined the four circles into two pairs.

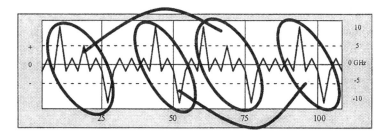

'This graph indicates *two* distinct signal patterns,' Schofield said. 'The first and the third. And then the second and fourth.'

'What are you saying?' the President asked.

'What I'm saying, Mister President, is that you're not the only man at this complex with a radio transmitter attached to his heart. It's Caesar's trump card, his last resort, so that even if he loses, he still wins. Caesar Russell has a transmitter attached to *his* heart. So now, if he dies, the devices at the airports go off.'

'But he's inside the complex,' Book II said, wincing with pain, 'and in exactly twenty minutes, the self-destruct sequence will be initiated.'

'I know,' Schofield said, 'and so does he. Which means I now have to do something that I never thought I'd *ever* want to do. I have to go back into Area 7 and stop Caesar Russell from getting killed.'

SEVENTH CONFRONTATION

3 July, 1045 Hours

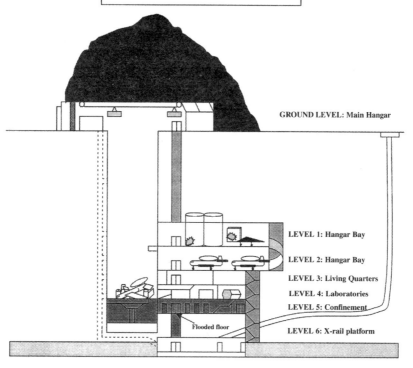

UNITED STATES AIR FORCE
SPECIAL AREA (RESTRICTED) NO.7
1045 HOURS

GROUND LEVEL: Main Hangar

LEVEL 1: Hangar Bay

LEVEL 2: Hangar Bay

LEVEL 3: Living Quarters

LEVEL 4: Laboratories

LEVEL 5: Confinement

Flooded floor

LEVEL 6: X-rail platform

Schofield re-armed himself.

With Book II and Juliet both wounded, he was going back inside alone.

He got his Maghook back from Book, slid it into the shotgun holster on his back. He also grabbed the P-90 that Seth Grimshaw had brought out of the complex. It only had about forty rounds left in it, but that was better than nothing. He jammed Book's M9 and his own Desert Eagle pistol into his thigh holsters. And last of all, he swapped his water-damaged wrist mike and earpiece for Juliet's working unit.

Book and Juliet would remain up in the tower armed with a P-90, guarding the President, the Football and Kevin until the Army and Marine forces arrived at the base.

Schofield pulled out Nicholas Tate's cell phone, dialled the operator. He got Dave Fairfax's voice straight away, cutting into the call.

'Mister Fairfax, I need a favour.'

'*What?*'

'I need the lockdown release codes for Special Area 7, the codes that turn off the self-destruct mechanism. Now, I can't imagine they're kept in a book somewhere. You're going to have to get onto the local network itself and somehow pull them out.'

'*How long have I got?*' Fairfax asked.

'You've got exactly nineteen minutes.'

'*I'm on it.*'

Fairfax hung up.

Schofield jammed a fresh clip into his M9. As he did so, a figure appeared at his side.

'I think she's still alive, too,' Kevin said suddenly.

Schofield looked up, appraised the little boy for a moment. 'How did you know I was thinking that?'

'I just know. I always know. I knew that Doctor Botha was lying to the Air Force men. And I could tell that you were a good man. I can't see exactly what someone's thinking, just what they're feeling. Right now, you're worried about someone, someone you care about. Someone who's still inside.'

'Is this how you knew it was me on the space shuttle?'

'Yes.'

Schofield finished loading his guns. 'Any final tips, then?' he asked Kevin.

The little boy said, 'I only saw her once, when you were both standing outside my cube. I only sensed one thing about her: she really likes you. So you'd better save her.'

Schofield gave him a wry smile. 'Thanks.'

And then he was away.

He tried the top door entrance first.

No luck.

Caesar had changed the code, manually it seemed. No time for Fairfax to crack that one.

That left only one other option: the Emergency Exit Vent.

Schofield ran for Caesar's abandoned Penetrator helicopter.

It was 10:48 a.m.

Two minutes later, Caesar's Penetrator—now flown by Schofield—landed next to the EEV in a swirling cloud of dust and sand.

The EEV hadn't been hard to find. Mr Hoeg's lime-green biplane—still sitting there on the desert floor—betrayed the exit's location quite unambiguously.

No sooner had the black helicopter touched the ground than Schofield was out of it and running toward the EEV.

He leaped down into the earthen trench and disappeared inside the exit's open steel doorway at a run.

It was 10:51 when Schofield stepped out onto the darkened X-rail tracks on Level 6, his gun raised.

The world down here was pitch black, save for the thin beam of his P-90's barrel-mounted flashlight.

He saw bodies laid out before him, shadows in the dim light—the remnants of the previous battles that day.

Air Force vs Secret Service.

South Africans vs Air Force.

Schofield and his Marines vs Air Force.

Christ ...

But another thing weighed on his mind. Kevin, of course, had been right. Apart from saving Caesar Russell, Schofield had a far more personal reason for entering Area 7 again.

He wanted to find Libby Gant.

He didn't know what had happened to her after the Sinovirus grenade had gone off up in the main hangar, but he refused to believe that she was dead.

Schofield brought his wrist mike to his lips. 'Fox. Fox. Are you out there? This is Scarecrow. I'm back inside. Can you hear me?'

In a dark place somewhere inside Area 7, Libby Gant stirred, a voice invading her dreams.

'*—you hear me?*'

She'd been unconscious for nearly an hour now, and she didn't have a clue where she was or what had happened to her.

Her last memory was of being inside the control room upstairs and seeing something important and then suddenly ... *nothing*.

As she blinked awake, she saw that she was still wearing

her bright yellow biohazard suit, except for the helmet. It had been removed.

It was only then that she became aware of a pain in her shoulders. Gant opened her eyes fully—

—and an ice-cold chill rippled down her spine.

Her entire upper body was bound to a pair of steel girders that had been arranged in the shape of an X. Her wrists were held high above her head—crucifix-style—affixed to the arms of the cross with duct tape, while more thick tape held her throat tightly up against the junction of the X. Her legs—duct-taped at the ankles—were laid out flat in front of her.

Gant began to breathe very very fast.

What the hell was this?

She was someone's *prisoner*.

As she hung helplessly from the cross, eyes wide and terrified, she slowly began to regain her senses. She took in the area around her.

The first thing she noticed about this place was that there was no electric lighting. Three small fires illuminated the immediate area.

It was in this grim firelight that she saw Hagerty.

Colonel Hot Rod Hagerty sat immediately to her right, similarly 'crucified'—his legs stretched out on the floor in front of him, his arms outstretched on his own cross. His eyes were shut, his head bent. Every few seconds he groaned.

Gant looked at the room around them.

She was sitting underneath an overhang of some sort, in dark shadow; a stage-like structure stood out in the open space in front of her. Some children's toys lay scattered about the stage, amid shards of glass.

It looked as if—once—a glass cube of some sort had encased the stage, but now only half of that cube remained standing.

Gant realised where she was.

She was in the area that had contained Kevin's sterilised

434

living area. Right now, she must be sitting directly underneath the observation lab that had overlooked the cube, beneath the overhang it created.

And then Gant saw the third crucified figure in the room, and she gasped in revulsion.

It was the Air Force colonel, Jerome Harper.

Or what was left of him.

He lay to Gant's left, also under the overhang, his arms taped to a cross high above his head, his head leaning as far forward as the duct tape around his throat would allow.

But it was his lower body that seized Gant's shocked attention.

Harper's legs were missing.

No, not just missing.

Hacked off.

Everything from the Air Force colonel's waist down had been brutally carved away—like a carcass in an abattoir—leaving a gigantic slab of raw hacked flesh around his hips. Indeed, Harper's whole waist region was just a foul bloody mess that ended at the curved bony hook of his spinal column.

It was the most disgusting thing Gant had ever seen in her life.

Her eyes swept the room, as the full extent of her predicament became clear.

She was the prisoner of a monster. An individual who, until today, had been a guest here at Area 7.

Lucifer Leary.

The Surgeon of Phoenix.

The serial killer who had terrorised hitch-hikers on the Vegas-to-Phoenix interstate—the former medical student who would kidnap his victims, take them home, and then *eat* their limbs in front of them.

Gant looked about herself in horror.

Leary—a big man, she recalled, at least six-eight, with a hideous facial tattoo—was nowhere to be seen.

Except for Hagerty and herself, the whole observation area was completely and utterly *empty*.

Which, in a strange way, was even more frightening.

Schofield made for the stairwell at the eastern end of Level 6.

He had to get to the control room overlooking the main hangar—to enter the termination codes before 11:05; or if he couldn't do that, to capture Caesar and get him out of Area 7 before the nuke went off at 11:15.

He threw open the stairwell doorway—

—and was instantly confronted by an enormous black bear, caught in the beam of his small flashlight, rearing up on its hind legs, baring its massive claws and bellowing loudly at him!

Schofield dived off the edge of the X-rail platform as the family of bears ambled out of the stairwell—papa bear, mama bear and three little baby bears, all in a row.

Nicholas Tate had been right.

There *were* bears on the loose.

Papa bear seemed to sniff the air for a moment. Then he headed westward, toward the other end of the underground railway station, followed by his brood.

As soon as they were a safe distance away, Schofield dashed into the open stairwell.

Dave Fairfax was tapping feverishly at the keyboard of his supercomputer.

After five minutes' work, the computer had found a source number that represented Area 7's self-destruct release code.

Not bad progress, really. There was only one problem.

The number had 640 million digits.

He kept typing.

10:52.

Schofield bounded up the stairwell, in near pitch darkness, his flashlight beam wobbling.

As he ran, he tried to get Gant on the airwaves. 'Fox, this is Scarecrow. Can you hear me?' he whispered. 'I repeat, Fox, this is Scarecrow . . .'

No reply.

He ran past the firedoor to Level 5—the door with the thin jets of water shooting out from its edges—then came to Level 4, the lab level, hurried past its open door, heading upward.

On the other side of Level 4, Gant heard the voice again. It sounded tinny and distant.

'—repeat, Fox, this is Scarecrow—'

Scarecrow . . .

The voice was coming from Gant's earpiece, which now hung loosely from her ear. It must have been dislodged when her captor had knocked her unconscious.

Gant looked up at her left wrist, duct-taped to the cross high above her head.

She still had her Secret Service wrist mike attached to it. But there was no way she could bring it to her mouth, and the mike only worked when you spoke into it at close range.

So she started tapping her finger on the top of the microphone.

Schofield came to the floor-door that opened onto Level 2 and suddenly stopped.

He'd heard a strange tapping in his earpiece.

Tap-tap-taap. Tap-taap-tap . . .

Long and short taps.

Morse code.

Morse code that read, 'F-O-X. F-O-X . . .'

'Fox, is that you? One tap for no, two taps for yes.'

Tap-tap.

'Are you okay?'

Tap.

'Where are you? Tap out the floor number.'

Tap-tap-tap-tap.

10:53.

Schofield burst through the Level 4 firedoor, scanning the decompression area down the barrel of his gun.

It was dark.

Very dark.

This end of the floor was completely deserted—the decompression chamber was empty, as were the test chambers opposite it, and the catwalks above. The sliding horizontal doorway in the floor—the one that led down to the Level 5 cell bay—however, was still open.

The water level down on Level 5 had risen considerably over the last few hours. It had levelled off flush against the floor of Level 4. Inky black wavelets lapped up against the edges of the horizontal opening so that it now looked like a little rectangular pool.

Level 5, it seemed, was completely underwater now.

Schofield stepped past the pool—just as something slashed quickly through its waves. He spun, whipped his gun around, but whatever it had been was long gone.

This was *not* what he needed.

Dark complex. Bears moving around the stairwells. Caesar and Logan in here somewhere. Water everywhere. Not to mention the possible presence of more prisoners.

He came to the wall that divided Level 4 in two, flung its door open and snapped his gun up . . .

... and immediately saw Gant on the far side, beyond the shattered remains of Kevin's cube, lying spread-eagled up against a bizarre steel cross.

Schofield ran across the observation area, slid to his knees in front of Gant.

As he arrived before her, he dropped his P-90, clasped her head gently in his hands and, without even thinking, *kissed* her on the lips.

At first, Gant was a little stunned, then she realised what was happening and she kissed him back.

When he pulled away, Schofield saw the two men on either side of her.

First he saw Hagerty, out cold, similarly crucified.

Then he saw the dead Colonel Harper—saw the raw pink flesh of his hacked-off lower body, saw his exposed tail bone.

'Holy *Christ* . . .' he breathed.

'Quickly,' Gant said. 'We don't have much time, he'll be back soon.'

'Who?' Schofield started unravelling her duct-taped throat.

'Lucifer Leary.'

'Oh, *shit* . . .' Schofield started working faster. The tape around Gant's neck came free. He started on her wrists—

There came a loud resonating *boom* from within the walls.

Schofield and Gant both looked up, eyes wide.

'The aircraft elevator . . .' Schofield said.

'He must have gone upstairs,' Gant breathed, 'and now he's back. *Hurry . . .*'

Faster now, Schofield continued untying the tape around Gant's left wrist, but it was done too tightly. His fingers fumbled with the tape. This was taking too long . . .

He spun, saw some glass shards lying over by Kevin's stage-like living area—shards that he could use to cut the duct tape. He slid over toward them and sifted through them, trying to find one that was sharp enough. He found one, just as Gant called, '*Scarecrow!*' and he stood and turned—

—and found himself confronted by an extremely tall broadshouldered figure.

Schofield froze.

The figure just stood there before him—perhaps a yard away, his face shrouded in shadow—absolutely motionless. He towered over Schofield, gazing at him silently. Schofield hadn't even heard him approach.

'Do you know why the weasel never steals from the alligator's nest?' the shadowy figure asked. Schofield couldn't even see the man's mouth move.

Schofield swallowed.

'Because,' the figure said, 'it never knows when the alligator will return.'

And then the giant man stepped into the firelight—

—and Schofield saw the most fearsome, evil-looking face he'd ever seen in his life. The face was big—like its owner— and it had a hideous black tattoo covering its entire left side, a tattoo depicting five ragged claw-marks scratched down the length of the man's face.

Lucifer Leary.

He was absolutely *enormous*, too, at least six-foot-eight, with massive muscular shoulders and gigantic tree-trunk legs; almost a full foot taller than Schofield. He wore prison-issue jeans and a sky-blue shirt with the sleeves ripped off. His black eyes revealed not a trace of humanity—they just stared at Schofield like empty black orbs.

Then Leary opened his mouth, smiling menacingly, revealing foul yellow teeth.

The effect was mesmerising, almost hypnotic.

Schofield shot a glance back over at Gant, at his P-90 lying on the floor in front of her. Then, in what he thought was a quick draw, he whipped his two pistols from his thigh holsters.

The guns barely got out of their sheaths. Leary had anticipated the move.

Quick as a rattlesnake, he lunged forward and clamped his fists around Schofield's gunhands, seizing them by the wrists.

And then the bigger man started to *squeeze*.

Schofield had never felt such intense pain in his life. He dropped to his knees, teeth clenched—his wrists held in Leary's giant paws. Bloodflow to his hands ceased. It felt as if his fingers—bulging with redness—were going to burst.

He released his pistols. They clattered to the floor. Leary kicked them away.

Then, with the guns gone, he seized Schofield by the throat, lifted him clear off the ground and hurled him across Kevin's living area.

Schofield went crashing across the stage, sliding through some toys, before he exploded through a still-upright section of glass and went tumbling off the far edge of the stage.

Lucifer stalked around the elevated platform after him, his every step crunching on broken glass.

Schofield groaned, tried to stand. He needn't have bothered. Within seconds, Leary was there.

The massive killer lifted Schofield off the floor by his combat webbing and punched him hard in the face, sending his head snapping backwards.

Gant could only watch helplessly from her cross—her hands still tightly bound, Schofield's P-90 lying on the floor only inches away from her—as Lucifer pounded Schofield.

The fight was all one-way traffic.

Lucifer hit, Schofield recoiled, collapsed in a heap to the floor.

Lucifer strode forward, Schofield struggled to stand up.

And then Lucifer hurled Schofield through the doorway

that divided Level 4, sending him sliding into the decompression area.

Lucifer followed him in.

Another kick and Schofield rolled—bleeding and gasping—up against the rim of the horizontal doorway in the floor, filled as it was with lapping water.

And then from out of nowhere, a giant reptilian head came bursting up out of the water and lunged at Schofield's head.

Schofield rolled quickly, avoiding the fast-moving jaws as they snapped down an inch away from his face.

Jesus!

It was a Komodo dragon. The largest lizard in the world, a known man-eater. The President had said they kept some of them here—along with the Kodiak bears, in cages down on Level 5—for use on the Sinovirus project.

The electric locks on their cages, it seemed, hadn't survived the power shutdown either.

At the sight of the Komodo dragon in the pool, a thin smile cracked Lucifer's hideous face.

He lifted Schofield off the ground and held him out over the reptile-infested pool.

As he hung above it, legs kicking, hands grappling at Lucifer's enormous fists, Schofield saw the dark alligator-like bodies of at least two dragons in the water beneath him.

Then without so much as a pause, Lucifer dropped Schofield into the pool.

Schofield splashed down into the water in an explosion of foam, a moment before Lucifer pressed a button in the floor beside the doorway, causing the hole's sliding garage-style door to close quickly over the ripples that marked the spot where Schofield had plunged into it.

Within seconds, the leading edge of the door met the opposite rim.

Ka-chunk.

Sealed. Shut.

Lucifer grunted a laugh as he heard Schofield's fists banging on the underside of the sliding door, heard the sloshing of water underneath the closed door—the sound of the dragons mauling the foolish Marine.

Lucifer smiled.

Then he headed back toward the other side of Level 4, where the pleasure of carving up the pretty female soldier awaited him.

Libby Gant gasped in horror as Lucifer Leary returned alone to the observation area of Level 4.

No.

Lucifer couldn't have . . .

No . . .

The giant serial killer strode confidently across the wide hall-like room, his head lowered, his eyes locked on Gant's.

He dropped to his knees in front of her, pushed his face close to hers. His breath was foul—it reeked of *eaten* human flesh.

He stroked her hair.

'Such a shame, such a shame,' he trilled, 'that your knight in shining armour was not the brave warrior he thought himself to be. Which only leaves us, now, to get . . . *better* acquainted.'

'Not likely,' said a voice from behind Lucifer.

The giant spun.

And there, in the doorway that led to the decompression area, his whole body dripping with water, stood Shane Schofield.

'You'll have to get rid of me,' he said grimly, 'before you lay a finger on her.'

Lucifer roared, snatched up Schofield's P-90 and let rip with an extended burst.

Schofield just stepped behind the doorway, out of sight, as the dividing wall all around the door was shredded by the hailstorm of gunfire.

Within seconds, however, the gun ran dry and Lucifer discarded it and stormed across the observation area, into the decompression area.

The horizontal door in its floor now lay open, wavelets still lapping against its rims. The large outlines of the Komodo dragons were still visible beneath the pool's rippling surface.

But, somehow, they hadn't killed Schofield.

And then Lucifer saw him, standing over by the decompression chamber, to the right of the pool.

He charged at Schofield, lashed out with a ferocious right.

Schofield ducked, walked under the punch. He was calmer now, collected. Not so caught-by-surprise. He had Lucifer's measure.

Lucifer spun, swung again. Another miss. Schofield punished the error with a crisp hit to Lucifer's face.

Crack.

Instantly broken nose.

Lucifer seemed more stunned than injured. He touched the blood that ran down from his nose as if it were an alien substance, as if no-one had ever hurt him before.

And then Schofield hit him again, a great powerful blow, and for the first time, the big man staggered slightly.

Again, harder this time, and Lucifer took an unsteady step backwards.

Again, another step backwards.

Again—the most violent punch Schofield had ever thrown—and Lucifer's back foot touched the rim of the pool. He turned slightly—just as Schofield nailed him in the nose, causing the big man to lose his footing completely and fall backwards . . .

. . . into the Komodo-infested pool.

446

There was a great splash as Lucifer entered the water, and as the foam subsided, the Komodos rushed him, swarming all over his body, turning it into a writhing mass of black reptilian skin, claws and tails, and in the middle of it all, Lucifer's kicking feet and agonised screams.

Then, abruptly, the pool turned a sickening shade of red and Lucifer's legs went still. The Komodos just continued to eat his body.

Schofield winced at the sight, but then, if anyone deserved to die such an horrific painful death, Lucifer Leary did.

Then Schofield hit the button that closed the floor-door, obliterating the foul sight, and hurried back to get Gant.

10:59.

Within a minute, Gant was unbound and standing next to Schofield as he freed the bleary-eyed Hot Rod Hagerty.

Gant said, 'You know, this birthday really has *sucked*.' She nodded toward the decompression area. 'What happened in there? I thought Leary had . . .'

'He did,' Schofield said. 'Bastard dropped me in a pool filled with Komodo dragons.'

'So how'd you get out?'

Schofield pulled out his Maghook. 'Apparently reptiles are exceptionally sensitive to magnetic discharges. I only learned that little fact this morning, from a little boy named Kevin. So I just flicked on my Maghook and they didn't want to come near me. Then I opened the floor-door up again from below and came back for you. Sadly, Lucifer didn't have a supercharged magnetic grappling hook on him when *he* fell in.'

'Nice,' Gant said. 'Very nice. So where's the President, and Kevin?'

'They're safe. They're outside the complex.'

'So why are you back in here?'

Schofield looked at his watch.

It was exactly 11:00 a.m.

'Two reasons. One, because in exactly five minutes this facility's self-destruct mechanism will be activated. Ten minutes after that, this whole place will be vapourised, and we can't allow that to happen while Caesar Russell is inside it. So we either *stop* it from going off, or, if we can't do that, we get Caesar Russell out of here before it does.'

'Wait a second,' Gant said, 'we have to *save* Caesar?'

'It seems our host decided to put a radio chip on his own heart as well as the President's. So if he dies, so does the country.'

'Son of a bitch,' Gant said. 'So what was the second reason?'

Schofield's face reddened slightly. 'I wanted to find you.'

Gant's face lit up, but she spoke matter-of-factly: 'You know, we can talk about this later.'

'I think that would be good,' Schofield said as Hagerty came free of his bonds, blinking out of his stupor. 'What do you say we do it on another date?'

Gant broke out in a grin. 'You bet.'

448

11:01.

Schofield and Gant rode the detachable mini-elevator swiftly up the main shaft, now armed only with Schofield's pistols—Gant with the M9, Schofield with the Desert Eagle.

Schofield had sent Hagerty down to Level 6, to escape via the Emergency Exit Vent. When he'd seen the hacked-up half-body of Colonel Harper, Hagerty hadn't argued. He was happy to get out of Area 7 as quickly as possible.

'I don't know if we'll be able to disarm the self-destruct system,' Gant said as Schofield gave her a shot of the Sinovirus vaccine to protect her against the contaminated hangar. 'You have to enter a lockdown code by 11:05 to call it off, and we don't know any of the codes.'

'I've been working on that,' Schofield said, pulling out his cell phone. He hit redial and Fairfax's voice came on the line straight away.

'Mister Fairfax, how goes it?'

'*The lockdown termination code is 10502,*' Fairfax said. '*Hacked into the system from behind, from the source code. Got it that way. Turns out it's the operator number of the head dude there, an Air Force colonel named Harper.*'

'I don't think he'll be needing it anymore,' Schofield said. 'Thank you, Mister Fairfax. If I get out of this alive, I'll buy you a beer sometime.'

He hung up and turned to Gant.

'Okay. Time to turn off this nuclear time-bomb. Then all we have to do is capture Caesar alive.'

They rose up the side of the darkened shaft.

Its great square-shaped opening up at ground level loomed above them, backlit by orange firelight.

It turned out that Lucifer Leary had indeed brought the main elevator platform down to Level 4. When they'd arrived at the elevator shaft from the Level 4 observation lab, Schofield and Gant had found the giant platform sitting right there in front of them, piled high with no less than *fifteen* bodies—prisoners, 7th Squadron commandos, Marines and White House staff—bodies which Leary no doubt planned to dismember in strange and unusual ways.

As such, the shaft now yawned wide above Schofield and Gant, open and airy.

As they travelled quickly up it, Gant reached underneath the moving platform. She emerged with her Maghook, which she'd left attached to the underside of the mini-elevator earlier.

'Get ready,' Schofield said.

They had arrived at the main hangar.

The hangar looked like hell.

Literally.

Fires burned all over the place, bathing the enormous space in a haunting orange glow. Bodies lay everywhere.

Assorted debris littered the area—the remains of blown-up helicopters, crumpled towing vehicles, the pieces of Bravo Unit's failed barricade over by the internal building.

Nothing, it seemed, lay unscarred.

The slanted windows of the control room overlooking the hangar were completely shattered. Even one of the giant wooden crates hanging from the overhead crane system had a gnarled piece of Nighthawk 2's tail rotor embedded in its side.

Amazingly, however, one object remained untouched by the day's mayhem.

Marine One.

It still stood on the western side of the aircraft elevator shaft, miraculously intact.

As their elevator jolted to a halt inside the hangar, Schofield and Gant looked about themselves cautiously.

11:02.

'The self-destruct computer is in the control room,' Gant said.

'Then that's where we're going,' Schofield said, heading for the internal building.

'Wait a minute,' Gant said, stopping suddenly, her eyes scanning the debris-covered floor around them.

'We don't have a minute,' Schofield said.

'You go then,' Gant said. 'Call me if you need any help. I'm gonna try something.'

'Okay,' Schofield said, charging off toward the internal building.

Gant, meanwhile, dropped to her knees and started searching through the bodies and debris around the mini-elevator platform.

Schofield burst inside the lower floor of the internal building, leading with his Desert Eagle.

He hit the stairs on the fly, charged up them. For the first time that day, he actually felt in control. He had the lockdown code—10502—and now all he had to do was punch it into the computer and disarm the nuke.

Then he would have plenty of time to find Caesar—whose men were now history—before he killed himself, and drag him out of Area 7 to face justice.

11:03.

Schofield came to the control room door, pushed it open, his gun levelled in front of him.

What he saw took him completely by surprise.

There, sitting in a swivel chair in the middle of the destroyed command room, waiting for Schofield and smiling broadly at him, was Caesar Russell.

'I thought you might be back,' Caesar said.

He was unarmed.

'You know, Captain,' he said, 'a man like you is wasted on this country. You're clever, you've got courage, and you'll do whatever it takes to win, including the bizarre and the illogical, such as saving me. You and your efforts would be unappreciated by the ignorant fools who make up this nation. Which is why,' he sighed, 'it is such a shame that you have to die.'

It was then that the gun cocked next to Schofield's head.

Schofield turned—

—to see Major Kurt Logan standing behind him, his silver SIG-Sauer pistol pointed right at Schofield's temple.

11:04.

'Come in,' Caesar said. 'Come in.'

Logan relieved Schofield of his Desert Eagle as the two of them stepped into the destroyed control room.

'Come and watch America's death sentence,' Caesar waved at an illuminated screen behind him. It was like the one Schofield had seen outside. It read:

LOCKDOWN PROTOCOL S.A.(R) 7-A
FAILSAFE SYSTEM ENACTED
AUTH CODE: 7-3-468201103

```
****************************WARNING!****************************
EMERGENCY PROTOCOL ACTIVATED.
IF YOU DO NOT ENTER AN AUTHORIZED LOCKDOWN EXTENSION
OR TERMINATION CODE BY 1105 HOURS, FACILITY
SELF-DESTRUCT SEQUENCE WILL BE ACTIVATED.
SELF-DESTRUCT SEQUENCE DURATION: 10:00 MINUTES.
****************************WARNING!****************************
```

Schofield saw a clock at the bottom corner of the computer screen ticking upward.

11:04:29

11:04:30

11:04:31

'Tick-tick-tick,' Caesar said deliciously. 'How frustrating this must be for you, Captain. No clever plans to save you now, no space shuttles, no secret exits. Once the ten-minute self-destruct sequence is set in motion, nothing can stop it from going off. I will die, and so will you, and so too will America.'

The clock on the screen ticked upward.

Covered by Logan, Schofield could only watch helplessly as it approached 11:05 a.m.

11:04:56

11:04:57

Schofield clenched his fists with frustration.

He knew the code! *He knew it*. But he couldn't *use* it. And where the hell was Gant? What was she doing?

11:04:58

11:04:59

11:05:00

'Lift-off,' Caesar smiled.

'Shit,' Schofield said.

The screen beeped.

LOCKDOWN PROTOCOL S.A.(R) 7-A

FACILITY SELF-DESTRUCT SEQUENCE ACTIVATED.
10:00 MINUTES TO DETONATION.

A blinking countdown commenced on the screen.
10:00
9:59
9:58
At that very same moment, an army of battery-powered revolving red lights exploded to life throughout the complex—inside the main hangar, down in the aircraft elevator shaft, even inside the control room.

An electronic voice boomed out from an emergency PA system.

'Warning. Ten minutes to facility self-destruct . . .'

And just then—as they were bathed in strobing red light—Schofield saw Kurt Logan take his eyes off him, just for a split-second, to look out at the lights.

Schofield took the chance.

He drove his body into Logan's, sending both of them crashing against a computer console.

Logan brought his gun around, but Schofield grabbed his wrist and banged it down against the console, causing the 7th Squadron commander to release the pistol.

Caesar just sat back, grinning with satisfaction, watching the fight in front of him with mad delight.

Schofield and Logan fought hard, covered in red emergency lighting. They looked like mirror images, two elite soldiers who had studied from the same manual, exchanging identical blows, employing identical evasive moves.

But Schofield was exhausted from his previous battle with Lucifer and he unleashed a loose swing which Logan punished without mercy.

He ducked beneath Schofield's wayward blow and then tackled him around the waist, lifting Schofield clear off the ground and driving him backwards toward the shattered windows of the control room.

Schofield blasted out through the destroyed windows of the command room, back-first, flying through the air. He shut his eyes and waited for the crushing impact with the floor thirty feet below.

It never came.

Instead, his fall was unexpectedly short.

Thud!

Schofield slammed down on a rough wooden surface that rocked beneath his weight.

He opened his eyes.

He was lying on top of one of the enormous wooden cargo crates that hung from the main hangar's ceiling-mounted rail network.

It had been parked just outside the control room, a little to the left, allowing the command centre a clear view of the hangar.

A triangle of thick chains connected the massive crate to the overhead rail system six feet above it. The chains were held together by a spring-loaded ring mechanism not unlike the closable circular latch one finds on a necklace.

Attached to the ring mechanism was a square control unit made up of three big buttons which presumably moved the crate back and forth along the rails.

Then suddenly, the crate rocked wildly and Schofield looked up to see that Kurt Logan had jumped out onto it after him.

Down on the hangar floor, Libby Gant had heard the crash of breaking glass and snapped to look up.

She had just found what she was looking for amid the debris on the floor when she saw Schofield come exploding out through the control room's windows and land hard on the wooden crate suspended high above the hangar floor.

Then she saw Kurt Logan jump out through the window, and land easily on the crate next to him.

'No . . .' Gant breathed.

456

She drew her gun, but abruptly, a barrage of bullet impact-sparks lit up the floor all around her.

She dived for cover behind a couple of dead bodies. When she finally looked up, she saw Caesar Russell leaning out from the destroyed control room windows, brandishing a P-90 and yelling, 'No, no, no! A fair fight, please!'

'Warning. Nine minutes to facility self-destruct . . .'

Up on the wooden crate, Logan kneeled astride Schofield, hit him hard in the face.

'You've made today a lot harder than it had to be, Captain.'

His face gleamed with anger in the strobe-like red light.

Another punch. Hard.

Schofield's head slammed back against the crate, his nose gushing with blood.

Logan then grabbed the control unit above his head and hit a button.

With a jolt and a sway and the clanking of mechanical gears, the crate began to move out across the hangar, toward the open aircraft elevator shaft. It was petrol-powered, so it hadn't been affected by the complex's power loss.

As the crate began to glide out over the hangar Logan kept pounding Schofield, talking as he did so.

'You know, I remember—'

Punch.

'—taking out you Marine pussies at the annual wargames—'

Punch.

'—Too fucking easy. You're a disgrace—'

Punch.

'—to the country, to the flag, and to your fucking bitch-whore mothers.'

Punch.

Schofield could barely keep his eyes open.

Christ, he was getting his ass kicked . . .

And then the crate swung out over the four-hundred-

457

foot-deep aircraft elevator shaft and Logan pressed a button on the control unit, stopping it.

The big crate swung to a halt directly above the wide, yawning shaft.

'Warning. Eight minutes to facility self-destruct . . .'

Schofield peered over the edge of the crate, saw the shaft's concrete walls, now lined with revolving red lights, plummeting like four matching vertical cliffs down into bottomless black.

'Goodbye, Captain Schofield,' Logan said, as he lifted Schofield by his lapels and stood him at the edge of the crate.

Schofield—battered, bloody, bruised and exhausted—couldn't resist. He stood unsteadily at the edge of the crate, the great hole of the elevator shaft yawning wide beneath him.

He thought about the Maghook on his back, but then saw the ceiling. It was made of sheer flat fibreglass. The Maghook wouldn't stick to it with its magnet, nor could it get a purchase on it with its hook.

In any case, he didn't have any energy left to fight.

No more guns.

No more Maghooks.

No more ejection seats.

He had nothing that Logan didn't have more of.

And then, just as Logan was about to push him off the edge of the crate, Schofield saw Gant—a shadow amid the redness—saw her taking cover behind some bodies next to the eastern rim of the elevator shaft.

Except friends . . .

He turned suddenly to face Logan . . .

. . . and to Logan's complete surprise, he smiled, and raised his open palm, revealing his Secret Service microphone.

Schofield then looked Logan deep in the eye and said 'Sydney Harbour Bridge, Gant. You take the negative.'

Logan frowned. 'Huh?'

And then before Logan could even think to do anything, with his last ounce of strength, Schofield reached over

Logan's shoulder and *unlatched* the spring-loaded ring mechanism holding the crate to the overhead rail system.

The result was instantaneous.

In a kind of hellish slow-motion that was only accentuated by the strobing red lighting, the crate—with both Schofield and Logan on it—just *fell away* from its ceiling-mounted rails, spilling the two combatants off its back . . .

. . . and the three of them—Schofield, Logan and the crate itself—dropped together into the four-hundred-foot abyss of the elevator shaft.

Schofield fell through the air.

Fast.

At first he saw the red-lit hangar rushing past him, swinging upwards—then suddenly that image was replaced by the rim of the elevator shaft, swooshing by him as he dropped into the shaft itself. Then all he saw were rapidly-rushing concrete walls speeding by in a blur of grey and he glanced up and saw the wide square up at the top of the shaft shrinking *very, very* quickly above him.

He saw Logan falling beside him, a look of absolute terror on his face. It looked as if Logan couldn't believe what Schofield had just done.

He'd just dropped *both of them* into the shaft, crate and all!

Schofield, however, just prayed that Gant had heard him.

And as he fell through the air, surrounded by red light, he coolly unslung his Maghook, initiated its magnet, selected a positive charge, and looked up in search of his only hope.

Gant *had* heard his call.

Now she lay on her stomach on the rim of the shaft, aiming her own Maghook—now charged negatively—down into it.

'Scarecrow,' she said into her radio mike, 'you fire first. I'll make the shot.'

As he fell down the elevator shaft, Schofield fired his positively charged Maghook into the air.

It rocketed up the shaft—flying perfectly vertical—its tail-rope wobbling through the air behind it.

Kurt Logan, falling alongside Schofield, saw what he was doing and yelled, 'No . . . !'

'Come on, Fox,' Schofield whispered. 'Don't let me die.'

Libby Gant's eyes narrowed as she gazed down the barrel of her Maghook.

Despite all the distractions around her—the flashing red lights, the klaxons, the droning electronic warning voice— she drew a bead on Schofield's flying Maghook: an arcing dot of glinting metal shooting up out of the blackness of the shaft, coming toward her.

'Nothing's impossible,' she whispered to herself.

Then, cool as ice, she pulled the trigger on her own Maghook.

Whump!

The bulbous magnetic head of her Maghook shot out of its launcher, rushed down into the shaft, trailing its own length of rope.

Schofield's Maghook shot *up* the shaft.

Gant's Maghook shot *down* the shaft.

Schofield fell, with Logan and the crate beside him.

Gant rode her Maghook all the way down. 'Come on, baby. Come on . . .' Since they were oppositely charged, they'd only have to pass by close to each other to—

Clang!

The two Maghooks hit—*in mid-air*—like twin missiles slamming into each other in the sky!

The Sydney Harbour Bridge.

Their powerful magnetic charges held them firmly together, and up in the hangar, Gant quickly hooked her launcher into a grate in the floor.

Two Maghooks equals three hundred feet of rope.

And a three-hundred-foot fall means one hell of a jolt.

When he saw Gant's flying magnetic hook connect with his own, Schofield—still falling fast—slung his launcher under his shoulders and around his chest. Then he tensed his arms around the rope, bracing himself for the impending jolt.

This was going to hurt.

It hurt.

With an outrageous *snap*, the ropes of the two Maghooks went taut and Schofield bounced up into the air, yanked upward like a skydiver opening his parachute—while below him, Kurt Logan and the wooden crate just kept on falling, and *slammed* into the aircraft platform below them.

The wooden crate just exploded, its walls shattering into splinters as it hit the platform.

Logan met a similar fate.

He landed hard—screaming—on the jagged remains of the AWACS plane that still littered the elevator platform. His head was separated from his shoulders as his throat hit an upwardly-pointed piece of wing. The rest of his body just *flattened* with the phenomenal impact, splatting like a tomato when it hit the platform.

As for Schofield, after he was snapped upward by the ropes of the two Maghooks, he swung in toward the side wall of the shaft. He slammed into it heavily, bounced off it, and was left hanging next to the sheer concrete wall a bare eighty feet above the elevator platform, breathing hard, his shoulders and arms aching from the jolt, but alive.

The two Maghooks reeled Schofield up the shaft quickly.

'Warning. Six minutes to facility self-destruct.'

It was 11:09 when Gant hauled him up over the rim of the great pit.

'I thought you said the Harbour Bridge was impossible,' she said drily.

'Believe me, that was a very nice way to be proved wrong,' Schofield said.

Gant smiled. 'Yeah, well I only did it because I wanted another—'

She was interrupted by a thunderous line of gunfire cutting through the air all around them, ripping across both their bodies.

A ragged bullet wound burst open near Gant's right foot—shattering her ankle—while another two appeared on Schofield's left shoulder. More bullets passed so close to his face he felt their air-trails swoosh past his nose.

Both Marines dropped, gritting their teeth, as Caesar Russell came charging out of the internal building nearby, his P-90 pressed against his shoulder, firing wildly, his eyes gleaming with madness.

Schofield—hurt for sure, but far more mobile than Gant—pushed Gant behind the remains of Bravo Unit's crate barricade.

Then he grabbed her Beretta and made a loping dash the *other* way, through the strobing red-on-black world, toward the remains of Nighthawk Two over by the personnel elevator, trying to draw Caesar's fire away from Gant.

The massive Marine Corps Super Stallion was still parked in front of the regular elevator's doors—battered and dented, its entire cockpit section blasted wide open.

Caesar's stream of bullets chewed up the ground at his heels, but it was loose fire, and in the flashing red light, Caesar missed wide.

Schofield made it to the Super Stallion, dived into its exploded-open cockpit, just as the chopper's walls erupted with bulletholes.

'Come on, hero!' Caesar yelled. 'What's the matter? *Can't shoot back?* What're you afraid of? Go on! Find a gun and shoot back!'

That, however, was the one thing Schofield couldn't do. If he killed Caesar, he killed every major city in northern America.

Goddamnit! he thought.

It was the worst possible situation.

He was being fired upon by a man he couldn't fire back at!

'Fox!' he yelled into his wrist mike. 'You okay?'

A stifled grimace over his earpiece. '*Yeah . . .*'

Schofield yelled, 'We have to grab him and get him out of here! Any ideas?'

Gant's reply was drowned out by the complex's electronic voice.

'*Warning. Five minutes to facility self-destruct . . .*'

Through a small door-window, Schofield saw Caesar approaching the semi-destroyed helicopter from the side, pummelling its flanks with his fire.

'You like that, hero?' the Air Force general yelled. 'You like that!'

Inside the blasted-open cockpit, everything was shuddering and shaking under the weight of Caesar's fire. Schofield clenched his teeth, gripped his gun. The two bullet holes in

464

his shoulder hurt like hell, but adrenalin was keeping him going.

Through the cracked door-window of the Super Stallion he saw Caesar—crazed and deranged—firing like a yee-ha cowboy at the chopper, striding cockily around it, heading toward its open cockpit.

Caesar would have him in about four seconds . . .

Then suddenly Gant's voice exploded through his earpiece.

'Scarecrow! Get ready to shoot. There might be another way . . .'

'But I *can't* shoot!' Schofield yelled.

'Just give me a second here!'

Over by the elevator shaft, Gant was crouched over the object she had been searching for earlier—the black box that she had pilfered from the AWACS plane down on Level 2 ninety minutes earlier, the black box that she had surreptitiously kicked away from the mini-elevator when she and the President had arrived in the main hangar before.

In the flashing light of the complex, she pulled a small red unit with a black stub antenna from the thigh pocket of her baggy biohazard suit.

It was Russell's initiate/terminate unit—with its two 'On–Off' switches marked '1' and '2'.

It was only now that Gant understood why there were *two* switches on the unit.

This unit not only started and stopped the radio transmitter on the President's heart, *it also started and stopped the transmitter on Caesar's heart.*

Caesar was almost at the blasted-open cockpit of the chopper, his P-90 raised.

In a few seconds, he would have a clear shot at Schofield.

'I'm *coming* . . . !' he cackled.

Schofield lay slumped on the floor inside the Super Stallion, pinned down, looking out through its exposed forward section.

Trapped.

'Fox—' he said into his mike.

'—*whatever you're going to do . . . please do it soon.*'

Gant was sweating, the world around her flashing red. Her ankle throbbed painfully, but she had to concentrate—

'*Warning. Four minutes to facility self-destruct . . .*'

She'd brought up the familiar spike pattern on the black box's small LCD screen. Now she turned to the I/T unit.

The only question was *which* switch on the unit controlled the President's transmitter and which controlled Caesar's—1 or 2?

Gant had no doubt.

Caesar would make himself Number 1.

Then—in time with the spike screen on the black box, *in between* its recurring search and return signals—she flicked the switch marked '1' on the initiate/terminate unit, *switching off* Caesar's microwave signal.

As soon as she did that, she switched *on* the black box's microwave signal—using it to impersonate Caesar's signal. If she'd done it right, the satellite in orbit above them wouldn't be able to tell that it was a new return signal coming back to it.

A tiny green strobe light on top of the black box started blinking.

Gant keyed her radio mike.

'Scarecrow! I just took care of the radio signal! Nail the bastard!'

As soon as Gant said it, Caesar came into Schofield's view.

The Air Force general smiled at the sight of Schofield, slumped in the cockpit of the destroyed Super Stallion, defiantly raising his ornamental pistol in defence.

Caesar wagged a finger at Schofield. 'Oh, no, no, no, Captain, you're not allowed to do that. Remember, no shooting Uncle Caesar.'

'No?' Schofield said.

'No.'

'Oh . . .' Schofield sighed.

Then—*blam!*—quick as a flash, he snapped his gun up and shot Caesar square in the chest.

A gout of blood erupted from Caesar's torso.

Blam! Blam! Blam!

Caesar reeled with each shot, staggering backwards, his eyes bulging in astonishment, his face completely aghast. He dropped his P-90 and fell unceremoniously to the floor, landing hard on his butt.

Schofield rose to his feet, stepped out of the chopper and strode over to the fallen Caesar, kicking the general's P-90 away from his clawing fingers.

Caesar was still alive, but only just.

A trickle of blood gurgled out the side of his mouth. He looked pathetic, helpless, a shadow of his former self.

Schofield stared down at him.

'How . . . how . . . ?' Caesar stammered through the blood. 'You . . . you can't kill me!'

'As a matter of fact, I could,' Schofield said. 'But I think I'll leave that to you.'

And then he hurried off to rejoin Gant and get the hell out of Area 7.

'Warning. Three minutes to facility self-destruct . . .'

Schofield carried Gant in his arms onto the detachable mini-elevator. Her right ankle had been completely shattered by Caesar's shot, and she couldn't walk on it at all.

But that didn't stop her contributing.

While Schofield carried her, she held the most important black box in the world in her lap.

Their goal now—more than saving their own lives—was to get that flight data recorder out of Area 7 before it was destroyed in the coming nuclear blast. If its signal died now, everything they had fought for would be for nothing.

'Okay, smart guy,' Gant said, 'how are we gonna get out of this seven-storey nuclear grenade?'

Schofield hit the floor panel of the mini-elevator and it began to whiz down the wall of the shaft. He looked at his watch.

11:12:30

11:12:31

'Well, we can't get out through the top door,' he said. 'Caesar changed the code, and it took my DIA guy ten minutes to crack the lockdown codes. And I don't like our chances of getting out through the EEV in time. It took Book and me a good minute to come *down* through that vent before. I can't imagine the two of us getting *up* it in less than ten. And by then, that Escape Vent is gonna be vapour.'

'So what are we going to do?'

'There's one way,' Schofield said, 'if we can get to it in time.'

11:12:49

11:12:50

Schofield stopped the mini-elevator at the Level 2 hangar, and still carrying Gant, hustled down its length, making for the entry to the stairwell at the other end.

'*Warning. Two minutes to facility self-destruct . . .*'

They reached the stairwell.

11:13:20

Schofield burst into it, leapt down it with Gant in his arms, taking the stairs three at a time.

They passed Level 3, the living quarters.

11:13:32

Level 4, the nightmare floor.

11:13:41

Level 5, the flooded floor.

11:13:50

Schofield kicked open the door to Level 6.

'*Warning. One minute to facility self-destruct . . .*'

He saw their escape vehicle right away.

The small X-rail maintenance vehicle still sat right next to the stairwell door, on the track that led out to Lake Powell, in the spot where it had been sitting all day.

Schofield remembered what Herbie Franklin had said about the maintenance car before. It was smaller than the other X-rail engines, and faster, too—just a round capsule and four long struts, with room for only two people in its pod-like cabin.

'*Forty-five seconds to facility self-destruct . . .*'

Schofield yanked open the pod's door, heaved Gant into it, then he clambered up into the small round capsule after her.

'Thirty seconds . . .'

Schofield hit the black start button on the pod's console.

The compact X-rail engine hummed to life.

'Twenty seconds . . . nineteen . . . eighteen . . .'

He looked at the tracks in front of him. They stretched away into flashing red darkness, four parallel tracks converging to a point in the far distance.

'Hit it!' Gant said.

Schofield jammed the throttle forward.

'Fifteen . . .'

The small X-rail pod leapt off the mark, thundered forward, shooting along the length of the underground subway station, crashing through the strobing red shadows.

'Fourteen . . .'

Schofield was thrust back into his seat by the speed.

The pod hit 50 mph.

'Thirteen . . .'

The X-rail pod gained speed quickly. Schofield saw the quartet of tracks both beneath and above the windshield rushing past them.

100 mph.

'Twelve . . . eleven . . .'

Then suddenly—*shoom!*—the X-shaped pod entered the tunnel leading out to Lake Powell, leaving Area 7 behind it.

150 mph.

'Ten . . .'

250 mph. Two hundred and fifty miles per hour equalled about 110 yards per second. In ten seconds, they'd be nearly a mile away from Area 7.

'Nine . . . eight . . .'

Schofield hoped a mile would be enough.

'Seven . . . six . . .'

He urged the little pod onward.

'Five . . . four . . .'

Gant groaned with pain.

'Three . . . two . . .'

The little maintenance pod rocketed through the tunnel,

shooting away from Area 7, banking with every bend, moving at phenomenal speed.

'One . . .

' . . . *facility self-destruct activated.*'

Boom time.

It sounded like the end of the universe.

The colossal *roar* of the nuclear explosion inside Area 7 was absolutely monstrous.

For a structure that had been designed in the Cold War to withstand a direct nuclear strike, it did quite well *containing* its own supernuclear demise.

The W-88 self-destruct warhead was situated inside the walls of Level 2, roughly in the centre of the underground facility. When it went off, the whole underground complex lit up like a light bulb, and a white-hot pulse of energy rocketed through its floors and walls—unstoppable, irresistible.

Everything inside the complex was obliterated in a nanosecond—aeroplanes, test chambers, elevator shafts. Even the bloodied and broken Caesar Russell.

From his position on the floor of the main hangar, the last thing he saw was a flash of blinding white light, followed by an instant's worth of the most intense heat he had ever felt in his life. And then nothing.

But to a large extent, the complex's two-foot-thick titanium outer wall contained the blast.

The concussion wave that the momentous explosion generated, however, shook the sandy earth well *beyond* the structure's titanium walls, making it shudder and shake for several *miles* around Area 7, the wave of expanding energy fanning outward in concentric circles, like ripples in a pond.

The first thing to go was the Emergency Exit Vent.

Its tight concrete walls were assaulted by the expanding wall of energy within a second of the blast. They were turned instantly to powder. Had Schofield and Gant been inside it, they would have been pulverised beyond recognition.

It was then, however, that the most spectacular sight of all appeared.

Since the entire complex had effectively become a hollowed-out shell, the super-heavy layer of granite above the underground section caved in on it.

From the sky above Area 7, it looked as if a *perfectly-circular* earthquake had struck the facility.

Without warning, an eight-hundred-yard-wide ring of earth around the complex just gave way, turned to rubble, and Area 7's buildings—the main hangar, the airfield tower, the other hangars—were just swallowed by the earth, dropping from sight, until all that remained in the place of Area 7 was a gigantic half-mile-wide crater in the desert floor.

From his position on board a Marine Corps Super Stallion that had arrived at the complex only ten minutes earlier, the President of the United States just watched it all go down.

Beside him, Book II, Juliet Janson and the boy named Kevin just stared in stunned awe at the spectacular end of Area 7.

Down in the X-rail tunnel, it wasn't over yet.

When the nuke had gone off, Schofield and Gant's maintenance pod had been shooting through the tunnel like a speeding bullet.

Then they'd heard the *boom* of the blast.

Felt the shudder of the earth all around them.

And then Schofield looked out through the rear window of the two-person pod.

'*Son of a* . . .' he breathed.

He saw an advancing wall of falling rock, *rampaging* through the tunnel behind them!

The roof of the tunnel was caving in, shattering into pieces as the expanding pulse of the concussion wave rippled outward from Area 7.

The problem was, it was catching up with them!

The X-rail pod shot through the tunnel at two hundred and fifty miles per hour.

The advancing wall of falling rock shot forward after it, doing at least two-sixty.

Chunks of falling rock rained down on the tunnel. It was as if the passageway was now a living creature biting down at the heels of the speeding X-rail pod.

Bang!

A chunk of concrete the size of a baseball landed on the roof of the pod. Schofield snapped to look up at the sound. And then—

Bang-bang-bang-bang-bang-bang-bang-bang-bang!

A deafening hailstorm of chunks rained down on top of the pod.

No! Schofield's mind screamed. *Not now! Not this close to the end!*

The advancing wall of collapsing rock had caught them.

Bang-bang-bang-bang-bang-bang-bang—

Chunks assaulted the pod's windscreen, shattering it. Glass exploded everywhere.

Bang-bang-bang-bang-bang-bang-bang—

Small chunks started entering the cockpit. The whole pod started to shudder violently, as if it were about to run off its . . .

And then all of a sudden the concrete rain slowed and the pod *blasted* clear of the falling chunks.

Schofield turned in his seat and saw the moving waterfall of concrete receding into the tunnel behind them, shrinking back behind a bend, falling back like a hungry monster that had given up on the chase. The ripple-like expansion of the concussion wave had run its course and petered out.

They'd outrun it.

474

Just.

And as the X-rail pod continued on its way down the tunnel, Shane Schofield fell back into his seat and breathed a long and deep sigh of relief.

By the time Schofield and Gant were airlifted from the canyonway outside the X-rail loading dock adjoining Lake Powell by a Marine CH-53E, there was a veritable armada of Army and Marine Corps helicopters in the air above Area 7.

They looked like a swarm of tiny insects, black dots hovering in the clear desert sky—all keeping at a safe distance to avoid any lingering radiation.

The President was now safely ensconced in his Marine helicopter, which itself was surrounded by no less than five other Marine Super Stallions. Until the radio transmitter attached to his heart was removed, the Marines would stay by his side.

And the moment he had been lifted off the tarmac at Area 7, he had issued a standing order that all Air Force aircraft in the continental United States be grounded pending further notice.

Schofield and Gant—and their precious microwave-transmitting black box—were reunited with the President, Book II, Juliet and Kevin at Area 8, which had been secured twenty minutes before their arrival by two Marine Recon units.

During their sweep of the base, the Marines had found

no live personnel except one Nicholas Tate III, Domestic Policy Adviser to the President of the United States, rambling incoherently, saying something about calling his stockbroker.

Gant was immediately placed on a stretcher and her ankle attended to by a corpsman. Schofield was given a temporary gauze dressing for his bullet wounds, a sling for his arm, and a dose of codeine for the pain.

'Nice to see you made it out, Captain,' the President said as he came over to where they sat. 'Not so Caesar, I take it?'

'I'm afraid he couldn't make it, sir,' Schofield said. He held up the black box, its green transmission light blinking. 'But he's with us in spirit.'

The President smiled. 'The Marines who swept this base said they found something *outside* it that you might like to see.'

Schofield didn't understand. 'Like what?'

'Like me, you *sexy* thing,' Mother roared as she stepped out from behind the President.

Schofield grinned from ear to ear. 'You made it!'

The last he had seen, Mother had been flipping end-over-end inside a speeding cockroach.

'Fucking *indestructible* is what I am,' Mother said. She was limping slightly on her real leg. 'When it got hit by that missile, I knew my cockroach was done for. And I didn't figure old Caesar and his buddies would take kindly to finding me in it. But when I ran off the runway, I kicked up a hell of a dustcloud. So I bailed out under the cover of the cloud. The cockroach flipped and smashed and I just dug a little hole for my head in the sand under its front bumper, ripped my fake leg off for added effect, and played dead until Caesar and his choppers flew off.'

'Ripped your fake leg off for added effect . . .' Schofield said. 'Nice touch.'

'I thought so,' she smiled. Then she jutted her chin at him. 'What about you? Last I saw, you and the Prez were heading off into outer space. Did you save the fucking day again?'

'I might have,' Schofield said.

'More to the point,' Mother whispered conspiratorially, 'did you do what I told you to do with You-Know-Who?' She nodded theatrically at Gant. 'Did you kiss the friggin' girl, Scarecrow?'

Schofield snuffed a laugh, cast a sideways look at Gant.

'You know what, Mother. As a matter of fact, I think I did.'

A short while later, Schofield sat alone with the President.

'So what's the word on the rest of the country?' he asked. 'Have they been watching all this every hour on the Emergency Broadcast System?'

The President smiled. 'It's funny you should ask. While you were gone, we examined the complex's power history, and we found this.'

He pulled out a printout of Area 7's source power history, pointed to one entry.

07:37:56	WARNING: Auxiliary power malfunction	System	Malfunction located at terminal 1-A2 Receiving no response from systems: TRACS; AUX SYS-1; RAD COM-SPHERE; MBN; EXT FAN

The President said, 'Remember you said that you blew up a junction box on one of the underground hangar levels earlier this morning? Sometime around 7:37.'

'Yeah . . .'

'Well, it seems that that junction box was kind of important. Among other things, it housed the controls for the base's auxiliary power system and its radiosphere. It also housed a system called the MBN. You know what "MBN" stands for?'

'No . . .'

'Stands for the Military Broadcast Network, the previous

name for the Emergency Broadcast System. Seems the MBN's outgoing transmission cable was destroyed in that blast. And because the LBJ Protocol was never initiated this morning, Caesar's transmissions over the Emergency Broadcast System were delayed by forty-five minutes.'

'But the system was destroyed at 7:37 . . .' Schofield said.

The President smiled.

'Correct,' he said, 'which means that every time Caesar Russell spoke into his digital camera this morning, he wasn't transmitting at all. He was speaking to no-one but the people at Area 7.'

Schofield blinked, trying to comprehend it all.

Then he said: 'So the country doesn't know this happened . . .'

The President nodded ruefully.

'It seems,' he said, 'that the people of America have been preoccupied all day with another drama, an accident involving Hollywood's highest paid actress and her actor fiancé.

'It appears that the unlucky couple have been trapped in the Swiss Alps all day, cut off by an avalanche while hiking illegally on Swiss military property. Sadly, their unscrupulous guide was killed, but I believe that just in the last hour our two superstars have been found safe and well.

'As I understand it, CNN has been covering the whole drama all day, updating the public every hour, recycling some amateur footage of the area, giving updates. Biggest news event since Diana's car crash, they tell me.'

Schofield almost laughed.

'So they really don't know,' he said.

'That's right,' the President said. 'And that, Captain, is the way it will stay.'

Exactly six hours later, the second X-38 space shuttle from Area 8 was launched off the back of a high-flying 747.

Its mission: the destruction of a rogue Air Force reconnaissance satellite hovering in a geosynchronous orbit above southern Utah.

So far as the shuttle's pilots could tell, it appeared that the satellite in question had been sending and receiving a peculiar microwave signal down into the Utah desert.

In the end, the pilots didn't care what it was doing. They had orders, which they followed to the letter.

And so they blasted the satellite out of the sky.

With the controlling satellite destroyed, the Type-240 plasma explosives in the airports were rendered useless, apart from their proximity sensors, which would take a little more time to disable.

Over the next few hours, all fourteen bombs would be disarmed and dismantled, and then taken away for analysis.

In addition to the disarming of the plasma bombs, the destruction of the satellite also allowed for the removal of the radio transmitter attached to the President's heart.

480

The procedure was conducted by a renowned civilian heart surgeon from Johns Hopkins University Hospital under the watchful eye of three other cardiac surgeons and armed supervision by the United States Secret Service and the United States Marine Corps.

Never was a surgeon more careful—or more nervous—during an operation.

Limited anaesthesia was used. Although the public was never notified of it, for twenty-eight minutes, the Vice-President was in charge of the United States of America.

An investigatory committee would later be formed to conduct an inquiry into the Air Force's role in the Area 7 incident.

As a result of that inquiry, no less than eighteen high-ranking Air Force officers in charge of a dozen bases across the south-western United States and *ninety-nine* junior officers and enlisted men stationed at those bases were tried for treason in closed session.

It appeared that all of the men linked to the day's events were either currently serving, or had once served, at either the Air Force Special Operations Command, based at Hurlbut Field, Florida, or with the 14th and 20th Air Forces at Warren and Falcon Air Force Bases in Wyoming and Colorado. All, at one time or another, had been under the direct command of Charles 'Caesar' Russell.

Overall, in a service of nearly 400,000 men and women, one hundred and seventeen traitors was not a very large group, barely a dozen to each tainted base. But considering the aircraft and ordnance at those bases, it was more than enough to carry out Caesar's plan.

It further emerged at the trials that five of the USAF personnel involved in the plot were Air Force surgeons who at various times had performed procedures on Congressional members, including the United States senator and one-time presidential hopeful, Jeremiah K Woolf.

Circumstantial evidence presented at all the trials also suggested that every Air Force man involved in the incident was a member of an informal racist society within the United States Air Force known as the Brotherhood.

All were sentenced to life imprisonment at an undisclosed military prison, with no hope of parole. Unfortunately, the plane delivering them to the secret prison inexplicably crashed during flight. There were no survivors.

In the investigatory committee's final report to the Joint Chiefs of Staff, the subject of 'informal anti-social interest groups' within the armed forces was raised. While it was acknowledged in the report that most such societies had been removed from the military during a purge in the 1980s, the report recommended that a new investigation be initiated into their continued presence.

The Joint Chiefs, however, did not accept that such societies existed, and therefore rejected the recommendations of the investigatory committee on this point.

Over the next six months, there would be a number of unconfirmed reports from tourists in the Lake Powell area concerning the sighting of a family of Kodiak bears around the north-eastern portion of the lake.

Officers of the US Fish and Wildlife Service investigated the reports, but no bears were ever found.

A couple of weeks later, a quiet ceremony was held in a dark underground meeting room beneath the White House.

Inside the room were nine people.

The President of the United States.

Captain Shane Schofield—with his arm in a sling.

Staff Sergeant Elizabeth Gant—with crutches on account of her broken ankle.

Gunnery Sergeant Gena 'Mother' Newman—with her small bald-headed trucker husband, Ralph.

Sergeant Buck Riley Junior—with sling.

United States Secret Service Agent Juliet Janson—with sling.

David Fairfax, of the Defense Intelligence Agency—wearing his good sneakers.

And a small boy named Kevin.

The President bestowed upon Schofield and his team of Marines the Congressional Medal of Honour (Classified), for acts of valour in the field of battle despite the endangerment of their own lives.

It was, however, an award they could tell no-one about.

But then again, they all agreed it was probably better that way.

★

While the others stayed to eat in the White House dining room—during which dinner the President had a particularly lively conversation with Mother and Ralph about the Teamsters—Schofield and Gant took their leave, and went out, alone, on their second date.

When they got to the venue, they found that they had the place to themselves.

A single candle-lit table stood in the centre of the wide wood-panelled room.

And so they took their places and dined.

Alone.

In the President's private dining room, on the upper floor of the White House, overlooking the Washington Monument.

'Give them whatever they want,' the President had instructed his personal chef. 'Just put it on my tab.'

By flickering candlelight, they talked and talked till late in the evening.

As dessert arrived, Schofield reached into his pocket.

'You know,' he said, 'I meant to give you this on your birthday, but the day kind of got away from me.'

He pulled a crumpled piece of cardboard from his pocket. It was only small, about the size of a Christmas card.

'What is it?' Gant asked.

'It *was* your birthday present,' Schofield said sadly. 'It was in my trouser pocket all day—I had to take it with me every time I changed uniforms—so I'm afraid it got a little, well, beat up.'

He handed it to Gant.

She looked at it, and she smiled.

It was a photograph.

A photograph of a group of people standing on a beautiful Hawaiian beach. Everyone was wearing boardshorts and loud Hawaiian shirts.

And standing next to each other at the very edge of the group, smiling for the camera, were Gant and Schofield. Gant's smile was a little uncomfortable, and Schofield's kind of sad, behind his reflective silver sunglasses.

Gant remembered the day as if it were yesterday.

It had been that barbecue held on a beach near Pearl Harbor, celebrating her promotion to Schofield's Recon Unit.

'It was the first time we met,' Schofield said.

'Yes,' Gant said. 'Yes, it was.'

'I've never forgotten it,' he said.

Gant beamed. 'You know, this is the nicest birthday present I've received this year.'

Then she lifted herself up out of her seat, leaned across the table and kissed him on the lips.

After their dinner, they arrived downstairs, where they were met by a Presidential limousine. It was flanked, however, from in front and behind, by four Marine Corps Humvees, six police cruisers and four motorcycle outriders.

Gant raised her eyebrows at the elaborate motorcade.

'Oh, yeah,' Schofield said sheepishly, 'there was something else I had to tell you about.'

'Yes?' Gant said.

Schofield opened the limousine's rear door wide—

—to reveal the small sleeping figure of Kevin lying on the back seat.

'He needed a place to stay, at least until they find him a new home,' Schofield shrugged. 'So I said I'd take him for as long as they needed. The government, however, insisted on providing a little extra security.'

Gant just shook her head and smiled.

'Come on,' she said. 'Let's go home.'

AN INTERVIEW WITH MATTHEW REILLY

THE WRITING OF *AREA 7*

How did you come up with the idea for **Area 7?**

I actually conceived the core idea for *Area 7*—namely, that a character has a transmitter attached to his heart and if his heart stops, something terrible happens—just after I finished *Ice Station*, way back in 1997. (I still remember finishing *Ice Station* and saying to myself, 'Okay, Matt, you now have two options for your next book: you can do that transmitter-on-the heart one or you can do that Incan two-stories-told-in-parallel novel.' Obviously, I chose the latter option, and it became *Temple*.)

The thing was, back then, I couldn't figure out a way to make the transmitter-on-the-heart idea work. My main problem was that I didn't know whose heart to put the transmitter on! I had this great idea, but didn't have a story to wrap it up in. Then, nearly three years later, when I decided to do a new Shane Schofield book, I said, 'Wait a second, what if I attached the transmitter to the US President's heart and made Schofield one of his bodyguards . . .' And so *Area 7* was born.

What was it like to write a sequel?

Area 7 is the first sequel I've ever written, and it was a very different experience to creating a wholly new novel. The first thing that must be said is that I didn't make the decision to do a sequel to *Ice Station* lightly. As a keen moviegoer, I am very conscious of sequels that ruin the original story. So I decided that if I was going to write a sequel to *Ice Station*, that book would have to (a) have a rip-roaringly original story that at least matched the story in *Ice Station*; and (b) somehow add to the experience of *Ice Station*. It was also important to me that *Area 7* should stand on its own, that readers who hadn't read *Ice Station* would still be able to enjoy it just as much as those who had read the earlier book. I reckon *Area 7* stands up to all three of those stipulations, but ultimately that's for my readers to decide.

So, to you, how does Area 7 'add to the experience of Ice Station'?

To my mind, a sequel should reveal some kind of extra dimension to the lead characters of the original. In *Area 7*, for example, we learn a little more about Schofield and Gant's relationship, and about Mother's home life. To my mind, the biggest addition comes in the character of Book II. (For those who haven't read *Ice Station*, I suggest, at this point, that you skip to the next question as I'm about to give away a couple of plot points.)

I loved the original 'Book' Riley in *Ice Station*. I loved his loyalty to Scarecrow, his nuggety strength, and his overall 'fatherly' influence on Schofield. As such, it was a big decision to kill him in *Ice Station* (his death, I've been told, shocked a lot of people; in fact, my girlfriend, Natalie, still hasn't forgiven me for doing that). And so, in *Area 7*, I thought I'd 'resurrect' Book in the shape of his son, Book II. I felt it might do two things: first, it would bring Book Snr back in the new book, at least in spirit; and second, it would add something to the *Ice Station* experience by showing that the story in *Ice Station* was not quite over at the end of the book, that the events depicted there had consequences, repercussions.

Now, I know what you're thinking: Matthew Reilly books aren't exactly known for their character development. Hey, one reviewer once said that the characters in my books don't live long enough to justify any 'development'. My response, however, is simple: I want to write about action and thrills and adventure, and if developing characters slow down the action, then developing characters get the chop! The introduction of Book II, however, was an effort to give a little more character depth than usual.

*Why did you choose to set **Area 7** in the American desert?*

Several reasons. First, because I love stories about Area 51, the top-secret base where the US government supposedly keeps aliens and crashed alien spacecraft. The second reason was far more pragmatic: a blazing hot desert was the diametric opposite to the Antarctic wasteland of *Ice Station* and I figured that, visually, a sequel to *Ice Station* should be as different as possible to the original. And once I learned about the extraordinary landscape of Lake Powell, with its incongruous mix of towering canyons and watery lakes and canals, the choice of location was settled. (And, hey, I'd been to the cold for *Ice Station*, the jungle for *Temple*, and the city for *Contest*, so why not tackle a desert environment for my fourth book?)

Have you been to Lake Powell?

Yes, I have. As part of my research for *Area 7*, I went to the Utah–Arizona border just to see the lake. I'd seen pictures of it in books (and on the Internet), but decided I had to see it for myself. It is absolutely awesome. Oddly, though, when you meet Americans and ask them, 'Have you been to Lake Powell?' they say, 'Lake what?' Granted, it is very close to the Grand Canyon, so it's probably just overshadowed by its more famous neighbour.

Some questions about technique. How do you go about writing? For example, do you set yourself certain hours in which to work each day, or are you a 'have to be in the mood' kind of writer?

I am, without question, a 'have to be in the mood' kind of writer. The simple reason for this is that I have tried writing when I *wasn't* in the mood, and I didn't like what I wrote. I had wasted my time. Now, if I'm not in the mood, I go to the library and do some research or see a movie (often just to give my mind a rest), and when I return, I am usually ready and raring to go.

The more complex reason, however, for this method of writing is that I just can't stand routine. I love variation, in the hours I work, in the amount of writing I do, in how I spend my day. (I also, it must be said, have a pathetically short attention span!) So rather than look at writing on a day-to-day basis—and say to myself, 'Okay, Matt, you *have* to write for six hours today between the hours of 9 a.m. and 3 p.m.'—I look at my writing on a weekly basis and say: 'All right, this week, I would like to get four good days' worth of writing done. Doesn't matter when I do it, as long as it gets done.' Now, I don't care if I get that writing done during the day, the evening, or the middle of the night (which can be a very good time to write since the phone—usually—doesn't ring at two o'clock in the morning!). So long as I get it done, I am happy. Working this way, on the average day, I get about eight hours of writing done.

Sounds like this would require considerable self-motivation. How do you motivate yourself to keep writing?

Generally speaking, motivation isn't a problem for me. Like everyone else, I have my bad days (who doesn't?), but they're not very common. Quite simply, I enjoy the act of writing. I am not a stereotypical 'tortured' writer, hunched over my keyboard, tearing my hair out, gnashing my teeth at the prospect of the next sentence. I like writing. I like creating. And I *love* creating big action scenes with words on a page. Since that's pretty much what I do each day, I find motivating myself fairly easy. Now, motivating myself to exercise, that's another story . . . !

Having said that, however, I should say something a little more *general* on the subject (because I am asked about motivation a lot). Writing a book does take a lot of *self*-motivation. It takes me about a year to write each novel. That's a long time to spend on a single project, so you have to really love what you're doing—and that means *wanting* to tell the story you're telling.

If you have a story to tell, no-one will force you to write it down. *You* have to do it. If you don't know the ending, no-one else is going to give it to you. *You* have to figure it out. Writing a book—to me—is one of the most invigorating mental challenges in the world. It can be hard (when I was finishing the writing of *Temple*, my head was nearly exploding with all the subplots running between the two parallel stories); it can be thrilling (it took me nearly two weeks to write the hovercraft chase in *Ice Station*, but every one of those days was just awesome; typing fast, living the action in my head); and it can be painful (I cut a killer action scene from *Temple*—before I actually wrote it, thank God—because I felt it was one too many) but when you see that manuscript sitting on your desk at the end of it all, it is enormously—*enormously*—satisfying.

On a more detailed note, when you write, do you work on a chapter-by-chapter basis?

No. I work on a scene-by-scene basis. I like to think that with my books, chapter endings are generally not the best place to stop reading. And, indeed, this is how I write—I don't stop writing when I reach the end of a chapter. I keep going, as I hope the reader will do. I stop my day's writing when I get the *scene* done. Again, the hovercraft chase in *Ice Station* is a good example. That forty-page action sequence took me nearly two weeks to write (sounds like making a movie, doesn't it?), but in it are a whole bunch of small interwoven mini-scenes—Schofield going under the hovercraft; Book Snr saving Holly; Renshaw and Schofield running alongside the cliff-edge. I did each of these mini-scenes on a different day.

Any other tips for aspiring writers?

Yes. There is no such thing as an 'aspiring writer'. You are a writer. Period. I was told that once, and I have never forgotten it.

So what's next for Matthew Reilly?

Hmmmm. Good question. With my next book, I want to re-invent what I do, and take the action thriller to the next level. It can go faster. I'm talking lean, mean and *totally* out of control. In the downtime I've had since finishing *Area 7*, I have been working on this idea, toying with new structures, figuring out ways to make the narrative just *zoom* along. I think if you want longevity as a creative individual (think of Madonna, or U2, or of great storytellers like Steven Spielberg, Michael Crichton or Joss Whedon) you have to evolve, constantly re-invent yourself, and take your craft to a new level. Reset the benchmark for yourself. So, to answer the question: the future involves pushing myself to a new level of *speed* in my next novel. And then I'm going to make a movie.

Any final comments?

As always, I just hope you enjoyed the book. Best wishes, and hopefully, I'll see you next time!

Matthew Reilly
Sydney, Australia
August, 2001

Matthew Reilly
Ice Station

At a remote ice station in Antarctica, a team of US scientists has made an amazing discovery. They have found something buried deep within a 100-million-year-old layer of ice. Something made of METAL.

Led by the enigmatic Lieutenant Shane Schofield, a team of crack United States Marines is sent to the station to secure this discovery for their country. They are a tight unit, tough and fearless. They would follow their leader into hell. They just did . . .

Matthew Reilly
Contest

'An electrifying . . . novel for the X-files generation'
JESSICA ADAMS, CLEO

The New York State Library. A silent sanctuary of
knowledge; a 100-year-old labyrinth of towering bookcases,
narrow aisles and spiralling staircases.

For Doctor Stephen Swain and his daughter, Holly, it is the
site of a nightmare. Because for one night this historic building is to be the venue for a contest. A contest in which Swain
is to compete—whether he likes it or not.

The rules are simple: Seven contestants will enter, only one
will leave.

With his daughter in his arms, Stephen Swain is plunged into
a terrifying fight for survival. The stakes are high, the odds
brutal. He can choose to run, to hide or fight—but if he wants
to live, he has to win.

For in this contest, unless you leave as the victor, you do not
leave at all.

'Matthew Reilly is our Michael Crichton'
DAILY TELEGRAPH

'If it is action you want then young Australian author Matthew
Reilly is your man'
ADELAIDE ADVERTISER

'a publishing phenomenon'
WEST AUSTRALIAN

Matthew Reilly
Temple

Deep in the jungles of Peru, the hunt for a legendary Incan idol is underway—an idol that in the present day could be used as the basis for a terrifying new weapon.

Guiding a US Army team is Professor William Race, a young linguist who must translate an ancient manuscript which contains the location of the idol.

What they find is an ominous stone temple, sealed tight. They open it—and soon discover that some doors are meant to remain unopened . . .

'There is no denying it. Matthew Reilly has really arrived'
DAILY TELEGRAPH

'Like *Ice Station*, *Temple* is well researched and technically adept. Diehard action buffs will enjoy'
WHO WEEKLY

'Probably the most breathless read in the history of airport fiction'
AUSTRALIAN BOOKSELLER & PUBLISHER

www.matthewreilly.com